THE SECRETS OF THE WAILING CASTLE

AMALINA DALCA
· EPISODE 1 ·

C.L. HOLMES

BAD HOUND PRESS

Episode 1

Dedicated to Mr. S.,
one undeniable master of inspiration

The Secrets of the Wailing Castle
Amalina Dalca, Episode 1
© 2019 C.L. Holmes

This text previously published as:

The Count at Play & Slaughter:
Episode 1: The Wailing Castle
© 2017 C.L. Holmes

Amalina and the
Secrets of the Wailing Castle
Episode 1 of the Count at Play and Slaughter
© 2019 C.L. Holmes

Bad Hound Press
A Division of Giant Dog Books
www.giantdogbooks.com
All rights reserved.

ISBN-13: **978-1949043-3**

Cover, design and layout by Dominic Wilde

THE SECRETS OF THE WAILING CASTLE

Prologue

The Open Window

His dead white hands locked onto her arms with a power she'd never felt before, while his heated eyes poured over her body in a searching, disbelieving way.

But why disbelief? She should be the one questioning. Even as the monster tore her bedclothes aside, all his effort aimed at her throat, she gaped in amazement: this is impossible.

Never had this deadly horror—never in her whole life—had it been known, suggested, or even hinted at in whispers.

No, she thought.

No, no, no.

Until this very moment everything in her life had always been so normal, so rational … so how could this be happening?

Her neck, freed of her dress now, felt the cool night air as he—he who had just killed someone before her eyes, the lower half of his face sheathed in blood, his body leaning almost casually through the window to take up his next victim—studied her for one more disbelieving moment (and she studied him right back; she wondering why she had opened the window in the first place; *cursing to herself for opening it*) just before she …

… just before she could …

Is this how I die? she thought as reality began to fall away.

Just as his mouth came down.

Part One
The Disappearing Daughter

1

Night Empress

Amalina Dalca had just seconds to build a story, to recite whatever excuses in the stuffy air beneath her blanket, as her father's footsteps crossed the floor and she waited for the inevitable. And though life had given her few reasons to lie to her father—which probably meant she was about to fail, and fail terribly—she would do all she could not to tell him the truth. No, she could never tell *anyone* the truth of what happened last night.

The worst of it: Amalina had opened her window. At night.

Unthinkable. Amazing breach. Principal sin.

But wasn't it really *his* fault by lending her the book on astronomy, which had then beguiled her into opening it with the promise of what she'd see on the other side: a spectacle beyond all compare? The window itself was easy enough to open, the cross bar over its wide panel had not been locked into place. There was never a doubt she would always honor the rule (the *absolute* rule—though a seldom spoken rule, it is true) to keep that window shut. How many times had her bedroom been too hot to rest comfortably, yet practice had kept her from acting? But now: here was an innocent girl with a pulsating new idea; a temptable youth pinched to her soul with curiosity.

So Amalina had lifted the bar and pried away the panel.

And the universe was revealed to her in the space of one gasp. No need to crane her neck after she stuck her head out, it was there in all direction. It was beyond what her father's book had promised, too—not just simple black ink squares and empty white circles as stars. With no roof to press everything down or walls to contain it, the real night sky was a vast, incredible gulf. Stretching from one end of the horizon to the other, in numbers outstripping any reasonable count, the stars were, for Amalina, a burst of brilliant white embers blown across, and into, and throughout a sideless, bottomless black. The book, though sparkling with novel allure, hadn't quite captured the magic.

As the air rushed in, caressing her body through the light fabric of her bedclothes, Amalina was entranced. The discoverer of an empire far beyond her little world of timber-and-daubing, tiled roofs and baking bread. The energy those far away constellations drew into her body gave her an unnatural, exciting—for lack of a better word—*power*. She rose to the tips of her toes.

Amalina had then supposed that other villagers had seen the night sky on their own, they having business to wander underneath it from time to time, yet they'd given little thought to the wonder above their heads. But since this was her first sight of it, and the evening was so calm, silent and solitary, night became all her own. She, in fulfilling her moment of curiosity, had conquered it. It left her feeling like a newly crowned queen, or empress.

Amalina, the night empress, then turned her gaze down to the village around her. Now in its premiere, unnatural setting, her village was dark and silent, and completely alien to what she knew in the daylight world. Here and there firelight escaped through windows and doorways, the street's generous jumble of homes becoming a panorama of glowing cracks in the stark emptiness.

At the street corners, the lamps which sputtered their paltry comfort when lit on dark or stormy days were, in this hour, vague, greasy yellow blots; barely brushing light on the front of the buildings and making the blackness blacker still.

• • •

But then, but then ...

A body lurched into view, breaking her reverie.

Amalina's heart hammered at the surprise as the figure stamped in from one of the side alleys and wobbled onto the street. Though at first a black shape, by the size, dress and halting gait, this could be no one else but Lucinda Skeldar; making her way from her home deep within the village, destined who knows where, or why. At its far ends the boulevard led either to the highway or the forest. Lucinda could be headed anywhere.

Amalina thought to wave or to shout, but she didn't know the girl too well. Lucinda was more a friend to her older cousin, Jenna, anyway—they being of a like age and hunting after boys now.

And really, the Skeldar girl was just an acquaintance to her cousin Jenna, at that.

• • •

And then, and then ...

Amalina sucked in a breath when she saw the second shape come prancing after Lucinda. One of the horrible forest wolves by the way it rolled its shoulders and advanced in careful, skittering lopes, from lamp light to lamp light, almost dancing after its prey.

She had seen this hackle-raising motion many times on her treks to the grain mill; accompanying her father in the cart, who would yell and fire bullets at the grey beasts as they attacked from the forest edge. And later still (until she woke with a scream), she would see the wolves again in her nightmares, where their fangs and claws tore her to shreds.

But, no, that wasn't it. Despite the familiar wolfish hop-creep, this second shape was not a wolf at all. It was human. It wore clothes: a heavy black cloak with hood, and seemingly strange white shoes.

But the way it moved like a wolf!

After closing on Lucinda, it reared and then launched. Not the muscular leap of a wolf, it was more like the lightning-fast spring of a spider. The shape caught Lucinda from behind, one hand over her mouth, while the other hand grabbed her shoulder. Arching backward, it pulled Lucinda's full weight onto its own legs. Its mouth then gnawed at her neck.

After a while its head pulsed in the same way spiders syphon their victims: an ecstatic emptiness to the motion. No sound was made.

Not even from Amalina, who watched as blood broke from the seal between the man's lips and Lucinda's neck. Black-red blood arcing out from the wound, worse than a goat or a pig's butchered throat—which Amalina had seen on occasion. It drenched the front of Lucinda's coat, and rapidly filled the grooves of the street's uneven cobble stones.

Amalina didn't have time to consider how amazing it was that this scene of murder was happening in the dim light of the street lamp instead of—and more sensibly—buried deep in some dark side alley.

Lucinda's face was hidden, half-turned away, half caught in the killer's hands, but Amalina stretched out of the window to see if she might glimpse her expression. Why was Lucinda not crying out for help ... if not in surprise?

But then, Amalina realized, why wasn't she herself crying out for her father, or for their neighbors, or for anyone?

She tried to say something, but the words caught in her throat. It was as if she were paralyzed. She could only twist her face in shock and anger, and wheeze.

The man turned.

The man at Lucinda's throat. *He* had heard Amalina.

In the cheap light, his face—a stranger's face—was deathly white, where it wasn't stained with Lucinda's blood. His hood had fallen aside, and she saw his thick, slicked-back hair, and his heavy eyebrows, and his over-large eyes, which were set at a symmetrically pleasing distance above the horror of his wide, gnashing mouth. (Was he speaking, or chewing on the gore? she wondered.)

His immense eyes were fastened on Amalina.

He appeared surprised at first, but then somehow his expression became even more so: eyes growing wider, even as the brows clamped evilly downward.

Lucinda's body collapsed in the distance, as his cloak became a black blur that sped along the street and then shot up the side of the house—faster than Amalina could scream—while making no sound.

. . .

And so, and so ...

When the man, framed in the window, had her in his arms, and his teeth fell to her neck, everything went black.

For some reason, at that moment, Amalina had closed her eyes and let herself go limp. The way some small animals do when a predator has its fatal, unassailable grip on them.

The motion felt serene and dreamlike.

She did not feel his teeth bite in.

Time passed ...

... or it did not.

All was darkness.

But she felt his breath building there on her skin, like a thick, warm breeze.

"No," she'd heard the man say, as he pulled back.

Her eyes had opened slightly. Her vision more watery than clear.

He'd said nothing then, but it was as if she could read his mind through his expression—his large, expressive eyes. *I want you*, she heard him think. *By all rights I have you ... but you are forbidden.*

He shook her in a sudden fit of rage; his golden conquest being so unjustly thwarted.

But why could he not kill her as he'd just done Lucinda? Amalina had wondered, with Lucinda's lifeless body still warm and trickling on the street below. Why could he not strike?

His fit ended and he seemed content to stare at her, to study her.

Then his round lips had pulled back into a red stained smile of sinister delight (Lucinda's fresh blood coating his teeth!).

"Perfect," he'd muttered aloud to himself. "She is perfect. Yes. Oh, so!" Then shaking his head slowly, "But not now. No. Not ... *now*."

He had shook Amalina's body again firmly, to make sure she was awake and listening. And then he'd exulted through his entire face: "Do not cry for the dead. They are mine. But fear for the lives of those you know and love ... should you dare even whisper what you've seen tonight. Never speak of it. It is a secret for you alone, lucky one. Not a word, you see. Or everyone around you will DIE!"

Then he had disappeared and Amalina collapsed to the floor.

She fell into a black sleep as deep and endless as the kind of abyss the village's minister would conjure from time to time in his sermons when he was going for a certain soul-shaking effect. She did not emerge until early morning, when she found herself on the floor and knew she had better not be discovered out of bed ... nor tell anyone what she'd seen.

She swam across the wood planks, up onto her peashell mattress and under her blanket, and fell unconscious again. Until her father came to wake her late in the morning, he entering loudly into her room, and she realizing with a start that she'd forgotten to close the window. And realizing, too, that she'd better come up with some good fib, because he was quick and certainly not a fool; and her bedclothes were ripped wide open at the throat.

2

The Day of Make Believe

"**A**malina, what have you done?" the voice repeated, more upset than before.

Amalina peeked over the blanket.

Her father, Dragomir Costin Dalca, dressed in work clothes with a worn apron over them, replaced the panel in the window. It was late in the morning, when the window, unless storming or winter, would have otherwise remained open. He repeated this action of opening then shutting the window a couple times, once fitting in the cross bar, too, before removing it again, as if making sure the process of it coming off could be done only by human means.

He glanced at Amalina, then returned his anxious gaze to the window, which framed a perfect spring blue sky with two fluffy white clouds. A fly blew in, insensitive to the drama about to play out.

Her father's expression, when he turned to his daughter again, became a confusion of doting smile and stern, and perplexed, and reprimanding eyes; the symptoms of an internal contest to puzzle out how the piece of wood (the bar) could have come off the window by itself. Because it must have! Amalina would never take it down during the night ...

... would she?

Didn't she *know?*

"How did this happen?" he asked.

"I opened it."

"You took it off! Why?"

"I wanted to see what it looked like."

"What *what* looked like?"

"Night."

"Silly girl, you know what night looks like."

"I do not," she said. "I've never seen it. Not once."

"You must have. More than once. It's not as if I was trying to hide it from you."

"Not ever, Papa."

"And the book I gave you: It shows you more than you could *ever* see by opening that window." He grunted ruefully as he realized giving her a book on astronomy might have been a terrible miscalculation. One never opens a door or a window *at night.* He added with a mutter: "And toward the waxing of the moon it is ..."

"What's the matter with opening my window, Papa?" she asked with sweet innocence.

"Never mind that," he dropped the panel and addressed her fully. "When did you open it?"

"I don't know …" Which was a relatively true statement, not so much a lie. How far was she willing to go?

"Before you went to bed? Or after you woke up; in the early morning?"

"Before I went to bed, Papa. After I read the 15th chapter, which describes the northern spring constellations. I thought I might go and see them." This was very true—if somehow tragic because of what was to come of it.

"The book," he grunted ruefully once more. "And you had that window open *all* night then?"

Amalina nodded. Still true. But again … *how far was she willing to go?*

His eyes widened now with curiosity and horror and dread—and also a flicker of pride at his young daughter's courage. "All night! What did you see?"

"All the stars," she told him. "There were so many it was confusing. I couldn't identify one constellation. I'm sorry, Papa."

A sincere apology. *Very nice.* To her relief, so far everything she had said was true. Maybe her father would be satisfied and fall for her subtle misdirection, which was, again, *based* on truth; with no need to flat out lie.

"No need to be sorry, Amalina," he nearly laughed, perhaps with relief at her naïvety. "It was your first time under the night heavens, after all. But I mean, did you *see* anything? Anything unusual? Anything strange?"

Dangerous territory. *Did he know already? He might* not *know.* It was hard enough not to keep staring at the window, knowing Lucinda lay dead at the street corner, or not to listen for the sounds of a gathering crowd down there, or a scream. She had already acted too calm and natural to now admit she knew about the dead body, and the stir it must be causing. She could show no interest or apprehension toward the open window unless a sound of alarm rang from the street. Or her father poked his head out and saw for himself and reacted.

"It was very dark," she answered him levelly, after clearing her throat. "Everything looks different."

"Did you see anything roaming *on the street?* An animal?" Dragomir paused and licked his lips. "Or a *man?*"

So there it was.

Amalina had feared her father would get to the question. Now he'd asked—and asked properly—what she'd seen last night. And she must decide whether to tell him the truth—the whole terrifying truth—or to lie. What excuses had she formulated while under her blanket? To her alarm, all she could recall in that moment were glimpses of the man's ghastly white face.

"Not a soul," she lied. "It was cold as ice. Who—or what—would be out in that?"

"You heard nothing?"

"Not ... now ..." she heard the man's voice say.

Amalina shook her head, compounding the lie.

Her father nodded in relief. Then his eyes narrowed.

"Are you all right, Amalina?"

"Yes."

"Your face is red. You're sweaty, I can see from here. Do you have a fever?"

He walked toward her. She jumped out of bed, holding the throat of her bedclothes together as if being modest or cold or both.

"I'm just surprised I slept in so late. And you, of all people, let me! There are so many things to be done!"

She went for her chest of drawers to find her dress. She felt the blush of nervousness and embarrassment, its redness radiating heat off her cheeks, forehead, and down her arms. She wiped the sweat away and tried to make it look as if she weren't scared and confused; as if she weren't still catching up from the night before; as if she weren't trying to avoid looking out the window; as if she were simply driven to a hysterical distraction by the lateness of the hour.

With her back turned to him, she half-hummed, half-sung a melody—her habit in the morning when she dressed—to sell her story of undisturbed innocence, planning to bury her ruined bedclothes deep in the drawer when he went away.

Satisfied, Dragomir smiled and concluded to her back as he put up the panel: "You'll catch your death of cold if you let the breezes in from the mountain. Foul air at night, I remind you, Amalina. Which is why you will never remove this board again, once it has gone up over the window—for the night."

"No, Papa ... I mean, yes, Papa ... I mean, no, Papa, I won't. I swear."

He would make sure of it. By noon, Dragomir Dalca had secured the panel in place with twenty iron nails.

· · ·

But by noon Amalina was already going about her business, moving by degrees within the village and would not learn what had happened in her bedroom—and to her window—until she returned that evening. And by that time she would little care. Why, even as she dressed for the day, Amalina's head felt light and the waking hours lying ahead of her seemed unreal, a dream produced by a fever: A day of make believe.

Yes, after so unusual and distressing a night, freighted with images she wished she had never seen (and knew she would never forget), and with the sun up and with her head softly buzzing, the light hurting her eyes, the colors popping like balloons, the smells itching her nose, the sounds ringing in her ears, daytime reality felt so *over-large*, so *over-stimulating*, and so *over-saturated*, it could only be a fiction. And so the day of surprises ahead of her— several shocking surprises over the next twelve hours—could almost be dismissed. But they couldn't be dismissed.

Instead they would overwhelm her.

· · ·

Surprise #1. The Conspiracy.

"Lucinda Skeldar, the armorer's daughter, is dead!"

This was crowed right into Amalina's face when, Amalina wishing to avoid the scene of the crime, she opened her back door to go fetch the water. In front of her stood Sadra, the minister's wife.

Sadra's dark declaration was blasted with trembling fervor, but through straight, bloodless lips which was neither a smile nor a frown, but could have been either. There was always a glee to this tall, thin, angular woman with a matching tall, thin, angular face when she reported sensational news. The worse a story was the harder it was for her to suppress the unseemly glow and the shifting of her angles. But all the while her lips would be strained into a cramped yet passable neutrality, so one could never with any confidence accuse the minister's wife of secretly harboring a barbarian's bloodthirstiness without the fear of her (and then her husband's) wrathful contradiction. Half the village children were suspicious of Sadra because of this unnatural ambiguity, while the rest bought wholesale her innocent mask. Sadra's lips were steely now, but the fire detectable behind her look could have melted cold iron.

In amateur fashion, Amalina attempted to mirror Sadra's sober-mask facade. She knew all about Lucinda Skeldar's death, but could never tell a soul she did, or give the truth away with even the slightest out-of-place expression. A flash memory of the man's brutal eyes and vicious teeth reminded her so. *Tell no one.*

"Went out in the night," Sadra continued. "Went out in the night and for what reason matters no more. The shameless slut toddled into the forest and what could you expect but the wolves ... the wolves!"

"Oh." said Amalina, acting as shocked and alarmed as Sadra could have expected, or wanted. "Oh! Oh! Oh!"

Amalina didn't question the news, but pushed on. Lucinda was dead. She knew this already.

What was that about the forest and the wolves, though?

Somehow Sadra had only heard rumors, Amalina concluded. She didn't know the full story of how ...

"... Her body was found by Gulgas the hunter returning to sell his furs," the story went on, from the Inn Keeper, who was as late as Amalina in sending a water bucket down into the well.

There was a large crowd in the village square, not just the Inn Keeper and Amalina, and most idlers were there without buckets. This sort of thing happened when a lively topic arrived overnight. The air hummed with voices.

"... Just off the road, a little ways into the wood," the Clockmaker expanded from behind the curious piece of glass set in front of his eye. "Gulgas spotted her clothes, naturally enough, as they look nothing like vegetation ... and then the blood!"

"He couldn't locate the wolves or he would have killed them," Amalina was assured, moments later, by the whispering Street Sweeper. "But let that be a lesson not to wander out of town, in the day much less the night! Lucinda might have had a bum leg, but those butchering beasts would have gotten her if she could sprint like a grey rabbit. Just as they would get *you* no matter how fast you think you can run, Amalina!"

Amalina nodded, her expression set appropriately to fear.

It went on like this.

And the hum was especially fervent today because none of the Skeldars were in the square, freeing the townsfolk from shame about the way they gossiped. Most deaths cloaked the village in a heavy, somber shroud. The rumormongering was hushed and mournful, and outfitted in genuine worry and grief; even while the victim's family mostly kept out of the streets to avoid social embarrassment.

The Skeldars were treated differently, because though prominent by money they were troublesome. The father a violent drunk. The mother of questionable sanity. The brothers bullies who'd gone off to war (and to everyone's relief never returned). The Skeldar's only hope to elevate their family name from the deep pit into which it had fallen—to rescue them to respectability—had been Lucinda; who, to everyone's dismay, soon after her birth, exhibited signs of the hobbled leg.

And so today the villagers carried on in the central square louder and more enthusiastic than they might in other cases.

But what they were telling Amalina though ... It was wrong! It wasn't true! Lucinda had died right here in the village! *I saw it*, thought Amalina.

But she said nothing and continued to wear Sadra's mask.

There was something to learn here, she sensed. And she knew never to question her elders.

Never.

But ... how could they claim something so false, when Lucinda's blood was all over the street? Had the man stolen her body away and dumped her in the forest? Had he cleared away the evidence of her death inside the village?

On her trip home, taking a roundabout route to the bakery's front door, buckets sloshing in either hand, rope handles burning into her palms, Amalina saw that Lucinda's blood, which last night had drowned the stone cobbles, was gone. Amalina passed by the artificially clean spot with an incurious glance downward—though she was *very* curious to study the area, but knew she couldn't be obvious about it—and after peeking, hurried on …

Only to almost drop both buckets when she nearly tripped over her own feet, her mouth falling open at the sight of the soapy wash bucket near the corner. The bucket was up against the lamp, with a bristle brush stuck into it. The water in the bucket and the brush bristles were dingy red. She turned around and walked back several paces. And now she did not hide the fact she was studying the place where, only hours before, Lucinda's blood had drenched the stones and the grooves between them.

"Here, little one, need help with those?" said the Street Sweeper, who had been trailing Amalina while giving the stones careless swats with his broom. Now he was hurrying to her side. "You all right? Did you fall down, Amalina? What were you doing there? But here, let's get you back to your store."

She didn't budge. She bowed her head and found little flecks of red in the chips and grooves of the stones, a red that did not match the old stones' natural grey color. "I'm fine. I just thought I saw something."

"I'm sure you didn't see anything," said the Street Sweeper with a worried look, trying not to even glance down at the cobblestones but turn her away from them. "I do a good job keeping these streets spotless."

"No question, but I saw—"

"What? A button or something?"

"No, it's actually—" she nodded at the dark crimson spots. But she was already amazed by the Sweeper's blossoming horrified expression, his eyes bugging, his tongue lapping inside his mouth, apparently disturbed by what he imagined she was going to say.

"Hey, hey, hey," warbled Lygo, whose house was on the corner, and whose door faced where the murder had occurred. He jostled his bulk off his small stoop, making his way to them. His worried eyes meeting with the Street Sweeper's, a silent conversation passing between them. "What's happening here, Amalina? Need help with those buckets, Amalina?"

"No, I was just saying—"

"Ah, did you fall or something? Best be careful. The street may still be a little *slippery* there. Sorry about that. All my fault."

"Your fault?"

"Oh, yes … Oops!" And now Lygo lumbered quickly to the water bucket and picked it up. He made a face at the Street Sweeper. "How I forget things! But it was so early in the morning."

"What was?"

"Oh, I—I was, um, washing the street there."

"Why?" asked Dreda, an old neighbor lady, who now joined the small group—as any gathering in the village was a magnet to pull in others, especially when there was the concern of missing out on a hot new rumor. In the excitement, Dreda's face, which looked something like a peach pit, seemed to lose a few of its hundred wrinkles.

"What?" Lygo said in surprise. "It's just that—Well, naturally—Well—Well, I dropped something there and I needed to clean it up."

"What did you drop?" asked Amalina.

"Yes, I thought I saw you scrubbing something hard this morning," Dreda added on.

"Did you? Well, of course you did. Had to clean it all up."

"What did you drop?" Amalina asked again.

"Just some water."

"Water?" Amalina nearly cried in disbelief.

"Why would you have to clean up water?" Dreda huffed impatiently. "You clean with water."

"No, no, it would make more sense," said the Street Sweeper helpfully to the stunned Lygo, "if you'd dropped the paint. The *paint*."

"Oh, yes, the paint. What did I say? I dropped some paint there and had to clean it up."

"Why did you say water, then?" said Dreda, hand planted on her hip, face thrust out, eye squinted at him. Really getting into the mode of Lygo's interrogation.

"I just got mixed up. I misheard. I'm too tired, you see. I was up so very early. And then with the news about poor Lucinda, I'm just not thinking right." He suddenly got a clever look. "As a matter of fact, that's why I dropped the paint. Sweeper here told me the news and I was so shocked, I dropped the paint right onto the ground."

Lygo grinned proudly, but the Street Sweeper was mortified.

"If you dropped it in front of Sweeper, why didn't *he* clean it up?" demanded Dreda, flustered by the continued nonsense. "It's his job, Lygo. You're too big and fat to be brushing away at the bricks, leave him to it. And you said you did it in the morning, but I saw you washing them very, very early. At dawn it was. And I asked myself, why is Lygo doing that, I'll have to ask him later. But that would mean you heard about Lucinda around sunrise—when the bell rang and my son opened the window—wouldn't it? But Gulgas didn't get into town with the news until—"

"Amalina, your father's calling you!" the Street Sweeper interrupted. "Get on home. Go, go, get! You have your answer, now away before he gets cross. And you, Dreda, you don't know what you're talking about. Isn't it time for your nap? Move along! Move!"

As the Street Sweeper pushed at Amalina with his broom, Dreda said to Lygo: "But what were you painting? And why so early? And why would you bring the paint bucket into the street?"

They sent the old woman along, too. And, looking back over her shoulder, Amalina saw the bizarre comedy playing out, with the Street Sweeper admonishing Lygo, Lygo's head drooping in shame, and they both glancing guiltily at the spot where Lucinda's blood had been. "What color paint?" Lygo asked the Sweeper. "Red, you idiot!" cried the Sweeper. "What else?"

No, the man—the killer—had not removed Lucinda's body to the forest. Or if he had, sparing the villagers the trouble of its removal, he hadn't swept away the blood. And there would be no sane reason for Lygo or the Street Sweeper (or anyone else) to wash away a massive pool of blood without wondering where it had come from. They knew! They must know! And yet ...

Her heart thumping, Amalina now recognized that the amazing truth— the real truth of last night—would indeed never be told: that Lucinda and her horrible murder at the hands—the teeth—of a man, and not a wolf (which was a second important alteration to the factual story)—had taken place *inside* the village proper.

No, no: To the last person, from Sadra on down, and forever onward through the rest of known history, it would be known that Lucinda's death happened by wolves and in the forest!

The world opened up for Amalina. It opened wide.

Her lightheadedness took her off her feet; as if she were floating, the heavy buckets unable to weigh her down.

As the book on astronomy had corrected Amalina's ignorance about stellar bodies—their very existence!—and she was willing to accept the new information, process it in a modern way, and reorient her position within the new, true, bona fide universe of planets and stars and countless celestial phenomena, so did Lucinda's "death by wolves in the forest" story—in plain truth a conspiracy of fiction by all around her—perform the same sort of miracle transformation with the daylight world, and those within it.

Now Amalina fully understood, after processing the shocking fact: the honest people she'd known her whole life—or at least most of them—were, instead, casual liars and conspirators. She reoriented herself to this truth as flawlessly as a cat tumbling out of a sudden whirlwind. She remained on her feet, if her fur mussed and her eyes more wary.

Amalina had liked Lucinda Skeldar—from a distance—as much as anyone else. Which caused her to feel a deep shame as she presently experienced gratefulness for the poor girl's death. Because, above all, Amalina appreciated the truth. And Lucinda Skeldar, in her death—and perhaps because the victim's inferior social standing gave everyone wider liberty to speak on it—had lifted from her world a strange, dark veil.

She wondered if her father was in on this conspiracy.

He wouldn't lie to me, would he?

But the day was still not finished gifting surprises upon Amalina Dalca.

. . .

"Just had to get herself killed last night, ruining all our plans for today," said Cristine, a slim, bright looking girl with cutting blue eyes, who had stopped Amalina on her second trip to the well. Cristine sneered past her own fear of the wolves in order to peck at the memory of newly finished Lucinda Skeldar. "It isn't too surprising, though, is it? Luci was like all the others, just like I told you before, Amalina. And see if I didn't turn out to be right! I told you it would happen. Happen to her, I mean. Of course it would happen. It always does, doesn't it?"

"Once or twice a year," Amalina said quickly, eager to hear more; hoping to add to her knowledge and understanding, and to further color in the world which, just the day before, she hadn't suspected had been so *intentionally* dull grey.

Cristine's eyes squinted like icy daggers in that perfectly sculpted face of hers, the coldness of her eyes not marring her beauty, only sharpening it. "Wait, do you know something, Amalina? It looks like you know *something*."

"No. I was just listening. And agreeing with you, that it happens a lot."

"Right. Too many wolves, they always say. Kill one and there are a thousand to replace it. And so we have our constant sacrifices ... like lambs. Chomp, chomp, chomp. And still, Amalina," Cristine assured with her elongating sneer, "we *know* which ones are the marked ones, don't we?"

"Do we?"

Astonished by Amalina's confusion, Cristine demanded: "Who always get caught out by the wolves, eh? Who're the idiots who leave their houses at night?"

"Many people, I suppose," said Amalina, maybe too naïvely.

Cristine made a nasty noise. "Don't play stupid. Why are you acting like that, Amalina?" Her eyes narrowed suspiciously. "You *do* know something, don't you? You know something and you aren't telling me!"

Amalina shook her head and feigned innocence as best she could. But she was visited by the memory of Lucinda's flailing arms. Then another of the man towering over Amalina in her window.

"Your family hears the most gossip of anyone in this town," said Cristine. "Tell me what I don't know. Tell me right now!"

"I only heard of what happened to Lucinda just now, when I went to get the water."

Cristine's eyes became cross. "You're playing stupid with me. I don't believe it! I'd never keep anything from you!"

"If I'd known about about Lucinda wouldn't I be wearing my mourning dress? Wouldn't I?"

She nodded slowly, chewing her lower lip, still unsure. "You have to tell me everything, Amalina. I never hear *anything*," she now pouted, "or anything good, until it's too late. You have to promise me, Amalina. Promise you'll tell."

"I already *have* promised you. We drew blood on it."

Another flash: Lucinda Skeldar's blood pouring over bricks.

Amalina gulped.

Cristine nodded again, with a laugh and a smile of satisfaction. No doubt she was remembering the enactment of their blood oath. Cristine seized Amalina's hand and squeezed it. "True. We drew blood on it. And don't you *ever* forget it."

More visions of Skeldar's blood over bricks.

Cristine leaned close. She pressed her forehead against Amalina's forehead at an angle, so her left eye and Amalina's right eye were staring into each other and nearly touching. With a wink, their eyelashes kissed. Then Cristine took her head away. Still staring into Amalina's eye, but smiling with contentment because she was convinced she had not lost her friend's confidence. Cristine's was a bright, heartwarming smile, despite all the hard lines.

Inside Amalina's head, Lucinda's body dropped to the street. Once. Twice. Three times.

Amalina's gut knotted; for withholding the truth from Cristine. By keeping silent, she violated their solemn pact: a blood oath of truth, loyalty and friendship. She wondered if Cristine understood the meaning of her blush—the guilt.

"I haven't forgotten our deal." Amalina squeezed Cristine's hand in return, enjoying the warmth and softness of her skin—Amalina's hand tingling at the contact, despite her guilty feelings. However, she could not bring herself to repeat the kiss of the eyes, for fear of cracking.

At least, from what she'd said so far, Cristine seemed innocent of the lie the adults were pushing. Most likely, Amalina supposed, because she, like Amalina, was too young to be trusted in it. Or, like both Amalina and Dreda, she was female. Maybe only the men were up to something (and Amalina up to something on her own, of course … she, who knew more than anyone else in the village!).

A flash of the man's large, depthless eyes.

Amalina wished she could shake her head to get rid of the recurring images. To blink and have them disappear. Instead, under Cristine's close scrutiny, she gripped onto her friend's hand and forced herself to listen.

Though Cristine was innocent of the village conspiracy, at this moment and within her own innocence she had her own poignant and reality-altering observation to make. Which Cristine, ignoring Amalina's strange looks of discomfort, and encouraged by how hard Amalina was squeezing her hand, she did presently:

Surprise #2: The Sacrifices.

· · ·

The Sacrifices.

"Lucinda, Lucinda, Lucinda … And all those other poor girls raised like lambs to be *sacrifices*," Cristine sighed falsely, returning to the original matter. She traced her finger along Amalina's white knuckles. "Oh, they all act as if they are so much better than us—better off than us—as if *we* are the unfortunate ones, because we're kept close by our parents, coddled and spoiled by them, and we're prevented from enjoying the freedom *they* have. They lord it over us, don't they? They brag about how they can do whatever they please, while *we're* worked like plow horses. Always at our parents' beck and call. Like slaves. *'Like slaves'*, those girls *laugh*."

Cristine gave an apologetic glance. "Well, *I'm* not worked like a slave, of course. But you are, Amalina, and the ones *like* us are. And I *would* be worked, too, if my parents could think of a way to work me. But father says his kind of work just isn't in me.

"But that's why they make fun of us, poor Lucinda and the rest," Cristine returned to her hissing indictment. "Because they're jealous at just how much our parents love and protect us, and in the end we're bound for a good life in the village. And yet how much *they* are star-crossed. So they braid their hair and put on too much make-up, and douse themselves in perfumes and wear outlandish dresses, and brazenly push their hips at the boys as if there were no laws to hold them back—and they act like it makes them better than us." She sighed falsely again, a false pity, after delivering what sounded more like a scolding Cristine's mother would give. "But it is all too *sad*, isn't it? Because they know how so cruelly separated they are—separated from the herd. And they know its coming for them, their fate. We all know. And then it does: Chomp, chomp, chomp."

"I wish you wouldn't be so mean about it," said Amalina.

"Mean?" Cristine cried. "Me?"

"It seems a little cruel. Lucinda just—"

"It's not like you knew her. You weren't her friend."

"Jenna knew her a little."

"Yesss," Cristine made a face. "Your cousin knew her, of course."

"I know you're angry … I don't like it when you get angry, because then you get cruel. I wish there was something I could say to—"

"Who's angry?" Despite her icy looks, Cristine's anger was scalding and spilled out on an acid tongue, her choicest bile measured in relentless doses that sometimes took Amalina's breath. Like now: "… Well, maybe just a little angry, I'll admit. Lucinda couldn't have chosen a worse time to get herself chewed to the last gristle. That was thoughtless of her. After all, to hell with that crippled creep, *we* had plans …" … Cristine went on.

But Amalina didn't share her friend's venom against the older girls. She'd never been bullied, having been lucky enough to have tragedy strike early. And so Amalina and her father, Dragomir, possessed a built-in buffer of sympathy within the village. Amalina was aware of this sympathy, and had used it sometimes, like an umbrella, to shelter Cristine; who was unfairly mocked by these girls, because in this time and place, like most times and places, it didn't pay to be pretty *and* be from a very rich family. The one or the other boy-lure was acceptable, but both at the same time unforgivable. Cristine was unforgivable. The bullying was bad, and Amalina tried not to think of it, and never mentioned it.

Cristine did not forget.

"… when they pull my hair, and gouge me with their fingernails, and kick me in the shins, and step on my foot, and tear my dresses, and steal my head scarves, and break my jewelry, and slap my face red, and how many times have they tripped me into the mud, and abandoned me in the woods, and the one time they tried to throw me down the well—you mean as mean and cruel as they are to me?" Cristine finished up.

"But you don't want to be like them, do you?"

"I'm not breaking anyone's skin, all I'm doing is talking."

"After awhile, it starts to feel a little like gloating," said Amalina, a new vivid flood of Lucinda's blood causing her to wipe her eyes. "And I kind of feel bad for Lucinda."

"Why?"

"I've always felt sorry for her."

"You hardly knew her. She might not have picked on me directly, but you know she was friends with all the girls who do. She was one of *them*."

"Well, you'd know better about it, she lived closer to your side of town." And Lucinda *had* been older and *was* dead now, Amalina reckoned, and so she *might* have fitted somewhere in that society of wild girls, the ones who tended to die more often than others.

Oh, if this was true, how the world was spinning round Amalina. If it were true, it was dizzying.

"You have to hate them with me, Amalina. Whose side are you on?"

"Ours, of course. I just don't know why you don't just ignore them instead of getting yourself worked up this way."

"Tell me how I can ignore them with one of their shoes on my face."

"But can't you just try to concentrate on better things?" Amalina knew it sounded lame even as she was saying it.

"And ignore them? No, no, no, no, no. The actual question—the *real* question—is, Amalina," Cristine turned now, with the cruelest smile yet on her lips, "why do *our parents* ignore them? Do they ignore, and estrange, and reject their death-bound daughters because all those *awful girls* have, from the years they've lived and the misdeeds they've done, proven themselves bad and willful? As it says in the bible: the daughter 'who disobeys her parents' should be killed? So the papas and mamas treat them to their backs and shoulders because they *want* to push them away and *encourage* them to get eaten? Or is it because they know from birth which daughters are fated, whatever the goodness or badness in them; so they don't want to get too close, knowing it'd be too painful when the wolves inevitably come to collect?"

Wolves? A flash: the man's gore-filled mouth. *It's not the wolves!* But Amalina couldn't dare whisper a thing about it.

"What's the matter with you? I said: Do the parents shun them because their daughters prove themselves bad and they want these 'nice ladies' to be eaten? or because they knew their daughters were condemned right when they were born, and neglected them because of it?"

"I, uh." Amalina couldn't answer. She was still processing the terrible possibility of a race of girls fated for execution; and the gruesome memories of the previous night were racing before her eyes. And also the question seemed so overly philosophical it seemed there must be a hidden point Cristine was getting to. "What difference does it make?"

"Because, Amalina," snarled Cristine, bitterly, "maybe if they *didn't* ignore them, if they would treat them a little better and pay them a little more attention, they wouldn't turn out to be such monsters, and I wouldn't have to look over my shoulder any time I step out of my house. Now, since I answered your question, will you answer mine?"

Amalina felt immensely sorry for her best friend, seeing how riled up she was. This time was so much worse, for some reason. "But I already said I don't know. You're smarter than me, what do you think?"

"I think your cousin is next," said Cristine, dagger-eyed. Amalina gasped. "This year or next. She will go to meet her boyfriend—ha, ha—or go to pick some flowers, or run off to Tsobl or something, and instead become wolves' meat hanging over the low branches."

"Oh!" Amalina gasped again.

Cristine paused because she knew it sounded insensitive, and maybe just too much.

"Jenna only poked your eyes that once," said Amalina. "And I told you she felt bad about it. And it was Bessa who told her to do it after she got your arms in a lock."

"But your cousin poked my eyes!"

"Because of Bessa! Who would say no to Bossy Bessa if she ordered you to do something?"

"Would *you* have poked me in the eyes? Even if it was Bossy Bessa telling you to?"

"Well ... no."

"Sorry, Amalina, but you should know better than I: your cousin, Jenna, is one of them."

"She doesn't have parents treating her bad, it's just my father and me."

"And that's my point," said Cristine. "Maybe you're too close to see it because you all live in the same house, my pet. Spy on your father like an outsider—like me—and see how he leaves your cousin Jenna well enough alone. He never speaks to her. I've only seen him scold her. And even then, he never looks at her. *Never* looks at her. I know it is too awful to think of— to think *about* your poor cousin Jenna and *against* your father. But see if it isn't true now that I've said it."

Amalina nodded immediately. She *had* noticed her father's wariness toward Jenna, and Jenna's contempt for both her and her father.

Up the street, Cristine's mother called to her. Her mother was dressed in a heavy black cloak that spoke of mourning and sorrow. With a lowered head she beckoned gloomily to her daughter.

"We'll meet tomorrow this same time," said Cristine, cheerily. "See if we haven't learned anything more about what happened to Lucinda. Like if they ever found her head!"

More flashes: Amalina saw Lucinda's head fall backward as her body dropped to the ground. And the head kept tipping backward at the nape of the neck, as if attached to the rest of the body by a loose hinge there. And there was a red-black hole just below the chin, as if she didn't have a neck at all. As if all the muscle and tissue were gone and the head was breaking loose.

Amalina shuddered and put a hand to her chest.

"What is it?" asked Cristine.

"I hope you'll feel better tomorrow," said Amalina, recovering herself and genuinely hoping her friend would push through this revengeful blood-lust and be a little more charming next time.

"No, wait a minute," Cristine said, her eyes pinning Amalina. "Just now, you … You know something. You do."

"No."

"You do!"

"You have to go," Amalina said.

"Cristine!" called her mother. "Come now! Come here!"

"No," said Cristine to Amalina. "What is it? Tell me!"

"I have to go, too." Amalina took up the buckets and turned quickly.

"Tell me, Amalina!"

"It's nothing. Nothing. I'm telling you."

"You're lying to me. I know you! You can't lie to me! Tell me, Amalina, tell me!"

Cristine followed Amalina who picked up her pace, heading directly away from Cristine's mother. Panic was setting in. If she didn't get away, she would break down. She would have to confess. She wanted to throw down the buckets and run home. She was sure she could beat Cristine in a foot race. Maybe even with the buckets.

"Don't you run from me. I can't believe you!"

"Your mother's calling."

"Keeping secrets! Keeping secrets! If you don't stop and tell me, we aren't friends anymore and we never were! Stop right now!"

"Wait, Bossy's coming!" said Amalina, a bit desperately, her ear in the air as if hearing Bessa's loud clomps; and feeling immediately awful for pulling such a trick.

Cristine came to a stop, her sharp eyes widened with surprise and fear as they searched for the large brunette bruiser.

"Cristine! Daughter! Come! Here! Now!"

Cristine whirled with a stamp of her foot and yelled back: "I'm coming! Oh, why do you have to be like that, Mama! Look what you've done! Scared my friend away! I can never have friends with you!"

Cristine hurried toward her mother.

Amalina took the first corner she could. The buckets sloshed dangerously. She steadied herself but did not stop, trying to put distance between her and Cristine in case she changed her mind and took after Amalina again.

She felt terrible, as if she'd just lost her best friend in that moment. It couldn't be that bad, could it? Not over something so little. It felt like she'd broken something, though. She'd definitely put a scare into her. What a day, what a day. She would have to beg Cristine's forgiveness when they met again. And maybe perform another blood oath just to reassure her. The only other option would be to tell her the truth. Tell her everything.

Amalina slowed her steps now, debating if she should tell Cristine the entire facts of last night—from Lucinda's death in the street, to the man responsible for it. Which would also, of course, reveal to her bitter but still innocent friend that Lucinda's murder was being covered up by their elders. Which would then unmask her parents, and all the adults of the village, as liars. How would that—any or all of it—affect her?

She wondered: *Should I tell the truth, in all its gory detail, to my sister in blood?*

* * *

The bakery was bustling with customers. Dark occasions dictated good business. A juicy scandal, a notable death, an announcement of war or approaching plague, decorated the store's walls with the town folk through the sleepy afternoon hours to the end of the day; they hoping to purchase just a little more excitement or commiseration than what they'd enjoyed earlier in the town square.

Amalina was always amused to see the people, upon finding another awful tidbit of the story, cross themselves religiously with a roll, or a loaf of bread she'd made.

But their superstitious gestures showered bread crumbs to the floor and the crumbs attracted mice.

Because of the brisk business, Amalina did not get to speak with her father beyond requesting loaves for the sideboard, or pieces of string to tie a package, or a broom to sweep the crumbs and smack the mice. Instead she spent time sifting the patrons, deciding which faces belonged to the conspiracy and which ones were clueless. Almost all, it appeared, were guilty. Men and women alike. The clueless ones hung credulously to every new lie, and not wanting to be left out, then lugged the story along with clunky exaggerations of their own. So who's to say which one was *really* in on it, then? In the case of her father being one of them: Dragomir was too caught up in business to provide clues.

She also fussed with the nagging question of what to do next. As far as she knew, she was the sole eyewitness to the crime ... and the only one who'd confronted the murderer himself. She was quite alone, then. Who best to approach with such startling information before she went mad by trying to contain it? How could Amalina not burst by holding it in? What a story to tell! It was like holding her breath, and with every ready ear tempting her to gasp for air.

Worst of all, though, she hated the thought of being one of the village conspirators now; *and against my own friend, at that!* Because Amalina appreciated the truth above all, she was loath to join them, to peddle their lies of village normalcy, much less add her own guilty silence to it! to be part of any secret, ever!

Only hadn't she just done so? Coldly losing Cristine for it?

But if Amalina confided the truth to Cristine, whether to relieve herself of guilt, or to get her best friend back, or both, that girl would never be able to keep such a powerful secret. Not even with their blood oath. She had a mouth that flowed worse than Sadra sometimes. And then, if word of Amalina's meeting with the man got out and spread, *wouldn't that be the very end!*

At the sound of the church bell, the doors were closed and the panels put up, just as it always had been in the village. A heartfelt prayer was given for the soul of Lucinda Skeldar, for her ill-fated parents, and for the preservation of the village against the ever-present wolves.

Cousin Jenna was sullen through the prayer and their meal. The depth of her sadness was unaccountable to Amalina. So far as she could tell, Jenna and Lucinda had never been very close. Her emotions must have sprung from the fact that Lucinda's loss was a direct threat to her life; a shrinking of the ranks of her peer group—allowing Cristine's theory as true: the village's unloved daughters being sacrifices to the wolf pack—which meant Jenna was now closer to facing sharp, snapping, bloody teeth.

This thought brought the man's blood-coated smile flashing before Amalina.

Dragomir ignored Jenna, just as Cristine had predicted. Dragomir had never bothered to explain his indifference to Jenna, or hers to him, for the years her cousin had been living with them. And for her part, Amalina had simply placed any curiosity she had about their odd behavior on a shelf for later examination, if she should have the time or interest in it. For some reason Jenna, as a human being *or* a subject, had never yet interested her.

Perhaps because … well, perhaps Amalina's disinterest in her cousin was born from the general village's attitude toward her—and that strange race of daughters pledged to wolf-fanged doom!

Cristine's theory *was* something to consider.

The three distracted nibblers, Amalina, Dragomir and Jenna, were quiet within their own considerable thoughts.

"Papa," said Amalina, breaking the hours-long silence with a sweet tone of undiluted innocence. "When you woke me this morning, did you know about Lucinda? That she … she was dead?"

He nodded grimly.

"You should have told me to wear my mourning dress. It was embarrassing, Papa, going out in colors."

"You're right. I forgot."

He gave her a smile and with his large hand patted her knee. He said nothing to Jenna, who sat next to him and who'd also gone out in a dress with bright embroidered flowers.

"Sorry, Jenna," said Amalina in a low voice, as if to apologize for something, but probably wasn't heard.

When the meal was over, Jenna headed with silent tears to her room. Amalina helped her father clean and prepare the store, and combine the ingredients for baking the next morning.

She also stole secretly to the sideboard, to collect some items for later use. She hid them in her dress.

"Papa," she picked up the questioning, as innocent as ever, now that they were alone, "why must we always cover the windows?"

"I already told you."

"Wolves can't climb as high as the second floor. They could never get in through my window if I left it open."

"I never said we do it to keep the wolves out," her father smiled. It was a broad, patronizing smile. As if to say he was always ready to be entertained by his daughter's simple, unexpected thoughts. "It's the bad air and the dust. Nobody in this village would suffer worse than us to let the mountain's air into their house at night. We would be ruined for the day, if not the week, should a contagion get into our supplies and wreck our dough."

"Sorry, Papa. I will be more careful."

"No need. I shut up the window. You only have to leave it alone."

"About the wolves …" and now her eyes grew large and her voice became low and breathy, as if she were about to ask for a favor she knew he would not grant her. "You asked me if I'd seen an animal last night, when I looked out the window. I thought you were worried I'd seen a wolf. And that it might get up through the window and attack me … like it did Lucinda … *in the forest*. I would have shut the window tight if I'd seen a wolf, believe me, Papa."

"I believe you," he smiled. "Wolves don't come into town. Not this far, anyway. It would be a very bad sign if they did."

"Why would it be a bad sign if they did?"

"It would mean something bigger—and worse—has moved into the forests. Something the wolves are more afraid of than us."

"Oh, I see," she said. "Then what animal did you mean when you asked if I'd seen one?"

He thought about it.

"A cat, or a deer, or a sheep, or a goat, or a dog. Something that might be scared into our streets by the wolves." He paused before he finally admitted: "I suppose I meant the wolves, too, Amalina."

"Who did you mean, when you asked if I'd seen a man?"

Her father's eyebrows went up. But he didn't answer.

Surprise #3: Dragomir was in on it.

. . .

When Amalina went to her bedroom, she saw the book on astronomy—which she had not yet finished—had been replaced with her favorite book on insects, the one with the delightful chapter about bees and honey making. She boiled angrily at her father. Until she realized this injustice fell in line with her new-found reality:

#1: There were secrets some of the adults kept from the young and innocent.

She half smiled at the image of the shadowy culprit, in sweaty desperation, swapping the offending book (the one that had caused her to open her window last night, against the rules), for a book far less dangerous. He worrying she'd notice the swap; or worse, that she would understand why it had been done.

Amalina's smile faltered only a little when she went to the window and saw twenty nails driven into and around the wood panel.

This could only be expected, she decided, because:

#2: There were people in the town—mostly young, almost all women—determined (by some means) to be sacrifices, who were ostracized and left for, if not outright encouraged to be killed by, dark forces.

While Lucinda and Cousin Jenna were of this fated number, Amalina and Cristine were not. And so her father had been forced to act; to protect Amalina. Not only because it wasn't her rightful destiny to be killed by the man, the monster, but because:

#3: Dragomir was one of *them*—the ones who knew. It was obvious now. And of course he would do anything he could to preserve his beloved daughter from the menace. So away went the book. And in went the long nails around Amalina's window. To close it for good and to keep her safe.

If nothing else, Amalina noted, as she quickly worked her torn bedclothes with needle and thread, her father had obviously never tested the murderer's strength, nor fully understood how powerful he was, or he wouldn't have bothered with the nails.

At this, the unreality of the day concluded with a nervous pang, which shot through Amalina's whole body. Just when dreams should be taking hold, and in minutes her head and limbs surrendering to fantastic thoughts ... her body chilled. Her mind hardened.

She was alone in a village of innocents and conspirators, all operating with their own set of facts. None of which applied to her dilemma, or helped her in any way. She shoved her repaired dress back into the drawer.

With a shrug to free herself from any further thoughts on the matter, Amalina got under the thin wool blanket and stared at the window—or where the window would be, as it was hidden in the warm gloom beyond the candlelight.

And then, gripping two large and sharp knives in each hand, she waited for the man to come.

3

Promises Broken ... and Kept

The room was dark and warm. Amalina's hands, gripping the large knives on either side of her body, became sweaty. Breathing calmly, she dried her palms on the rough blanket, and then she took up the knives again.

He is coming ...

. . .

The vision of the man, the feeling of his body and his arms and hands locked around her, the consuming look in his eyes, haunted Amalina's every thought. She heard his voice, the few words he'd spoken, over and over again: "Perfect, yes. But, not now ... No ... Not now. Not ... *now.*"

His threat to kill everyone she loved did not bother her. It seemed only natural for him to have said it. More intriguing to Amalina were those words he'd said to himself—*for himself*—when he thought she wasn't listening: "... Not now. Not ... *now.*"

These words repeated in her head. Relentlessly, as if chasing her; or her them.

Throughout the previous day, Amalina had been irritated by visions of blood flying from Lucinda's neck. The sight being so singular, so horrifying, so unexpected—the memory like a wound that would not close, bursting again before her eyes like a vivid piece of nightmare at every mention of Lucinda Skeldar's name. But those were just phantom flashes, causing her a small gulp of surprise and disgust, to be pushed down.

But the memory of him and his words: "Not now. Not ... *now* ..." they came voluntarily, and in a heated way. She took the words as a promise that he would return. A prospect that—just like his threat to kill everyone—did not outright frighten her.

There was good reason not to be frightened. The monster had had Amalina in his arms, he could have killed her. But he had not. He'd warned of death for everyone else, if she should tell anyone what she'd seen of the murder, but he had not threatened *her* directly. Amalina had faced death then, and finding herself immune to it—even without good reason for the immunity, but there it was—she was emboldened.

This murderer, this villain, could pluck the strongest man from the earth and tear throats out with his teeth. But Amalina was more powerful than him. For some reason.

How amazing. How intoxicating. The world became ever more interesting than it had been. She had grown beyond simply being a self-styled queen of the night. In reality, she was now an equal to ... to whatever powerful thing he was. The world was more alive, as she was more alive. As the colors became more vibrant, even in the dark.

And her thoughts kept circling:

He is coming for me, what shall I do?

... Amalina couldn't wait for him to return ...

He is coming for me, what shall I do?

... To test her strength against him ...?

He is coming for me, what shall I do?

... To learn more about him ...?

He is coming for me, what shall I do?

... To challenge him—to persuade him by logic or force—to leave the village alone ...? (at which point she would become a hero. A hero above all heroes of all time!)

He is coming for me, what shall I do?

... She dreamed of every possibility ...

He is coming for me ...

... But if he were to return, she knew in her heart there was only one answer when facing such a villain: She must strike him down.

... *What shall I do?*

...

While preparing the ingredients for the next morning's dough, Amalina had hid two large and razor sharp knives in her dress. She held these weapons on either side of her prone body. The plan was that when the man came for her she would fall limp as she had the first time. But before he could speak, or commence whatever evil he had planned, the trap would spring: She would plunge a blade into his chest. She would do so, again and again, until he fell out of the window, foul monster dead, never to threaten another life.

Oh, that would make Amalina a great legend, certainly.

The prospect thrilled and terrified her. The confrontation, its outcome, was impossible to predict. But think if she should succeed!

It was the joy-giving, body-electrifying charge only the crisis of life and death brings. She only had to wait for him to come.

Which he had promised to do.

But, in the end, he did not.

$\bullet\;\bullet\;\bullet$

Which was just as well.

Because Amalina's excitement, her feeling of invulnerability, her bold confidence that she could survive the man's return—and also succeed in her heroic attack—lasted not much longer than a quarter hour. Sitting alone in her bedroom staring into the darkness (toward the boarded window), she recalled his terrifying power, and knew, in reality, there wasn't much she could do to hurt him.

He was too fast. He was too strong.

And what had his words meant, really? "Perfect"? And "Not ... now"?

It certainly wasn't a guarantee he could not hurt her. She had no real proof of that. Her idea that she was forbidden to him were words she'd taken from his look; ones she'd fancied she'd heard in his thoughts. He hadn't actually spoken them aloud.

So those words he *had* said were all she was left to interpret. And what of them?

"Perfect," he'd said. How was she perfect? Perfect for another victim?

"Not ... now"? Maybe he'd already had enough blood from Lucinda and he wanted to save Amalina for another meal, when he had a stronger appetite.

Could that be?

A shiver ran up Amalina's back and across her arms and made her hair stand up. She imagined him right outside the nailed up window, ready to break through. He could easily destroy the board. With the gentlest rap of his hand. He was so powerful. She could be sitting in bed and he'd blow in like a sharp wind and snap her throat right open. She held back a whimper.

What if this was true?

What if he was coming for her tonight—to kill her?

It was all the better she'd taken the knives from the cupboard, because now she was in a fight for her life. She dare not warn her father. The man would make Dragomir suffer for it, too.

She could not tell anyone. No. And especially not Dragomir.

It was just the man and her, pitted against each other.

Her thoughts turned feverishly to how exactly she should strike with her knives. How she would spring this deadly trap. Should she follow her original plan, playing limp and innocent? But in a sudden nervous turn, she crouched just below the window, muscles coiled tight like a depressed spring, the business end of the knives pointing upward, ready to launch toward the ceiling when he broke through.

Next, she was hiding—shivering—behind her dresser.

Or, after that, now turtled beneath her covers, ready to flee or lash out if and when he found her.

But he did not come.

Night after night he failed to show.

And Amalina grew ever more tired, like the fizzling candles she held, as she waited through the night, staring without blinking. Expecting him to be there. The terror and anticipation glutting her veins, but sapping her strength.

Sometimes she couldn't help but fall asleep, and she'd wake with a start, stabbing at the air.

She grew tired of staring at the wood plank. In the midnight hours she could imagine all kinds of horrible creatures outside of it, waiting to pour in. It was frustrating. She began to resent that piece of wood.

Knowing the nailed-in plank was useless to stop the man, she carved a small hole in it, just so she could see outside, to see if he was there in the street. Doing so rid Amalina of the speculative imaginings of beasts lurking behind it. She saw what was really there and what wasn't. And she could prepare, she told herself, if she saw him coming.

He did not appear.

Was it because he could not see her in the window, see her whole body, as he had on that first night?

Or was he—for some reason—biding his time?

She couldn't wait like this forever.

"... Now," she caught herself mumbling, as if a command, into the chilly night air.

• • •

"How did this happen, little one?" asked Amalina's father, a number of nights later, pointing to the hole she'd made in the panel. It looked like an animal had gnawed through the wood from the inside. "How did this happen?"

"I don't know," she said. She moved uncomfortably under the covers. He could tell she was still wearing her day dress and not her night clothes.

She hadn't changed for sleep!

"You did this," he said with purple exasperation. "Why? I told you not to open the window."

"I didn't open it. It's still nailed shut."

"You broke it. I patched it up. I put a cork seal on it and you broke that. Again and again, Amalina. You've done it every night since—"

"The cork fell out. It's not my fault. And the board split open in the first place probably because you nailed it so much, Papa. And then the wind comes at night and blows out the seal."

"The wind blows from the outside. Which means pushing *against* the window. Pushing it *inward*, into the room, not *outward*," her father said.

"The cork is lying on the ground outside. So something pushed it out. Which was you."

"I just wanted to see the moon," she said quickly. "The window isn't really open, is it? Not if there's just a little hole in it. No wind comes in. Look, I can seal it with the cork again when I'm done looking and it's fine."

"Do as I say," he commanded her.

"Yes, Papa."

• • •

The next seal was a wedge perfectly matched to the opening.

When the wedge didn't work, came wedge and pitch.

When the wedge and pitch didn't work, it was wood and nails, covering the crack entirely.

When this covering failed, as everything else had, her father, more purple than ever, stood outside Amalina's little attic room; while inside, Sadra, the minister's wife, and Alexei, the old village doctor, carefully and dutifully inspected Amalina's body.

The first site the doctor visited with his trembling hands was Amalina's smooth neck. All the way around her throat they tickled.

His breath smelled of sausages.

The minister's wife, who brought with her a scent of acid and wood fire (which hatcheted through the sausages), couldn't decide whether to smile or frown as she observed closely. And so she just glowered.

When the doctor and Sadra didn't find what they were looking for, the search carried on to Amalina's arms and legs. Then her clothes were removed, piece by piece, and the doctor's hands got shakier.

Sadra croaked suggestions, leading Alexei's hands to painful areas, contorting Amalina into positions of torture on her bed. And in moments where the minister's wife could not speak, struck dumb by a gulping, lip licking triumph, Sadra's eyes blazed so maliciously the heat concentrated like hot coals tossed onto Amalina's gooseflesh.

Amalina complained she was cold. Sadra slapped her and held her down, the peashell mattress crunching under their combined weight, while the doctor inspected so unquestioningly every length and fold Sadra sent him.

In the end, old Alexei shook his head and shrugged. They had no answers.

After thanking them, her father whispered hopefully on their way out, turning an eye back toward Amalina: "A delicate matter. You will not speak of this to others?"

"Secrets last as long as God pleases," said Sadra.

• • •

Dragomir paced about, unable to formulate words. What would he do? she wondered, nervously.

He could switch her bedroom just to get her away from that window.

He could insist that he, or Jenna, or both, sleep alongside her at night—to prevent her from opening it.

He could board the window altogether and seal the new wall with tar.

He paced the small, simply furnished room, his head shaking, looking like a bear that was losing its mind.

Amalina watched old Dragomir caught in a novel state of upset.

She was responsible for her father's condition, of course. And she felt guilty for it.

But how could it be helped? She couldn't tell him the truth, could she?

Whether it was true that the killer was powerless against her (a fantasy she still entertained from time to time, always during the day when everything felt safe), or it was not, his threat to destroy her loved ones carried weight. A throat ripping was perhaps quicker and more merciful than a lingering death from plague—which Amalina had seen carry off a good number of neighbors and friends ... but death, no matter how quick, was something she would not wish on her father—or anyone else—much less suffer on her account.

It seemed impossible old Dragomir could be killed as easily as Lucinda Skeldar. He was the strongest man Amalina knew (except maybe the loggers who visited the village from time to time). And for some years, when she was a child, she had even assumed her father was near eternal. But having seen and felt the killer's power, she knew down to her toes the man could carry through with his threat to destroy Dragomir; if Amalina were to violate the man's one condition, and admit to her father the truth.

"We have to open the shop," was all her father could come up with when he finished pacing. But before he could make it to the door—satisfied he'd said *something*—he stopped. "Amalina, what has come over you?"

"I don't understand why you're so upset. I want to see outside. I don't see the harm."

"You defy me."

The pain in his eyes. Something she'd never seen before. It was hurtful.

And the killer's threat, though she'd considered it dangerous just a moment before, was, in truth, waning. He'd promised to visit again, hadn't he? Yet he hadn't returned. Were his threats just as credible as his promises?

And with the guilt at disobeying her father, and the explosive desire to tell someone—anyone—what she'd seen and knew, and the crushing isolation of keeping it all in, she could barely keep her lips from moving; her throat giving voice to something she should not. She started. And then stopped. Then started again. She couldn't think of what to say. She wanted to say something, but knew what she most wanted to say she could never reveal.

For relief, she settled on a counterattack: "Why don't *you* tell *me* the truth, Papa?"

"What do you mean?"

"When I tell you why I open my window, I am telling the truth. But you aren't satisfied. When I ask you the reason why opening it is wrong, you won't tell me."

"It's wrong, daughter, because I told you not to open the window and yet you do it anyway."

"But, Papa, *why* must you tell me not to? There must be some good reason. A little hole won't let anything in that will hurt me. *Will it?* I can keep my door closed when I—"

"If you do not stop this, you will bring embarrassment down on this family. Don't you understand? Now Sadra knows. Now everyone will."

"You're the one who had them come here, Papa."

"That's not the point. Why won't you obey me, even when it threatens my standing, and your standing, and the standing of our business in this town? Something I've worked hard for my whole life! My whole life!"

"And that's all you care about!" cried Amalina. "Your standing!"

"What?" He looked very surprised by what she said.

So did Amalina. And she didn't know how to follow it up.

"We have to open the shop." He left.

Amalina noticed her father's absence as she tended to the customers. Tired as ever, she didn't give it much thought and pushed on, half lost in fading memories of Lucinda's killer. Even now, the thought of Lucinda's bleeding neck did not produce more than a blackened, worthless image. She wondered if the same devaluing would happen to *him*, the man. At some point the watchmaker asked Amalina what her father was doing outside.

She found Dragomir on a borrowed ladder hanging a bundle of garlic outside her boarded window. She had never questioned why almost every house in the village had a fresh string or round of garlic posted beside its doorway. The purpose had seemed decorative. Now it did not. And the world gained a new, if disagreeable, color. Her father came off the ladder, passed her with an exaggerated stride, and told her: "Get back inside."

For most of the afternoon Dragomir was out of the store. Amalina had no time to sneak off to meet with Cristine. To apologize to her friend, to hopefully mend their relationship and trade information. She had missed their rendezvous for nearly a week now. Who knows how it was affecting Cristine, who'd been in such a bitter mood when they last met. But Amalina was more distracted with the mystery of what her father might be up to— added to the occasional visions of the murderer—to be bothered at the thwarting of her plans.

Helpfully, Cristine came to the store behind the tailcoats of her mother. Cristine at first wouldn't look at Amalina, but after awhile began shooting scouting glances from below her hood. When their eyes finally met, there was a small jolt of electricity. Cristine didn't smile though. Her mouth was set straight and cold. Only, she continued glancing.

"What?" Amalina mouthed to her friend on the next glance, as Cristine's mother continued to chat with old Widow Lidsz, oblivious to her daughter behind her.

Cristine shook her head.

"What?" Amalina mouthed again.

"Where were you?" Cristine mouthed back, her icy eyes rounding into something a little more vulnerable, if critical.

Amalina made a gesture while she handed bread to her next customer, indicating how helplessly busy she was.

"Are you still mad at me?" Cristine mouthed to Amalina.

Amalina made a face that said, "Don't be ridiculous."

"I'm still mad at you," Cristine mouthed back. But then she cracked a smile. And Amalina smiled, too.

Cristine lifted the hem of her skirt discreetly and showed a large bruise on her shin. A gift from the mean girls, of course. They'd done it after Lucinda's death to release their rage and fear on their costumary victim. Or Cristine had tempted them into it with a vicious, ill-considered taunt. She pursed her lips and shook her head.

Amalina rolled her eyes. Then made a gesture over her heart.

As Cristine followed her mother out of the store, she left Amalina with a sly wink. They were still sisters of soul and blood, and in good standing. This boosted Amalina's withering spirits.

It was the highlight of her working day.

• • •

The iron bell rang the day's end from the church tower, just as it always had.

And then, across the village all the households wound up their businesses and shut tight their doors and windows, just as they always had.

Then the families sat for a prayer and a meal around their hearths, with the bright snap of the hearth fire, the whisper of the wind, and the far off howl of the wolves threading through their supper silences, just as they always had.

Only on this evening, in the Dalca house, the stew got the worst of it: A hearty mix of vegetables, with several chunks of beef, and spiced with wild herbs, it was one of their best meals they'd ever prepared; all the participants were invigorated when they began to eat it. But leaden by their mutual standoff, Amalina didn't clap or sing over the pot, and Dragomir didn't bestow so much as a dissatisfied grunt on it, and, instead, in a miserly way, forced each ladle into his mouth to become a bite of ashes. Amalina could never *dare* think she could continue putting holes in the window and be forgiven, he smoldered.

And then, to finish things, Dragomir informed Jenna, who seemed in danger of making a favorable remark on the stew: "You will take Amalina's room."

Jenna looked surprised, befuddled.

"No," said Amalina.

"Yes, she *will*," Dragomir growled, leaning his reddening face toward his daughter, which brought out the details of soup drops and random crumbs in his voluminous beard.

"No, I won't," said Cousin Jenna, suddenly aflame.

Surprised by the attack from his left flank, his face reddened even more. "You will."

"I don't want it," Jenna snapped. "It's drafty, and small, and the smell of the ovens and the customers' dirty boots collects up there. I like my own room and I won't trade with her."

He folded his arms, frowning at a space between the two girls.

"Papa, I don't want hers, she doesn't want mine."

"Neither of those rooms are *either* of yours," he said to both. But then he turned to Jenna. "This is *my* house and they are *my* rooms. And for her mother's love, I will not dispossess my daughter Amalina. Defy me, dear niece, and you will be without a room, and moreover a house. You can take up with the cats or the dogs for all I care."

Jenna threw her bowl down, it landed with a solid splash. She was already at her bedroom door when Amalina's father called to her.

"Where do you think you're going?"

"Where do you think, Uncle?" Jenna shouted. "You'd have no trouble forcing me into Amalina's shabby little dresses, no matter how much it hurt me to squeeze into them. But you'd never let Amalina be seen in the street in *my* clothes, would you?"

That shut him up.

The guiltless and delicious stew went cold, and Dragomir dumped it without so much as a last swipe of a finger for a final taste. While the transfer of the ladies' wardrobes between bedrooms was conducted in the gloom of unhappy muttering. "Bet her bed's smaller, too," Jenna complained.

Amalina lay her dresses on her new bed—which smelled of Jenna's favorite flowery perfume—and then looked to Jenna's window. The window was small, and the panel fastened over it was solidified with riveted metal bands. It looked like a miniature armored door that a tiny hawk might make use of.

Amalina blew out a frustrated sigh, which she was sure her father enjoyed hearing. He must be listening, she thought.

Later that evening, during their nightly preparations for baking the next morning, she made certain to disappear at strategic moments to the closet.

And later still, when she was alone in Jenna's first floor bedroom—now her own bedroom!—she took from under her dress the block hammer and chisel she'd smuggled, and went for the window. She could picture the opening she was going to make, and tried to imagine the man outside—the memory of him fading to where his features were becoming indistinct (which was maddening)—whether he might be on the street close by, or only to be glimpsed in the very dark distance. But there he would finally be, and her weapons would be ready.

"Amalina!"

Her father stood in the doorway.

"What?" She thrust her jaw out the way she'd seen him do it, to show defiance.

"Why?"

The candle flickered in his hand, he was trembling. It was all too much. His eyes were watery. It looked like he might cry. The old bear had never cried. Not for her. Not that she had ever seen. It was an expression of emotion she did not want to have mar the might and dignity of the man who had raised her. She almost broke down at the thought of it.

The hammer and chisel felt very heavy. But she kept them poised, ready to make their mark. Something had to happen. She had to open the window and find the man waiting outside or she had to relieve her father's pain; to explain her actions.

Her father—her kind father—would understand if she told him. As he'd always forgiven her for anything she apologized for.

But she couldn't tell him! There was no way to tell him. Was there?

Now she wanted to cry.

"Leave me alone!"

"Put those down and get into bed this instant."

"It doesn't make any sense."

"I don't have to make sense, I'm your father."

"You just like bossing me around!"

"I like you to obey, like a good daughter. What do *you* like, Amalina? Does disobeying your father feel good to you?"

This made her think of Jenna. And Lucinda. And the girls destined for death. But she wasn't one of *them*.

"Why don't you tell me the truth?" she challenged.

"What truth?"

"Why you don't want me to open the window! It's because of the strange man, isn't it?"

Her father gasped. He shot forward, out of control. He almost dropped the candle. "What man? Who are you talking about, Amalina?"

Now it was out, wasn't it? She felt her secrets pressing out the small puncture she'd just made in the air between them, with the full force of a cask of wine shoving out a spigot. Shooting out like the crimson gout from Lucinda's neck.

"The man who kills people," she answered.

He gulped.

She gulped.

"You've heard about him," her father said. "In rumors. And you want to see him. But you can't. And even though you can't, you should never try."

"But I *have* seen him, Papa. When he killed Lucinda."

"You saw!"

"It was horrible," she blurted. "But *everyone* said the wolves attacked Lucinda in the forest. Even *you* told me that."

"You saw him. You are lucky you are alive, Amalina."

"Who is he?"

"You are lucky you are alive. Do you understand that?"

"Oh, he wouldn't hurt me. If he wanted to hurt me, or kill me, he would have done it then. But he didn't."

"He saw you?"

"Yes, Papa. I was in the window."

Within an hour Amalina was in a space she never knew existed. It was a basement cell below the deputy's small jail. There was an old bench and straw and a pitcher of water. She supposed this was a real life dungeon.

The men (including her father) had left her down there with a torch. Above the torch's calm hiss, she could hear their excited voices upstairs. They were deciding who would stand guard for the night.

Amalina tested the strength of the iron bars caging her in, then sighed once more with frustration. This time she was without options to free herself—without any alternatives she could think of.

Maybe this was for the best, she thought. She didn't know how strong the bars were but they *might* stop the man, should he come for her. And he would come for her, wouldn't he? She'd broken his command of silence. She was defenseless without her knives now. Her father had found them and taken them. So what good was escaping? Instead, she lay down to sleep, trusting to the bars for her protection.

• • •

The man moved out of the shadows as if through the wall itself. He stopped outside her cell, watching her.

"You will help me." His voice was deep and imposing, and sent vibrations along her limbs. His pose was solid and still, something like a statue, but also suggested an immense spring ready to give way. Then he moved *through* the metal bars, like they were silk curtains. His eyebrow lowered to become a remonstrating check mark over his right eye. "Come, Amalina. We haven't much time."

4

Adventure in Moonlight

The largest cemetery within the Ardeelian mountain ranges was said to be the graveyard adjoining the St. Grigori Cathedral. This because of its gratuitous amount of level land—level being a relative term in the mountains. But St. Grigori's yard could *never* boast of the most occupants. How many anonymous mass graves, stocked during the country's darkest days of plagues and Tartar invasions, would produce more bodies if they could only reveal themselves; with their knee-shivering, worm-glutted stacks upon stacks of forgotten bones?

St. Grigori rightfully claimed the longest and widest plot, however. Spread over seven luxurious rolling hills, with room enough—besides the graves—for many copses of trees and its own portion of lakefront. All bounded by high iron fencing, as if the modest headstones of the pious poor, or soaring tombs of the nobler families, might need to repel an invasion force even from the water.

Somewhere within the St. Grigori cemetery, Neku Jonker plodded a course through a section of headstones that were crammed close together. The wood handle of the shovel in one hand and the iron feet of the cage lamp in the other both together knocked and dinged without rhythm, but in a tuneful way, on the corners and tops of the stones. Neku swore lightly at the small pains the collisions made, afraid the next might make him drop one item or the other.

Panting, already out of breath, his mind was distracted in the work still lying ahead for him. The *fun*, as he would call it.

• • •

Maintaining the graveyard had not always been Neku Jonker's charge. If circumstances hadn't happened the way they had, it rightly never would have. From an early age he was considered too slow for any job requiring responsibility. As well, armed with a top row of teeth sticking far out past the bottom jaw; googly, bulging eyes; strange hairy warts on his chin; head hair that shot out on all sides like a carelessly dropped haystack: he wasn't cut out for work in any position dealing upfront with the public.

His drawbacks dropped him into the charitable orbit of St Grigori's Cathedral, which claimed all the unwanted souls, dead or sometimes living.

And the cathedral's dark and reluctantly traveled burial grounds seemed—to the cardinal and populace alike—the best place to stock Neku Jonker.

So Neku fell into the graces of the graveyard's lifelong intendant, Ilya the Grave Digger. Ilya was a big-bellied, big-chested, big-hearted man with sympathetic eyes, and a mouth pleasingly noncommittal. He accepted everyone with his kind, gentle manner, whether they be dragged bawling in through the iron gates by a parent to visit some ancestor's resting place, or they needed the final piece of dirt to be cast over their bones. He was the perfect man for the job, and he had been so for decades.

In his customary good spirits, he accepted Neku as a gift from the Lord above—if not a singular burden from the cardinal—as a way to ease his back now that he was getting on in years.

Neku had no sense for order but took direction well, Ilya would boast. And anyone can dig a hole, even an idiot like Neku.

. . .

Presently, Neku found the site he wanted and closed the hood over his lamp before setting it on the grass. The moon was enough to do tonight's work. First he used a knife to reveal and remove the carpet of grass before the gravestone. Then he swung the shovel, spun its shaft in his hand, before he sent its blade into the ground. It bit deep, his muscles strained, and the first load of dirt broke free. Ilya the Grave Digger roundly admitted Neku had a knack with the shovel. Neku was quick and tireless (once he was in motion). So more and more he'd given over his work to the gangly boy. And sometimes he'd eat his meals with him. And he'd drink hard spirits with him. And he would, in his loneliness, talk to him.

One evening, Ilya had drunk more wine than usual and saw they would not have the grave finished before sunset. He called Neku up from the hole to rest for a moment. The two talked after a while.

Ilya, with a wink, asked Neku if he wanted to know the troubles of being the intendant of the world's largest cemetery. Seeing the mischief in his boss' eyes, he nodded; Neku liked mischief on a molecular level.

"You may think we sit on the lowest rung of society, Neku, my child," said Ilya, with another wink and a nudge with his knuckle. "Oh, most people do consider us lowly and worthless, of course. But not all. There are some ... I tell you, I could be *rich*. Do you believe me? A very rich man. One of the richest, even all the way to Tsobl.

"You see," Ilya continued to the quiet but now indecently attentive Neku, "but maybe I shouldn't say. But I must ... Yes, I must tell you. Because some day you might encounter the same temptation, and you must know how to respond to it:

"Years ago, a merchant, who I shall not name, took me aside ..." he stopped himself. "Oh, this was a few days after I had shut away a high placed woman—who I again will not name—a wife of—no, I should not say ... Even *you* might be able to figure it out. This merchant came to me, with tears in his eyes, vibrating at the farthest ends," Ilya demonstrated the merchant's vibrations by shaking his hands in front of Neku, "unable to control his emotions. He asked me, begged me, that I might do him a favor when he died (a dire moment he felt was fast approaching—and it turned out he was right, you see). He confided to me that he and this woman I'd recently buried—a high placed woman, did I say? who was married to a powerful lord—were lovers!

"... Please, Neku, don't be shocked. This world is full of sinners, and some find their way here, into our consecrated ground. Now, he asked that I might discover a way to remove her—his lover—from her crypt, and place her inside his own vault—next to him—when the time came. I denied him as politely as I could, telling him he must be out of his mind with grief to ask for such a thing, but he'd soon recover. However, he did not stop. No, the horny devil persisted. I told him it would not be proper. What if someone should find out? Whatever private crimes these two sinners had committed while they lived, shouldn't her husband have the right to have his beloved wife beside him in their final rest? Shouldn't the innocent husband, who had conducted his life righteously and without sin, be the one to claim eternal rewards, and the adulterers punished?

"This merchant plied me with bribes of every order and degree, and baited me with modifications to his request. He promised a bequeathment of all his wealth if I should just—*on one night of the year*: the date of his birth— carry her body to his, or his to hers, so they might lie together ... at least once a year! He assured me this foul deed is what *she* would want.

"He showed me tokens of their betrayal and infidelity— which he called 'love'— against the powerful lord: trinkets and letters which I did not want to cast my eye upon, even if I could read their filthy words. He read them to me, and I could barely keep from throwing him out.

"But he was in earnest, and fell to my feet, pleading. I saw he was withering away and would die soon. I felt my withholding this favor was aiding in doing him in. Still, I could not bring myself to agree to the terms. I said I could not, not in all good conscience. And besides, how foolish it would look, how odd, for the wealthiest man in town to name the graveman his heir. There would be questions— and my station would be so elevated upon such a gift—his entire fortune? Can you think of it!—there would be no way for me to render the service he requested. You see, I would no longer *be* Ilya the *digger*. I'd be Ilya the Richest Man in the World.

"The day before he died, he came to me, skinnier than you, Neku, with a solution. He would secretly pay me more than I'd ever dare dream to possess. Before dying, when he understood the moment of his death was at hand, he would swallow a whole bag of gold coins. He would swallow several rings— one being one of the love tokens, aforementioned, which the woman had given him—and I could have it all; if I would just remove him from his resting place on his day of birth, remove the treasure from inside his corpse, and let him on those occasions to lie alongside his love."

After this disquieting story, Ilya assured Neku Jonker that he'd never taken the merchant's offer. Even now, years since the poor fool had died of pining away, Ilya the grave digger had not once visited the man's site after burying him, much less succumbed to the temptation to open the grave, to take his tribute or perform the service.

Ilya nodded happily, satisfied he was in the right, crowing to Neku that the Lord was on his side.

Neku, however, was fascinated by the ghastly deal. Totally entranced.

Old Ilya might have noticed a small gleam in Neku's eye, but if he did, he did not understand its meaning. The gravedigger was near to passing out from strong wine, and the sun was down and there was only the paltry light of a partial moon obscured by clouds, so there was still the chance he hadn't seen it at all.

The next morning, when the cardinal learned of Ilya's tragic death during the night—a drunken Ilya having fallen into an open grave—he charitably allowed Neku the chance to prove himself as the new intendant of the grounds.

This allowed Neku to confirm, on the next full moon, that the merchant—whose identity Neku had no difficulty in determining—indeed had himself buried with a digestive system full of gold and jewelry. He'd nearly burst his (now leathery) stomach, and the riches extended down into a good portion of the shriveled entrails.

Neku sensibly withheld removing from the exterior of the corpse any of the rings and other gold ornaments, for fear of being detected and called a common graverobber.

. . .

Neku's shovel struck wood. In short order he cleared the dirt away from the box, having learned through experience how to prevent the surrounding soil from falling into—and desecrating—the coffin. He used his special tool and removed the already loose nails.

Though the full moon was bright and his eyes well-adjusted to his purpose, he took down and removed the hood from the lamp. He wanted to see everything.

When the lid came off he saw the collapsed face of the woman. Now a simple puppet of dried flesh on bone, hair disheveled by use, and wearing a simple, clean dress—save a number of slashes and holes in the torso—she was someone who, when alive, had been a perpetual victim. Though the medical diagnosis had not been invented yet in that remote time, and the very concept would have been foreign to the hearty and industrious mountain people of Ardeel (whose purpose was to survive any possible calamity), today she would be diagnosed in modern terms as a *morbid masochist*.

Neku had known her when she was alive, but only from a distance, and when he was younger. His youth and general idiocy didn't prevent him understanding that her insistence on blaming everyone else for her problems was the very cause of her problems. Accusing them of plotting against her, and, it would seem, arranging situations where she would be taken advantage of, stolen from, and punished. She died young, though surviving longer than she should have. But her last days were spent wandering the streets pointing a dirty fingernail of accusation at anyone who would pass— *you have done this to me!* she would cry—and then challenge them to hit her, beat her, pull her hair out, stone her; kill her.

She was a perpetual victim, which made her perfect. Staring down at her half rotted, now mummified face, Neku felt the initial jolt, the thrill he'd been waiting for. Here was the night's victim, his work was nearly done. His teeth chattered with excitement.

He hauled her body out of the box and didn't bother with the lamp, but dragged her along, excited to get this business over with ... he'd waited so long.

It was a full moon, when he could see well enough without a lamp and so not attract, by the movement of a swinging light, the attention of the cardinal or his servants inside the cathedral—or any passerby of the cemetery—and then be whipped, or hanged. Or worse.

Though, according to Neku's conscious mind, which was a playground of lies and falsehoods, his fun was merely a service to keep the souls of the graves happy—even though, deep within his twisted soul, it was more truly the illicit thrill of the act that fired his engine and drove him—he knew clearly that to his superiors what he did with the bodies would, without a doubt, be found abominable.

The woman's heels made a soft, halting hiss through the grass on the route to the small woods.

Not far into the tree line he arrived at another body outfitted in a marvelous, if greying, lavender dress. This woman—or rather, the remains of one—opulently clothed, haunted the very air with her presence. Even on a night with no moon and a full cloud cover, Neku believed he could spot her in the deepest forest. She was one of a kind. And on this night, every year since he'd discovered her in *his* yard, she came alive once more.

Neku grew contempt for the body in his arms—a similar revulsion the one in the lavender dress would have had for the *masochistic* worm he was holding, this underling, this *slave. Yes.* And though the body he pulled toward her was in much better condition—a couple centuries fresher—and she— this one in the dress—a simple skeleton with flecks of wooden flesh, a shower of hair that was no better than a wig, and with joints stitched together by ribbons to keep it all of a piece, she was superior, a highborn, even in ancientified death.

Neku celebrated her superiority—enacted it—the way the woman in the lavender dress would have: bringing the poor masochist forward, the maggot mumbling and reproachful and blaming. Neku sent the dagger, clutched in the noble woman's hand, into the worm's crumbling chest. Once. Twice. Three times. Some of the thrusts which would have killed the poor wretch fell into the same holes that had already been made on previous anniversaries.

Yes, this is what the woman in the beautiful dress would have done to the slave, laughing sadistically as she did so, the forever-tormentor giving the forever-victim what they each most desired.

He stopped when he noticed the noble woman's head wobbling dangerously on the ribbon-tether, which linked the neck to the torso. He threw the newly savaged victim to the ground, and shook the noblewoman; to represent the laugh, the loud, cruel laugh, that would have convulsed her at such a moment.

And now—just as it was shortly ago—just as it'd been the moment for the poor slave to rise from her perpetual rest to play the victim, the noblewoman was to meet *her* perpetual fate.

Seizing the great lady around the waist, as if he were the servant of destiny and she his majestic, if helpless, ward, breathlessly he swept her toward St. Grigori's tower.

While repetition dulls one's appreciation for even the most spectacular events, with the height of passion experienced the first time never to be recaptured, Neku's simplicity allowed him to enjoy on every occasion the peak of an old thrill as if it were new. This brought him out to brave his occupation's dangers with the relentlessness of a famished dog slipping into a butcher's market; his mouth watering, every scrap a treat.

He would swear to any judge who might catch his case, Neku Jonker brought the souls of the cemetery to life, allowed their physical halves to reenact their sins once more in the material realm. He could sense their spirit-pleasure—whether they were in heaven or in hell, he did not know—and they cried their support, hurried him on, begged him to be the next one to live again, if for just a handful of hours.

So it went: Men and women carried on their affairs. Thieves stole valuables from their neighbors. Rapists had their satisfaction with the most beautiful and highly stationed women. Sadists and violent citizens had their way with sniveling worms. Zealots boiled the sinners, or bored to numbness the undeserving with their drawn out sermonizing. Husbands beat wives. Wives reduced husbands. Nearly everybody who entered these sanctified grounds on their back was considered an epitome of Christian sainthood, or a deserving martyr, or the Cardinal would never have allowed their entrance, instead condemning them to an anonymous mass grave in the bordering forest. But Neku knew their secrets. Or he could learn them easily enough by observing and listening to talkative mourners. And each new body—or rather, the spirit-person who'd inhabited the dead shell—would live again, truly live, on some special moonlit night.

Even if they were dissolved to nothing more than a skull, or clattering rib cage, or piece of bone.

Neku hurried on towards the church tower, gasping excitedly. It would not be long now.

He shot off the ground.

He realized why he'd done so when he landed, staggering on the grass, and fully comprehended what his unconscious mind had more quickly noticed: the blood- drained woman standing amidst the stones, watching him.

He fell backward, losing his grip on the woman in lavender.

He shook his head. He blinked. He cocked his head. The gaunt woman remained standing there.

No, he thought.

He doubted his eyes. *It couldn't be.*

It shouldn't be.

And night was running out, and his work would be left undone if he didn't move.

He gave the strange apparition a second look, and then readjusted his grip on the woman in lavender, and, convincing himself he was seeing things, stepped toward the Cathedral tower.

"What are you doing?"

He froze.

She'd talked!

He wanted to drop the noblewoman's body away from him, to hide it.

Another thought made him want to hold it up to hide himself.

"Who ... ?" he began to ask.

"What are you doing?" the ghostly figure demanded, her expression unchanging.

"Who is you?"

"You don't recognize me?"

"H-Hedy ... Frau Hedwigga," he whispered hoarsely and gulped. "Meine Damen, my love. My wife."

"Then answer me, Neku Jonker: What are you doing?"

"But can't be," he said, amazed, forgetting the woman in his frozen hands. He stepped forward screwing his eyes this way and that, trying to see her better. The shadows across her face were too deep. He wished the moon was the sun. He could not believe it was her. He repeated: "It, er ... uh, can't."

"It is."

"But, but ... you ... died."

"So I am dead," said the spirit, sternly. "And so is that woman in your hands!"

"Yeh," Neku agreed, still turning his head in many directions, trying to get a better look somehow at Hedwigga. "Her *is* dead. Very, very dead. Her not move. Only me move her. Her not talk. Only me make her talk. But, but, Hedy, you ... right there ... stand on feet ... without me help you. And ... you talk ... talk out your lips."

"And I command you, Neku Jonker," she said. "Stop what you are doing."

"But, but ... you is you?" asked Neku. "Neku no believe."

"Why can't you?"

"Dead no rise by self. It be imp-possible."

"Unless there's a good reason."

"What reason?"

"To warn you that this awful thing you're doing must stop. To think this is what you got up to all those nights you left me alone!"

Neku unconsciously gripped the noblewoman harder, protectively. Her lavender dress crunching tightly between his fingers.

"It is wrong, Neku."

"You look as Hedwigga, miene liebchen," he said. "But, but ... on night, *this* night, rise from dead, you say ... how me know is *very* you?"

"Look at me. Who else could I be?"

"A trick."

"'A trick'? Is it 'a trick' to tell you to do right by the dead? 'A trick' to tell you to be a *good* man?"

"Me feel," he began, after allowing a notion that this ghostly figure might be who she swore to be—and very much seemed to be—his dead wife—and that that he *was indeed* wrong for playing these body games, "what I do ... it be a good work, liebchen. Me feel is so."

"Neku, I am your wife: Hedwigga Jonker, born Hedwigga Von Schiederhausen, daughter of the Duke of—"

"Please, please," said Neku, now feeling confused and suddenly doubtful. "But, but, you know name. Every people know name of beau-ti-ful woman she marry poor Neku, so poor Neku. They know what she look as and know what she wear in bury box. All know. You famous, meine liebchen ..."

"As your wife I command you—!"

"But, but ... *is* you, Hedy, meine liebchen? Is very you?"

"Must I prove myself?"

"Me listens to just one womans, me obeys just one womans ... to God me so promises. If you not Hedy ... oh, oh, Hedy, long rest her soul"—(this phrase, 'long rest her soul', seemingly memorized judging by its perfection)—"she be very unhappy ... to me," At this Neku's eyes looked shrewdly at her.

"Errant husband, ugly fool, you try the very patience of the spirit of the dead," she said.

"You look like Hedwigga, that you do ... But no *sound* much like," he said.

"My voice is hoarse," she said through her teeth. "My throat is dry. I'm not used to speaking in the ground. How does a spirit from the dead sound?"

He became restless. His body shifted back and forth with the urge to continue to the tower, to forget the apparition.

"Prove me you Hedwigga," said Neku finally. "Or me ignore you. Me go now. Very busy."

He even took a daring, impertinent step toward the tower, to push this 'Hedwigga' into action.

"And how shall I prove to you who I rightly am, if you cannot see for yourself? How?"

"Me *will* see for me self," he said, licking his lips. "You dress: shuck it!"

Get naked?

Amalina, who was clothed in the coarse, binding fabric of Hedwigga's funeral dress, and with the plain burial shroud removed and dangling over her shoulder, almost fell backwards. Neku's doubting her, doubting in her appearance, had been only lightly anticipated. And it'd been only more-than-lightly prepared for. This sudden demand—outrageous as it was—that she remove her clothes—called for every nerve Amalina had to keep herself in check, to stand unflinchingly before him instead of crying in alarm.

Neku's arm moved. Suddenly there was a pistol in his hand.

What to do now? She wondered.

The man hadn't told her.

* * *

The man hadn't told her many things. Though he had been with Amalina for almost four hours—which seemed an eternity, every second of it—the whole proceedings had been rushed.

After having led Amalina unseen past her father, the deputy sheriff and the quickly assembling posse, the man had delivered her to a carriage with two horses attached, which then whisked them unnoticed out of the village. Little red curtains covered the carriage's windows, hiding them from sight; and also prevented Amalina from knowing where they were going—if she would have thought to do so.

Her mind had scrambled at every possible opportunity for a weapon, or some method of defense, en route to the carriage. But inside it, the carriage was lit by four small, expensive, glassed-in lamps, and all she could see or think of was *the man* himself. He dressed in very old fashioned, very worn clothes; velvety ones a nobleman might have been proud of, once upon a time. And appearing very large, taking up half the space of the plush, padded compartment. This is what consumed her mind. She didn't even notice the speed or the sway of the carriage as it raced along toward its mysterious destination. *He* had returned as he'd promised ... for her.

What now?

This was the climax of so many sleepless nights. Her heart hammered. She was fully awake.

"Your name is Amalina Dalca," he said.

"Yes."

He nodded as if content with himself: "You know how to speak Deutsch." It was a statement, not a question.

She nodded. "How do you know?"

"The book in your room. It was written in High Deutsch. And of course you are a baker's daughter—daughter of Dragomir Costin Dalca"—he pronounced her father's name with a strange tone, as if in admiration or contempt, his black eyes showed no difference. But the amusement within it was for himself and not to impress Amalina one way or another. He stroked the ends of his long mustache with this same self-pleasure—"a learned man who would make sure his daughter was learned, too, as your mother was, and can speak the many languages of the foreigners who pass through your village on their way to Tsobl. Clever man. Splendid for business ... and diplomatic relations."

Amalina's heart had skipped. "You knew my mother?"

"Let me hear you speak Deutsch for me, Amalina."

"You knew my mother?" she asked in Deutsch.

"Something else," he encouraged.

"What do you want me to say?" again in Deutsch.

His face burst with a smile. "Perfect! Perfect! Yes, that is what I thought when I first saw you, and now my intuition is proved ... and my plan has *improved* 100 fold. Clever man, Dragomir, clever man." He broke from his reverie, though his eyes concentrated more on her surface, observing her but generally and speaking laterally, as if to a merchant who was selling her. "You speak very well, Amalina. Without an accent."

"I have a tutor."

"And your look," the man continued, ignoring her, lost in his own thoughts, "Perfect, just as I thought. But now we shall make certain."

The man shifted position. There was a small trunk at his side. He opened its gold clasp and lifted the lid. Out came a stiff, off-white, charmless dress. He presented it as if measuring her with it, or it with her. His eyes ticked one- two, one-two, between them.

"You will dress yourself in this costume," he said in Deutsch.

"When?"

"Now."

"Where?" she asked, horrified by the single-most option.

His eyes were on her.

"Inside," he said. The dress was in her hands. She saw the last of his shoe as he disappeared out the window and went atop the carriage. "Let me know when it is on and you're ready," he said clearly. He did not shout, but his low rumbled words filled the carriage as if he were still inside.

The dress was rough, and tight, and pinched, and smelled of old wood and smoke. Her nose wrinkled as she changed in the confined space.

"I'm ready," she said.

The man returned gracefully through the window, like water pouring into a glass, his eyes alight and showing the same delight as before he'd left. He nodded again and again. "Perfect." Then he reconsidered. "Almost."

He took out a small box from within the trunk. Opening it, he picked out several even smaller, flat, decorated boxes. One he opened in his palm, and dabbed into it three fingers. They came up covered with a white, creamy substance. He held his fingers toward her face.

"I will apply this to your skin," he said. "I have the skill and I know how you should appear."

"What ... ?"

"Make up, Amalina," he said. "An opaque cream, the acting troupes use it to create their fantastic characters. And tonight that is what you shall be for me: a fantastic character. Oh, you look almost perfect. But you must lose color; face, chest and arms. And your cheeks must be hollow," he applied the end of a burnt cork just below her cheekbone. "And you must have at least some wrinkles now," the cork skipped lightly here and there. "And your eyebrows must be more severe, if you are to fool him."

She submitted to his ministrations, watching his appraising eyes and the excited movement of his lips—his expressions demonstrating how to contort her face properly.

"Perfect," he said as he pulled back into the corner of the carriage and viewed her in whole.

"I don't know how to act. Who am I to play?" asked Amalina.

"You have only to say no more than a few words," he answered. "It should be enough. You look just like her."

"Who?"

"Amalina," he began, "There is a very nasty man, a dire criminal who needs to be stopped. And you must help me stop him. In fact, in all the mountains, you are the only one who can help me. You *will* help me."

"You ..." Amalina ventured, then stopped.

"I? I, what?"

"I don't know who you are."

"You've never heard of me? in whispers around your village? Your father never *warned* you about me?"

She shook her head.

"Innocence only gets you so far in life, little one," the man pontificated. "And only when you are young. And though you are young to me, so is all of humanity. But *you*, child, are too old not to know who *I* am."

"My father is afraid of you."

"Who is not?"

"I saw you kill her. A girl. Lucinda." Then Amalina added from excitement, but without good reason: "My good friend."

Her eyes twitched and goggled, and her teeth gritted in upset, as she worked herself toward reproach at the murderer. It was as if the horror (and the rightful anger) of the crime—of *his* crime, do not forget!—dissolved in his presence, and she needed to pump herself to the level of fear (and hatred!) she should truly have for him, instead of this powerful but oddly neutral hysteria flitting through her body. It made her giddy. She couldn't tell if her act was convincing enough. She was supposed to be upset to the point of madness.

"We haven't much time," he answered. "We know all this, and its better left unsaid, isn't it? So unpleasant. Decorum, please. You are here to assist me tonight."

"And what am I supposed to do?" she answered, still stoking outrage.

"This nasty man, this criminal I spoke of, he lives far from your village. He doesn't know you, has never seen you, or heard of you. So that is why you will be all the more perfect for our plan. To stop him."

"Who is he?"

"You've never heard of him, but his name is Neku. Neku Jonker. He runs the graveyard of his town. On this night, every year, he pulls a woman—a beautiful, innocent woman—from her place within the graveyard that is his charge, and does horrible, unthinkable things to her."

Amalina made a face, to which the man patted the air with his hand in the stately and calming gesture of a gentile aristocrat.

"That's awful," she said. "I can't imagine why someone would—"

"No need to bother," he assured. "You need only help me stop him. You have no problem preventing such a despicable crime from taking place?"

"No ... I mean, yes ... I mean ... no, I would rather help anyone stop such a person. But it does surprise me. You, I mean—"

"What about me?"

Again she pumped her organs for fear, for anger.

"You murder innocent people—!"

"Have I not already warned you away from this subject?" he sniffed.

It was all so disarming, as if he weren't Lucinda's murderer after all; convincingly so, in his refined and noble temperament.

"But what horrible things you do to the living ... and yet you care so much about this man, Neku?" Amalina persisted "and what he does to someone who is beyond caring ... who is *already* dead?"

"That is the last of your interruptions. You know nothing of me, and so what can I say in my defense? And why should I bother? I have my reasons for why I do what I do. But understand, child, this villain operates with impunity year round. Each and every full moon he pulls the dead from their graves or their crypts—not just this one woman, but many others—and makes them perform the most offensive and grotesque acts."

"He does?"

"So it is in your interest to stop him, my dear. Should your father, Dragomir, by some chance, be buried there, his corpse would be enslaved by Neku ... just as *your* body would become his plaything, should you by chance be interred within his domain ... upon the eventuality of your death. You *do* understand that you will die someday, Amalina?"

She nodded. And bolstered by the free-roaming energy seeking some outlet in her body, she felt the familiar tear grow in the corner of her eye, which erupts whenever she considers the dark subject of her mortality. Her mother having already died, she knew it was her destiny to perish, too. As was her father's destiny and all others'. A new tear formed at the building thoughts.

"Heaven help you if your body becomes Neku's," the man smirked, smoothing his mustache. "And so you must help me, because he *must* be stopped."

She asked why he couldn't write a note to the sheriff, or the council.

"They wouldn't listen."

"Why not?"

"They'd reward Neku ... if he told them the whole story. Which he would do if cornered by such an accusation as playing with the dead. They'd encourage his despicable wrong doings if they knew the entire truth."

"They would?"

"You see," he began, leaning back, lowering his eyelids, "The woman he mistreats on this night is my wife. He removes her from her mausoleum and he does unthinkable things to her body; mocks it; dances with it; makes her say and do things she would never have done in life. And when he is done, he takes her to the top of the tower, to recreate the tragic end of her life, when she was thrown off the top of our castle by our enemies." His voice did not carry emotion as it had when he'd clucked over Amalina's costuming. The explanation's cold delivery sounded lethal, and matched the dull, deadly look in his eye. "My beloved is tormented, even in death. Such innocence, a soul so immaculate, so undeserving. Yet she is sullied and tortured by a monster. Any punishment the sheriff might propose against Neku for such a crime—and mind you the sheriff would never—no, not ever—propose a punishment for Neku, out of spite for me and my name!— any punishment pronounced for that Neku Jonker could never satisfy me. I must have my personal accounting in this affair."

"You can't stop him on your own?"

"I've tried, Amalina," said the man. "But he knows not to venture outside his graveyard at night, a place where he is beyond my reach. It is sanctified ground, you see. He has sanctuary."

"Oh." She didn't understand the logic. But the man being convinced of its truth was enough for the moment. "But why me? You have servants."

"Neku carries two pistols and he is a deadly marksman. He killed one of my men, and wounded my last. He will shoot anyone he does not know or trust. And believe me, I have tried to reason with him outside of violence," said the man, with a detectable note of sadness. "I have asked him to stop. I have warned him. I have offered him a fortune in gold, if he would only leave my love alone, or to give her to me. But he is cruel and evil. He enjoys his work. Nothing on earth could persuade him to stop his unholy activity."

The corner of the man's mouth and mustache lifted into an uneven, contemplative smile.

"*Neku* had a wife," the man said. "Her name was Hedwigga. She drifted in from the western frontier, fleeing the war where her family had suffered tremendously. She spoke only her native language when she arrived, and she was reduced to limited means. She resorted to marrying Neku in order to have a legitimate claim to citizenship, and have a new Ardeelian name and identity in which to hide from her family's pursuers ... if they should ever travel this far east.

"Hedwigga was never very happy as Neku's wife," the story went on, "as you could imagine. But she made due. She was a very strong woman and forced our dolt Neku to learn her tongue and not the other way 'round. Then she ruled her pauper's fief as if she were still in a royal family, and he her servant. She was of aristocratic birth, you see. She died several months ago ... and she is buried in his yard. And while I cannot enter that place, there is nothing stopping you. And you, dear Amalina, drawn up in this magnificent disguise, you look just like her and wear the very fashion she was buried in.

"You will enter his yard tonight," he informed her. "And you will pretend you are Hedwigga's spirit. You will stop him from desecrating my wife and you will convince him never to do so again ... and thereby save from his depraved injustices not just my own beloved, but those countless other innocents who are already buried within ... " he added with a pointed look, "and all who might ever be.

"Don't worry, you are perfectly safe," he assured Amalina, upon seeing her look of distress and doubt. "If he believes you are Hedwigga, he will not harm you ... And more, if he believes you are she, he will listen to you and obey you."

"Because he loved Hedwigga," Amalina said to convince herself.

"Because he feared her," the man corrected. "Feared her more than he ever feared me. In her religion, Hedwigga was as charming as a rod of barbed iron."

5

The Last Laugh

The man spent the rest of the time coaching Amalina. Quickly grasping the mission's dangers, she listened to his instructions and did not divert him with unnecessary questions. Nor did she distract herself with thoughts of attacking him (impossible) or escaping (improbable). She had a role to play this evening and sensed that if she performed flawlessly, and helped him away from his own suffering at Neku's hands, there would be some reward in it.

What her reward might be she could not guess and did not ask, but she knew all the same that it would be worth it. Several times she caught herself imagining the possibilities—if nothing better than a fresh chance to stab him with a knife and so end his bloody reign … and, catching herself, would return her attention to what the man was saying.

She *had* paid close attention.

She was certain she hadn't missed him mention what to do if Neku pulled a pistol and demanded she undress; to get naked right there in the cemetery, under the full moon.

And so this moment, upon the grave digger's demand for her to "shuck" her clothes, to verify she was truly his Hedwigga, Amalina was without direction and felt quite alone.

And more, in that instant, her mind was full of rebellion. She was now safely out of the monster's range. He'd said he couldn't enter the graveyard. Here she was gated within it, and he outside it. He'd said Neku Jonker was an expert shot with his pistols and had thwarted the man's previous attempts to get what he wanted. Why couldn't she just run to Neku now, reveal the play-act, and rely on him for protection? Why was she so willing to help the monster? to play the part in a deadly charade without question? It was as if by just being in his presence had sapped her of her own will, had turned her into his slavering subject. It was as if the man had spun her like a top in that carriage, and in a mindless whirl she'd taken his direction, moved where he guided her, following a trail he'd set for her. But why should she continue his programmed course?

He'd given her good reason to dislike Neku Jonker, and good reason for her to stop him from continuing his misdeeds. As it was, Neku was standing there in front of her with a corpse in hand, performing the loathsome necromancy the man had accused him of doing.

But wasn't the man even worse than Neku? If she should take sides, shouldn't it be with the side that did not cause the death of innocents, no matter what unfortunate crimes the lesser evil committed? Why should she, for one more moment, labor in the cause of the greatest criminal creature she could conceive?

Because of the reward, she reminded herself. *The reward! Were you not just thinking of it? If you help him do justice here, there may be a way to purchase more justice—from* him*!*

And more still, beyond her reward, there was the punishment if she should not obey. If she gave up the game, if she defied the monster, *she* might be safe from harm, but he would return to her village—much quicker than she could ever hope to—and carry out his own bloody retribution against those she most loved.

There was *that* to consider.

There was no real choice then, was there? But to succeed at her given task, and hope for the best.

Once again, she tried to remember everything he'd told her, looking for clues of what she should do.

"I say 'shuck dress,' Hedy," Neku reminded her, looking oddly hopeful, and then terrified, and then commanding, in that order. The pistol shook slightly, but pointed in her direction. He pulled back its hammer with a click. Amalina could already feel the explosion from its small, compact body, and then the whirr and smack of the lead ball into hers. "You know what I say. Shuck it."

She had to do something. She couldn't continue to ignore him. She had to rejoin the match.

So she did, concentrating fully.

. . .

Amalina ignored the pistol and the corpse. She also forced herself not to glance around for the man who had brought her here. It would only damage the ruse by alerting Neku of another person within, or near, the graveyard. She did not take her eyes off Neku. She bore her eyes into his.

Getting naked did not upset Amalina. Her first concern was, by doing so, her body would not match Hedwigga's own—her body being young. Who knows how old Hedwigga had been? She also understood that the white cream the man used to make her skin look deathly pale had only been spread to the margins of her clothing. Stripped bare, her body would reveal all her darker parts, and so reveal, very clearly, the weakest facet of the deception. She could not remove the clothes. At all costs.

So she shook her head.

"Must see you, Hedy," Neku insisted.

"You would have me take off my clothes, Neku? Bare my entire body—which should be known only to God and my stupid husband—to all?"

"Maybe *is* you," he wondered. "But who 'all' watch? We alone. Must see, Hedy. Must see!" He jabbed the pistol's barrel at her.

"Put the woman down," Amalina ordered, pointedly ignoring the thrusting pistol. What ghost would be threatened by such a thing? She prayed he couldn't see the sweat building around her forehead.

Insecurity bit her then, and she suddenly felt awkward. Like her body was made of six jangling, uncontrollable pieces. She wasn't a real actor, she realized—how much play-acting can be had inside a bakery? The whole moment began to feel like a bad joke that she couldn't carry through to the end. But she had to try! If she flagged now, what would become of her and all the people she loved? She pictured the man beginning to lick his teeth in anger as he watched the scene from his hiding place. Amalina got an idea. She summoned the voice and hard bearing of Sadra, the minister's wife, who she imagined was how the living Hedwigga once was: Imperious, righteous. Her lips tightened.

She croaked: "Do as I tell you, or you will suffer!"

"*Must* know it very you, Hedy," Neku frowned. "If me no can see you body ..." His brain went to work. There was a pause over which the swaying trees creaked. He blinked several times and then developed a peculiar grin. "Instead you tell answer of me question ... Must be asked by me, and only Hedy know answer. Only Hedy know *real* answer."

"Do you think I'm a child? And you would treat me to games?" blustered Amalina.

Neku continued: "If you Hedwigga, you—you very real you—you know answer: Where is spec-ial mark on me—on me very body? ... an', an' what ani-mal it look as?"

Amalina nearly blew out a breath.

Had she understood correctly?

Where was a 'special mark' on his body? And what animal does it look like?

Amalina wanted to throw her arms in the air. To give up.

But of course she couldn't give up. The man was there. Somewhere. Watching.

In a stroke of improvised brilliance (if unintentional), she wrinkled her nose, recoiled from the question and growled: "Neku! Don't be disgusting! How revolting! You should ask me such a thing, and you think I would answer that question? Sick! You are sick in the head!"

The mouth of the pistol barrel bobbled and shook. Then came down.

"It *very* you!" Neku shouted, stepping forward a couple paces. "Hedwigga!"

Then it was as if he remembered his place. He shrank back half a step into a hunched cower before her. The position he must have taken regularly under wife Hedwigga.

"Now you will return that unfortunate woman to where she belongs. And you will never remove the bodies from their coffins. Do you understand?"

"But, but ... they *want* me do!"

"Do not lie to yourself. It is a desecration of sacred material, only the Lord can call the dead from the ground, and you will be lost to eternity in hellfire should you continue this abomination just one more night!"

"But, but ... why god care, Hedy? He has they souls. Or, but, but ... he knows where they be pun-ish-ed. Why he care?"

"Don't question me!"

"No, no ... But, but—"

"Even now," said Amalina, delivering the words as the man had carefully directed her, picking up the train of the script where it connected here. She began to step backward, slowly. "Even now, Neku, with your hands on her, offending her soul and the spirits of heaven, I suffer—"

"You ... suffer?" Neku asked, wide-eyed, and taking a step forward to maintain an even distance as she slowly retreated.

"I am your wife," said Amalina. "My soul is bound to yours, just as yours is to mine. And what crimes you perform on this earth, I pay the consequences in purgatory. I was only set free from my sufferings because the Saints ordered me to come here, in favor to those innocent souls you've upset. I was given one chance to warn you, Neku. One chance to reason. One chance to save us both. But, but, Neku ... now I feel the pull of death, taking me, pulling me even from this place where I thought I should find my forever rest ... to be thrown outside of it!"

Amalina walked backwards steadily and with small gestures of her hands, which begged Neku to come after her, to take her hands. To save her. Her eyes pleaded. She tried to fill her expression with pain and accusation. She had only to walk backwards a straight line. A perfect line was the path the man had sent her into the graves. A perfect line she took back out, and since she knew the course, and did not have to worry about tripping into a random headstone, or a closed side gate—which the man had opened with a wave— she did as she was instructed, with Neku following her, and began to pick up her pace.

Neku's chin hung out far beyond his chest. He let the woman in the lavender dress drag in an unseemly way, that unfortunate woman, the man's wife, now forgotten in the presence of Hedwigga. Amalina tried not to pay attention to the body. It was not the first decrepit corpse she'd ever seen, but the sight never got familiar enough for her to feel comfortable against the shock of witnessing one anew. In fact, the body coming nearer, as Neku absently pulled it along, repelled Amalina, encouraging her backwards flight. The pistol was no longer a threat, he'd shoved it back alongside its brother in his belt.

"Help me, Neku," said Amalina. "They are taking me away! Banishing poor Hedwigga! The daughter of a Duke! A saintly Christian in conduct and

           C.L. Holmes

merit. My! Their invisible hands burn me at the touch! They wound! Help, Neku! Help me! Help!"

Neku's eyes were wide, his mouth hung open stupidly as he strived to see the punishing demons pulling his bride out of the yard. He shook his head the way the slow-witted do, to see if reality wouldn't somehow rearrange itself the way the rocks inside their skulls would sometimes fall into line. He stamped his feet with knees raised high; obviously confused and agitated.

"Help!" Amalina cried pitiably, arms outstretched for him, feeling the joy of the seduction—savoring the power and the excitement of animating another human with your own words and movement, which she had never experienced, or fully understood was a possibility. "Help! Help!"

When Neku stepped beyond the churchyard gate—he hadn't noticed how strange it was that the gate was standing open—the man was behind him. He batted Neku's hand, paralyzing his arm and causing him to drop the ancient corpse.

Then, with one hand holding Neku's neck, the other around Neku's waistband, the man stretched Neku's body out in front of him. He pulled and yanked Neku's torso to a painful length. The gravedigger's eyes were wide with terror now. Those eyes pleaded for Amalina—for his wife—to rescue him.

Those eyes begged for help. But they did only after they'd flicked up from the wild grasses which he knew encircled the St. Grigori cemetery like a moat—the surrounding wild grasses *outside the fence*. Which was the moment he'd realized what he'd done: he'd left sanctuary. At night.

His pistols were worthless now as they dropped from his waistband.

The man laughed. Amalina turned away.

• • •

At some point, the man swept Amalina up, as a hawk would a sparrow; flew her from the graveyard and returned her to the carriage, which took off immediately.

He held Amalina in his arms as a gentleman, as she recovered from the same paralysis Neku Jonker had seemed to gain at the man's touch. The man laughed—most likely at the thought of Neku's death. It was a deep and reverberating laugh.

"That was great fun! Great fun, Amalina! How long have I waited to have my revenge on him! Perfect! Perfect! He laughed at me inside his fortress. Now I found the means to lure him out ... Who laughs now, eh, Neku? Eh? Ha! Ha!" His laughs continued into a thunder-like roll that stretched off into the distance. The animals in the passing forests, perhaps on the other side of the mountains, could tell how pleased he was. "I've put the past behind."

She lay in the comfort of his arms ... they were strong arms, solid as wood. But the flesh was soft enough to allow her to pretend that her bed's mattress had come to surround her. The only difference was the dark fabric of the man's clothes and the smell of herbs—with a hint of some animal musk—which she could not identify but she'd begun to notice. It was hard to reconcile the comfort she felt within the nest of his body with the violence—which she' d heard but not seen (though hearing was enough)— the terrible violence this same body had wrought moments ago.

After a while, his rumbling laughs stopped, and the man fell into a contemplative silence. A little later he looked out the window and nodded.

"The sky lightens in the east. I will leave you now. I must return to my castle. Genadie will take you near your village. Go to your home. Tell them that, in their haste and panic, they left your cell unlocked, and you wanted to sleep in your own bed. They will believe you, no matter how long you've been away. Or your father will believe you, and he will convince the others."

"Now that you are done with me ... " she began, a strain of fear growing.

"What?"

"You aren't going to punish me?" she asked.

"You performed spectacularly, why should I do something like that?"

"But ... I told ..." she prompted. "... Told my father, you know ... and the others ... that I *saw* you ... told them what you did to Lucinda Skeldar ..."

"Oh, yes," he said, but was caught off guard by what problem she was trying to introduce. He'd been so happy, and the subject she brought up lay so far afield from his moment of victory that he obviously did not know what Amalina was talking about. But he was one of those types who concealed their moments of ignorance in head nods and general positive mutterings until they retrieved their bearings. Which, shortly enough, he did, with the stroke of his mustache. "Oh, yes," he said more definitely now, and curtailed a benevolent smile before it became too obvious to Amalina that maybe his threat to kill everyone she loved had been an idle one. "That *was* a dangerous thing to do, betraying my command of silence. But you have done me this good service, and there's nothing to do about your infraction now, anyway. They know, and that is that. I know you will do better next time, as to disobey me is *very* dangerous."

She nodded, her eyes closed. The darkness suddenly filled with the haunting vision of Neku—her final sight of him: emptied of blood, his wide eyes blanked by eternity.

"Who are you?" she asked.

"I am a man of great dignity and suffering, but I have my means to survive and that is what I do. I haven't time to tell you more. But if you are curious, when they put you in that cell again, you may use this key," the man handed her a key. "It will open the door. The mayor has a book they keep hidden inside the deputy sheriff's desk. It is large, and old, and red as fresh blood, and you will know it when you see it. Read that book, and you will know who I am. And when you know who I am, you won't take my warnings so lightly.

"And ... make sure they don't catch you wandering into the village," he added. "They will likely put you to the torch as my accomplice. And I cannot rescue you in the coming burning hours."

6

Exposition of the Count:
The Secret History of the Sheriff of Korr

The old book he sent Amalina to look for, which bore the unofficial title (the title being crudely scribbled across its first page) "The Secret History of the Sheriff of Korr", was not well hidden, nor was it difficult to find. Not locked away as foretold, it lay out in the open, weighing down the left side of the deputy sheriff's tiny desk. The old book's most important passage, written in the ancient sheriff of Korr's precise hand, was even easier to locate, marked off by a tattered purple sash:

> The rumor of a darker cause to our recent tragedies, beyond the natural guilt of the wolves, was today confirmed by ambassadors from the villages of Netz and Kirgyl and—
>
> (... and here there were several small holes burned lengthwise into the page, obliterating whatever other names had once been written upon it...)
>
> —who arrived on horseback, twelve in all, and to a man appeared distraught and agitated as they greeted us, and as a body they were as spent as their hard-driven horses. These towns have suffered the same bloody deaths of their citizens as we have. It could only be for this reason they would come to us in such a group and with determined disposition.
> Netz and Kirgyl and—
>
> (... then several small holes ...)
>
> —'s letter of appeal to Tsobl, written two months ago, for lawful aid against the menace, resulted in the assignment of the high council magistrate, who arrived in Netz—Netz being closest to Tsobl—to conduct his investigation.
> However, Tsobl's magistrate disappeared while performing his duties.

The magistrate missing, the mayor of Netz and its physician, both learned men, convened their own investigation of the slayings. The many pieces of evidence discovered a greater truth, which the riders shared with us at once, without dismounting.

Our town council heard these sound men and their evidence, whose summation was this: the wolves are responsible for only a handful of the dead. But those wolves are under the sovereign control of an entity that is, not coincidentally, also responsible for the remaining deaths. This entity being a single man—one who recently, and so quietly that no one was aware, took residence in the high castle in the mountains. His servants, who number on a single hand, represent him as a high nobleman, a former knight and count, and a member of the great and terrible family who, until recently, controlled our several valleys for some time.

The reason he has waged this quiet war against our female population is unknown. He cannot be contacted personally, all dialogue conducted through his dark and evasive manservants (who confirm his guilt through their own furtive ways and their suspicious looks, though they deny all questions and direct accusations). But if he is a member of this high-stationed and infamous family, it is then not impossible. He could be quite mad and capable of anything.

We were easily convinced of his responsibility, and determined to set forth against him.

But the ambassadors from Netz cautioned us. Such a group of their own <u>had already been formed</u>, and brought against the castle and its criminal; they were killed, with no survivors or hostages taken. The wolves took them.

A superior number, we declared, must be joined to meet his threat. This impulse, too, was dismissed by the ambassadors.

Their purpose coming to Korr, it was revealed after the whole of their history was imparted, was to collect us at this count's request. There is to be an embassy at his castle, to come to an arrangement of peace.

After a short deliberation, our mayor has accepted to go, along with the deputy sheriff and several others in high standing, to conduct this council with the criminal count.

But not one of our number can think of a sufficient or satisfactory outcome, other than the count's death.

Therefore, a second party is formed from our strongest and bravest, to plan a well-armed assault on his castle, while the mayor and the rest are gone to meet him in cold-blooded diplomacy.

So this was how it began? Amalina thought. *Our village's first brush with the monster?* And the sheriff, in his dry, stern, and stiff language, presenting the discovery of the darkest threat against them as a matter-of-fact force to be reckoned with? to be dealt with in a routine, if heavily martial way?

The handwriting changed after this passage, Amalina noticed. The letters became shaky, with wilder strokes splattering ink across the page. Was this even the same person writing here? wondered Amalina. Or someone new? If so, what had become of the sheriff? If still the sheriff, then what had happened to him to change his hand so dramatically?

Dear God, <u>have mercy</u>!

The newest words whimpered in uneven, underlined strokes.

If we do not succeed, all is lost! Give us Strength! Give us Victory against the cruel and unjust!

It comes down to us: The men of this city, to remind that cruel despot in his lofty fortress, <u>the light of day conquers all shadow</u>!

It sounded, and looked by the uneven scrawl itself, to be a desperate cry of hope more than confidence.

A separate parchment was fastened here to the book's page, in the upper margin, by a wood pin. This sheet was also (coincidentally) stuck there by the remnant of a wax seal. By the look of it, it was an official document, written boldly, and in a learned man's sure script, and read like a legal proclamation:

This accord of peace, and its attendant price, is acceptable by all men who find its purchase reasonable in the face of its unacceptable alternative. Should Heaven wish for Evil to exist, as evidenced by events that have now occurred before our eyes, reasonable men know that they must desire not for Good to perish irretrievably, in fruitless pursuit of vanquishing that which good men are inclined to find naturally offensive. For Heaven is completed by both day and night in harmony, and as day is pleasurable and good, and night the provenance of evil and death, it is Heaven's desire for one to follow the next, in countless years, each dawn of one complementing the settling of the next. It is natural that if day, no matter how good, should seek out and vanquish night, it would displease Heaven more than if night should do the opposite. Heaven created day from darkness, light being the beacon of Good, which shines in the cold of Evil, and that light could not demonstrate its Good without the example of Evil, while Evil may exist freely of Good itself. Good is not meant to destroy, but to thrive in spite of destruction, and should never seek wanton annihilation of Evil, but only humble submission to Heaven.

With such being our understanding, and the knowledge any further vain effort to rid our land of this pestilence would only, by inciting Heaven's reprisal, obliterate everything that is Good, we accept the branch of peace proffered by what is undoubted Evil, with the purchase price set high above what would be palatable in any human venture; understanding and accepting that our present dealing is not a human venture whatsoever, but a new covenant between Heaven and man, thus priced beyond our ability to contain it within reasonable boundaries, thus submitting ourselves humbly to the unknowable ordinances of Heaven itself.

As this professed Count of Ardeel, a possession of Heaven, evidenced by his astounding power, cares not to sign any compact, but only wishes to know our compliance, this contract is signed by our hands alone, to make it understood between us, the good souls, what heavy burden we have accepted, so that Heaven's light shall persist in these lands in the face of our Almighty's permitted Champion of Evil.

From this day forward, it is agreed by our surviving men—and it is an understanding that shall be vouchsafed by them—never the knowledge to be transmitted to outsiders, or any others—that:

The Count of Ardeel shall stay in his keep in the mountain outside of Netz, or others, as is his demand, and shall not be troubled by any assembly of good men of our various towns, this being his foremost demand.

This Count—as his inhuman evil reaches further into infamy—will have permission to take from our people a body, when he so requires it, and without retribution. For this sacrifice the Count assures we will continue in peace within our homes, our towns, our borders, so much as peace can be said of allowing such a heavy pay-price.

This Count will, with our compliance guaranteed, stay his hand against us—a device with which he could remove us down to the last soul from the mountains, as if his hand were the hand of Heavenly Grace itself.

We shall mark out the homes of those who have entered into this accord, so the Count will know who is an ally in this act. All others are numbered as <u>the Count's foe</u> and open to reaping by that fell hand. We shall not mark out for protection those visitors or foreigners who have no knowledge of our agreement, no matter how we may cherish their safety—better that they keep away. And all those marked by our compact will have the freedom to move about in the light of day without threat.

Be it known that any body, even those in homes that are so marked and who are credited for protection, who would roam in the darkness of night from the protection of their mark, who do so for whatever reason, are numbered as prey. Should we prove too conservative in our ways, or conspicuous in our means, or protective of our number, thereby depriving the Count of his <u>wants</u>, the Count vows to retract his peace to gain his <u>required body</u>.

We enter into this agreement as good and reasonable men, with no recourse to our safety besides what has been offered. And so this contract shall remain valid, and in perpetuity, and is to include all descendants of our homes and families, however the distance it need carry, as long as we remain faithful to it. Knowing not where our fault lie, for the reason we have been so fairly and justly cursed, we pray that Heaven will not be long in sending its divine hand down into our land to reclaim this creature and spare us.

Bishop of Tsobl

Many signatures extended down the flowing length of the compact's page, which was folded several times. Some of the names had been removed by small burn marks.

Continuing on in the book itself, to the page the agreement was pinned, the handwriting changes once again, from the sheriff's and the frantic scrawler's (who had requested God's mercy and assistance), to a more stately penmanship; resembling the finest script Amalina had seen in bibles, and hymnals from the local monasteries; and with a tenor strangely detached— or perhaps loftier—than were the previous entries. It apparently picks up the narrative where it had originally left off, from before the attached compact was written.

The Four knights who rode in support of Tsobl's cause, the mayors of Netz and Kirgyl—

(... then four burned holes ...)

—and our own Mayor Jorgas Hachal, along with their representatives and our own Deputy Sheriff, Alexandru Bisner, Miller Lasser the Miller, and his two cousins Laszu and Lagra, were dead by the time our body arrived, each segment having met their end by the might of the Knight of Ardeel. The Tsobl Knights' helmets, visors raised, exposing their waxen faces, greeted us from spikes along the fortress battlements. Men from the previous parties, assorted followers, pages and retainers, milled about the forest outside the castle's sealed gate, appearing purposeless and lost before the remnants of their dead.

A new embassy was being quietly formed among these leftover pieces. Our arrival enlivened some, and hope shone in their eyes. They expected a new champion would be taken from our party to meet with the bloody noble within the castle.

Our initial offense at, and then final acceding to, their desires for a diplomatic party was not a long road. Combat against this mad count had been tried and failed long before our arrival. The evidence of the attempted raising of a siege against the fortress lay throughout the bedraggled camp. No engine for scaling, or penetrating, or bombardment had ever survived a single night beyond their construction, reduced to a hail of shredded timbers or burning embers long before dawn; the night being the mad count's preferred province for conducting business, whether holding court or challenging his enemies; though it was reported that he could also repel invasions attempted in the daylight hours as well. This creature, with monstrous power and the speed of lightning itself, destroyed all instruments of siege by his own hand and means, so it was observed by many, and killed all who stood against him as if they were no more than circling gnats.

It was incredible to believe, and we refused to believe. But the truth of it lay beyond their words and deep inside their eyes, their courage and spirit carried aft by their shrinking, impotent, sunken souls. We must believe them.

This Knight of Ardeel, this Mad Count, this King of the mountain fortress, this creature of unheard of power and abilities, had slain all knights who'd challenged him. He had welcomed the first embassy from Tsobl, Netz and Kirgyl—

(… then four small burns obliterating more words or names …)

—they entered. Later the Mountain King opened the gate and announced the death of that embassy, called for another set of leaders to parley, and warned the same fate would befall this second embassy as had visited the first, should they prove as inflexible in their diplomacy. Later again, the gate was opened and a new embassy was called, and not long after that the King of Death pushed out a cowering member of the latest party, who stood as witness to the seriousness of that man, and proclaimed that all who had entered of the third party, save him, had died at this mad knight's hands. The next leaders were elected and sent in. Again, one man was returned, who spoke of the need to accede to the Knight's will, the creature's will, or all would be lost. The next leaders were selected, and one returned shaking and white, no longer the same man who had entered.

Again leaders were selected, and admonished at the threshold by the Knight: to listen earnestly to the appeals of the witnesses to the previous failed negotiations. The new-found ambassadors insisted on bringing in a brace of twenty footmen with swords at the ready. The Knight allowed this, only for the mad count to return in four hours requesting a fresh embassy, the newest ambassadors and their armed retinue having been slain utterly.

The next man to return from an embassy described the scene he encountered upon entering the main room of the fortress. The floors were awash with blood, so that treading there was either sticky or slippery, depending where one stepped. The Knight had laid out a carpet to make their footing easier and it was soaked through with the previous embassy's blood. The heads and bodies of those brave and honorable men were still in the room, shoved to the corners or thrown up over the rafters, the look of surprise or horror on their faces. Still, in spite of this gruesome setting and its cautionary portent, these newest men could not agree to the Knight of Ardeel's demands, demands this trembling ghost before us could dare not speak of, but which I learned later, though I dare not admit here on this page, lest I curse our whole population. These men then met the same fate as the first.

Every embassy fell, one after the other, and it mattered not whether it was conducted within the castle or outside in a tent, whether attended by a handful of wise men or protected by a squadron of pikes and archers, those who would not agree with the Knight fell to him. As a science, it was an established law. And yet brave men volunteered for the next embassy, filled with conviction they could—

(... the burns on the opposite side of the page unevenly broke this sentence here ...)

—and find a way to stem the wrath of this being who remains unsatisfied and uncontent, even with a moat of honorable men's blood surrounding his keep. And all fell until what remained were the scraps of leadership we found when we'd first entered the scene.

I tried to exorcise the castle and grounds and remove this Knight by means spiritual, which led to nothing, my light of divinity curdling within the intense midnight of the hour which persisted even in the noon-day sun.

The next embassy was agreed to, just so that fresh blood could be tried, with the result that fresh blood was spilled, and we, the new comers, could experience what had been experienced by others ten times before.

We were left with nothing but the remainder of spent men and futile hopes. Pages and messengers who were dispatched to Tsobl to appeal for more negotiators, for an army, for a force of interdiction, soon hung out on the ramparts along with the bodiless knights. No messages would escape this castle's lands.

Finally, there was nothing more to be accomplished by our steadfast resistance to the triumphant Knight of Ardeel, this mad count, than the emptying of the mountains of we, the good people, and all those we cherished, young and old, all reduced to clay and ashes.

Any army would surrender facing these circumstances which rivaled even the legendary bloody incursion of the Khan of the Steppes.

I, the bishop, the representative of the church and the sole representative of our village, entered the Knight of Ardeel's castle with the remaining ministers of Netz and Kirgyl—

(… and, as always, there followed four burnt holes …)

—, and three other hearty men who could be encouraged to do so, along with those who had been spared, those shaken witnesses to the previous embassies.

The setting inside the castle resembled the horror of what had been recounted by those frail, shaking, warning ghosts who had escaped the past parleys, with the only added bits of disgust being the stickiness of the blood at our feet, and the stench of nearly two hundred bodies rotting, that we were forced to cover our faces with cloths and nosegays. The Knight did not appear to notice the carnage beyond drawing our attention to it in order to instruct us, and beg humbly that we learn from our eyes and to be humble in our own right.

What bravery had been shown by every one of these bodies, which had spilled their blood in this chamber. What constancy to God's love, and faith to His promises. What boldness in confronting the unconfrontable. How had these men faced the foul eyes of this agent of evil and never given in, despite what was the obvious evidence of their impending fate? No man, with seeing eyes in his head, could have understood anything less than he would not exist beyond the hour, torn limb from limb, if he should not submit to the count's demands. And they did not submit. They were men of great, unshakeable honor.

But they were also the possessors of no urgent need for the ultimate survival of good in the face of evil.

We arrived at terms agreeable to both sides in less than an hour, the demands of which chills my soul but must be carried out or nobody shall survive but the Knight himself. A circumstance Heaven would not allow.

God save us.

After a generous empty space, the narrative takes up again in the same hand.

Clarifications have been made. Those who were entrusted with the knowledge of the treaty and yet resisted its articles met the fate of all who have ever resisted the creature at the keep. Those who understood what needs be done have been sworn to an oath, from ever forward, to preserve the secrecy of this regretful compact. All future men who reach maturity—and please it the Almighty that this should not extend a single generation beyond our own—shall be sworn to the oath and make their mark in these pages to serve as witness.

God save us.

Further clarification: The Knight of Ardeel shall know who is allied in this compact by the placement of a sign upon their home. He appears to be a man of his word as much as he is a beast in the satisfying of his hunger, but we shall not allow for mistakes. The creature's senses are heightened like that of a wolf. We will mark ourselves and our family homes out by the placement of flowers or some other bright or pungent vegetation upon them, on, at, or above the entrance, which shall appear as innocuous decoration to outsiders, but cannot be claimed to be overlooked by this sensitive enemy of ours. He shall know who is untouchable, without uncertainty.

God save us.

There follows below these amendments a list of signatures that vary wildly in their confidence and ability to print a letter, but never faltering in the strength of the signer's conviction to be read. A few times names are crossed out, or repeated in clearer print, or—(and in these notable cases, there are many more of them in the beginning of the contract, than later on)—a name is removed entirely by a hole in the paper, suggesting the application of the tip of a candle.

After a couple pages, there is an additional comment:

Flowers are useless or unattainable in the Fall, Winter, and Early Spring. Even in the fairest of weather they wither quickly, lose color and emit no smell. The floral bunches or berries are offensive and provide no logical excuse to remain on a home, and require too frequent replacement. An oversight on my part. A substitute will be found.

God save us.

Then follows page after page of signatures. Never a date. Amalina knew most of the names as they all originated in the village, family names which have persisted over the ages. She browsed through them, finding members from her own family (from paternal *and* maternal branches) repeating again and again as the years stretched forward from the origination of the contract. Eventually she found the signature of her grandfathers. Flipping forward, she glanced over the rest, noting how similar all signatures were, from generation to generation, even in their variance.

Each one of these men were committed to a hideous secret, upon signing to a deal with a creature whose purpose was to delight in evil and death, threatening even their own wives or children should those innocents be so careless as to step outside on the wrong night. They were, these signers, committing to the compact, but you could never know from the steady handed, or shaky scratching of their name (with some names written in with an illiterate's verifying X splatted next to it) what was going through their mind. Any signature could be read as guiltless as the signing to the receipt of a delivery of wheat.

The simple, blank faces of sinners, Amalina mused. *Columns and columns of them.* According to the date of the initial contract, many had been dead for a couple centuries. Amazing how old this book was.

But why had portions of the text and specific names of signers been removed? she wondered. And removed by the drastic means of burning them out? Who were they, and what was meant by erasing them so?

In Amalina's eyes this deputy sheriff's logbook, the *Secret History,* originating from an ancient past, was a book of the damned. She suppressed a small, clever smile at the thought of adding her own name to it.

Hadn't she become an ally to the count, just like them?

She'd done more than any of them, in fact. She had come to his aid. And she would keep his secret, as all these other men had. Wouldn't she? At this point, didn't she have to?

Even with Amalina's surprisingly glib attitude in that moment—and wry smile at her conspiracy with danger and darkness—when she reached the final page of signatures, she could not force herself to look for Dragomir's name, but shut the leaves as fast as she could.

7

A Step Forward

"**A**malina stays home tonight," said the deputy sheriff to his friend Dragomir, employing a light but matter-of-fact tone.

They stood outside the sheriff's small building, and when Dragomir faltered, he caught himself on the standing horse hitch. It felt as if a boulder had crashed into his gut. But he had to maintain control. He couldn't lose the deputy's respect. The deputy could never be allowed to see Dragomir panic, even though:

"She isn't safe," countered Dragomir in a calm voice, though desperation was gnawing at him. He resented the un-reined feelings; the powerlessness and weakness—the *fear*—that was gripping him, changing him. He'd always been considered a strong pillar of the community.

And now, to increase Dragomir's anxiety, the deputy's eye was on him. Perhaps reconsidering his good opinion of the once *solid and trustworthy* Dragomir the Baker. It was happening: the Dalca family's diminution.

"We can't have your child here every night," the deputy sheriff said casually, if firmly. "And with a secret watch detail for her, too. A secret watch which is growing ever less secret within our village, dear friend. It's wearing everyone out. And it can't be good for Amalina. To spend her nights in a barred cell is not an education to which you'd wish her grow accustomed. Bad precedent, playing her childhood out inside the Iron Inn."

"We should call a general council and I'll talk to Daniel," said Dragomir, casually (but pointedly) mentioning the mayor. And for another point, using with familiarity the mayor's Christian name. "*Daniel* might have some constructive ideas."

"My dear, dear friend ... ha, ha, ha ... the threat is *over*," the deputy sheriff patted Dragomir's shoulder with resolve, his voice louder now; and bursting a confident laugh in the middle, as if to further emphasize just how over— and for his part he pointedly stressed that word, too—how *over* it really was.

But on the completion of the deputy's statement a denying chill fell over them. A chill that caused them both to shudder uncomfortably. The deputy sheriff looked to the sky, seeking the cool breeze that had just blown, for it must have been an errant piece of weather and not a ... No, he wouldn't allow his confidence to be spoiled by omens of wind. The threat to Dragomir's daughter was *definitely* over.

If their conversation had been at an end, the deputy sheriff would have, as was his habit, pulled out an iron key, and with off-hand authority, and a hint of impatience, plopped it into his hand. It was his signature move. Everyone in the village knew when the key appeared it was time to pack your bag and leave. But there was no need to be brutal to Dragomir, the deputy thought sympathetically, to shove their meeting along. He did not want to upset his friend—a true friend—any more than he must be already. Why, on that first night, when they'd put Amalina under watch, anticipating the arrival of their most feared enemy, the Knight of Ardeel, he—the deputy sheriff—had been just as upset and fearful as Dragomir had been. Only now, time had passed. The threat had petered.

The deputy's worry—and his worry-tainted look—now transferred from Amalina's safety to his friend's stability.

"Our foe is a man of honor," said the deputy sheriff in a low but reassuring voice, "and a man of his word. It was your daughter's mistake, you know. She opened her window. But he will abide our agreement, as he always has." Before the deputy sheriff let a good word fall on the man who was the subject of the conversation, he spat on the floor twice, "Heaven destroy him."

"There's no reason for him to be confined by our compact," Dragomir fretted glumly, "should he find some reason, any reason to ignore it, and he wanted to have his way. We could not stop him."

"Even more reason to keep Amalina at home, no? The Iron Inn can do nothing more than announce our will against his desires. It wouldn't hold him back. But take heart, dear Dragomir. I understand your concern. Considering Dasha—forgive me for reminding you of her, but you are—you must be—thinking of your beloved wife at this time—but these are not the same circumstances as when she died. And you have said it yourself: He could take your daughter at will. If that was his wish, he would have done so already. Let Amalina then stay at home with you, and allow her to enjoy a well cooked meal—not my miserable bachelor's stew—and let her sleep in her own bed."

The iron key emerged from the deputy's front pocket and slapped loudly on his palm. Now the matter was finished.

Dragomir nodded.

But, no, it wasn't finished.

As he walked away from his old friend, Dragomir knew the town council was not his final resource, only his first. He had close ties whose strength neither the deputy sheriff, nor Daniel Hokz, the mayor, could guess at.

He headed across the village to its distant edge, where he could smell the baking bread and already picture in his mind the thin smile of Argus, the village's other baker, who was, as Dragomir was, in the Merchant and Baking Guild. In time of need, any brother of the guild would aid another ... even against the village itself. Their bond fitted into a steel network that spanned like a spider's web across Ardeel, and presumably the rest of Europe. It was a bond older and more durable than anything like the town council. The town council, Dragomir thought testily, was just a pack of stranger-dogs with the capacity to conspire from time to time for their own self interests.

Yes, he thought with warming hope, Argus the baker would hide Amalina for the night. This would do. Dragomir had to keep her safe from that creature. He had to protect her at all cost!

As Dragomir caught sight of Argus' shop, however, he decided against it. There was nothing wrong with the shop itself, it being squat and solid, like any building of industry in the village, but the clientele, the downcast laborers, willing to nibble at the pieces of plaster and straw that Argus fortified the bulk of his loaves with, reminded him of their different stations in life. Dragomir was an honest breadmaker. Argus was a miserly profiteer, who knew a life-sustaining staple product was a moneymaking product, and who was utterly unconcerned with quality. So, then, he wasn't a very *good* man.

On the back foot, Dragomir pivoted, and swung himself in the direction he'd come.

He was alone, after all. If there was a solution to his dilemma, Dragomir would have to secure it himself.

The plan came soon enough, as unsatisfying as it was. And it begged some further consideration.

Dragomir plotted how to move Amalina into his bedroom for the night in a way which required minimum diplomacy. And he debated the need (and trouble) of dressing her in shackles. And … should he leave his rifles cocked and within reach? Or hold one in his arms, at the ready, for the entire night? And what kind of shot would be most effective against such a creature? A solid ball, or some kind of mixed small shot?

He dispatched Amalina on an errand to buy twenty long-burning candles and a candlestick that fit three. He would explain their necessity later, he told her.

He could tell that she could tell that he was up to something.

• • •

In the heat of preparations, Dragomir was startled to find the stranger in his shop.

"You'd like some bread?" Dragomir suggested helpfully. But the stranger's stilted posture and fixed gaze suggested he had another purpose for having so quietly materialized inside the door.

The man bowed and presented a large envelope, fitted between thumb and forefinger of both hands. His hair was greasy, his clothes unwashed. But the gesture was the height of polite society. Even his front foot was extended forward, with muddy-shoed toe pointed out. Dragomir accepted the envelope cautiously, confusion ticking in the corner of his eye. His eyes stayed on the curious stranger, who looked to have run through the countryside in his shoes, run a great distance to be here. And run in haste, through puddles of mud or over sooted walls, or any other dirty obstacle, to deliver this post. The envelope was not sealed. It contained a small, folded slip of vellum.

At the sight of the handwriting, with its thin lines and blotted, brutal stops, Dragomir's stomach turned. He read the cramped paragraphs feeling ever more lightheaded.

"No," said Dragomir to the stranger, eyes now hostile, his breath blowing hard; his worst fears confirmed, and amplified, by the letter. "This can't be ... He isn't serious."

The stranger remained impassive.

"Of course I reject this request," said Dragomir, blood boiling, shaking the paper in his limp hand, wishing he could cast the paper in the stranger's face or dash it to the floor. But it stayed in his hand as if glued there. "I reject this letter, I reject you, I reject *HIM*."

"This," the stranger pointed to the letter, his voice low, breathy, rasping, "it is not a letter of request, sir."

"What is it?"

"You've read it."

"Just now. In front of your face."

"Then you understand."

"I understand nothing," Dragomir flushed with anger. "I don't understand *how*. And certainly I don't understand *why*."

"Take heart, there is nothing to fear—" but Dragomir scoffed so loud and fast the stranger couldn't finish his thought. "Sir, it's in the letter: what my master plans for her."

"This is an insult. Why, I ask you. Why is he doing this to me?"

"To you?"

"He wishes to steal from me my most precious possession, does he not?"

"It's not theft, sir," the stranger's voice scraped through the air on his raspy breath.

"It's abduction."

"But, sir," the stranger persisted, his dull expression lifting slightly with incredulity, "your daughter might have died that night and the blame would have been yours. All yours. Master spared her, sir. He spares her, yet. But he will have a fair exchange for what mercy his honorable hand grants you."

"You say he spares her?" Dragomir shook the letter at the stranger again. "Get out of my store. Never come again. I know your face, you rat. You'll be recognized. Be warned, you won't enter this village without finding yourself thrown back into the forest—with arms broken. If you're lucky enough not to be torn to bloody shreds."

The stranger bowed his strange, deep bow, as he retreated, looking like he was the performer in a sickly dance; with Dragomir's raging and ranting sweeping him out the door and into the street.

Dragomir's fiery gaze burned at the stranger as he made an unhurried departure from the village, the stranger's head turning this way and that. Was he checking to see if he'd been noticed by any of the other villagers? Was he taking note of the street? and its details? Details on which he'd base a plan of action, after he reported this encounter to his master?

What have I done? Dragomir wondered, grabbing hold of his whiskers. To defy the monster meant death. How many lives would his anger cost the village? And the punishment would be much worse for Amalina—the very person he'd sought to protect!—by rejecting the letter.

Oh! he rubbed his face. *Now what's to happen, you ungrateful wretch?*

• • •

That afternoon, before dinner, Amalina noticed her father's worried expression: his eyes darting at the windows and doorways at every turn, anticipating—with obvious fear—something that was never quite there.

What was he expecting? she wondered.

But she didn't let him know she was aware of his strange behavior. She kept her head down as they cleared out the store, sweeping it clean of dust, crumbs and the odd mouse that had found its way in.

"There's just no keeping anything out if it wants in," her father grumbled ruefully at the scampering mice. "You did not use your head ..."

He was mumbling to himself.

It was difficult not to ask her father what he was talking about. But if she spoke to him now, she knew it would lead to the subject of the Count of Ardeel. But, of course, any interaction with Dragomir would bend that way. This unwanted conversation would happen one way or another, she realized, no matter the starting point. There had to be, and there would be, a final, dreadful confrontation about the darkness that had entered their lives. So she avoided so much as clearing her throat in his presence.

"You will sleep in my bed tonight," Dragomir announced between grumblings.

"Yes, Papa," she said, feeling warmed by the idea, rather than taking offence. The way she would have been offended a few days ago when she was still in her mania to see the man again, and saw her father only as an obstacle to what she wanted.

For his part, Dragomir nodded at her willingness to do as commanded, satisfied she'd finally come to her senses.

But what had changed that she now understood the danger?

He didn't much care what had happened or why. He was steeling himself for the coming night and its inevitable battle.

. . .

The two of them—father and daughter—closed the store, quietly, automatically; their thoughts differing but sharing a complementary vision of the night to come. They were conspiring with each other, but so secretly that not even they knew it. They would finish their chores and have their meal, and do all the preparations for tomorrow. Then silently they would move towards the same room, they would change into their night clothes and then they would climb into bed. There they would find peace for the night, with no possibility of her being drawn to the window, or even securing some means to open it, to allow the man entrance into their home.

Amalina caught her father looking at her with a vague sadness in his eye. He turned away quickly. But through the rest of the evening she sensed his closeness; following her from room to room as if attached to her by an invisible rope. He mumbled or hummed here and there. And he would pat her and poke her as he passed by, as he used to do when she was a small child. He gave her an encouraging laugh. She might have found it fun and pleasing. She did at first. Then she realized these actions weren't affectionate tokens of the old, jovial Dragomir, but something pairing with the sadness in his eyes. Expressions of nostalgia, of melancholy. As if he were mourning her by reciting those actions instead of spontaneously delivering them, and as if she were already a ghost.

And then she caught him mumbling again: "Without you I would be devastated. I can't lose you to him ..." he sighed heavily. "I need your help here."

Her father, she realized, was much more worried for her life than she'd ever expected.

But he doesn't have to be! she thought sadly. After what she'd done for the Count, and the fact that he'd used her to assist him instead of outright killing her, made it so much easier to believe her initial notion that she was somehow protected from him was true—had always been true. He couldn't touch her. She was somehow off limits. The Count could only employ her, and threaten the lives of people she cared about to compel her compliance, in whatever else he had planned for her. Ultimately, she was safe. The fiend was powerless against her, so there was nothing to worry about, so far as her immediate mortal life was concerned.

But, unable to confide to Dragomir the reason why she wasn't afraid of the Count, the reason he truly had nothing to fear for her, it made her pity him. And pity for her father is something she had never wanted, much less expected. *Maybe I could pity him when he gets old and rotten and can't run the store anymore*, she thought, *but ...*

But why couldn't she tell him?

The Count hadn't seemed too upset when Amalina let slip his secret the first time around. He *had* reiterated his threat to kill the people she loved if she betrayed his confidence again. But he didn't seem too serious about it. Not at all. So why couldn't she tell her father everything: that she'd gone off to a graveyard with the man, on a mission to mete out justice upon a far worse criminal than the Count—*(now, was* that *true?)*—and so she was more the Count's accomplice than a victim?

Her father needn't worry. No. And why shouldn't she tell him?

She could swear him to secrecy. As long as he told no one else, the count wouldn't mind. She was sure of it.

8

The Final Hesitation

The Count of Ardeel was coming for her. The promise of his return was contained in his parting words. And that presented a problem. She could not bear the thought of seeing him again. He was too confusing: He was an honorable gentleman of nobility in bearing and letter. But, as well, he was a monster.

Though she'd willingly assist him as long as he continued to do good and noble things, she was ultimately sworn to kill him. He'd murdered Lucinda Skeldar right before her eyes. And that girl was innocent, nothing like the loathsome Neku. And he'd killed many more like the innocent Lucinda, and had been doing so for a very long time. All the reason to resist him, to exterminate him, was contained in the very book he had insisted she read; a tale of the village's first violent encounter with him stretching back through the centuries. He was a beast, a superhuman monster. Unnatural and evil, no matter how gentile he smoothed his mustache and patted his clothes free of lint and animal hair, and eyed her with delight. She had to kill him.

And so all the better she not say a thing to Dragomir, and happily acquiesce to her father's cautious plan to keep her alongside him at night. Better for her to abandon her room and share his, so she could put off having to face the inevitable moment of confrontation with the monster, and make the incredible decision: the decision to intentionally put her life in jeopardy and do what must be done.

All this internal debate bubbled as she continued in her mechanical motions. Her motions syncing with her father's as they went about their business, with his odd tickle, or hum of a tune they used to sing together cutting into her thoughts at just the wrong moments. Cutting in all too frequently. Honestly, it was getting too much for her, with her father's maudlin, so un-Dragomir-like behavior. It became irritating.

They continued on, not acknowledging the undercurrent of dark reasons why they were about to do what they were about to do.

No difference or oddity was acknowledged. Even when, before heading for bed, Amalina picked up the shiny new candlestick and lit the ridiculously long tapered candles in its three sockets; even as she saw Dragomir quietly pouring gunpowder down the barrel of his long rifle, the table littered with shot and wadding.

"You know," Dragomir mumbled to her, not looking up from his work, "I wish I'd paid attention to how we made that soup the other night. I've been thinking of it all week. Didn't you find it delicious?"

Amalina wandered off to the bedroom. The one on the left, leading into her father's room. As if it were all natural and routine that she did so.

Inside the bedroom she found her nightdress laid out on the dresser. She set down the candlestick and changed clothes. Also on the dresser was the book on insects. The one she liked so much. The one with the chapter on the bees. She might actually enjoy reading it tonight. Maybe she would share the chapter with her father, as they'd done with other books when she was little. It would be fun, she thought.

But the problem was, she caught sight of the window. Just out of the corner of her eye, and she then turned to face it. The window was as small as the one in Jenna's room (now her own room). But it was not fastened by bolts as Jenna's—(now hers)—was.

There was a simple bar across it.

The bar was not yet locked into place.

The bar seemed loosely placed, actually. As if it might accidently fall away without so much as a touch, and allow the covering panel to drop from the window.

It didn't matter Amalina removed the candlestick from the dresser to the small bedside table, or that she snipped out two of the candles. The window remained in the light.

It called to her.

Would *he* be coming tonight? Would he know what room she was in? Could he get in through such a small window?

Was he outside?

Annoyed, agitated, Amalina did not get into the bed. She took the candlestick up and stamped to the window. She stared at it.

What view did the window give her into the street? What did it look like outside?

For some reason, the question was too much for her. She wanted to know. And worse, she could not settle her mind. It would only take a couple seconds to satisfy her curiosity. Just lift the bar and pull away the panel ... and look outside.

Her father would never know she'd opened it. And if she did do it, her stampeding mind would be quieted. She could return to the bed and read her book and be content to fall asleep. If she didn't do it she would be wracked with wonder and disappointment, and consumed by the curiosity clamming up her throat, crushing her breast, preventing her breath.

She did not have a weapon.

But there was no reason for one, she confidently knew.

Her mind pictured the street in an early evening light with the sun still filling in the shadows, though the light was dimming, and dimming. It wouldn't be time yet for him to come, she thought. She thought all this, even though she knew the bell had rung long ago, and they'd taken their time with their meal and preparations for the next morning, and so it would be very dark outside. In truth, it would be full night. But she did not picture it that way. In her lying mind, if she were to open the window, right now, she would find the street in a soft-focus, grey-blue twilight. Still too early for him to be there.

Best to get it over with, she thought, rather than suffering the agony of tossing and turning all night; sweaty and unhappy.

She could hear Jenna scraping something around upstairs. Maybe she was rearranging the dresser. She couldn't hear her father, but cleaning and loading rifles wasn't loud work unless one did it wrong. But also, cleaning and loading rifles wasn't time consuming either. She didn't have much time.

Dragomir's last words to her—some silly thing about the other night's soup—still murmured in her head as she took a step forward.

She removed the bar. Then she opened the window.

9

Only the Beginning

It felt like a dream. She was in the carriage once more, with the plush upholstery and the vibrant red drapes hiding the windows, and the interior tossing about violently as the carriage attacked the road at the speed of eight horses. It all seemed impossible. Impossible for everything to be just as it had been before when this whole adventure began.

But it was true. She was here, and it was happening. All over again.

And how?

The Count hadn't shown the night Amalina went to her father's room and opened the window.

When she'd opened the window the street had been dark and empty. And Dragomir, unaware the window had been opened (and then quickly shut), had come into the room and sat in a chair beside the bed, with one rifle across his chest, his finger near the trigger. A second rifle leaned beside the chair at the ready.

She didn't know if he ever fell asleep. His eyes were still open when morning came.

But she'd finally drifted off to sleep at some point, feeling comforted by her father's presence.

And the Count did not come to disturb them.

Not in the real world.

In her dreams, though ...

When Amalina had finally drifted away from the book with the chapter of the bees and sunk into a deep sleep, she'd found herself in the room, but alone. The candlelight was dim and casting soft shadows.

But she could see the window.

Though she'd opened it earlier, she was filled with the same curiosity to open it again. This time, she felt, the Count would be there.

She opened the window. He was not there.

The dream went on.

Later, she opened the window again, when she found herself returned to the room for a second time. Just like the first, though, there was only the empty street.

The dream went on.

Once more, for a third time, she found herself in the room. Unable to prevent herself, she opened the window. This time the street was that soft-focus, blue-grey of dusk she had expected. But there was nobody outside.

Her dream carried on.

But her dreams returned her to the room once more. Hot, sweaty and impatient, wondering why she was back for a fourth time, she opened the window. The window peered not into the village, as it should, but out onto a field of flowers that rounded at the horizon. Birds and insects were in the air. It was midday, bright and pleasing.

The only thing unpleasant was the sight of Lucinda Skeldar's head bobbing in the distance, as she skipped through the field. Amalina turned away, disturbed by the song Lucinda was singing. And then she heard her father's muffled voice in the next room: "Without you I would be devastated."

It took much longer for Amalina to return to the room for the fifth time, but eventually she found herself in her father's bed, with the all-consuming window facing her. She thought she'd woken up. When she looked to her right, her father wasn't there. So it must be a dream, mustn't it?

But it felt real. She believed she was awake. And she had to—yes, she just had to—*was compelled beyond reason*—to go to the window and open it. She would die if she did not. So she went to the window, threw off the cross bar and pulled away the panel.

It was night. At first she thought she was alone. Then she noticed the boots hanging down outside the window above her. The boots moved as if the body above them, which was out of sight, was twisting and turning maniacally. The Count had come for her but was at the window on the second floor—the attic window, Amalina's old room. The boots shook and she heard him complaining, "This isn't your room. This isn't your home."

. . .

She woke in the morning to find nothing had happened at all, though she was as tired as if she'd stayed up all night.

To her relief—and to her father's—the Count hadn't come. Not that it broke any spell. The Count's return was still a threat. But it was daylight now and they could breathe easy for the moment.

Amalina snipped out the candles and threw off the cross bar and opened the window. The fresh morning air blew in, and the street was in a golden soft-focus, with all the shadows shortening and hardening.

A new day.

Amalina went to her own room and chose a bright, colorful dress, the special one she would normally shy away from on a day of work.

She joined her father in the bakery. He didn't bother her with pokes or forlorn tickles, his eyes were dark and baggy, and he only grunted at Amalina if she got in the way.

Fine, she thought.

. . .

It was midday when Amalina went for a second time to get water. With no murder to cover up—and the outrage of Lucinda's death finally fading—the town square was without the gossips and lightly attended. She dumped the buckets in quickly, and with no sign of Cristine around to talk to, she headed back to the shop.

But she caught a familiar scent as she neared an alley. And she was not too surprised, then, when she saw the *very* familiar man hidden inside it, out of the light, beckoning to her.

"Genadie," said Amalina.

"Yes," he motioned her into the alley. "Please, come."

These were the first words he'd spoken to her, having conducted all their other business with simple gestures and bows. His voice was thin but gravelly. His strangely stooped bow, which he seemed to travel with, made her feel like she towered over him, though he must be much larger when fully extended. She looked around for the Count, but he was not there.

"Please, I can't be seen here," said Genadie, still gesturing her to him.

It didn't seem like a trap—the exact idea of it being a trap not entering her mind, as he really seemed like one of the helpless mice she swept into the street every day—and so she took a step in, checking behind her to make sure she and Genadie were not observed.

"What do you want?" she asked.

"You must come. The Master wants you."

"What? Now?"

"Yes."

"I'm getting the water—"

"No, you must come along with me now," Genadie's voice scraped, a ridiculous smile sliced into his face.

"No," she said sternly. "Don't you see these buckets? I'm working."

"Leave the buckets here. We are to leave immediately. Immediately, girl. Your father knows."

"What!" It seemed preposterous. It should be. She didn't know whether to laugh or be angry.

Genadie pulled out a piece of parchment. He held it out to her, pressed under the thumbs of both hands.

"What is this?" Amalina took the paper from him and unfolded it.

The paper was very familiar to her. It came from the bakery. They used it to wrap bread or jot tallies. This had been used for a private note. Amalina's stomach lurched.

> Daughter,
> You are to leave with the man who presents this letter. Do
> so without delay. Understand that I know all that has

transpired. We are now indebted to a person whose name I do not dare spell out. But you know of whom I write, and we are obligated to him for your very life, and you must assist him when he calls. He calls on you now.

Forgive me, it is better you leave without returning from the well. It is a matter of urgency, as I understand. And in truth, my heart would break to see you leave our home with your eyes in tears, or to say a dreadful goodbye to you on your way to help this person whose name I still dare not mention. It would shatter me. It is best I pretend you have gone off to fetch the water, and you have just lost your way and taken a while to return.

You will return, my daughter. But for now, you must obey, and go.

D.

Just as the paper was from the bakery, the handwriting was her father's. She'd seen it enough in the ledger and on notes, and when he had helped her learn writing.

So it was true! He knew everything! Or … was that true? Maybe he knew only a little, and he thought he knew everything?

But she did not want to leave with Genadie.

"You must come. Master wants it."

"I don't care. I have to bring the buckets—"

"You read the letter."

"I don't care. I want to say goodbye, at least." The corner of Amalina's lips began to tremble. She pictured poor Dragomir in tears behind the counter.

"No, no. No goodbyes. There is no time, girl. We must go. You read the letter."

"I don't care what the letter says," Amalina snapped. She felt like tossing the bucket over his head and marching back to the store. In a sudden fury, she couldn't believe her father was so cowardly that he'd write such a letter and mean it. Now she wasn't sorry for him at all, she could smack him in the arm.

"He doesn't want you to return. Not now. You must come with me."

"He isn't the only one who gets a say in this," Amalina bucked.

"No, girl. You obey Master. Or there will be consequences. Come. Come."

Her sadness and anger smoothed quickly at the memory of the Count. Best not to get too willful. Who knows what the emergency was. Maybe he was dying, or in some bad way, and she could help him reach his death.

"And what am I supposed to do with the buckets?" she smirked.

"Leave them." He indicated the ground helpfully with a sweep of his arm.

And so she let the buckets go and followed him to the carriage using alleys and checking for bodies in the streets and faces in windows.

Oh, this had to have been arranged, she smoldered. Midday, when the sun was up and baking, and people would be at their work, or eating, or sleeping indoors, or otherwise preferring to be inside and away from a hot window. This was the plan: Send her to the well at noon, have her be intercepted and snuck away unobserved.

The carriage had been hidden just outside the village, the same place Genadie had let her out the other morning. Very good. Very clever.

She got in and they were off. The window drapes were shut against the bright sun. It seemed gloomy in the cabin, especially when her thoughts returned to how she'd arrived inside that carriage.

The cabin warmed to that of an oven, and the jostling of the compartment on the uneven road became even more irritating. Why wasn't the carriage stopping? How long could Genadie drive these horses under the sun without stopping for water and rest, or at least a change of horses? Amalina pulled back a drape to let in some air. She didn't recognize the road. She stuck out her head.

"Genadie!"

It took several attempts before he turned around.

"Where are we going?"

He said something that sounded like "Olympus."

"Where?"

"To our Master," he said over his shoulder.

"You mean the Count?"

"I mean our *'Master'*," said Genadie.

"He isn't *my* master. He is the Count of Ardeel. Isn't he?"

Genadie shook his head violently. "Count! Count! What a thing to say! Count! He is 'Master', girl."

"I said: He isn't *my* master," she repeated, louder this time. "He can be yours. I don't count as my master anyone who kills innocent people."

Genadie waved a dismissive hand. "That man! That Neku was a very, very bad man! He is not 'innocent'!"

"Not him! The others!"

"What others?"

"Lucinda! She was innocent. I saw what he did to her!"

"That girl?" Genadie shook his head again. "That wasn't his fault."

"Wasn't his fault? I saw him do it!"

"It wasn't his fault. You don't understand. You're a child and you know nothing. Now be quiet and let me drive. Hyaah, hyaah. Nk. Nk."

"You still haven't told me where we're going."

"To Master."

"*Where* is he, Genadie? *Where?*"

He repeated the word which she couldn't quite make out. Was he really saying 'Olympus'?

"Where?"

"The mountain. The high castle"

"How long will it take to get to there? Which mountain?"

"We'll arrive by night."

Night!

"How long will I be gone?"

Genadie shook his head.

"Tell me!"

"Not long, girl. You'll be back home before you know it."

"Tomorrow?"

Genadie shrugged. "Not long, Master says. And so be quiet. You'll be home before you know it."

"I have nothing to wear tonight. I don't have any other clothes but what's on me. It's cold in the mountains ... and at night!" And while this was true, she only wanted to hear further confirmation that it would not be long before she returned.

"Your father has sent some of your clothes." Genadie pointed a gloved finger over his shoulder to indicate the roof, or the rear of the carriage. "And there are fine clothes at the castle that would be better than any of them."

Her father had given Genadie her clothes? When?

Dragomir had become so sneaky; running off, out of her sight, plotting and planning things against her. It made her blood boil. But, then again, she had plotted and planned things privately against *him*, hadn't she? But still, the thought of Genadie's hands on her personal items ... And Genadie, that little filthy thing, judging her clothes as inferior!

"How long, though, Genadie? Heh? Tell me!"

"You'll be home before you know it."

"My father needs me there! I need to help make the bread! I can't be gone too long!"

"You'll be home before you know it! You'll be home before you know it! You'll be home before you know it!" Genadie chanted angrily, sending a warning look down at her.

But the phrase meant nothing and told her nothing. The last time she'd helped the Count—the monster—she'd been gone for just a short adventure. It could be so again. But if her clothes had been sent along, that meant it could be days, or weeks.

And in the hours that followed, with the heat and jostling adding a slow-cooking misery to Amalina, she felt a terrible distance growing between her and her home. When she peeked out there were only the jagged walls of the mountains growing on every side. Sheer grey rocks were biting off her routes of return. And after a while the feeling grew that she was leaving forever. She would never see her father, her home, or her village ever again. It was the same awful feeling she used to experience when accompanying her father to the mill when she was little. But she was older now and the prospect in this instance was more real. Her stomach shrank.

• • •

That very same stomach-knotting dread visited Dragomir when Amalina did not return from fetching the water. She'd been gone a long time, but he hadn't realized it until Jenna came asking where Amalina was.

With incredible calm, he closed up his shop and followed the route to the well. He found the buckets, still full of water, hidden in an alley.

He tried to picture the scene in his mind, hoping she wasn't frightened, or hurt. He could not cry out; the way his whole body wanted.

He lugged the water back—the rope biting softly into his calloused palms; which made him remember and inwardly weep over his daughter's little hands, hands that had been on those ropes only an hour or so ago—and he opened up the store and growled at Jenna never mind about Amalina.

He would have to do all the worrying alone.

And he was plagued with a most empty feeling: that there was nothing to worry about, because there was nothing to be done about it. She was gone. Amalina, his daughter, gone forever. He would never see her again. There was nothing he could do.

• • •

But there was something Amalina could do. She was not as helpless against the monster as Dragomir was, because she knew her strength against him. She considered bolting from the carriage whenever it might stop, and simply walking back. In full defiance.

But the carriage never stopped. And so, waiting patiently for her moment, she carried on planning and strategizing wild escapes, through deep forests, across broken ramparts, over colossal mountains, down rampaging rivers, through confounding mazes, one glorious slip more daring and impossible than the last.

And eventually her thoughts smoothed out and became dreams. And in every dream there was a small shadow in pursuit, way off in the distance; always closing on her, but getting no nearer. She was the master of the land, especially in warm daylight. Her pursuer was just a shimmering piece of black air, buzzing persistently on the horizon but without power. And in her dream she finally found the road to the village. Why, there was Jenz Timer walking alongside Gulgas the Hunter, both coming up the road, having just sold a great bargain for their wares, and each with a small loaf of dark bread in their hands. They waved to her, throwing crumbs all over the ground which the mice hurried to eat.

She did not stop to talk to them, but ran, ran all the way back to the bakery and her home. She pushed through the front door and knew she must go into her father's bedroom. She would go there and tell him he didn't need to sit with his rifles all night because she was back and the Count was dead (for some reason). It all seemed logical of course. And so she ran into Dragomir's bedroom only to find his chair was empty ... though the candles were burning brightly and he *should* be there. It was night, for sure, because it was as dark as midnight except for the glow of the candles.

That's when she spotted the boots dangling outside the open window, kicking around angrily. It was very quiet, and unlike last night's dream, the monster wasn't complaining how she was not in her proper room. Not grumbling how this wasn't her home. No, it was eerily quiet. She just heard the violent shuffling of the black suede boots against the upper sill, and the hissing of the velvet leggings above them.

But then she heard his laugh. The same rolling laugh, like thunder, that she'd heard in the carriage after he'd obliterated Neku. It started small, outside the window, with the shaking, shivering boots, but then it carried inside the room and grew and grew. The laughter of revenge, of triumph.

"She's here!" The boots jangled. "She's here! You did it! Yes. Perfect! Perfect!"

• • •

Amalina woke and was utterly astonished. As she heard the words continue to roll "Perfect! Perfect!"

The interior of the cabin was lit by candles, it was deep into the night, and the whole carriage was still jerking around, perhaps even faster and more madly than before.

Jutting through the window into the compartment, as if he'd been stopped halfway as he climbed in, his left arm hooked over the window's bottom sill, his other arm stretched upward in a white silk sleeve, his hand steady on the wall, was the Count. He appeared huge, as if he filled the whole space with his upper half, and especially his head and face. The face was monstrously large, the flesh blown up, saturated under the translucent skin with a cloudy flow of black-crimson blood. His whole head looking like a pustule about to pop. His eyes were bloodshot, too—or better to say, engorged with thick red ropes of veins—the knotted orbs looking as if they were about to shoot out of his head, the pupils pointing like sharp knives at her. And it was all completed with an unsettling, hungry smile of impossibly large teeth, erupting from behind his stretched, blood-red lips, with two teeth, on either side of the whole ivory set, descending like daggers. And he was laughing his laugh of triumph again, while he looked at Amalina like a wolf who'd cornered his favorite rabbit. Which in the end is what Amalina was, wasn't she? Prey.

So no, she would not be seeing her father again.

'Perfect!' indeed.

PART TWO
THE WAILING CASTLE

10

Neku Jonker

Earlier—a day before the previous chapter's events—the low constable—who was sent from Tsobl to Netz at haste to investigate a pressing matter—peered down at the riven and desiccated corpse of Margit Bincy, his eyes half-closed in boredom. Bored so it seemed to the men beside him. His next words, however, betrayed this artificial construction: this constable's facade of 'disinterest'.

"You say," he asked, swishing the sides of his long cloak absently, "That she was found this way?"

"Found this way, yes," said the Cardinal's right hand man, who stood between him and the Cardinal.

"But as I understand, not here in the church. Not lying on this stone slab, conveniently within the very room you prepare a body for services?"

"No, not here, no," the right hand man agreed, somewhat breathlessly. "She was in the graveyard."

The low constable stared.

"We would not just leave her exposed in the yard, of course," the Cardinal's right hand man added quickly, finding more to say by the instruction of a subtle motion of the Cardinal's fingers, "not so anyone else might see her. And we didn't return her corpse to the grave because she's beyond decay. Mummified, that is; and mummified in a *natural* way and not in an *unnatural* way. We thought you'd wish to see her state yourself to make your own *independent* determination; so you could then put those who found her at ease."

Just below his hip, the Cardinal tickled the ends of his fingers, indicating the right hand man had finished saying what was expected of him, and now it was time to shut up.

"Show me where she was found in the yard," the low constable said blandly, his eyes hooded and half-lowered still.

As they walked, the constable nodded internally, his stomach creaking and crying for some food, his distracted head knowing what his purpose— or what the Cardinal's purpose for him—was: *By my being here*, he thought, *I will add an external sobriety to events which the Cardinal cannot manage to calm on his own, and so put to rest—before matters get out of hand—any rumors of magic or the supernatural. Because the one who found Margit Bincy's body is not a simpleton, nor a minor citizen of the town, whom the Cardinal, or one of his subordinates, can crush.*

. . .

The mayor's wife, the one who'd found Margit's body, had entered the graveyard early in the morning on some recent day, with the idea of visiting the headstones of her parents. She'd tripped over Margit Bincy in a way that sent the body lurching upward from the ground, like a wraith made of paper scraps, chomping teeth and clawing fingernails. Frightening enough to convince the mayor's wife that she was under attack by the corpse, and send her screaming into the church, telling anyone who would listen what had happened: she had only narrowly escaped with her life, and the graveyard was opening and sending forth its dead.

"An excitable woman," as the right hand man had described her to the low constable.

The low constable, though just a junior officer, would now be the official stamp and seal of the Tsobl governorship; an administrative institution superior to, and outside of, the local power structure owned by the Cardinal—who was currently feuding with the mayor—and thereby lend authenticity to the Cardinal's assessment of the situation; because the Cardinal's haughty and arrogant manner had him commonly mistrusted, even by his friends. The mayor's wife needed to hear from this reliable man of bureaucracy, the low constable of Tsobl, Margit Bincy had not sprung from her grave by magical means; perhaps summoned to molest her by the vindictive Cardinal himself.

"Here?" the low constable asked when he was shown a spot of mashed, spun and trampled grass just inside a copse of trees. He returned their nods.

His eyes studied the grass with his deceptive look of profound boredom. Without moving his head, the light grey disks stirred around in many directions. Then he walked away, pulling the Cardinal and his subordinate along behind him as if by a powerful magnet attached to his backside. The Cardinal sped up when the low constable picked up his pace. This brought out a smile on the constable, which the two men trotting behind him could not see. The smile, more a sneer, really, was stowed away when he slowed down.

The Cardinal and the subordinate were out of breath.

It had been a wandering loop of the grounds, stretching to another copse of trees, zig-zagging later through the headstones, terminating at a decrepit vault, where the low constable prodded at its door with his finger.

The low constable made an agreeable noise, though looking as if his time was being wasted. The Cardinal leaned forward in anticipation of some declaration. The Cardinal's right hand man leaned forward, too.

"How," began the low constable very slowly, "do you shave your beard?"

The right hand man looked to the Cardinal's fingers, which twitched irritably.

"I don't understand," said the right hand man, irritably, too. What was this about beards? What had it to do with Margit Bincy or where they'd found her in the graveyard?

The low constable pointed to the Cardinal, "I meant to ask the Cardinal, not you. Do you shave your beard, Cardinal?"

Of course there was no way for the right hand man to answer the question himself unless he did the Cardinal's shaving. So the Cardinal would have to answer. Was this sudden, inane digression by the low constable a ruse—some *impertinent* ruse—by a minor functionary to get the Cardinal to speak to him personally? To elevate his own importance among his friends back in Tsobl when recounting this visit—that he'd conversed directly with the powerful and renowned holy figure in Netz? The Cardinal's fingers (which the right hand man looked to immediately) galloped in the air like the legs of a nerve-struck spider, frightened out of its wits by the nearby lifting of a shoe. He did not know where to run for safety.

"Eh. What did you say?" said the Cardinal finally, with profound reluctance.

"Your beard is so very short, very narrow, and with exceptionally fine definition to its edges," the constable admired; seemingly keen about something for the first time since he'd arrived. "How you keep it that way is remarkable. I don't have much hair on my face as of yet, and so I just shave it all off. But my elders, no matter how they trim their beards, there is a volume to their whiskers, a natural unruliness they cannot tame. Your hairs are low to the skin, as if new growth, but they are so thick in number the beard is solid. How do you manage this? Do you have a special blade?"

"Just a razor," answered the Cardinal.

"Kept very sharp."

"I suppose so."

"And a narrow comb, to style and measure the cut."

The Cardinal did not answer but waited for the next revelation, his eyes opening then narrowing, as if sighing with impatience. 'What is this about?' his expression seemed to demand, 'you are wasting my valuable time, you meaningless—'

"And you must have an exceptional looking glass," the constable barreled on, "one situated near a window, I would think. You don't have the eyes of a young man."

"The dust upon my eyes are covered in dust," the Cardinal smirked, but then nodded 'yes'. He also huffed now with deliberate, obvious impatience, in case this low constable wasn't getting the hint by his expressions alone.

The low constable nodded once, and raised a finger to oppose the Cardinal's agitation. He was presently coming to his definite and important point, and leaned his back casually against the ill-kept vault where he'd concluded their walk.

"All of these are individual pieces: the blade, the comb, the looking glass ..." began the low constable. "If I were to see your blade, or the comb, or both, sitting on a table in your chamber, I would not be able to tell what kind of beard you have. If I saw your looking glass, I might remark on its clearness and resolution, but think nothing on its placement near the large window. And neither clarity nor position would tell me what kind of beard the Cardinal wore, or if he wore a beard at all."

The Cardinal nodded. The Cardinal's right hand man's lips puckered and his eyes pushed out of his head.

"But perceiving your beard," the low constable continued lazily, "I can deduce all these separate and specific pieces—your blade, your comb, and your glass, and just how it is positioned near a bright window—without having set eyes upon them, as they fall in a straight line from the first, mundane observation: your *superbly manicured* beard. You follow? With one piece—the right one—I can perceive everything that comes attached to it— anything and everything associated with it—with the utmost precision. "

"I see." The Cardinal turned red. He was used to giving sermons, but was unaccustomed to receiving them. And now it was as if the low constable had looked up the Cardinal's skirt and announced what he'd found. The Cardinal, flustered, grumbled, "So gleaning from my beard you could relate the contents of my private inner chambers ..."

The low constable noted his subject's interesting reaction without changing expression. His eyes were still bored.

And yet.

"Never mind. I just wanted you to understand a small measure of my 'parsing ways', as the high constable calls it. Nothing more to it."

"This was a trick of some kind," countered the Cardinal. "To impress."

"Impress the Cardinal of Netz?" There was a slight pause, then, after an equivocal sweep of his grey eyes, the low constable poured out quickly and suddenly, in an all-business manner: "You will be relieved to hear there was nothing of the spirit world to Margit Bincy's resurrection."

"Sensible," said the Cardinal, taking the switch in stride. "Good."

The low Constable wasn't done: "But how you report this to your people, without upsetting them, I leave to you."

"What do you mean?"

The Constable nodded: "Margit Bincy was removed from her grave, which means a grave robber has gained access to your grounds. This woman was not well-liked by the community, judging from her clothing and hair and the location of her plot, and so she will not tax the pity of your congregation. But she isn't the only one who has suffered defilement. No, if you return to the woman's grave you will discover the tools that removed her from her resting place—if you have not already found them and hidden them yourselves. Did you find these tools and hide them away?"

"No!" the right hand man protested.

"No? Well, you and I both know she didn't jump out of the hole. When they are found: a couple of these tools, besides a hooded lamp, will be specialized. They tear open the ground and pull the nails from the coffins. And you will find, hidden in the copse of trees where Margit was found, a sharpened knife that made a good number of the holes in her dress and her breast.

"I mean to say," murmured the low constable, "your intendant has gotten up to some very dark work inside your grounds. Over a period of years, perhaps decades, he has systematically disturbed the rest of the souls buried here, with the sole purpose of plying his insidious trade upon their bodies. His trade: not to steal from them, but to play with them like life-sized dolls. The man must be a simpleton, an idiot, and one lacking in empathy and religious morality, to have turned over the graves of countless innocents."

"Rosczy," the Cardinal's right nostril lifted as if getting scent of a sewer. "Find Neku. Find him and bring him to me. Do not tell him why, but seize him and bind him so he does not escape. Then bring him—"

"He's dead," said the low constable.

The Cardinal's head swung so fast the cross he wore tinkled across the beads on his robes. "What?"

"Or else he would have returned Margit to her grave, which he did not."

"You are certain he's dead?"

The low constable nodded.

"Just as certain as everything else you have claimed here—claimed to me now—gathered up by your so-called 'parsing ways'—to be true?"

"You will find the intendant's body outside the gate, or an entry point furthest from view of your cathedral, where he was done in. The killer did not have time to return Margit to her grave, you see. As well, he will not have bothered to dispose of Neku."

"Who killed Neku?"

"Tell your people whatever you like," said the low constable. "It doesn't matter. The villain in the story, for all they will be concerned, was Neku Jonker. Tell them you executed him yourself and hadn't told anyone for fear of embarrassing the church, and they should be satisfied."

"And if we do not find his body?"

"You will find it soon enough, unless it was dumped in the lake, in which case it may take a month or so for the body to reveal itself on the surface, or along the shore."

"But can you tell me who killed Neku? Do you know?"

"Not yet. But it's just a matter of proper perspective. While I have my suspicions, I haven't found the item to align my eye with the facts' true path. Not yet. I dare not say anything until I do."

"You will be willing to sign a report that Margit's presence in the graveyard was the work of a grave robber, and nothing more?" asked the Cardinal.

"Whatever you'd like your people to think, as long as it is within the bounds of the truth."

The Cardinal's lips moved slightly. His eyes narrowed, but then he nodded. He motioned with his finger.

"Thank you," said the right hand man.

Then the low constable was left alone. The two men swung their robes back toward the big church. Just before reaching it, the right hand man, Rosczy, shot off to the right, following a trail that led to a far off point along the fence. A gate. Where he would perhaps find Neku's body.

But less than a half hour later, Rosczy located the Cardinal in his chambers and reported: "I couldn't find the body."

"Of course you couldn't," the Cardinal sniffed, running a finger over the stubble of his beard. *Should I cut it off?* he wondered. That the low constable had been eyeing him so closely, and making such a sport of his whiskers during his little game of 'Impress the Cardinal', it had made them tingle in an annoying way. "Neku's gone. I told you that myself, did I not?"

"But you sent me to find him."

"I sent you away so as to pretend I believed the constable. Which I do not. Neku, that disgusting wretch, is not dead at all, but probably miles from here already, hiding. Our only misfortune is he is too stupid to think for himself, and is limited in thought, and he will eventually return to the town, if not our church, because it is most familiar to him. The cur. We do need to find him, though. To make sure he's never seen again."

"Of course," Rosczy nodded low, not able to look at his superior for too long a time. Not in the face anyway. "Well, I thought you'd believed the constable."

"Why should I have?" the Cardinal blew out a breath of contempt. "You heard how he went on. His special ways; his vain *inanities*."

The Cardinal nearly laughed. There was no 'crystal-clear mirror' next to a 'large bright window', as the low constable had crowed with pride at his cleverness. As a matter of fact, the Cardinal had no mirrors in the entire cathedral. If he could banish reflections on the surface of liquids he would do so. His eyes were as sharp as a hunting hawk's, even at this age, and he hated the look of his own face. Every time he'd seen it, it had blown his self-image of a grand noble, the face of a great leader, which he had painted in his own head. His eyes were too perceptive, he saw too clearly the faults and the artifices hidden on, and behind, the skin and muscles of his reflection.

His weaknesses penetrated deep enough, apparently, to reshape—to deform—the bones of his skull.

No, there was no mirror. In fact, the trimming of his beard was done not by his own hand, but by a servant who was skilled in such things, a former barber. The Cardinal had simply pointed out the portrait of a beloved saint who he so wished he could resemble, and ordered this servant to cut his beard to match it. And the servant complied. It was to the Cardinal's ultimate pleasure that he could, every morning, sit back in his chair and know his power was enough that he could get quality work out of this servant. The Cardinal watched the man's eyes as he worked his idol's face, and thrilled as the fear of failure in them was replaced by the gleam of pride; that he hadn't destroyed the Cardinal's heavenly skin with a nick or a slice or a cut.

It wasn't even a special blade or a specialized comb the man used to trim the beard, but a common razor and pair of scissors.

The only thing the low constable had gotten right was the razor was sharp, but how surprising is that? What a *glittering generality*.

No, the low constable had gotten it all wrong. It was a wonder he'd been perceptive enough to detect what Neku Jonker had been up to ... and perhaps had glimpsed some truth as to what had happened to the sickening toad to make him abandon his work. But it was luck or a miracle the low constable had understood this much about Neku's antics. And the Cardinal had been lucky for the constable to serve his purpose anyway, to act as witness against the paranoid, supernatural ravings of the mayor's wife.

"The man Tsobl sent us was useful," the Cardinal summed up for his right hand man, thinking sourly to himself: *even if he was a complete insult, sending such a minor-ranked novice of law when I'd requested the high constable himself.* "But, he is an idiot and was wrong on all counts."

"Anything else?" asked Rosczy.

"He can live."

• • •

The low constable's stomach gurgled hungrily, but he would not eat or drink until he was outside the Cardinal's sphere of influence.

As he pondered the Cardinal, the image of the man's face presented itself.

Of course the Cardinal doesn't have a mirror next to a window, the low constable thought, a tricky little sneer buried under his expression of grim determination. And how could a nearly blind Cardinal—which he is *not*, because the text he writes is infinitesimally small—cut away so precisely at a beard anyway, crippled with a shaky hand (which the Cardinal's infinitesimal, yet *squiggled*, writing did reveal) and equipped with the mind of an outrageous bore who enjoys the sight of toadies scrambling to do his bidding? No, no. There was no mirror next to a window. There was no dedicated sharp blade—other than a rather pointed dagger meant for personal defense … and probably not even a comb. One quiet trip through the cathedral and its grounds before presenting himself to the Cardinal had told him all he needed to know about the Cardinal's personality and habits.

And then, by the Cardinal's allowing him to make all these false assertions, yet at no time correcting him, the low constable had learned even more: the Cardinal regarded him as nothing above one of his lowly subjects, to be patronized and treated with bemused condescension.

And perhaps he knows more about Neku, and what actually happened in the church grounds, doesn't he? the low constable mused.

But maybe not.

Nobody was paying attention to the low constable anymore.

Now he arrived at the vault at which he'd concluded the tour of the grounds with the Cardinal and his right hand man. A large, plain, dilapidated vault. Those two were not around, and the low constable was alone and unobserved.

The low constable pried at the old door. The latch fell away and the door opened easily enough. He swung it all the way so the daylight could reach as far in as it could. Then he stepped inside.

The low constable had been wrong after all.

They would not find Neku Jonker outside the gate. Neku had been killed beyond the church grounds, but that is not where he'd been left.

Neku Jonker's body, naked and twisted like a rag, squeezed of blood, lay atop the torn-aside lid of the vault's central crypt. After peering into the crypt's hole and seeing it was empty, the low constable shoved Neku's body in. Then, with grunts and groans, he replaced the marble lid.

It's true, the low constable thought, his heart beating wildly. *All my suppositions were correct. The spirit world has come to life.*

He steadied his shaking left hand by gripping it with his right. His eyes were wild and darting about. If he was correct and the spirit world had come to life, it had revealed a monster out of all proportions. But that thing didn't yet know of him or who he was, or that he was now aware of its existence. And, the low constable understood greedily, if he returned to Tsobl safely to report what he'd found, and then lead them back here to kill this beast before it discovered him and his plan, he would free the world of an unholy terror. He would become a hero of absolute legend, the greatest ever to have served the people of these mountains. A freedom-bringer, a divine-justice deliverer. *It can all be true!*

He could hardly contain his thoughts. One thought did outshine all others, though:

Now I must act.

11

The Castle by Night

When the carriage stopped Amalina woke. She leapt to the door, but having been stuck in a cramped posture for so long her body was slow and difficult to move. Genadie reached in and pulled her out.

Now in the courtyard, Amalina found she was surrounded by a breathtaking upsweep of grey stones; mammoth, rough blocks which constituted the surrounding castle courtyard's walls and the castle's body in whole. Everything was the same stone it seemed, even under foot.

So I've made it inside the castle Genadie told me about. It is very—

Her attention was stolen by the Count, who stood at the end of the carriage, once again observing her with the greatest appetite, his features stretched and blood-bloated.

But then ghastly echoes filled the courtyard. A disturbing wheezing and grunting.

Amalina gulped.

It was the horses.

The horses were still in their fetters. Their black hair was soaked, matted, and foamed over at their shoulders and rumps. Steam burst in clouds from them, and their eyes were wild in terror. They sucked in and gusted out breaths that suggested they could not actually get enough of the air they needed to live—cold air that might extinguish the fires inside them. Though they stood as rigid as statues, just beneath their hides their muscles rippled and shivered as if the sinew, which had pulled the carriage at such speed for so many hours, had torn free from the bone, and whipped around like so many wriggling snakes and worms.

The count saw Amalina's concern for the horses and patted one.

"Genadie, we've pushed them to their limit," he observed.

"Yes, master. I prepared their graves yesterday. I will bury them when I have put Ms. Dalca in her room."

"Good thinking," he said. He smiled and brought his eyes to bear on Amalina. He said nothing.

"I'm cold," she told him, finding it difficult to look into his eyes—there was something of a blank infinity in them—but forced herself to do so. To defy him. She wrapped her arms around her torso.

"Yes," said the Count. He pulled off his cloak and handed it to Genadie, who then scrambled over and placed the cloak on Amalina's shoulders in the humorous way a child decorates a Christmas tree: carefully, and eagerly, but with uneven, awkward, and unsure plucking movements. Once it was on, the cloak lacked warmth.

"Did you bring my overcoat?" she asked Genadie, but then remembered to swing her eyes back at the Count, accusing him with her question. He was the one responsible for this abduction, after all.

"Bring your coat—?" began the Count.

"Oh," Genadie leapt to interrupt, jumping between her and the Count and waved his hands above his head. "No, do not worry about this, Ms. Dalca. There is plenty for you to wear inside the castle. I have only to bring you to your room, you will have plenty to wear."

"But did you bring my overcoat?" she asked again, beginning to suspect something by the fear in his eyes.

"Don't worry about this matter, Ms. Dalca."

"I will worry. I like my coat and prefer to wear my own clothes, and if you or my father forgot to pack it in with my belongings, I will insist you go back and get it for me. Or you can bring me back home so I can make sure you take the right one."

"Oh, Ms. Dalca," Genadie frowned miserably. "But the coat was packed, I am sure of it. Your father is most thorough."

But, by his tone and delivery, it was clear there was something being left unsaid.

"Get to the point," demanded the Count, irritably.

"Yes," Genadie nodded to his master, "Yes, yes. But, you see, Ms. Dalca, your clothes—the chest and boxes, the luggage—look, Master, they have fallen off the carriage."

"What!" Amalina ran to the rear of the carriage and then, finding it empty, jumped to see if the luggage might be on the carriage's roof. She felt a terrible pull in her chest when she found no cases at all. "My clothes! My books!"

The terrible pull inside her was erased by the sudden brutal stroke of the Count, who struck Genadie in the middle of his back. Genadie smashed down onto the courtyard's stones, like a bug swatted there, a crunching sound coming with it. The Count's eyes were red with fire (or blood, who could really tell?). He stepped forward over his servant's shivering body.

"You lost the lady's clothes?" thundered the count.

"So sorry, my master," said Genadie in a rasping voice. "The wolves ..."

"The wolves!" the count smashed Genadie again. Blood was left on the stones.

"I'm sure I tied them well enough," the poor servant coughed and muttered when he'd recovered.

"Bring Amalina Dalca to her room, while you still have limbs left to move. I will search for her crates and boxes along the road for as long as I can. Before the sun ..."

"Yes, Master," said Genadie with a relieved groan.

The relief Genadie was enjoying, she could tell, was that he would not die. Not today. Not at his masters' hands.

Limping, and with an uncomfortable hunch, Genadie led Amalina into the castle.

The castle was so dark he had to hold her hand as he wound her through the rooms and corridors to her chambers. The rooms they passed through were smaller than she'd imagined were inside a large, old castle. But it was cozy enough, and familiar to her senses, even if she couldn't see how they were decorated.

Genadie seemed to move through the entirety by memory as he limped them along.

"Are you all right?" she asked him. "Are you injured?"

He did not answer. His breath was heavy and rasping.

"Genadie, are you hurt?"

Up a number of stairways, he deposited her, finally, in a room that was larger than her own bedroom at home. It was square, and had wide windows along two walls. The moon and distant mountains sat outside one of the windows. The moon was the very same moon, she reflected, which had thrilled her from the window she'd opened just a few weeks ago.

My bedroom. The thought repeated like a fading echo.

She now felt the loss of her home, of her father, of Cristine, and her village. The loss of so much ...

"I'm still cold," Amalina complained. "And I still don't know what I'm doing here, what the Count wants with me. How long *am* I going to be here?"

No answer.

Genadie had left the room long before she realized he was gone.

She turned around twice to make sure he wasn't scurrying behind her like a small rodent. Then she stood, alone in the room, still cold but wrapped in the monster's cloak.

She went to the windows. At an angle, she could see down into the courtyard, and there she saw the horses. They were released from their fetters and sprawled, limb over limb, on the ground. They were dead.

But Amalina was not.

She had been spared. She lived. Something she had not expected.

Even with the loss of everything dear to her, it was a great release that she was alive and would, apparently, continue to live for some time to come.

A faint wailing of the wind—sounding grotesquely human—drove Amalina from the window.

Now, why am I still alive? she wondered.

She still didn't know. The count had some plan. It must be a clever one, because, after all, he *was* very clever. As she considered everything that had happened so far, he had not only swept her into his own plottings, but while doing so he'd kept himself at a safe distance. Whether he knew it or not—*but he must know, mustn't he!*—she was intent on doing him considerable harm: skewering him with a knife, slashing him with a razor, immolating him with a torch, venting him with a bullet, clawing his eyes, biting out his neck. And yet he had always appeared at times inconvenient to her plans, she with no weapon at the ready or awkwardly positioned, and always with Amalina unprepared both physically and mentally.

The Count only came to her when he was assured a commanding position, one of safety and superiority.

But he came to her. Because he needed her.

Why does he need me?

12

The Castle by Day

Genadie visited Amalina in the morning, his eyes wrinkled and tired, and his whole body carrying the same limp as the night before. But his energy ... what incredible energy! His movements projected excitable power. No matter what damage now restricted the motion of his limbs, he seemed capable of dancing up a wall, or blowing off his tight-fitting clothes with a sudden lurch, by the way he went about tidying the room and sweeping out the fireplace.

"You will come with me, Ms. Dalca," he said when done, after lowering his incongruously tired looking eyes in a show of respect.

She was still in bed, having woke there some time before but finding no reason to open her eyes until the Count's servant had arrived and began rattling around. Now fully awake, she still felt like she could use more rest.

Last night, with the strange, faint, almost human-like wailing of the wind, she had thought she would never fall asleep. But when she'd found the door locked, she was quick to throw herself into bed and wait for the sun to rise. Unaware when she did fall asleep, despite the wail, it was not enough to satisfy. Her whole body felt as tired as Genadie's face looked.

She sighed.

Presently, sunlight filled the chamber and all was quiet, except the birds chirping somewhere outside. The wailing of the wind had disappeared with morning.

"Why will I come with you?" she asked, not moving, only her head visible above the covers.

"Breakfast," he said.

"I need to dress first."

"Are you not already dressed?" His eyes leapt to her body. An odd hunger in them.

"I need to prepare myself for the meal."

"Oh," said Genadie. Then he chided her: "As you wish. Be not too long, Ms. Dalca."

There was little to prepare, as she could not find a wash basin and she had no other clothes to wear.

Inspecting the clothes she did have, the ones she wore, she found patches of dried bread dough on her skirt, arm and leg. She sensed the distance between her smudgy leg—here inside this room—and her home and bakery, where the dough smudge had been created. She knew what her father must be doing right now, with the sun up and all those chores that must be performed, which he was now performing without her. He was all alone.

Her breath swelled and she felt like she might cry. How must he be feeling?

He should be regretting! He deserves every ache and pout for handing me over like a coward to the monster!

She smiled at the thought of his being overwhelmed by customers, and fumbling overcooked loaves. But for her it was a short-lived smile. She returned to wanting to cry at the thought of missing her home and loved ones. But that brief smile was adequate, anyway, to generate enough spirit for her to lift her feet and leave the room.

Genadie led her through the castle at the speed of his limp and her shuffling funk. The corner of his mouth ticked painfully at each step. His eye winced. But it seemed he could continue for hours, the way he powered along, almost eagerly.

"Are we going to have breakfast?" she asked.

"That is where we are headed right now, Ms. Dalca."

Amalina wondered where they were going to wind up. Where would they eat in such a place? Were they going to dine in a large hall? dedicated, in days of old, to feasts and to the entertainment of barons and ambassadors? Or would it be a private chamber, reserved for intimate meals and quiet conversation? She'd never been inside a castle before—had never seen one in real life—and knew them only from songs and poems and stories, which had built in her mind the most romantic of structures, with high battlements and massive rooms stocked with expensive tapestries, furniture of the finest craft, and every implement and trinket composed of gold and inlaid with gems.

From the night before, what little she'd seen of the exterior of the castle confirmed the immensity of her imaginary one, but the smallness of the few rooms they had blindly wound through hadn't suggested anything of a great hall. But, still, her mind began fitting itself with a grand reception by the Count, on the occasion of her first meal there, with a feast of extraordinary size and delicacy. Which she thought the Count, in his high station, might expect, even if he were simply dining alone and without a special guest.

As they passed through one corridor after another—some turned inwardly, made of stone, timber and tapestry, lit by Genadie's tallow candle; some lined with high, thin windows looking out onto slopes of grass that died away into a surrounding forest shot through with a mist that looked like it was made of cream—all picturesque, and step-by-step quieting her melancholy, and distracting her from the wonder and agitation of why she was there—Amalina felt a growing excitement that overshadowed any dread of her circumstance. She could not believe she was not kneading dough, or fetching water, or sweeping, sweeping, sweeping—a sensation so worked into her body after lifetime of it that her muscles almost insisted she do it right then and there—but was instead treading the halls of royalty and fairytales.

But the breakfast meal was not to be served in any castle room dedicated to feasts, no matter how powerful Amalina imagined it. They winced gingerly down several flights of stairs, then out the main building, and then round behind it and entered into what appeared to be a small, dilapidated barn sandwiched between, and underneath, a small, high bridge which linked, the castle and the castle's wall.

This was Genadie's hovel. It was constructed not of a romantic imagination, but of blacked boards and timbers, which held together loosely, allowing light to sift in through thin, randomly placed fissures. The whole room shared the blackness and greyness of the room's surrounding planks and boards. From bedframe to bedding to cabinets to furniture, it was a monochromatic presentation. It wasn't sad, or depressing, or gloomy, Amalina noted, but it held the darkness of a perpetual dusk.

Genadie pointed Amalina to a black chair at his grey table.

"We won't be eating in the castle?"

"Us?" Genadie nearly howled. He shook his head as if her question was beyond all reason. He pointed her to the chair again. He moved to the fireplace where there was a meager fire smoldering, and fetched out a pot using a blunt length of iron with an angled, flattened bill on one end.

In the pot was a porridge. It should have been yellow, if prepared properly. It was more of an orange-brown, and fell off the ladle onto her plate in lumps. It resembled enough what it should be, though, to encourage Amalina's stomach to growl.

Genadie smacked a round of bread between them on the table and she saw, even in the ill-light of the room, it was too dark, suggesting it had lounged too long in the oven. The sound of it landing on the table was of a large wood plank landing on another. The way he had to crack the crust open with strong blows of the edge of his hand, and ripping at it with his fingers, and prying at it with his dirty fingernails, did not encourage her to think it was edible in any way.

"How old is this bread?"

"Excuse me, Ms. Dalca?" he asked as he handed her a bowl shaped shard of the loaf. She studied it in the dim light.

"Sawdust!" she shouted accusingly at the piece. "Where did you get this bread? You couldn't eat such a thing if you've been starving for a month."

Genadie pulled his piece out of the porridge and gnawed a hunk of it into his mouth.

"I eat it," he said.

"It isn't good for you, unless you are a termite."

"A what?"

"Where did you get this bread?" she demanded again. "You've been cheated."

"Made it myself."

"Oh," said Amalina. "But you left it in too long. Look how it's burned."

"I thought you didn't like the sawdust."

"I haven't gotten back to that," she said. "Why did you put sawdust in the dough?"

"Fills it out, doesn't it?"

"Only poor bakers who want to cheat people do that."

"How is it cheating?"

"It makes people think they are getting more bread than they really are."

"But they are getting more bread," protested Genadie, chewing off another hunk, making the bread look edible. And maybe tasty. He traded that bite with a chomp on a round, pink vegetable that might have been a raw radish.

"You aren't getting more bread," she said. "You are getting less bread, and more wood."

"If the sawdust is baked inside the bread then it is part of the bread, just like nuts and seeds."

"Nuts and seeds are sweet and healthy. You'd never think of eating a tree, would you?"

"You've never been too hungry," Genadie remarked sagely. "If one were to suppose about you, one could suppose—by your particular and refined tastes—you're some kind of princess."

"Stewing bark I've heard of, but you should never eat wood. Never."

"Not a branch or a chair leg," Genadie allowed charitably. "Sawdust is soft. Much easier to get down."

"Well, there's no reason to get it down. Just don't eat it. I can't imagine where you got the idea. I can make bread better than this."

"Can you?" Genadie looked at her with interest, a sparkle in his hooded eye.

"Don't you remember that my family's trade is making bread?"

"Hmm. Never tried your bread, though." He thought for a moment. "Smelled very nice."

"It's the best in the village!"

"It isn't your purpose in the castle, though."

"What is my purpose here?"

"Let's finish our meal first. Much to do."

"I think I'm done with breakfast, thank you."

"You haven't touched a thing."

"There's no cook here?"

"Me."

"There's nobody else in the castle?"

"There is our Master."

"Besides him. I mean servants. Someone who knows how to cook, specifically."

Genadie shook his head. "No."

"It's only you!"

"Master needs only me," said Genadie, hooking his crooked thumb at his nose. "At least that was, until now. There's no one else here but Master, you and me … and the animals."

"You show me where you store your ingredients, and I will make the meals from now on."

"Will you?" Genadie looked very pleased.

"Sure."

"But that isn't what you are here for."

"I'll do whatever I'm here for *and* prepare the meals. I'm sure you are very busy, too, aren't you Genadie?"

"Yes, Ms. Dalca. Very busy."

"Then leave the meals to me. I may have to rise early, and we may have to work a little later, but we'll have something that will fill our stomachs properly. That's assuming your cabinets are well provisioned."

"That would be very nice of you. And very kind." Genadie winced as he smiled. "I'd like that very much. Something made from female hands. They know how to cook. My grandmother's mamaliga was delicious, I remember it now," he said fondly, staring off into the air. Then he looked at Amalina with some admiration. "It's good you know how to cook, Ms. Dalca."

"It will be my pleasure. If I have anything to do with it, you'll have the best bread you've ever tasted."

Amalina was so pleased at the thought of some proper bread, it caused her to feel sorry for Genadie, who'd at least made an earnest effort at preparing her food. And, anyway, she began to feel real hunger. So she dug into the off-color porridge and small plate of vegetables, thinking she'd fill her belly, no matter how poorly it tasted, and smile and compliment Genadie on his amateur cooking.

The food—all of it—had no flavor. Even the vegetables, the radishes, held not the barest of a scent. Amalina had to choke it down, and wondered through her plastered on smile whether Genadie had any spices to work with. Probably not.

"The wood from a cherry tree tastes best," Genadie remarked in the meantime, absently.

. . .

After breakfast, Genadie led Amalina out of his hovel and to the front of the castle's main building. In the fore-courtyard, the carriage was parked, its fetters coiled loosely on the ground. The horses were gone.

Genadie put his ear to one of the main building's mammoth front doors and listened. Then he used a large key to unlock it.

The first room they entered, the same one they'd entered last night, was much larger in the light of day—a light which shoved warmly between them through the open door. The room had seemed very small in the darkness, but that was because the room was cramped on every side with all kinds of glass, and metal, and wood, and boxes upon boxes, which reduced what she should have sensed to be a cavern, as Genadie led her through it last night, into what she perceived was a series of closet-sized rooms and narrow halls. Within the clutter of this single large room were makeshift alcoves filled with desks and benches, with mysterious apparatus set upon them: assemblies of pots and glass bulbs, filled with faintly colored liquids, or crusted with burnt material. Amalina had never seen anything like it before, but she imagined it to be the den of an alchemist. She also spotted loose leaves of paper, and scrolls of vellum, scattered within these alcoves, as if they'd blown in and landed like large flakes of snow, gathering in careless drifts and lumps.

Genadie winced painfully, and shook his head with a beleaguered look as he glanced back at the cluttered room. He sighed. Then he turned to a single massive solid door set in the wall. He did not need a key for this one but threw back a bolt.

The next room was perhaps even larger than the first one, but it was packed just as closely, filled halfway to the chandelier with stacks of books. Thousands of books, of all sizes, shapes and colors, and seeming no order but that they could balance on the ones below, reaching for the ceiling in uneven towers. Every stack was like a ten foot tree, each trunk knocked inward or outward into a new width after so many inches. So this collection was a forest. A deep, dark forest of knowledge and learning. It was amazing to her. It held so much promise. She wished she were alone, to search and discover.

Genadie stopped. He turned in circles, looking randomly at the stacks. The index finger on his right hand, barely protruding past the cuff of his sleeve, went to his lower lip.

"I am here, Master," Genadie shouted. "We are ready!"

Amalina hadn't been prepared for the loud blast from small Genadie. She fell back a step.

The Count entered from a side door. He held a black cloak over his head as if he were protecting himself from a rain or a blinding light. In the darkness of the folds of his cloak, the Count's face was a light grey rectangle, and Amalina could see his eyes clearly. He was no longer red and swollen, like last night. He appeared emptied.

But he smiled.

"Yes," he said with his rumbling voice. "She is here. And ready to begin. To begin today. Perfect timing."

"Master," Genadie groveled on the ground.

"Amalina Dalca," said the count, slowly. "You are here to do me service."

"I know. But … what can *I* do for *you*?"

"It will be difficult at first, for there is much to do. But it will all be completed in due time, in due time." He said what he had to say as much to himself as to anyone else in the room. It was as if he was reminding himself to be patient, to mentally prepare himself for the, as-yet undefined, task, and how long it might take.

"Several things," the Count said, turning his head to regard the books. "This is my collection: Manuscripts, tomes, scrolls, drawn from all corners of the world. A wealth and treasury rivaling even some of the great libraries of the Ottomans."

He didn't look as pleased as he sounded when he spoke that last word. He swiped the corner of his large mustache.

"Amalina Dalca, you are fluent in high Deutsche. You know Polish. You know Hungarian. You know some Latin. You are familiar with Greek. This is good and helpful, yes. And it means you are special at accepting and excelling at languages. This is very important. In the mornings, after breakfast, you will commence learning French."

Amalina glanced at the Count in surprise. But he was still admiring the room.

"You will be trained until you are conversant in that language. In the afternoons," he continued, "you will have instruction in Italian. In the evenings you will study Flemish. You will be instructed until you are judged to be excellent and fluent in speaking, reading, and writing these languages.

"During the week, you will have two and a half days," he said now, turning to her, "when you will catalog the books in this room, and you will organize them, so that they will be properly inventoried and placed in the great library of this castle, which is empty and waiting to receive."

While Amalina immediately understood this was a daunting task, and would take a very long time to accomplish—a very long time to accomplish any one of the many steps in his plan—she found herself unable to lift her voice to complain. It was too much to rail against, because it was too much to take in.

"You understand what I have told you," said the Count.

"All these books?"

"They must be made ready for when the time comes. And there is little time to spare before the moment arrives. Yes, it will be coming soon enough."

"French, Italian ... and Flemish?" she asked.

"Yes."

"No Spanish?"

"The Spaniards have taken too closely to the Muslims." The Count spat. "I will not bear any strain of the Ottomans if I do not have to."

"And that is why no Turkish," Amalina surmised. "Or Arabic."

The Count stared at her, not coldly, but with a strange flash behind the eyes. Then he stalked away to a far door at the edge of the forest, his hands still holding the cape over his head. "And you will begin today. There isn't much time. There is very little time, at that."

His tone and delivery seemed so far from his cheerful 'Yes's' and 'Perfect's', with which he'd sprinkled her on their previous encounters.

But he was out the door and that was all she was left with. Besides the quaking Genadie.

And the lingering question: *'Little time' before* what?

13

The Invasion Bells

"What brings you, Attila?" asked the old fat man with a smile that was friendly enough; because he wished he could warm, with doses of congeniality, the young thin man who stood before him, so that this young thin man would not remain such an uncomfortable threat.

The low constable of Tsobl bowed, returning the smile in a friendly enough way. But the smile was lined with the hunger to be heard, to be acknowledged, to be believed, and to be respected. And an impatience to be rid of the old fat man, so he would not have to bear these insufferable hurdles of bending and scraping before relics of command. "A matter of importance, sir," he answered.

The high constable wiped his mouth and grizzled jowls with a stained napkin. He pushed aside his plate of lamb. He drank slowly from a large bronze cup, one eye lowered to keep the low constable in his sight. Then: "Tell me."

"Well, this is very important, you see—"

"You already said that, Attila."

"Yes sir. I just wanted to make clear—"

"Calm yourself, Attila, my boy. I can see you are out of breath. Calm is paramount to our profession, as calm spreads reassurance; that one comfort which others look for us to provide. I understand you have something important to say, but nothing is ever so dire you need not retain your composure."

"An invasion—a raid."

The constable's eyebrows rose high up his forehead. But then he chortled.

"That's what the bell towers are for," he said, resettling. "You haven't come here—here before me—to announce an invasion."

The low constable gripped his left hand and ticked his head to one side.

"Well, now ..." the low constable began, holding off the rest of his statement with a dramatic pause.

"This isn't a theatre, Attila. Out with it!"

"First off, I should let you know that I have read the book."

"What book?"

"*The* book."

"What book, Attila? Be clear."

"The Secret Account of the Tsobl Constabulary."

"Have you? That was very naughty of you. You took it from my safe?"

"I read it in your office, when you went home at night."

"You broke into my safe, you little thief."

"A talent I learned from our criminal element, but I stole nothing," said the low constable, his eyelids drooping, taking on a dull, bored look.

"You stole a bit of knowledge. Forbidden knowledge. It is a crime as old as Eden." The high constable didn't look concerned, and tossed away Attila's petty espionage with a laugh. "Did you find anything else of interest to you?"

"The book, sir—"

"It's from a bygone time. Not many people know about it. Anymore. And nobody who does know it believes it. I hope you haven't thought, because it is routinely kept out of sight, that it has some kind of validity."

"Well ..."

"'Well', 'Well', what are you getting on about? My lamb will soon be cold and I'll have to reheat it. I don't like reheated lamb."

"The Cardinal of the great Grigori church is in imminent danger. He is under threat by none other than the Count of Ardeel."

"Who is the Count of Ardeel? I've never heard of that title."

"The book."

"The book? ... The Count? The Knight? The ... that one? The monster?"

"He has recovered his wife from her tomb within the cemetery. His power must be growing. He is able to penetrate the consecrated grounds of our Lord God."

"That thing had no wife, nor was he real. He was a fiction, drawn up by fear, and believed by the old elements, the yokels."

"He was nothing less than the Voivod of this land, the king, the controller, before he became the knight of all that is unholy."

"Voivod? Voivod Teppes, you mean?" The high constable took a bite of lamb and chewed on it, staring blankly into space. "What imagination you must have, Attila. Not a recommendable trait in a man of the law."

"You believe me," the low constable accused with his bored eyes. "You're thinking about it, and you're considering what I say is true."

"How old he must be, if it were true."

"He sold his soul, he is near immortal. But I must see the book, to make certain I am right."

"The Tepp queen," the high constable spat on the floor at her name, "her body was stolen? Grave robbers."

The low constable shook his head slowly, his half-closed eyes looking sleepy.

"How do you know?"

"All the evidence. The Cardinal must have done something to awaken the monster's wrath, and the first challenge has been made. We are in danger, high constable, if this game of theirs should get out of hand."

"The Cardinal confessed this nonsense to you?"

"The Cardinal said nothing. He was glad to see me leave as quickly as I did. He wishes to contain his troubles within his own circle of power. But that changes none of the facts. The monster has invaded sacred ground, and he has killed blood that is untouchable—"

"Whose?"

"I need to see the book to confirm it. I know I saw the name, but I need to confirm, high constable, if you will just let me look."

"Who did he kill?"

"No one of importance yet. But someone who should have been beyond his reach."

"Who? And I will ask no more. Who, Attila?"

The name, when the low constable told him, meant nothing to the fat old man. *Neku Jonker?* A worthless wretch? The Cardinal had probably killed the man himself, finding his cemetery's intendant stealing from the graves.

The low constable was sent away—kicking and screaming in his peculiarly quiet, brooding way—with a reprimand for having disturbed a good meal, and the promise that the book on the secret history of the Tsobl Constabulary would be relocated, so he couldn't bother it again.

The low constable, with his bored eyes, went to a tavern and drank more than his narrow body could tolerate.

Or, that is, that is what everyone in the tavern thought they saw: a young, skinny man downing cup after cup of cheap wine, until his body swayed and he could barely walk. Then he staggered out the door.

And just a little later the bells in the northern bell tower rang before the sun was down. Rang loud and continuously.

Invasion!

. . .

When the city's panic was quelled, order restored, and Tsobl's bloodthirsty militias disbanded, the low constable was pried from the swinging rope of the bells, removed from the bell tower, and remanded to the custody of the high constable, who put him in irons and shut him up in the small jail below his office.

"Verrry wellll," the low constable trilled drunkenly as his eyes rolled into the back of his head. "As always, high constable, you win."

"You are the only one playing games around here, Attila," the high constable sniffed.

And when the reproving old fat high constable went home, confident his subordinate was subdued for the evening by drink, and perhaps had finally had his dangerous ambitions thwarted forever by such a stupid act, the low constable shook himself twice and stared very soberly through the bars of his jail.

The object of his interest was, of course, the safe just behind the old fat man's desk. Or more precisely, the musty old book contained within it.

14

Amalina's Discoveries

Shortly after the morning meal, Amalina realized someone was knocking at the door.

"Hello?"

"*Pardonnez-Moi, Mademoiselle!*" came the response from behind the thick oak.

"Oh, *bon jour!*"

If it had been the afternoon, she supposed, the conversation would have been in Italian. Or the evening, Flemish. But it was the morning, so, naturally, French.

Amalina opened the door to her language instructor. Still limping, and squinting on every other step, Genadie entered.

"*Bon Jour, mademoiselle Dalca,*" he said.

"*Bon Jour, Bon Jour,*" she returned.

How surprised Amalina was when she'd learned Genadie was to be her French teacher, that he was a man of learning and a linguist at that. He was her professor for French, Italian *and* Flemish. And every time he entered her room for the next language, he brought with him a completely different air. If Amalina didn't know any better, she'd swear he brought in, as well, a different limp and squint. His demeanor reflected the spirit of the culture that undergirded the language itself. And the change in his attitude and bearing wasn't a silly exaggeration on his part, a pretense to entertain a small child with overblown performance. It was a natural alteration, of which Genadie was most likely unaware, the particular tongue being like a rigid garment he slipped into, and was thereby forced into its requisite poses.

How different he was in his role as instructor than the toadying wretch he was before his "Master": a shivering puddle which he melted into at every appearance, passing shadow, or imagined sound from the adjoining room, of the Count.

The days had become so long with labor, and with the Count's hours of operation seemingly restricted to the evening and night, within less than a month it began to feel as if the castle was Amalina and Genadie's alone. A circumstance that would have reinforced her loneliness and longing for home, if there wasn't always a language lesson, and the forest of books— and the almost mystical and phantasmic views from the high castle windows—to distract her young mind. Which brought her to the natural question.

"But teacher," Amalina said in French. "Why are you here? Isn't today the day I catalogue books, and you ... you work in the other room?"

"Yes, my student," Genadie nodded. "But I am not here to instruct you, I am here to request your help."

"My help?"

"I am a man," he said, "and so naturally stronger than you, a young woman. But you're stronger than most young women, and you have smaller hands and fingers than I ... And so you might help. Come with me, if you please."

Amalina understood most of what he said. She followed him into the next room, where Genadie seemed to be shifting the boxes and instruments back and forth without much of a change in its overall crowded appearance.

"How goes your work in the ... uh ... uh ..." Amalina stumbled in the new language. "How do you say 'hall' in French?"

"Do you mean 'hall' as in 'great room'?" he asked. "As in, '*la Grande Salle*?'"

"Ah! *Grande salle*. Yes, that is what I meant, great room. Grande Salle."

"But you are mistaken, mademoiselle Dalca," Genadie continued, and chided, in French. "This is not a *grande salle* I am clearing; if that is what you mean to discuss—*ma travaille*, my work. When you're sorting the books in *la grande salle*, which is the room *you* are working in, I am packing up the items found here in the entrance area, *l'entrée grande*. For that is what this place is, simply the entrance to the castle."

"So large for an ... uh ... entry ... way?" Amalina tried experimenting with her new words.

"If you think this is a large entrance, you have not been to the Black Castle outside Tsobl. This castle is very small by comparison."

"There's more than one castle?"

"There are many castles. Only Master knows and has seen them all."

"Well, the entry here is larger than any room I've ever seen. Even the main room of our village's church. But, anyway, how goes your work here in *l'entrée grande*, then? I hear you banging and clanking all the time. Even into the night sometimes, after Flemish."

"There is a lot to do," he said sadly. He was leading her carefully through the mess, counting his steps. "And how is your cataloguing going?"

"Slow, of course. I don't recognize most of the languages, and so I am setting them aside for you or the Count—"

"Master," Genadie blurted the correction, as he always did.

"—to help me. But, anyway, it can take as long as it might. I don't really care, because I love touching these books, and opening them, and studying them. Even smelling them. Each one is so different, so interesting. If I were not a baker, I'd want to be the librarian in the great archives of Athens or Rome."

"Glad you're a baker, though," Genadie interrupted. "A librarian would never make such delicious and fortifying bread ... and your *mamaliga! Excellente.*"

"Thank you! But, uh, Genadie, what *is* in this room? What're all these instruments and devices for?"

"They *are* ... to be put away," he said as they arrived at a desk. An apparatus made of thin metal bars and glass bulbs lay on its side. It looked like a fantastic insect. He pointed her to a fly-wing screw holding two segments of rods together at a hinge. "And that is why I need your help, here, Ms. Amalina. If you would turn this screw, counter-clockwise, it would be most helpful. My hands are old and knotted and I just can't get my fingers on that stupidly small wheel."

"Yes, let me try. Counter-clockwise means ...?"

"Turn it to the left," Genadie motioned with one of his knotted fingers. The finger was more than a bit crooked, she noticed. It looked like a malformed stick.

She grabbed the top of the screw and turned. But the screw did not move. She tried again, holding her breath and concentrating all her effort. The metal wings bit into her fingers.

"It is stuck then," huffed Genadie in their native tongue.

"*Non,*" she replied in French. Amalina lowered her weight and braced the instrument against the table and turned at the top of the screw with all her strength. "Je—Rahhh!" The screw popped. She thought she'd broken the wings, but saw instead that it had broken free from whatever was holding it fast. She tried the screw again and it turned slowly, loosening as it pulled from the hole. "There we are. But, uh, Genadie, what is this thing? What are all these? I've never seen anything like them."

"These? Well, they were the Master's latest fling," he dismissed the room with a small flip of his hand.

"*Fling?*" Amalina didn't understand the word as expressed in French. Genadie explained in their own language what he meant.

"Master grew an interest in the sciences, you see," he continued, returning to French. "Chemistry and Physics. He purchased all the equipment known to the practice of those particular arts in order to study and explore them." Genadie didn't look happy at his Master's choice of hobby. "Why he chooses to play the alchemist is not to be questioned."

"I wasn't questioning, just wondering what it is. It looks very interesting."

"I suppose it is. And when our Master decides he is interested in something he is very thorough and acquires everything in that vein. And always it piles up in the entrance of our castle, builds into a mountain until nothing more can fit. So you see. He plays with it for a while, and decides, in the end, whether it's worth his time. If it is, then the items here move to the next room, and those in the next room into the next, and so on, marching along like a centipede until they eventually find a permanent room within the castle. And it is up to me, or whoever serves our Master, to transfer it all exactly and carefully from one room to the next until they reach their destination. If our Master is displeased with the subject, *l'entrée grande* is cleared, the trash tossed out of the castle from this entrance, and all the items are destroyed, set like a bonfire, never to bother him again. Something he should do more often."

"The way you describe it," observed Amalina, "the castle is like a head. The entryway is a mouth. It is there the Count—"

"Master."

"—has his taste of something. If he likes it, the castle swallows. If not, it spits it out."

"Clever girl," Genadie allowed with an errant squint. "The Master said as much."

"Books are in the next room. So reading was his latest interest, before Chemistry and Physics, then?"

"I suppose you're right."

"After my books are transferred to the library, you have to move all that equipment into the great hall? It seems we could cut down on how long this takes: As I catalogue, I can move the books, and you can place some of the equipment in the newly opened space."

Genadie shook his head. "No, no. The equipment won't be going in there."

"He didn't like science?" She exclaimed in amazement. Then, thinking what a waste it'd be to burn all this fascinating equipment: "He's going to destroy all of it?"

"The opposite. He finds this study very interesting and profitable ..." Then he added in a moody tone: "Though I don't see why." Then he patted the metal brace and bottles Amalina was taking apart and said: "But I am moving it all to the northern tower, where it will be housed permanently."

"Then why do I have to clear the great hall?"

"It isn't a matter of clearing it as much as putting it in order, and creating a proper library of it. Although, it's also a matter of clearing that room, too. You see, he wants both *l'entrée grande* and your great audience chamber to be cleared out and readied."

"Readied for what?"

"For his next interest."

"It will take all two great rooms … um, uh, *both* rooms?" she corrected in French.

"It is going to take the whole castle, mademoiselle Dalca."

"What is it?"

"What is what?"

"What is his next interest?"

· · ·

Not much happened in the next several months, besides Amalina and Genadie's tireless work, but three moments do stand out.

The first was more of a gradual realization.

Amalina missed her home and her friends, most especially her father and Cristine. She missed them terribly. The pain from the shock of their separation, and the anger at just how unjust that separation was, gradually quieted with the overwhelming distractions of work, and the calming hands of time. What remained was a background pulse of unhappiness, which rose in quiet moments, mostly at night.

She'd grown used to Genadie and their meals together, and the pitiless charms of the fairytale castle. But the discontent was always there to remind her that this castle was not her place—no, not at all. Maybe her old village had been nothing more than a familiar setting, and when she'd grown older she'd find herself at home in another setting just as easily in a different part of the world—perhaps in the great and fantastic palace of the Kublai Khan (the palace and the Khan an amazing—and terrifying—discovery in one of the books she'd peeked into while cataloguing). But Genadie and the Count were not her true family or friends, this was beyond doubt. Nor was the castle the place where she should be.

It could not have been made clearer when she was put to work on the very first Sunday.

"But this is the Sabbath."

"There is no Sabbath here," Genadie informed her.

"How can there be no Sabbath here if there is Sabbath everywhere else in the world?"

"It is not everywhere else in the world. Go ask a pagan or a heathen. And even if Sabbath were everywhere else in the world, it is not *here*. In Olymp—" he cut himself off.

"'Olymp' what?"

"There are timetables and schedules we have to meet. There is no room for pottering around with the ridiculous."

"Well the Sabbath exists here if I'm here. And Sundays and Tuesdays are for worship, and that is what I'm going to do." She then asked: "There is no church?"

"There used to be a chapel in this castle, but I can't tell you where it was. But you're only looking for a reason to frustrate me. I'd think with your family's history, Ms. Dalca, you'd be an atheist."

She wasn't familiar with the word "atheist", but she was suddenly in the mood to argue.

"What is my family's history, stinky? My father and I attend church every Sunday and Tuesday. Everyone in the village does. Even those from out of town go to church, if they are in town, on the Sabbath or the semi-Sabbath."

"Well," harrumphed Genadie, as if to say 'There's no figuring some people.' "Be that as it may, that particular religion does not exist here. Nor does any other. But one."

"Which one is that?"

"Our Master," he said in the most matter-of-fact tone possible, without dramatic lilt or dogmatic ire or patronizing instruction, as if it was the ultimate truth and he was simply reciting from a rote book. "And if you want to worship him on your precious Sabbath days—for worship's sake, or out of habit, or form, or whatever your reason—do as he commands you, eh?"

So everything in the castle was bent towards one being: the Count. This fact confirmed and compounded the primary fact that the castle was not her home. She was then, in some sense, very alone.

At night, if dreams came to Amalina, she dreamt of escaping back to her village and seeing her family. She saw her father, wracked with sadness and guilt, his hair careworn to white, his face a mess of wrinkles, crying in lamentation over the loaves he could barely handle with his squeezing, twitching hands. A pitiful sight. And no matter how she called to him, he did not hear her, or see her, or recognize she was there.

Also in the dreams, Cristine was being picked on by the other girls, now that she was no longer protected by her more popular friend. She hid her head under her hood and scurried through the unwelcoming streets to the protection of her home, reduced to a scared and lonely shadow. Again, as with her father, Amalina could not attract her friend's attention no matter how hard she tried.

The dreams, and the feelings of helplessness and unhappiness, and the sense that she should not be away from them and instead tucked away in the mountain castle, waxed and waned, but persisted to the point of burden for Amalina. She felt tired, and listless, and didn't even find wonder in the new books she opened.

Until she opened a book with beautiful illustrations that took her breath away. Mechanical illustrations of inventions that lifted things and moved things and contained things. Dragomir's favorite studies had always been in the realm of the physical. And so when she saw the precise lines, with markings and footnotes so specific, she was taken. And one of those swells of sadness rose in her breast, almost causing her to gasp.

But the feeling burst upon an idea so enlivening that Amalina jumped off the stump of books she was sitting on. She pounded at the adjoining door.

"Genadie, are you there?" she called in Italian, as she noted what time in the day it was. "Genadie!"

"What is it?" he said from far beyond the door.

"Come quick. Come quick."

He opened the door. He did not look at Amalina but searched the room for what cataclysm would have caused her to become so loud and excited.

"What's happened, Signora Dalca?" he asked in Italian.

"Please, Genadie, you must help me. This book. It is something my father would love to read. Could you give it to him?"

"What?"

"I mean ..." here she switched back to her native tongue, "I don't know how to say 'lend' in Italian. But to lend it to him. Just for a little while."

"This book belongs in the great library."

"Yes, of course. That's where it'll go. But it isn't going in now. I can just catalogue it, as I am supposed to. Look, you can see me write it right here into the entry, and I will make a mark that it's been given out and should be returned. And you can get it back from him before the books go into the library. What do you think?"

"The master said there is to be no communication between you and your father until the work here is done."

"This isn't communication, Genadie, it is a book. Just a book. You see? And I know you travel for supplies. Couldn't you go to my village just once and give this book to my father? You don't even have to tell him it's from me. Just a present from the Count—"

"—Master—"

"—as a way to thank him for allowing me to be here. And you can tell him I am well or anything you like. And you might even fetch a bible from him, so I might conduct Sabbath here properly ... by myself of course, quietly, before I go to bed. An exchange of books, if you like."

Genadie curled his whole face at being presented with this unexpected and perplexing request. But he didn't say "no", which is exactly what Amalina was hoping for.

"Thank you, Genadie," she said, touching his hand in place of throwing her arms around him. Her smile glowed and seemed to brighten him up. "It will make me so happy, I'll work twice as fast."

"You have been slow recently ... and gloomy," Genadie admitted.

"Ten times as fast! Thank you, Genadie, thank you, Genadie, thank you, Genadie."

"Don't forget your place, my student," he corrected her in Italian.

"Yes, Signor. But thank you."

"I will ask our Master if it is acceptable."

Master!

Amalina's exploding enthusiasm extinguished as fast as it had come. But what could she expect from Genadie? She could never fully poach his loyalty from the man he worshipped. She would have to wait, and hope, and pray.

And when Genadie returned with the Count, and the Count studied the book, turning it over and over in his dead white hands, and inspected it with a wild toss of the pages, and finally nodded (the nod as good as a lazy shrug), Amalina almost shouted with joy. "But no bible," said the Count as he left.

• • •

The second notable event followed closely on the first. That day's excitement—or maybe, instead, her increased appetite for the meals she prepared—stirred the internal workings of Amalina's body. Besides vivid, exciting dreams, there came other results.

Before Amalina felt the first trickle on her inner thigh, she heard a loud, masculine howl. A disturbing basso sound that traveled and echoed throughout the castle and continued for some minutes, winding up the stairs from some corner of the castle to just outside the threshold of her door.

The door burst open, nearly breaking off the hinges. And there, in the doorway, stood the Count.

Amalina yelped in surprise.

He held one hand over his nose and mouth, gripping them as if to cut all flow into those outraged orifices. With the other hand he pointed to her, as if he were pointing out his murderer.

"It'ssss … you!" he hissed and bellowed at the same time, almost in shock. "You! Blood! Foul blood! Foul blood!"

He disappeared, only to be replaced a few seconds later by a sheepish Genadie. Genadie seemed to weakly imitate his master's reluctance to enter into the room. He stood at the entrance, shoulders rounded, head bowed.

"Dame Dalca," said Genadie apologetically in Flemish, "Please, if you will come with me."

Genadie led her downstairs, through the building, upstairs, up, up and away, until they were in an incredibly high tower, in the opposite corner of the castle from where her previous bedroom was. This room was small and cold, and their flight there so unanticipated that the fireplace was swept and barren, much less stocked with already burning logs (a service Genadie always thoughtfully provided for Amalina).

"You will stay here," he told her. "This will be your room from now on."

"Why?" asked Amalina, still unaware of the reason, and still shocked by the Count's appearance in her doorway.

"Master's senses are acute," explained Genadie. "They surpass anything, man or animal, that lives on this earth."

Genadie's answer greatly satisfied him, and he smiled.

"Yes," said Amalina. "And what does that have to do with moving me here?"

"It will be easier for him not to smell you."

Amalina felt thoroughly offended, then embarrassed and ashamed. And completely confused because he had been free to smell her all along. Hadn't he inhaled once since their first encounter? And could she smell worse than Genadie?

But then she realized what was happening with her body, and knew, with some annoyance, what had caused the Count to fly into such a rage.

With a muted sigh, Amalina excused herself from work the next day and had Genadie escort her from the castle (in so long!), and ride her to the nearest wet forest where she could find a swamp growing the moss she required.

It was refreshing to be outside the castle. Almost surprising to be free of its high, cold walls, and at liberty amid tall grass and flowers and under the warm sun. She was pleased she'd thought to bring along a chunk of bread and fat, so they might have a picnic if they liked. And they might have had a picnic, too, if Genadie hadn't been acting annoyed and resentful, and looking like a wounded dog.

"Come on, Genadie," she chided. "Don't act like that. You're being that way just because *he*'s acting that way. There's no need. You're your own person. We've become friends, haven't we? So why don't we have a language lesson or something fun, and not pretend as if I'm made of poison."

Genadie couldn't bring himself to answer but kept quiet and avoided turning his face toward her, and brought her to the sun dappled swamp to get things over with.

She quickly located the moss she was looking for, Genadie nodding dumbly as she pointed it out. He fetched the amount she instructed in a bucket. This is what Amalina would need if ever the time came again: a supply of this moss, which she could use to soak up the spilling blood from her body.

The monster was offended by the smell of blood?

She dragged her feet on the way back to the cart. But then she darted off in all directions, gathering bear berries, dog flowers, lilacs, and any other colorful leaf that might complement the bunch she was gathering. "It will brighten the castle," she told Genadie. Add some life to it. Too bad tulips were out of season!

Genadie only muttered his worries: that the bouquet, so alien to the castle's austerity and neglect, might smell too strongly for his master.

Amalina's clothes—well, the old, ancient clothes the castle provided her—were brought up to the tower when they returned, the bed was made properly, the flowers arranged in a large-mouthed pot, and the fire stoked to keep the air warm.

And so Amalina had a new home within the castle. As far away, apparently, from the Count as possible. And she didn't mind it much, except for how much she had to climb and wind around to get to—or get away from—the rest of the building. The view from the narrow windows was even more spectacular here, and there was some comfort at knowing she was more to herself. On her own.

The solitude allowed her to relax, and contemplate. And the odd thing of it was, her mind continued to return to the moment the Count had burst into her room. The look on his face.

No. The look in his eyes.

It was fear.

But it wasn't the fear itself that distracted Amalina's thoughts—strange though it was. The striking thing in his reaction, in those eyes, was something else altogether.

• • •

The third and final matter of note within those several months, was as gradual as the first, but, in the end, as sudden as the second.

Over her entire stay, Amalina had grown used to the wind crying outside the castle, which picked up around sunset and did not let up until near dawn, and was a constant companion every night. To the point she sometimes forgot it, the noise receding into the background unconscious. Other times, the longer she listened, Amalina fancied the cry was from a human throat, and not of the wind at all. But it was too variable in its pitch, and so angry in its voice. But also it was too impossibly constant for any human to keep up. Impossible for it to be anything more than a nasty trick of the air as it screeched up across the mountain crags around the castle.

Amalina once considered it the cry of a ghost. She didn't know what ghosts sounded like, but she felt they wouldn't be so inexhaustible and inarticulate. In stories, they always came in startling glimpses, and bleated the clearest warnings, or accusations, or demands for revenge.

The subject of the wailing cry, and its many necessary questions, all came to a head on the day Genadie dropped into Amalina's book-forest a book he'd found in his science room. It was written in Latin, a language she was just barely familiar with. And she was utterly unfamiliar with the words here, they pertaining to scientific matters, and with no helpful illustrations to suggest their meaning. She idly flipped around the pages, intent on dropping the book on a nearby stack, to be inventoried later, but then spotted the several sheets of handwritten notes inside. The notes were from the Count himself. Long ranks of numbers. Tabulations and calculations and formulations.

The count was at work here.

On the final page was a note that read: *In here you will find all that you require.* Then, scrawled below that was written another message—a reply from its recipient: *Most helpful indeed. Thank you, estimable Count. I am indebted to all your help, as you are to mine.* Then it was signed with the initials: *A. X. P.*

There was something intriguing about this brief exchange. Amalina could not decide what it was, but she wanted to explore its mystery more. She found a way to sneak the book, large as it was, up to her room for further study. She figured the tome would not be missed—no matter its great size— until her inventory and transfer of the books to the great library was finished. So she had plenty of time for deeper investigation.

That night, Amalina went page by page through the book, looking for any other hidden notes. She remarked on the numbers and figures, in the Count's hand, that had been written into the margins of the book itself.

That's when her candle went out.

There was no relighting its plug end from the dying embers in the fireplace. She hauled the book to the window hoping the moon (it was a full moon) would be enough to complete her inspection.

The cry of the wind was much louder on this side of the castle. But at this particular window it was louder than Amalina had ever heard it before. And worse, with a sickening tug at her guts, she now realized that it was not the wind alone, and it had never been. Combining harmonically with the upward sonic sweep of air across the craggy mountain's face was the unmistakable shriek of a woman, which carried on without let up until dawn.

And the shriek, the awful wail, swirling as it did outside, came from somewhere within the castle.

15

The Wail

"What's that horrible sound?" Amalina asked eagerly, with little thought to discretion. She was tired, having not slept, and wanted her answer as soon as she could get it. "That one I hear all night long, from outside my window ..."

Though Genadie's limp and wince had improved steadily since the night of her arrival, it returned as bad as ever when some particular matter stressed him. As it returned now, when she asked the question. He winced twice.

"You know the sound I'm talking about?"

"The wind?"

"No, it is more like a woman screaming."

"You?"

"Why would I ask you about it if it was me doing the screaming?"

"I don't know," his eye ticked. "Is it you?"

"No."

"Why do you ask me?"

"Because you would know, wouldn't you? That wailing, it's awful to listen to. I want to know what it is—who it is— and why she screams so every night."

"I don't know. Why would I know?"

"You know what I'm talking about, Genadie. You've heard it just as I have."

"I don't know. I thought it was the wind. It must be the wind."

"It isn't. And it's coming from inside this castle."

"You burnt the bread this morning," said Genadie, spinning away from her. "Tastes awful."

"Still better than anything you've ever made," Amalina returned forcefully, caught up with frustration at his ridiculous evasion, but being led easily onto its track.

Genadie slunk off to work before she could renew the assault.

The screaming woman must be on my side of the castle, Amalina thought as she blindly sorted through the books, not doing more than shifting them from one pile to the other. *That's why her voice is louder, she's on my side of the castle. And she must be near a window.*

"Who are you?" Amalina shouted that night from her own window. "Hello! Hello! Are you all right? Where are you?"

The scream carried on. But it was a human voice she heard, she was absolutely certain now. Not the wind.

Well, if she won't answer, I'll go find her! Amalina thought with a tug of excitement and dread.

Amalina covered herself in a long house coat, took a candle, and opened her bedroom door.

At the end of the hall stood the Count: as solid, and still, and as menacing as a tree trunk blacked and scarred by lightning. Amalina fell back half a step under his gaze.

But the Count couldn't have known where she was headed. Could he?

She pretended not to have seen him and turned in the other direction, towards the stairs that would take her to the side hall where the privy chamber was. From there she could cut back in a cross-wise direction and find the servants' stairs leading to the main floor.

As she rounded the corner, stepping quickly in the opposite direction of the Count, there he presently stood, just as still and menacing as seconds before. How? He would have had to have flown right through the stone walls to get there. He wore no expression. But his eyes burrowed into her, in their large and dark way.

"Hello," Amalina said, hesitating before she continued forward, toward him, with very slow but determined steps. His eyes had the power of an opposing wind, or the pushing charge of a magnet. Her steps slowed, and then she began to retreat from him, saying absently but for the Count's ears, "Oh, I guess I went the wrong way. Right the first time. I get so confused in these halls at night ... sometimes."

Amalina headed back where she came, then picking up her pace, took up the first route again.

And the Count was impossibly facing her once more, blocking this direction. Yes, she thought in amazement, he would have had to have gone through several walls of stone at least, just to get where he is. But he stood there, just as he had before, just as he had blocked her in the other direction. Silent. Emanating the impenetrability of the castle's walls from his body. He being one of its stones apparently, but one that can move its place at will and instantly. To block her.

"Oh, there again," she said lightly. But she pushed forward, toward him. Each step needing more effort, taking longer to complete. "Well, sir, I ... Well, I ..."

"Where is my guest, Ms. Dalca, going?" asked the Count in his deep voice.

The sound broke the tension in the hall. She could breathe and walk more freely.

"For a walk, sir," she said. "I can't sleep."

"No," he said. "There's more to it, of course ... of course. Going *somewhere*. Hunting, Ms. Dalca?"

"I'm going downstairs," said Amalina, daring to walk past him and down the stairs. She found him blocking her path at the bottom. "To find the reason I can't sleep. Who is she, may I ask?"

"Nobody knows her but me," said the Count. "And no one can find her but me."

"But it's too much. Every night. All night. Are you torturing her, sir?"

Around the corner, another flight of stairs, and there the Count was at the bottom of them, eyes glowing dully at the edge of the candle light.

"I'm here," he said.

"Sounds like she's being tortured. Genadie is torturing her, then? No, I don't believe—"

"Where would a young woman like Ms. Dalca have heard someone being tortured that she could recognize such a sound?"

The way he spoke irritated her. So roundly. Never directly. The way his large eyes looked more through her than at her. Not like the other night, when she'd seen fear in his eyes, after her menstrual cycle had begun—in his disturbed expression then was, finally, a true recognition of her.

Yes! she thought at the realization. That's what had been nagging her ever since that moment, the Count frozen in her doorway, hands covering his nose and mouth, eyes aflame! It was a moment where he was completely focused on her as an entity of equal value—of equal threat—not an apparition, or a vague toy.

And here he was returning to that annoying level of casual, removed discourse, even as he impossibly pursued her, miraculously materializing there in front of her at every turn in the hall.

"What are you doing up here, sir? I thought you didn't like my smell. Or was it bothering you again, and you've come to tell me?"

She saw a flash in his eyes. A small spark of immediate distress.

"What?"

"I don't like the way you talk to me, sir," she said. "Pardon my saying so, sir. But you must talk to me like I am more than a trained animal. You must treat me with respect and kindly, if you want me to work for you. And work well for you."

Down the hall.

"Of course, Ms. Dalca, you are not to be mistreated. Never."

"I can't sleep. All that screaming. Can't you make it stop?"

"It's not as easy as one thinks."

'Round the bend.

"What is it? Why does she do it?"

"I can't say."

"You will say. You will tell me."

Down the hall.

"Whether I would acknowledge you the way you wish I'd acknowledge you, you can't order me about. I am your master."

"You are not my master and you never will be."

"I am your master and you will obey me."

Down more cramped stone stairs.

"My father is my master. The mayor is my master, I suppose. Our priest is master of my soul, along with the Lord and God, perhaps. Perhaps the king is also my master besides the mayor, now that I think of it—though I know nothing about him and he lives in another land. But that's all that I can think of. You are not my master, you've only kidnapped me."

"I am your master because I am the master of everything in the world."

Another set of stairs. The Count at the bottom, of course.

"And how can that be, if I don't allow you to be my master?"

"Allow me?" he laughed that roaring laugh he'd had at Neku's death. "You will now obey me, Ms. Dalca."

"I will find her and I will release her."

"You will do as I command."

"I will do as I wish. Just you try to stop me. I know you can't."

"I can."

"Try." She began to wonder if she wasn't pushing things too far. "You can't hurt me. You can't touch me. I know it! I'm more powerful than you, even if you won't admit it. So let's see you try. Just try to stop me!"

"I will."

Amalina barked a hearty laugh that didn't compare to his, but it was enough to deliver her intent: to remain free and independent. When she came to the top of the next hall, he wasn't at the end of it.

"Because I am the master of you, and everything else in the world," the Count's voice rang out from all directions, "for I am the master of darkness."

His head came over her shoulder and blew out her candle. She yelped in surprise. And then she laughed at her own stupidity. Trapped in an ink-black limbo.

16

The Strike

"Once, long ago," said Amalina, "something really scary happened."

"Oh, a story?" said Genadie around a mouthful of bread. "I like stories. Scary ones not so much, but—"

"It's not a story. It really happened. Do you like the bread?"

"Of course. It's very good. Thank you, Ms. Dalca."

"Better than your blocks of sawdust, yes?"

"Let's not be hurtful, Ms. Dalca. Let's just agree your bread is tender and a little nutty, and that is 'very good'. Be nice and pleasant when we can."

"Are you trying to teach me manners, Genadie?"

"You're a child and still have things to learn, of course. Manners are a good start. I am your teacher, never forget."

"Not during breakfast. Anyway, my story is about bread. Do you want to hear it or not?"

"I thought you said it was scary."

"It is."

"Scary bread?"

"You're usually a good listener."

"Well, go on."

Amalina took in a breath. Then: "Maybe you heard of the war-feud between the fraternity of bakers and the new government? It was long ago."

Genadie made a face but continued to eat.

"My papa was drawn into the trouble. All the bakers in the country were. The king's newest governor and the new assembly declared a special tax on our common bread. They said they needed it to make up for the grain shortage from the bad harvest and the tonnage of wheat and rye the governor's new army was eating; and to help compensate the mill owners, who were losing money by the shortage."

"I seem to remember a shortage of some kind," said Genadie. "But then, there are always shortages, and I don't eat much, you see, and so not *quite* sure ..."

"Well, never mind the shortage, that tax wasn't fair. And that's the point. The governor and the assembly and all their friends didn't have to pay it, they exempted themselves in the law. And that isn't fair, is it?"

"On what grounds did they do so?"

"And for one thing, they could have just disbanded the army to make things easier, couldn't they? But worse, they and their friends had seized mills from us during the invasion and bought the rest in the years after, so a lot of the taxes would be going right to them. That isn't fair, is it?"

"No." Genadie winked: "Can't say it is very scary, either."

"Well, it wasn't fair. They don't have to pay the tax and so get their bread cheap, but the regular citizens have to pay it? Why should anyone pay more for bread than anyone else, as we're all the same, aren't we?"

"We're not including Master in this, right?"

"Papa even made a great speech against it to the Tsobl assembly. He said: 'Any man working a trade which brings them right up close to humanity, from physician, to undertaker, to ditch digger, to baker, they can all tell you this one fundamental truth—um, this one deep-grained truth: Every living creature, no matter their station in life, their background, or their ancestry, is born helpless, it helplessly dies, and, while living, it helplessly *shits*—and it eats in order to do so; *equally.*'"

"Your papa said all that?"

"Papa fights for what is fair and right. But the government in Tsobl didn't care, because they were the new people and were proud and nervous about—"

"Oh, yes, Ms. Dalca. That's very true. Even today they are quite smug about their superiority, aren't they? Morally and intellectually. ... Well, that's what Poor John used to say, anyway."

"Who's Poor John?"

"Neku killed that one. Didn't Master tell you? And Old Torga said they're still devoted to advancing their economic might and consolidating their grasp on power."

"Wait, who's Old Torga?"

"Another one, also politically inclined."

"Another one?"

"Well ... well, that's another story. But returning to the governor, the assembly and the occupiers, you see, these King's Tsoblers, as Old Torga would call them: they want to elevate themselves above their fellow countrymen in the most absolute sense. To advantage themselves, and to tyrannize the rest."

"You sound like you're giving me a lesson. Let me finish first, *teacher*."

"Go on. But this *is* history. Maybe history lessons during the morning meal *would* be a good idea. I'm familiar with—"

"You know, my papa has part of their blood, on my grand mama's side."

"Oh, I didn't know."

"But we were here long before the war. Not part of the occupation."

"I see. I'm sure Master knows. He knows everything."

"And my papa's not like them at all. He could have gone along with the tax because he's one of them. He can prove it by the records, if he wanted. And it would have helped him a lot if he'd gone along with it, because they would have been grateful and rewarded him. But my mama wasn't one of them, she's true Ardeelian, you see. And papa loved her, and he said it would have been an insult to her. Because she was the most beautiful and kindest woman he ever met."

This seemed to bring a tear to Genadie's eye.

"But all that doesn't matter, because the tax was bad, anyway. Even if papa is one of the 'preferred' citizens, as they called it. In our village, most people, according to them, aren't. Most don't have money, and they couldn't afford the tax. Never. Not even Argus could stuff enough woodchips, dirt and straw in his loaves to make them cheap enough for a profit. With the tax, our village would either go in debt or starve."

Genadie made a satisfied harrumphing noise. "Yes, certainly, that would serve the new King's Tsoblers, all right. Serve the new King's Tsoblers to *perfection*, as Young Clever Brabas would say."

"Young Clever Brabas? Now who's that?"

"Oh, that one. Well … that one … Well … I don't think I should … I don't think I'm allowed to talk about … well … This is your story anyway and I shouldn't keep interrupting. But as Young Clever Brabas would say, starving the good people would serve them Tsoblers to perfection: to watch from their windows as the majority of Ardeel, the ones who've lived here since the mountains were created, the unfortunate ones who've lost control of the country's businesses and government, to fall to the curb as skeletons." Genadie shrugged. "Or the people could just leave off eating bread. Or they could bake at home."

"No, Genadie. They would revolt. It would be an uprising! And the baker's guild knew it! And there's no profit-making in a time of rebellion, so they weren't for the tax either. They refused it." Amalina lifted her arm and called defiantly into the air: "'Cut the peoples' rights if you will, Governor, but those wretches will cut their bread at home for the same price as you.'"

"Your father said that?"

"The head of the guild."

"Are you in the guild?"

"No, I'm a girl."

"You should be in it, with this very good bread of yours."

"Now listen: the governor and the assembly sent the army to enforce the tax. So papa's union ordered a general strike. No bread, no tax. Like I said, papa fights for what is fair and right, and he'd strike for it. All the bakers of Ardeel shut down their ovens. But guess what?"

"What?"

"That upset everyone!"

"Yes?"

"The hungry people came to the bakeries with pitchforks, the army with their swords and rifles. Everyone demanded the strike over, the ovens be fired and the bread made."

"Ah, yes!" said Genadie, with a scratchy giggle. "Master told me of the event, now that I recall. It happened some years ago and when I was up here in the castle, safely away, so that I didn't even know it happened. But wasn't that a turn-around, eh? From the way Master described it: The soldiers meeting face-to-face with the regular population—each side intent on opening the shops by force—only to realize they all belonged to the same 'inferior' race. And they immediately banded together!" He itched with excitement the cheek of his grinning, grimy face. "Yes, in an instant the rising crest of a civil war was reduced to a bloodless march of solidarity against the King's lawmakers. Who had to've recognized with (as Master said) 'dead-faced horror' from their windows—their high, richly leaded windows reflecting the glow of the torches coming at *them*—the folly of stepping so gratuitously on the feet of a people who outnumbered them ... and who controlled the weaponry! Yes, ha, ha! Quite an end to what Master said was an unfair, prejudicial, ill-conceived, mean-spirited, corrupt and stupidly impossible tax policy. That's how it was related to me, anyway. Master found it entertaining enough to tell me about it, Ms. Dalca. He was very amused. Now that I think of it, he didn't tell me as much as he said it to himself, but I was in the room. So he must have wanted me to hear, mustn't he? That was kind of him."

"The point," muttered Amalina, annoyed at her story being diverted so by the rat, "is that when they came to papa's store, when their bloodlust was at its height," here she gestured to simulate what she was describing, for effect, "when the torches were bobbing outside the bakery, and the nooses being stretched as a promise of what was to become of papa should he not open his doors and fire the ovens, still my papa held the strike."

"Oh."

"Isn't that scary?"

"Very good. Now, let's get to work, Ms. Dalca." And she heard him say to himself on their way out of the hovel, "It's interesting what little girls find scary."

Genadie did not ask why she had thought to tell him the story over their morning meal, and Amalina did not explain. She also omitted from the recounting that in the corner of the besieged bakery, when the hour was darkest, a very, very young Amalina had sat watching and learning from her brave papa.

. . .

"Is something wrong?" Genadie inquired softly in French.

Amalina did not answer.

"You don't appear to be making much progress," he said, trying Italian.

Amalina stood. Genadie bent a little and gave her a curious squint of anticipation, expecting an answer from her action.

She took one step. Then she took another step. Standing beside a short stack of books, she took up the topmost book into her hand. Each movement was very slow. She did not look toward Genadie or acknowledge him. She was like a ghost performing its regularly plotted task, oblivious to the haunted onlookers.

Book in hand, Amalina turned round. Then she took one step. Then she took another. Then she spun slowly. Then she sat on the stack of books she'd been using for a seat. She sat there with the new book on her lap, her eyes looking blankly at its cover. She sat that way for some time. Genadie shifted uneasily.

"Ms. Dalca? Ms. Dalca?" asked Genadie, coming close to her. She smelled his mildewy clothes. "Pardon, me, Ms. Dalca. Is everything all right?"

Amalina stared at the book in her hands and did not answer. She had the library ledger open at her side. A quill was stuck into an open bottle of ink next to it.

"Are you all right?" Genadie leaned in closer. Amalina had become a statue, it seemed. "Amalina—?"

Amalina slapped open the cover, revealing the book's first page.

She froze again. Her eyes went blank.

"Amalina," Genadie's voice scraped with concern, "Do you need water? Are you hungry? Tell me, Amalina, my student, what is wrong with you?"

"Noth-inng," Amalina answered.

"It seems something's wrong. Oh, quite wrong. You catalogued so many books in so little time. But now, it's been … and … and you haven't done a thing, I think. No, you haven't done a thing." He sounded increasingly worried about the last point, about how long it'd been without notable progress, more so than about her strange behavior.

"I *have* 'done a thing', Genadie," said Amalina. She pointed a finger to the stack to her right. There were three books.

"No, no," Genadie's voice rose. "It's been over a week. A week! I wondered why you hadn't called me to bring down the high books. Oh, I wondered and I said to myself there must be something wrong, but I wouldn't question Master's confidence in you. No, I would not. Not even when you played dumb in our language lessons, and you forgot all your vocabulary and syntax. But coming here, I see I was right all along. Something has happened and you are not working."

"I am working, Genadie," Amalina said, slowly. She pointed to the stack of three books again.

"No, no," Genadie scratched hoarsely. "No, no, no, no, no. You tell me now what's happening here."

"I'm working."

"You tell me now or I'll tell Master."

"Go tell master," Amalina said, slowly.

"What?" Genadie's legs buckled.

"Go … tell … master," She almost broke into a smile, but got control of her mouth when she sensed the crisis. She had to appear as lifeless as a doll. She forced her lips into a deadened neutrality.

"I *will*. I will go to him," Genadie threatened unhappily.

"He won't like being wakened at this hour," Amalina tormented him still, and, as always, slowly. "It's only midday."

"He won't like knowing what you're doing … eh, what you *aren't* doing, Ms. Dalca."

"A lot of people in this castle don't like a lot of things that are happening in this castle, Genadie. Don't you think?"

"What do you mean? You *are* up to something." He became placating. He lowered his head to below her eyes, almost subservient. "Please tell me what you are up to, Amalina. You can confide in me. But tell me. Tell me so that I don't have to disturb his meditation. Do you want him to hurt me? You couldn't want that. That isn't like you."

"Tell me who screams at night."

Genadie gasped. He shook his head.

"I will know the answer to my question, or I will make your master's life difficult."

"You already have," he growled. "You mean to say you're going to make it worse? There's only so much he will permit, Ms. Dalca. And you know the consequences if you go too far."

"Go too far? I only want the answer to one simple question: Who screams at night?" Amalina put her finger on the title on the first page. She noted the title's letters, one at a time, at the crawl of a caterpillar, with the tip of her finger. "It shouldn't be too much trouble to answer. Either you or him, it doesn't matter to me. But I want to know, and I want to know the *truth*."

"Master says the source shall not be known to anyone!"

"Do you know the source, Genadie?"

Genadie bit his lower lip. His grimy cheeks blushed. His whole face answered for him.

"*You* are anyone," she said, "and, look, *you* know the answer."

"Don't make me go to him, girl," he bowed at her.

"If you feel you have to."

"You understand the consequences." His knees trembled. "Ms. Dalca knows the trouble she is making against the will of our Master. It's not as if the answer will benefit you in any way, and here you are deliberately sowing the storm."

"You say your Master doesn't want anyone to know. Tell me, Genadie, how the mystery of that scream wouldn't be wondered about *by* anyone, with it going on all night long, hm? How can the answer—the source of this piteous wail—not, in the end, be revealed, when all one can think about is: What is it? Who is it? And why won't it stop? It's the *only* question that this horrible place *begs* to be answered. I will know it!"

Amalina licked her finger (slowly) then turned the title page over (slowly) to reveal the following page.

"Horrible place … " Genadie's voice scratched indignantly as he shrunk away from her, his head shaking from side to side, his squint ticking nervously.

Genadie disappeared. She waited for him to show with his Master at his side. Him pointing her out with a crooked finger, looking like a wounded animal at her affrontery, and having put him to so much trouble.

At supper, she ate alone. She felt a bit scared. At night unexplained sounds in the castle were more mysterious and foreboding. But Amalina summoned the courage and the resolve she'd seen her father display during the baker's strike, and calmly lit the candle she needed to get to her room, and there retired. Seemingly the only living person in the dark, spider-ridden castle.

The only living person in the castle, until an hour or so past sunset, when the forever scream sounded from somewhere below.

. . .

The Count, his features bloated, entered Amalina's room with a blow to the door. It was late, the fire down to glowing coals, but it was enough to see by. Blood trickled from the corner of his mouth. He was dressed in his long cloak. Genadie, behind him and holding a candle, gawked guiltily at Amalina in her bed.

"Work must be done," said the Count. "That is what you are here for, Ms. Dalca. That is why I brought you to the castle."

There was a look in his eyes that was a modification of the terror she'd seen in them a month or so ago. Now there was brilliance to the look, as if he was not terrified but in wonder.

I should be terrified, Amalina thought. *With the horrific way he looks—and the blood.*

Some poor girl's blood was pouring over his lips, the value of her life, taken just hours ago, worthless to him. As insignificant as the lives of his countless victims before.

It was always disturbing to be reminded of the Count's true nature. She could not get used to it, no matter how many times it happened, or to square it with his more mundane appearances within the castle, when he wasn't transformed into that inhuman beast, consumed with the urge to murder and feed, but appearing as a benign, if distracted, aristocrat.

"You are master of the night," Amalina said from her bed, controlling not only her face now but her whole quivering body. "But you are not master of the day—"

"Master is always *the Master!*" Genadie shouted.

The Count swatted Genadie into the wall. Genadie groaned.

Amalina didn't react.

"You are comfortable," he said. "You are clothed. You are provisioned. You have the promise to return to your village when your work is done. There is no reason for you to seek to trouble me. You've only to do your work."

"If, because of the noise, I can't sleep at night," she continued from where she left off, "I can't work in the day."

"Then you will work at night," answered the Count, not smiling. "You will sleep during the day."

"Who screams at night?"

The Count bared his teeth. They were crimson, coated in blood. They had the look of a wolf.

"This again," he said.

"That's all I want to know. I promise no more trouble if you just tell me."

Suddenly, the covers to the bed were ripped away and hit the wall. The force of their removal almost took Amalina with them. Stripping them from her hands had burned her palms and fingers. She yelped in surprise, and felt naked on the bed.

The Count was at her side, his chest heaving, his body so much larger, his fangs gnashing.

"Master, no!" Genadie shouted.

The Count was suddenly on his servant. Amalina hadn't even seen the move, he was just close to her one moment, the next moment he was pressing Genadie into the stone wall. Genadie cried. She feared the snap of bone.

"Stop it!" said Amalina, though she had had all the intention of remaining as immovable as stone, no matter what.

"I want peace in my home," said the Count, still full of fury. "If it takes death to quiet things, so be it."

Genadie cried again.

"Stop!" Amalina burst out once more.

The Count was on her. As her face mashed into the bedpost she tasted blood. Recovering her composure, she refused to scream, even as she was driven harder into the wood.

"No!" cried Genadie. "Master, you mustn't!"

It felt like her cheekbone might break.

Don't scream. Please don't scream.

"I mustn't?" asked the Count with a detached, curious tone. "*Mustn't?*"

"No," said Genadie, sounding very relieved. No one was being killed, presently. For Amalina, she was still being crushed to the post, her skull felt like it would shatter, and she was trying everything not to react, to remain cold and seeming careless of what he might do to her. That is how negotiations were won—she'd seen it before, when her father talked down the angry mob outside his door—wasn't it?

In the quiet, there was only Genadie and Amalina's panting, the hiss from the coals in the fireplace, and the terrible wail winding in at the window.

There was a shift in the Count's arm. Peering back, eye watery from pain, her blurry sight told Amalina that the wailing had distracted him. He was looking at the window.

"You can hear it, Genadie?" he asked.

Genadie nodded.

"And *is* it very loud?"

"You mustn't hurt her, Master," said Genadie.

"That is not what I asked you," the words dripped from his mouth.

"Sorry, Master. I know you can hear an ant crawling ten miles away, so you might not be able to fathom mortal ears. But it is very loud, even to me, Master." Enthusiasm sprouted in his voice as he realized he was drawing the Count's attention, slackening the anger. "But Ms. Dalca is wrong of course, and she must pay it no mind!"

"Very well," said the Count, ignoring Genadie and answering some hidden thought in his own head. "Very well ..."

Something felt like a punch to Amalina's stomach. She barely registered the loud bang of wood against stone, and the crack of a lock, as she tried to recover her breath. She did feel something else—a cold breeze on her skin. All was dark presently, except a window lit by starlight. The window looked much like the one in her own room. But as her eyes adjusted she noticed around her a different bed and more ancient decorations. Genadie was thrown against the wall.

"Can you hear it here?" asked the Count.

The scream was faint, but still audible.

"Yes, Master."

Another punch, another bang, another room.

"And here, Genadie, can you hear it here?"

The wail was faintest here, much like in the room Amalina had first been shown when she'd arrived at the castle. But the sound was, of course, something that could still be heard. And now that she knew what it was, it was unrecognizable as anything other than the sound of a human scream. Never the wind. It seemed impossible she had once thought it was anything else.

"Genadie?"

"Yes, Mas—"

Bang!

Amalina coughed. Genadie rolled across the floor of the newest room.

"And here, too?"

The ever-present scream was louder here than in the last. They must be visiting the castle's high corner towers, and circling back around the building, they were now closer to Amalina's room, closer to the source of the voice again. Genadie didn't have to answer.

The Count's blood-filled face winced.

"Master, may I speak with you?" Genadie asked softly.

The Count took a step toward Amalina, his hands clenching and unclenching. But inside the anger there was an odd air of amusement in his expression.

Amalina thrust out her jaw in bold defiance.

The Count licked his teeth clean. His body hunched over. His skin darkened in patches and it began to look as if hair would grow from these patches, as his features became more canine in appearance. He began to resemble a wolf.

A wolf that was preparing to pounce.

"You will be *torn apart*," he said in a wolf's growl. But it was as flat as if he were ordering an item from a menu.

Genadie leapt in front of him, grabbing him at the wrist. "Stop, Master!" cried Genadie. "You mustn't! Not her! Not *her!*"

The Count suddenly rounded on Genadie and had him in his awful grasp, pulling his body in opposing directions as he had with Neku Jonker. But his red eyes were on Amalina. They never left her.

"You will do as you're told," he said to her dispassionately, as if talking through her, as if talking to the air.

Genadie howled in pain.

Amalina stared into those awful red eyes, holding back a shiver of fear.

"You will do as I bid you," it was the voice of finality.

This was not to be a bargaining session.

But Amalina, determined to hold steady, did not relent.

Neither did the Count.

A red streak, as if the beginning of a tear, zagged across Genadie's exposed belly.

Amalina's fear grew, pushed by a swell of panic at Genadie's seeping blood.

But she must hold out, mustn't she? The Count wouldn't possibly hurt—

"Everything is replaceable," the Count concluded.

Then the Count twisted his servant's body like it was a rag. Genadie squealed. Blood fell in a gush from the rend in his body.

"No!" screamed Amalina. "Stop! Oh, please, leave him alone! I will do anything—"

Bang!

Amalina rolled head over foot onto the mattress of her own bed.

She was alone in the room. She still tasted blood in her mouth. The side of her face which had been run into the bedpost felt as it were pulsing with fire. Her eye socket throbbed painfully.

She wanted to cry, to send forth a fountain of tears and drown out the scream coming in the window by a torrent of sobs of her own, but she thought better of it. There was no telling if the Count would return, or that he wasn't still watching from a place she could not see.

She didn't want to cry from the pain, though that was bad enough. It was the thought of Genadie. The monster could have killed her. It *would* have killed her—*and why didn't I find a weapon to use against him?* she hissed reproachfully—it would have killed her if not for Genadie. And Genadie had suffered for it. He had willingly taken a beating, perhaps might have even died, to save her. Why? Had he actually grown to care for her during their long hours of labor and lessons? Developed some fondness or attachment to her because of the many meals she'd prepared for him in their isolation?

And she realized, too, she had cried out involuntarily when the Count began to crush Genadie into the wall. And then again when he began to rip Genadie like a helpless toy. Because deep inside her she feared for his life. She could not see the groveling little sycophantic servant suffer any longer for her, on her own account; despite her determination to press his master: to force this powerful monster into giving in to her demand.

She had wanted to test her mettle against the Count. Like a stupid, bored child. And she had even been willing to risk her own life to face him down, to push him to the ultimate act against her. But with the threat of Genadie's torture, or painful death, she'd lost her nerve. Would her father have faltered just the same, on that night so long ago when the lynch-team was at the door, if instead of attacking him directly they had gotten hold of her?

Well, anyway, Amalina thought to herself, I *gave in for Genadie.* Much to her surprise, she had grown fond of the little groveler.

17

Genadie Convalescent

The next morning, since Genadie had not lit his hovel's hearth, Amalina used a torch to get the logs going, while trying not to make anything out of his absence. She carried on, skipping the baking of bread, but preparing the mamaliga as she always did, making sure there was plenty for two. When Genadie did not appear at meal time, her worry for him throbbed.

Ordinarily, she would have searched the castle to find where Genadie'd gotten to. Now she felt that if she did not do as the monster expected of her—*exactly* as he expected of her—the consequences would be dire. Well, so then, Genadie wasn't there? She could do nothing about it. She wasn't hungry? She forced down the meal anyway, so as not to upset the order of things. Not that Genadie was very talkative (outside of their lessons, of course), but she missed his presence and felt all the more alone and anxious as she spooned her portion of the tasteless yellow-orange mamaliga mash— his favorite—into her mouth. This was the way things were going to be? Because of it, she grew resentful of the Count.

This being a morning for language study and her instructor was absent, she was at a bit of a loss for how to proceed. Occasionally Genadie had left the castle on business and she could not receive proper tutoring. When that happened, before departing, he'd told her to read from her language primers. Other times, he'd ordered her to continue cataloguing books into the register for the Great Library. This was not the case today. The last she'd seen of him was his mouth, screaming, and blood firing out of a thin seam in his midsection. He'd left no instructions for the following day.

Since she knew she could not concentrate on her studies while fearing for Genadie's life, she decided to do something non-taxing and go to the great audience chamber to record books. She would log them at top speed, to make up for all the time she had wasted during her ill-conceived strike. Maybe if she were to work fast enough, she thought remorsefully, and prayed, it would somehow spare Genadie any more pain ... or bring him back to life if he hadn't survived the wounds of last night. Amalina wept and wiped the tears from her cheeks at the thought of what had happened to the sad, rat-like man, and what might have been the fatal results; not knowing if learning how things had turned out for him would make things better or worse.

The book forest was waiting for her as it always was, quiet and restful, as if nothing noteworthy had transpired the night before. Finding her ledger, she realized that she'd stopped working yesterday when she'd run out of reachable books. This was a problem. Whenever Amalina needed to start a new stack, which sometimes was near as high as the ceiling, Genadie would always be the one to cut it down to a reasonable height, halving and quartering a tower into manageable pillars for Amalina to work from. But here she'd left off when there were no books she could safely reach or pull down.

And Genadie wasn't there to help her.

What could she do?

With a distracted eye, she studied the problem for a few minutes.

She'd never dare to pull a book from the middle of a stack, which would send the higher ones raining down, nor would she think to push a pile over for fear of setting off a greater chain reaction of toppling stacks. Both options potentially damaging or destroying ancient and valuable creations.

She could go to the adjoining room, she thought with a sudden burst of excitement, and trepidation: *l'entrée grande*. She could go there to see if Genadie had skipped breakfast this morning to start work early.

She would find out if he were alive or dead.

In the pit of her stomach, she knew he would not be there.

But she went to the door. She put her ear to it.

Inside *l'entrée grande* she heard a metallic tapping noise. It was not mechanical, with regularly spaced taps, but something curiously uneven yet with some bit of rhythm. A cadence which suggested thought behind it. Someone was in there.

Amalina opened the door.

The entrance hall had been cleared of most of its clutter since she'd first arrived. Who knows where Genadie put it all, but now some walls were visible as was most of the floor. Several sets of unpolished but imposing suits of armor were nailed to the stone walls, along with some stained weapons and dusty tapestries. There was also a hexagonal wood stand with a lead chalice on it, set near the fireplace.

The tapping came from inside the remaining mountain of scientific debris; inside one of the crate-and-box hills. This hill had a deep alcove cut into it that could almost be considered a room. Tucked into that alcove was a large table, and on the table were several sets of apparatus resembling the wiry insect Amalina had helped Genadie disassemble.

Sitting before it all was a small, hunched shape that wore a thick, hooded black cloak, the kind of garb she'd seen traveling monks use. The figure's hand, which was hidden inside the cloak's wide sleeve, idly rapped a metal rod against one apparatus. The owner of that hand, whose head was buried within the hood, was distractedly tapping away while reading a page from a book which was also laid out on the table.

Genadie?

He'd never worn anything but his old moldy gentleman's suit, unless he put a large green wool coat over it, when he went into the cold. But maybe he was so badly mangled that he felt the need to hide himself from sight. It must be him. Who else could it be? And what was he reading there so intently that he'd ignore her knock?

Before she was halfway to him, the hood spun toward her with unnatural speed, causing its cloth to cinch closed with a loud snap. A sleeve came up to part the opening.

The Count stared icily at Amalina. She was almost blown backward at the surprise. How could the Count, who seemed so outsized in his dimensions, fit inside a small black cloak?

"Oh," she said. "I thought you were Genadie."

She stepped closer to better see his face. It was protected by shadow, but she could see it had drained significantly since the previous night. The flesh, while not loose, did not bulge as before. His cheeks were white. His eyes had returned to an ivory color, and weren't covered with the ropy red veins. Usually, on returning from an (apparently successful) night's hunt, the Count seemed to grow in proportion to the size of a giant, now his scale had collapsed to that of a normal human. A tired human.

"I thought you were Genadie, *sir*," she repeated, tacking on the proper deference.

The Count shook his head, and he was still tapping the rod against the structure. The eyes looked through her.

"What did you want from Genadie?"

"The books are too high for me," she explained. "He would help me when—"

A sudden black blur hummed past Amalina, catching her in its draft. She spun and grabbed the table to keep from falling. Before the metal rod finished clattering on the floor, where he'd dropped it, she heard from the next room the heavy thump of leather and wood onto stone. Then the Count materialized at the table, accompanied by the small vortex of air that followed him, and was bent over the book he'd been reading before she interrupted.

Peering into the great chamber, she saw the remaining stacks had all been halved, so that she could reach their tops with only slight difficulty—maybe by standing on a tall stool—and not require her to bother him or Genadie again.

Once more, she approached the hunched black robe.

"Excuse me, sir."

He didn't respond.

She called again.

He did not react.

She felt she should return to her work, but then reconsidered. There might be a deeper meaning to the Count's somber mood and the black robes. Black was a color long associated with death. The Count might not just be protecting himself, she thought, he might be in mourning.

"Genadie, sir," Amalina dared to continue. "Might I know? Is he all right?"

One large sleeve rose from the body, and without hand or finger visible he pointed to a door across the entrance chamber.

She'd never seen the door before, but maybe she hadn't paid enough attention. Or maybe it hadn't become visible until recently. Revealed now after a wall of crates had been removed.

And so what was through the door he pointed to so dramatically?

Genadie, of course. That was his answer.

But what was that room? Why would Genadie be in there? Was the rat working on some new project for the Count? Or was his bloody corpse callously laid out on the floor? Or perhaps bundled up in reverence, with candles burning for him?

The Count was reading the book again, his sleeves folded in front.

Amalina went to the door. She paused, took a breath, and then opened it.

This room was much smaller than the entrance, narrower than it was long, and was completely empty. There was a door at its far end. She went to it and, pausing to suck in another bracing breath, she opened this one.

Another empty room. This one much smaller and narrower still. As was the case in the previous room, there was one door at its end. She trotted to it, her nerves feeling worked over, frustrated, and resolved to push all the way through to the end of this game.

She opened the door.

. . .

"Genadie!"

Genadie tried to sit up from the bed. He managed only to tilt his head. And though he couldn't manage that for more than a second, he could, after collapsing back to the straw pillow, maintain his wide grin.

"Amalina," he beamed brightly at her. "You're well."

Amalina ran to him and tried to understand what was happening. He was lying fully exposed on a cheap frame bed, resting atop dirty looking blankets. His midsection and his left arm were wrapped in material similar to cheese cloth, his moldy gentleman's suit covering the rest. The gauzy cloth was stiff and brown and blood-soaked. When he breathed there was a rattle in his encapsulated chest.

"Look at me," Genadie's voice scraped merrily, and proudly. "I am sleeping in the castle!"

Amalina had never seen such open-faced delight in a grown man, it was like looking at a tickled baby. And she'd never have believed Genadie would be found in such a state. She wondered if he was delirious.

"You're well, Genadie?" she asked softly, not wanting to excite him too much.

"Of course! Look at me! I am sleeping in the castle! *Inside* the castle!"

"Yes, I see that. Try not to excite yourself. Here, have some water." She ladled water from a bucket beside the bed, pouring it onto his parched lips. "That's better, isn't it?"

"Yes, thank you. You're so kind. Making … Making our meals and all, I— I mean, you—"

"Just rest yourself," she quieted him. "You need to heal."

"I will," he said, closing his eyes. The smile remained.

"Genadie," she whispered near his ear, feeling a terrible swell of guilt, and remorse, and empathy for this tortured man. "I'm so sorry what happened. It's all my fault."

"What's your fault?"

"What happened to you."

"What happened to me?"

"Don't you remember?"

"What nonsense are you talking about, Ms. Dalca?"

"What the Count—"

"—Master—"

"—did to you last night."

His eyes opened and he glanced down to take in his bloodied chest and belly. Then he shook his head and mashed his lips into a smile.

"Oh, this is nothing," he said, dismissively. "He's done much worse to this silly body."

"Has he?" Amalina said in wonder. She couldn't believe he'd survived what happened to him last night. He'd suffered worse?

"Never mind all that."

"But it was so awful."

"It was nothing. T'was a misunderstanding. He didn't mean to go as far as it went. But when Master is in one of his moods," he winked knowingly, "it is best to be careful."

"And it was all my fault," said Amalina, now having to force herself to cry; in opposition to the unrelenting cheer of the victim. "I was selfish, and I thought I could push him around—"

"No, no," Genadie cut in quickly, his smile vanishing. "This wasn't your fault! Don't you try to take credit for my being inside the castle! It was my own actions that did it. Don't dare rob me of the honor!"

"No, I wouldn't think to," she said, feeling confused. But his blissful smile returned when she said it, and his head settled back down onto the pillow. "It's just that I wouldn't want to see you suffer because of my—I mean to say, for daring to help me so courageously."

"I saw it in your eyes, you didn't want me to suffer," Genadie said, serenely. "And that is good of you, Ms. Dalca. But think: if I hadn't acted as I had, I wouldn't be here now. Master would not have allowed me to enter Olympus."

"Where?"

"Olympus."

"What do you mean?"

"Olympus, Olympus," he repeated the word happily, savoring the word. "Come, Ms. Dalca, do you really not know where you are?"

"The Count's castle in the mountains."

"Olympus."

"I've heard you say that name, Genadie, but I don't understand."

"This the home of the gods," he swooned. "Olympus! Master, he is the father of us all. Master is the god of all gods. Master is ..." his whole body trembled as if it took effort to say it, or to hold back from saying it, but then he overcame the obstacle in a burst: "Zeus!"

He looked to be more in religious ecstasy than a wild delirium. Amalina's eyebrows rose three inches.

"Does it hurt?" Amalina asked him, not knowing what to say but knowing never to agitate someone so near the precipice of death, for fear he might slip over it. She lightly touched his cloth wrapping. "Oh, I really didn't think he would actually *hurt* you."

Genadie had settled down. He murmured, almost barely there, "Why not?"

"You're loyal to him. With a devotion that ... well, a devotion I've never seen before."

"Anyone who is not serving Master ..." He'd gone back to calling him Master, not Zeus, a small relief. His thought lingered as he breathed in and out with a faint gargling sound. "Anyone ... is dispensable."

Amalina felt uneasy. "Even me? You told him he couldn't ..."

"As long as you are serving him ..." He didn't bother to finish the sentence.

"But when I'm done ... But ... He did promise I could go home when I'm done here. That I'd be safe. And returned."

Genadie nodded slowly. But his eyes were dull, vacant. His face slack. He was trying to reassure her, while avoiding the question. Whatever he was thinking yet not wanting to say spoke louder: In other circumstances, without a thought, she could have been in his place. And if she weren't more careful in the future, would be.

The promise of immunity to punishment, or even a return to her village, was not—and had never been—guaranteed.

"Ms. Dalca, more water, please," he said, settling deeper in to the straw pillow, his eyes, two dark smudges, closed. He was exhausted.

Amalina fed Genadie the water carefully, observing his crude bandages. Had he wrapped himself? Or was this the Count's work?

. . .

Amalina left her candle in the room. She passed through the entrance hall with careful, quiet steps in the hope she would not draw the Count's attention.

He was still there, fully absorbed in the book. His back was turned. She glanced at it with hatred. A shock of deep, deep hatred. Any sensible fear of what he could do in return to her reduced to a small bead beneath her growing rage.

This thing had nearly killed Genadie, she stormed. Silly little Genadie. And that meant nothing to him.

How easy it was now, looking around the room, to picture the way it'd appeared centuries ago: all the bodies of the knights, butchered beyond recognition, their various parts thrown carelessly to the walls, stacked in loose piles, soaking foot-deep in their mingled blood. The culprit, the Count, wading through it without a glance at them. Caring nothing for the preciousness of life. She pictured the horrific display in her mind with a small shiver.

Such cold arrogance deserves punishment.

Look at him, he doesn't even care about me!

Staring murder at his back as she passed him, he not even looking up, she imagined how she might attack the Count.

Just one swift blow!

But she felt the hopelessness of even attempting it.

That hopelessness enraged her further. For the unfairness, the unjustness of it. If only the Count could be treated the same way he had done Genadie, if he could suffer the casual mistreatment, the bland tortures and the offhand terrors he put on others, she didn't doubt that he would conduct himself much differently. He would, and could, never be the monster that he was if he ever experienced the helplessness of the weak. It was merely a matter of securing the power—the superior force—necessary to teach the monster a lesson in humility. A lesson that he richly deserved ... if he couldn't be, more justly, killed outright for his crimes (both past and future).

But how does one kill a god? she sneered.

What a mind Genadie had! She could easily write off Genadie's odd assertion that the Count was Zeus, the king of all the Grecian gods, as a lapse into delirium, if he hadn't invoked the name 'Olympus' before his injury, in easier times.

But why not believe him? By all the written and firsthand observations, the Count possessed the extreme power and the attributes of a god. So ... could he be one?

Was the Count truly Zeus? And this neglected castle Olympus?

Am I going mad? she wondered unhappily.

No. This is a house of insanity, and I'll go mad if I start believing!

Or, she reconsidered coolly, *might it be true, after all?*

Well ... no ... it couldn't be.

Whatever power the Count had, no matter how invulnerable and immortal he appeared, he did not control the sky. He did not control the earth. He seemed to need to hunt victims and drink their blood for his vitality, instead of being the sole source of universal energy.

But still ...

Doing any work was impossible. After last night's carnage, and this morning's relief at finding Genadie still alive, and then her general confusion and renewed hatred of her employer, it was all too unmanageable. She plopped herself on a chair, and sat motionless but for the thoughts swirling in her head.

What was to be done now? It was almost as if she'd been transported back to the very first moment she set foot in the castle, all the intervening months, with her preoccupation with work and lessons, and the tamping of her hatred of the Count and the soothing of her determination to kill him—to bring him to a final justice—had not happened. It was as if all her initial dark, vengeful feelings were returned to her, fresh and unsettled, by Genadie's wounds, and by coming to understand just how fragile her safety was: once she was done with her work it was a matter of the creature against her, life or death. It put her on edge. And, unfortunately, along with those overwhelming feelings came the realization she could not do anything about it.

He might as well be Zeus, she thought sourly. *Here I am in 'Olympus', the champion for my people—as the story would be told—and I have as much a chance to stop him as any mortal would against the most powerful deity in creation.*

She knew that in most tales of a mortal against a god, a mouse versus a lion, this was the moment the powerless being would become clever, would discover a cunning method to take advantage of a flaw the superior being had but was unaware of—hubris was standard—and trick the being into using against itself its own power.

With a sigh and a smirk, she regretted how she did not know who the Count really was, what he was, or what he was capable of. The months had revealed nothing new or useful. Her only inkling into him was the old book in the deputy sheriff's office, which recounted his abilities in the most fantastic of terms, likening him to a punishing creation of heaven. That and Genadie's fawning belief that he was none other than the supreme lord of the Greek Pantheon. All disheartening.

She would have to disregard all that or it would sap her will and prevent her from acting. Instead, she'd have to analyze for herself everything she'd seen of the Count. To systematically break down her observations of the monster into smaller pieces. Coldly dissect and study them from many angles, searching for clues, to determine who he really was as a being of this earth. By understanding his true nature, she would find his weakness—as all creatures of the earth have a weakness—which she could then exploit.

Her reward for beating him—besides proving Genadie wrong about what his master was—was she could leave the castle and return home.

But first, the hard work. She had to scour her memory. See if by sifting through those paltry pieces, she could figure her adversary out.

Feeling a slight stirring of energy—and knowing so much more energy and effort would be required to take even this first step in the eventual punishment of the Count—she stood on her toes and retrieved the topmost book on the nearest stack.

When she sat down, she experienced what happens from time to time in everyone's life: There are always several moments in one's life when you feel the most powerless, or the most out of sorts, and suddenly, without the least effort on your part, what you need most is … simply delivered to you. Such a moment is declared "serendipity" by poets, while the faithful call it "divine providence" and the proof of the will of their God.

At just the moment Amalina was at her lowest, vulnerable and powerless against her enemy the Count, and with no real understanding of just what he was and how she might defeat him, she looked down at the cover of the slim book she had picked off the stack and she read its title.

Amalina forced herself not to scream.

18

Monster Killer

The Count was about to die and he did not know it.

The trap had been carefully prepared, and it waited in all its deadliness for his arrival. For him to step easily and unwittingly into it.

Amalina waited, too, with strangled breath. She could hardly breathe from anxiety over whether it would work. Because, if it should not …

But it should, she told herself confidently. A startling number of the creatures detailed in the book she had found could be vanquished by the power of the Christian cross. While she did not know which of the creatures the Count was—as many fit his particulars to some degree—almost every one resembling his description had this certain vulnerability.

So then it was decided. He would die by the cross.

It was well into Autumn, almost winter now. Reading the book, 'Demonologae: Monsters In Our Lands And How To Destroy Them', then assessing which monster the Count could be, and then developing a strategy and planning the attack had taken longer than expected. The first drifts of snow had already plumped the hard lines of the mountains and the castle, and ice overlaid almost every surface within it—locking shut doors and windows, solidifying water buckets and crusting over the well. And the Count, when he wasn't laboring over bitter smelling bubbling liquids or obscure equations in books, or ministering to Genadie in his few idle moments, had returned from too many hunting trips happily engorged with blood. Innocent blood. A bland, complacent look of satisfaction on his ruby-red lips.

The Count would die, she calmed herself. By the cross.

The type or manufacture of the cross did not matter, nor did it need to be blessed by a priest or have been used in a church. In one of the book's anecdotes recounting the destruction of an unwholesome entity, it assured that a common serf had, by reflex, brought two scythes together in front of her face in order to protect her head during an unholy assault, inadvertently creating a wood cross with the handles. The molesting creature disappeared in a shriek of lightning, never to reappear.

Inspired by this, Amalina had constructed a holy cross out of the logs she split for firewood, lying one long chopped piece perpendicularly over a shorter one—even praying over this crude, makeshift cross for added effect—and presently waited, with puffs of breath in the firelight, for the Count to come.

To come … and explode.

She set down the bell she'd been ringing. She was between Genadie's hovel and the door leading to the kitchens. The greater pile of logs was stacked next to the door, with a few just inside. The ones designated for the set-piece of the trap, and the ones she'd already chopped, lay beside the large, short flat stump where the chopping was done. The axe was stuck wedge-first into the stump. The monster-killing cross was out front of all of this.

"What is it, Ms. Dalca?" the Count asked blandly from the doorway.

He did not seem too bothered by the cross, which stood right before him.

Amalina complained she was too weak to cut more wood, that there wouldn't be enough logs to last them through winter.

Far from exploding, the Count was put immediately into a lively but contradictory mood. He launched into the debate, questioning this way and and then that way who should cut the wood, Genadie being too hobbled and still recovering, and she overtaxed physically by maintaining the castle (and while also fulfilling her normal duties). He himself didn't require the wood or the fires, he reasoned, so he didn't see how it was his business at all.

Amalina tried to draw his eyes to the cross. She stepped forward and positioned herself near it.

His only reaction was to casually rearrange the logs with the tip of his boot, looking more put off by the awkward arrangement of the wood pieces than by the fear of a godly presence created by them.

She remembered now, with an inward moan, that the very Bishop of Tsobl, a man of great heavenly might, had failed to work any religious method of wounding him. The cross was a bust. She should never have tried it.

• • •

The count was about to die and he did not know it.

Death for him rested in a goblet on the table.

Amalina watched the goblet—and its contents—with a bit of worry, but also pride. It had been some work in creating this particular trap.

To accomplish it took a week of plotting and getting the Count to allow her and Genadie (who was still very lame) to return to the swamp on the next warm day, so she could get more of the moss that she required.

From a safe distance, the Count, with his nose pinched precautiously, had motioned that she could do whatever the hell she wanted when she was "in that way". So she'd spent an exhausting winter's afternoon outside the castle, both making sure Genadie was warm and comfortable in the sleigh, while turning her fingers to icicles searching for—instead of the moss—the ugly, fatal roots she needed.

She'd nearly killed them both on that adventure, the Count rescuing her and Genadie after sundown—after finding them dragging along the road, both half-succumbed to the death-sleep of cold—by driving the horse at top speed back to the castle and setting them to thaw by a roaring fireplace.

But she'd made it back to the castle alive.

And two malevolent forces (described in the book, of course) could be killed by ingesting, or at least introducing into its mouth, the bitter roots of a certain flower. A root which she had found near the swamp and pulled from the frozen ground.

She almost could not bring herself to dice the roots and put them in the wine, having had her life saved by her would-be victim.

But upon seeing the Count return the following night, his face a mask of blood, with long hairs from a blond woman's scalp caught in his teeth, he giggling in an inhuman way, she set to work. *Him or me*. The wine bottle was infused with the bitter root and placed on Amalina's table for dinner.

She rang the bell that would summon the Count.

When he came, she thanked him for saving her and Genadie, and offered him the cup.

She drank a cup of her own, and despite the rancid, bitter taste of the wine, smiled and encouraged him to drink. He took up the cup.

He was about to die.

The Count downed the wine with one throw. Then he made a terrible face, and his hands grabbed at his throat.

"Where did you get this wine?" he asked, his tongue rolling and smacking disagreeably against his teeth, not dying.

"In Genadie's hovel."

"You've been drinking it? You like it? This tastes good to you?" his face puckered.

Amalina nodded sheepishly, still surveying him in the hopes that the poison was slow acting.

"It tastes like Genadie's been eating roots and pissed into the bottle," the Count railed on, his face continuing to twist, the flavor of the spiked wine causing him to lose all sense of manners and decorum. Perhaps this was the sign of impending death, she crossed her fingers. "You might have poisoned yourself!"

"You don't know wine at all," was his final opinion, before leaving the castle for the night. Returning early next morning, with the sun just about to rise over the mountains, to complain it had taken two bodies' blood to relieve him of the bitter taste.

• • •

Two unsuccessful attempts.

Amalina had to be much more careful now. The first two tries were reasonable to explain as accidents and circumstance. So easy to deny any ill intent, counter any accusation of malice if he didn't fall to the blows and survived to question what had happened. But all the remaining options to kill the Count—to test the ability to kill him, anyway—would be more obvious in method. And if they should fail, it would mark her as his enemy. Very fatal without the ability to kill him.

So was it worth the risk?

The next weapon against the Count was to be a spear.

An even riskier proposition because the spear would have to be manufactured. There were none in the castle. The few potential sharp or pointy objects which could be used in the creation of a spear of spears were so hard to locate it almost seemed deliberate. And deliberate, too, those she did find—even the crude, wooden pitchfork—were blunted and dulled as rounded river stones.

So the spear, she determined in the end, would have to be crafted from the long iron rod she found in the stable.

But, in all fairness, was it worth the risk?

• • •

The only place inside the castle grounds where she could fashion the spear's blade without detection was Genadie's hovel.

She dragged in a makeshift anvil-rock and positioned it next to the well stoked fireplace. The fireplace itself, its stocky shape, its mouth, and an ancient built-in bellows system on one side, suggesting that this shack might have actually been the castle's smithy in its earlier days. She took a splintered wooden hammer up in one hand, and struck it hard onto the red-hot end of the iron rod. There was no clank, or ringing sound, or the shower of sparks she'd thrilled to as a child when visiting the village blacksmith. There was only a dull thump. Lifting the hammer, the glowing tip of the iron had not flattened or lengthened in any way.

Maybe the metal wasn't hot enough, she thought.

She sighed in frustration.

Even with Genadie out of the way, she had only so much time to herself in the mornings and evenings before she had to attend to her duties, or she would risk drawing the Count's attention. Fussing with the fire, figuring how to make it hotter, or getting the rod to accept its heat more readily would be time consuming.

She groaned now and threw the rod into the water bucket, where it uttered a mellow hiss.

Amalina knew this weapon was really her only hope, if she could only forge it.

But.

But …

Should I even be trying to kill him? She wondered.

The feeling it was her duty to do so, that it was her ultimate fate to do so, had been so strong when the Count had first taken her into his arms—after witnessing what he'd done to Lucinda. And that feeling of grim responsibility returned to her with some regularity—returned along with the recurring dream of Lucinda's head bouncing through the tall barley, while singing a haunting song. The dream seeming to suggest that Lucinda was waiting for justice to be done. Waiting for Amalina to do something about it.

That it was Amalina's duty, and her fate, and her responsibility to do in the Count couldn't have been more underlined—shouted by the world into her ear—than when she—feeling at her lowest ebb, questioning her purpose for even remaining in the castle—blindly picked up the book with the provocative title: 'Demonologae: Monsters In Our Lands And How To Destroy Them'. That miraculous happening, in an instant, made it clear that ridding the Ardeel Mountains of this creature was her sole destiny.

Or so she'd once thought.

Could it have been plain coincidence that I discovered the book just then? she considered now. Or maybe—could it be?—the Count had set the book there on purpose, to see if she would take the bait. To test her trustworthiness. And it was only out of dumb luck he didn't suspect she was already taking direct instruction from it.

Or did he suspect that she was already using the book to fashion weapons against him? Or did he know? And he was laughing at her, knowing her fate was sealed, and he had all the time he wanted to have his revenge for attempting to kill him.

Encircled by doubt and feeling powerless, she fell into a funk.

She thought: Who said I'm supposed to do anything about him? If knights and bishops couldn't bring him down, why should I think I'm the one to do it?

And anyway, her thoughts continued heavier now, *shouldn't I admit what I've been feeling all along? That I can't really kill him. I couldn't kill something that looks so human, even if it is a monster from hell? It walks, it talks, it thinks, it has feelings. It has sheltered me and provided for me …*

Yes, it's true, I've felt that way from the very beginning, haven't I?

No matter how monstrous his crimes, she could not see herself delivering a true deathblow to the Count. Her other attempts on his life had been entirely passive—the arranging of sticks of wood, the spiking of a bottle of wine. With these methods she would, in the end, only be a witness to his destruction. His death would be accidental. Out of her hands. And even then, at those critical moments when he was about to fall into her trap, she felt short of breath, a sweat trickling down the side of her face, a coldness in her cheeks and a knotting in her gut, as she watched the Count in anticipation of his demise. And she felt that she might just die alongside him out of guilt and pity if he were to die because of her.

Mice and other rodents, which she'd killed with the flick of a wrist, were one thing to cull without feeling. He was human. Or was once human. Or appeared human, anyway.

And now to actually penetrate his body with a weapon, it sent shudders of mortal sympathy through her body. She could feel it happening already, and her entire being rebelled at the thought. She wasn't a natural murderer, she understood deep down that she would never be.

Am I really the one to do it? she questioned again, more serious than before.

She considered her father, alone in their bakery, so far away. How many times had he told her, when he was lonely, or when he was feeling melancholy and remembering Amalina's mother: "What would I do without you, Amalina? You are all I have in this world. I can't ever lose you. I'd be completely lost without you."

Yes, yes. Who had declared she was supposed to slay this monster? And what if all she did in the effort was to die herself? Never mind she'd miss out on the delights, the untold experiences that were in her future, she thought, what would become of old Dragomir? Even now, he must be falling apart, if he hadn't already done so. The only remedy would be to return to him, as he'd said she would; as the Count promised she would; as she had vowed to herself she would!

As she saw it now, her only purpose at this castle was to survive. To escape the Count's dark hold. To go home. To cheer her father's heart. To return to a true life.

That afternoon she tried to get the fire hotter than it had ever been before, by stacking the hearth with the best-burning logs, and pumping two sets of bellows into it, to urge its flames ever higher. The fire needed to be hot enough to soften iron. Even though she had resolved not to kill the Count but to do as he instructed with perfect obedience and to simply survive this perilous passage of her life, this iron weapon still felt necessary. It felt so crucial for her to build it, and for a reason that she couldn't understand, but sensed its righness to the marrow.

To create the weapon became like an overheated obsession.

19

Amalina's Last Lonely Day in the Castle

Amalina was about to die. She saw this very clearly. The cold bit into her hands, her legs, her face. Numbing them where it didn't lance them with pain. But there was nothing she could do about it. And, in just a few minutes, if she did not immediately die from losing control of her limbs, she would slip into a fatal slumber.

She wanted to cry out or to laugh madly, and would have if she could work her jaw and lips.

There was no reason for this to have happened.

How she'd gotten to this point had been a mistake. A foolish one. Caused by the creeping madness of her prolonged isolation.

Lonely as they are, winter months were always troublesome for Amalina. Her mind tended to wander into odd, dark areas.

But here in the castle? The winter months inside the castle—secluded mentally and emotionally, until suffering from what we in the modern age would describe as cabin fever—were a playground for obsessions.

With the accounting of the books almost completed, and their physical transfer to the Great Library partly begun but put off until Spring—when it was assumed Genadie's strength would be fully recovered—Amalina's duties had fallen to cooking meals, tending to the remaining small animals, light maintenance of the castle, and learning languages. Cooking and eating was restricted to Genadie's ramshackle cottage (with Genadie's meals transferred to him inside his castle closet). The animals she fed and fattened in a roofed dormitory next to the cottage. Maintenance was mainly hauling logs into the castle, keeping burning the fires in the rooms that were used, and preparing and keeping stocked the supply of torches (an annoying chore which stank of tar oil, and delivered hundreds of splinters to her fingers and palms). The languages, if she was not being directly instructed by Genadie in his closet on the ground floor, she preferred to study from the primers in her own room.

With the Count preoccupied with mysterious experiments, resting, and hunting, this had left Amalina plenty of time—perhaps too much time—to think.

Her weapon had been coming along slowly. She was still figuring out tricks to bring the temperature up quickly and to sustain the extreme heat needed to play with the iron rod's shape, to fashion it to a spear-like wedge and point.

The madness grew.

When she'd grown bored with that, she found herself inventorying their meager supplies, comparing the amount of grain or flour used on a daily or weekly basis, with how many months they had left before the first thaw, which would allow them safe travel to the nearest village to resupply ... and calculating just when starvation would set in before that happened.

The madness grew.

When that no longer interested her, she decided to explore the castle. Scribbling with chalk on one of her wardrobe's ancient linen skirts, she set out to map what she could of the grand structure. Not only to fully appreciate its daunting design, but Amalina understood a detailed map might one day come in handy. She knew most of the doors would be locked against her prying, of course, and that the Count would unfailingly materialize to redirect her wanderings. And, as well, the main building tended to be locked up at night, especially when the Count was away, sealing her up like a prisoner and preventing her from exploring more thoroughly— and discreetly—the extent of the castle grounds. But in a week she'd developed a good picture of the castle's layout, even if her hand drawn map sent some rooms' dimensions absurdly outside the main building's walls. She'd discovered where the Great Library would be (the room was enormous and when filled would be quite spectacular), and had learned which tower the scientific equipment had been deposited (where a Great Laboratory would someday be housed). And, at length, by his preventing her from going this way or that, she knew keenly what areas of the castle the Count was most sensitive to remain private and kept off limits.

The madness grew.

A week of tremendous snow storms filled the courtyard and made the outer castle walls disappear. She'd thought of her village, of Cristine, and of her father. Each one had their own turn of hours-long feverish contemplation. What must the village look like today? Were the passes cut off by the snow? Did everyone have enough to eat? Were they safe from sickness, or were they shut in their own homes against an epidemic? Was Cristine still hurting from Amalina's sudden departure? Had she turned her sadness against herself, or was she finally standing bravely against the taunts of the other girls? And Dragomir ... well, Amalina's torture and worry over his health and his ability to cope with her loss as a business partner, a daughter, and a companion, has already been well established. And all of that was magnified out of proportion to the point that she cried herself sick.

The madness grew.

Careful observation confirmed a strange suspicion, by having recorded the details (secretly) in the margins of the library catalog, that the Count's hunts could be detected—easily detected—by the sounds of several of the wild animal species inhabiting the mountains and forests around the castle. His departures and arrivals, she'd noted, were announced by either the wild howl of wolves, or the screech of bats, or the tooting of owls. The sounds erupting suddenly upon a sunset, dying out shortly after they started, only to begin again many hours later, often just before dawn, presaging his return by about half an hour. On nights he didn't hunt, but stayed in to rest or amuse himself with scientific experiments, the mountainside remained quiet (except the wail and the wind, of course). Why it was one animal or the other on any given night Amalina didn't know, but she'd found their behavior novel and interesting, and she began to associate these animals with him.

The madness grew.

And finally, the obsession of the screaming woman had taken hold. Even with the windows shut tight, the wailing penetrated into her room. Its sound welled up from somewhere below—far beyond the parts of the castle she was allowed to visit (though other times it seemed closer). She thought the wail so sad to listen to, so pathetic. The need to see this person, to comfort her, to silence her pain became as needful a desire as anything she had ever experienced in her life. She felt she must see the face that produced such a horrible sound. She must, as her thoughts had turned, free her from her torment. Whatever torment that might be. Even if, in the end, she could not bring herself to kill the Count, she could easily dare to rescue this poor woman.

When Amalina's service to the Count was over, and it was time to leave the castle for good, she had promised—promised to this woman privately, somewhere in a midnight hour, while listening to that heartrending sound— that she would rescue the wailing woman, and take her to her village.

To this end, Amalina had begun to hoard lengths of cloth: table and furniture coverings, unused drapes from closets, thinner velvet tapestries from abandoned rooms, unwanted old dresses from the castle's supplies. All had found their way to her room and been hidden from sight. As she had read of princesses doing in various fables, she took these pieces and tied them together, end to end, and then, securing one end to the leg of her four poster bed, hung its full length out her window. The rough-but-ready rope nearly touched the snow drifts below. If she should ever dare to use it, it would allow Amalina access to the windows of almost every off-limits room in this tower. One of them, she figured by the closeness of the sound (on some nights), could be the room that contained the screaming woman.

Before the rescue happened she would need to confirm where this woman was, and that this woman would be easy to free, and that she would be healthy enough to travel.

• • •

For several days the weather had warmed in the mountains, and Genadie, barely limping, had sprung from his closet with a strange air of numb-bodied determination matched with a peculiar miserableness. Grumbling, he'd folded and set aside his blood-encrusted bandages (perhaps for another day), had gathered what seemed to be wild horses that had strangely wandered up to the castle gates, harnessed them, and then stuck them to what looked like a massive angled shovel bolted to the front of a sledge. Cracking a whip above their heads, the horses moved, and with this ingenious device, acting like a plough, he'd begun clearing away the snow from the courtyard. The horses had whinnied in protest, the dull blade of this plough scraping with a clatter on the icy stones. It was noisy. And that was before he added the great squeaking, rolling bar that compacted the snow in his wake, which went on just before they quit the castle, to attack the keep's approach and the road to the village.

In the afternoon, when Genadie had disappeared outside the castle walls for over an hour, and she couldn't hear the clamor of the sledge and horses anymore, she'd opened her window and thrown the full length of the multi-knotted rope down the side of the tower.

The air was cool, but compared to other days it felt no colder than a brisk spring day. Amalina hadn't bothered to warm her hands in the fire before wrapping the rope around her leg and arm, and, trying not to look down, shimmied out of her room, with the idea of testing the rope's strength for the night when she would put it into use.

As soon as she was out of the window, and her feet had touched the large stones, and she had felt her full weight catch in her arms, and her eyes had seen only the outside of the castle and the long drop below her, she knew she'd made a mistake. The reality—or the stupidity—of her decision to quit the warmth and safety of the uppermost room of the tower, trusting a descent to her malnourished limbs on a makeshift rope, had sunk in as fast as the wind cutting coldly through her dress.

Amalina had tried to shimmy upward, back up and onto the window ledge. But she could only bob her capped head, before feeling her weight tell her she would really be moving in one direction only—downward—and the little control she had over her drop would be how fast. She could wrap her legs in the rope and hope to stay at her altitude until she froze into an icicle, or she could let go entirely and fall to the welcoming stones that were hidden under the snow below. Or, she'd decided, she could carefully—oh so carefully—let one arm lower and secure it as best she could in the rope, and then repeat that action with the next limb, and proceed steadily downward.

She'd unwound the rope from her legs so that there was some slack, enough to let the uneven knots pass between her thighs without adding stress, and lowered herself some more.

She'd then let go with her upper hand and brought that one down below the left, which clutched the rope with white knuckles, the creases of skin filling in with a scary pink color.

Amalina had tried not to think of the bitter cold biting into her, or the fatal fall that seemed to be sucking at her legs and shoulders. She had concentrated on the simple work she had to perform to save her life. One arm, then the other, then one leg, then the other, one after the next, crawling backwards, never letting go.

She had reached a window and, unable to kick the wood covering in, had waited there for a time, the window's shallow edge giving her only a little rest. Just a little rest. A very short rest.

. . .

And this is where she remained. Stuck. Losing her body to the cold. Knowing she was either going to freeze to death there, or abandon control and fall. How dumb she felt, having gotten herself needlessly into this position.

She didn't know how long she'd waited, but she knew she had to try the next window down, or the next, or eventually reach the ground, or it was all over. She wanted to cry. She wanted to give up.

There was no shouting for help. If Genadie or the Count discovered her in this predicament, there was no telling the reaction. She breathed a sigh of relief that there were no boot prints, and no streaks of blood in the snow below, the way there were in other parts of the courtyard. The Count did not come to this section of the castle grounds. It was daylight, so the Count should be safely tucked away, anyway, wherever his chambers were. She was safe from detection as long as she made it down before Genadie returned.

So get going!

One arm, one arm. One leg, one leg. Down, down, down. Ignore the pain. Ignore the pounding rush of blood. Ignore the dangerous numbness. Keep the breath steady. Keep your eyes closed. It will all be over at some point. *It is nothing worse, Amalina, than kneading the endless balls of dough, or slopping those damned buckets of water from the well, or chopping, chopping, chopping the hard, fat logs into fire wood.*

She found another window ledge, this one narrower than the last. She couldn't kick its shutters open. And she couldn't stop, of course. Was this the room the woman cried from at night? Oh, well. She wouldn't find out today.

Down.

Down.

Down.

Another window. Another ledge.

How far was she from the ground?

Oh, don't look down! Too far!

She tried to swing her leg to kick the window's shutter open. Her foot bounded off it. She wanted to scream.

Is the woman inside here? Can she hear me? Open the window! Let me in!

Now Amalina needed the wailing woman to rescue her! What a laugh.

Amalina laughed madly. And she kicked the shutter again.

The board covering the window shoved out at her, opening wide, knocking her backward.

A very handsome man's face was there inside. She'd never seen it before: this young, good-looking face.

His eyes went wide. Probably as wide as hers.

"Who in the world—?" he said.

But at that instant Amalina lost her grip on the rope, and as she rushed to the ground, she heard nothing more.

20

The Most Talented People Alive

"Welcome," said the Count with a warm but measured tone, as he eyed these two strangers with a look that was both glistening and hungry, while stroking the right side of his mustache with long, soothing pulls. So while his delivery was stately, he resembled a cat recently awoke from a nap, debating whether he wanted to play with his toys or to commence eating them.

"Welcome all … to the High Castle of House Tepsji."

"Don't be so formal," the woman wearing the fur coat laughed. "We aren't one of your *aristocrats*."

"How else should one welcome one's dearest friends into one's home?" he asked with genuine curiosity, still pulling at the mustache.

"Friends?" She threw her head back and laughed even louder.

Her voice was low and sultry, the laugh was very deep for a woman. Its vibrations made Amalina's head throb.

"Home?" asked the handsome man just after her, echoing the Count's final word with disbelief (this was the handsome man who'd been at the window when Amalina fell). He stood just behind the woman, and added to her under his breath: "Anyone who calls a castle his 'home' I'll gladly accept as a 'friend'. He can call himself anything he wants, if he lets me in the door."

"Well," the Count began with an affected purr to the woman, "If not friends, what are we?"

The woman pointed to herself, showing off large, glittering rings on three of her fingers, "Katrina." She pointed at the Count, "Patron."

"Ah, yes," the Count chortled. His low growling laugh meshed with hers as they stared into each other's eyes, as if they were sharing a joke Amalina didn't quite understand. They both looked predatory. "Yes. Perfect."

"Well, you have us here," she said, surveying with dismay the entrance hall, which was almost empty now but for some remaining scientific debris, numerous candles and torches to light the cavern, the dull suits of armor and such, and a roaring fire in the giant fireplace. "But it doesn't look like you prepared for our arrival."

"I told you not to expect much," said the Count. "I have only my manservant—you of course remember him, and you saw him on the castle approach: Genadie—who is recovering from an injury, presently. I don't expect much from him, or any more help until we get closer to the arrival of our guests. So living conditions will be a bit bare-boned. Which is why I thought it a good idea for you to bring your own attendants along."

The Count nodded at the quaking peasants who were still standing at the entrance door, planted there as if too nerve-struck to enter. Their eyes were hard and shifted about nervously.

"I'm sure they can see well enough to your needs with what we have. And make you comfortable."

"Who is this?" the handsome man pointed to Amalina.

"I call her 'Mouse'," said the Count, glancing at her. "You will find her scurrying about and discover her in the most surprising places, no doubt. Quite curious what she gets up to."

The handsome man lifted an eyebrow and shot Amalina a look of knowing amusement.

Please don't say anything, she thought furiously, trying to signal him with her thoughts, her eyes. Her head throbbed, and she blinked wetly.

The handsome man winked at her, assuring her he held her confidence, and then said, "But she isn't a servant, then."

"More of a student, and my guest," the count answered. "But she's not so elevated within society that she can't help with service now and again if it is required of her. Isn't that so, Mouse?"

"Yes, sir."

"Don't hesitate to ask her for anything you might wish," said the Count.

"Empress Cleopatra's golden headdress—fitted with countless, oh, countless rubies," Katrina challenged.

"Within reason, of course," he said. "Our mouse is only a young woman and not an elemental, of which there are no such things in this world. Which is why I adore you, Katrina, as you come the closest on this inadequate plane to a divine spirit."

Katrina nodded, with her eyes closed, bending at the waist and spreading her arms aside, in a dramatic show of accepting his flattery. Then she gave a low laugh. Was it mockery? Or was she really some kind of creature as he was? Her shape was hidden within the fur, but she had a dark olive complexion, with large eyes, high cheekbones, a small (almost piggish) nose, and fat, round lips.

"Of course I haven't introduced you. How forgetful. Mouse, this is Katrina. And this is her partner Erik. Two of the most talented people alive."

"There are not many talented people who are dead," Erik joked, while half bowing to Amalina in a theatrical way. The Count shrugged at the statement. Katrina's interest was invested in counting the decorations in the entrance hall.

"I must attend to business," the Count said, withdrawing. "I just wanted to welcome you personally, and make sure all is acceptable to you. We will meet later tonight to talk. I will have Genadie escort you."

"Something to eat?" Erik mentioned, sounding off-hand.

"Oh, yes," the Count looked surprised. "Yes, I'd forgotten. Food ..."

"Katrina exists on flattery," Erik began another joke, his handsome, bright blue eyes still glancing at Amalina, to include her in his humorous act. "But as you know, I tend to eat like a moose, and I'm confident our attendants will have developed something of a hunger after being trapped on the sleigh for days."

"Yes, yes, of course." The Count looked annoyed. "It's unforgivable that I should forget such a detail as your host. It's been too long. Well, then, I didn't know exactly when you'd arrive, did I? But, no matter. I know you've already been to your rooms, Mouse can show your attendants to the kitchens, of course, of course. Everything is at their disposal to make you two as comfortable as can be. Mouse?"

"Yes, sir."

"Oh," said Katrina with a note of disappointment. She'd locked her eyes on the Count's. "I suppose the rooms are fine. But still, the castle is so ... empty. It feels so lonely."

"As I said before ... "

"Is there some reason my room has to be on one side of the castle and Erik's all the way on the other?"

"I wanted to give you the finest room, of course, my Katrina: the suite reserved for queens." the Count smiled but tugged at his mustache a little too severely. He levelled his deadly eyes at Erik. "Erik, as any man does in this world, does not care about where he lays his head at night. Isn't that so? And to obey the customs of this land, and to be respectful of my ancestors, he will stay in the bachelors' quarters."

"It's really no problem," Erik said quickly, assuring the Count that he wasn't the one who'd protested.

"Reserved for queens?" asked Katrina. "Are you sure you won't be disrespecting your ancestors by putting me in there?"

"You are as a queen to me," said the Count, bowing, but still pulling on the mustache.

Katrina pursed her lips, unhappy with the answer. "But your ancestors ..."

"I won't say a thing to them. Now, if there are no more complaints, I must return to my work."

The Count retreated through a door which locked behind him. A door Amalina had never yet been through.

Katrina and Erik exchanged curious looks. Her wide, sardonic smile had gone. Her round purple lips formed a pout.

Erik's handsome eyes, now showing irritation, or at least concern, gave Amalina one last wink, before everyone, in silence, left the chamber.

• • •

"This is all you have?" Katrina's female attendant Odetta said to Amalina with a worried, distracted air. She was a middle-aged woman who had obviously been fat once upon a time but was aging into thinness, her innate power wearing out her cheeks as she flew about with the energy of a small, nervous child. "Worse than I ever could have imagined when I caught sight of this place! Kralov will tell you, won't you, Kralov? When we rounded the mountain and I saw this castle I swore to him it didn't look right. I swore to him it would be bad inside. Didn't I Kralov? Eh, Kralov?"

Kralov, an old man still in his coat and fur hat, eyeing the decrepit kitchen, shrugged as if to say 'Leave me out of it.'

"I'm very sorry," said Amalina with embarrassment. She was opening cabinets hoping for anything edible she might have missed in her inventory—something that would at least seem acceptable to minor noble guests. "I didn't know anyone was coming. The Count didn't tell me. Neither did Genadie. I could have readied things. I could have ordered supplies. I could have made it look better and gotten it into shape. Maybe the chicken has laid an egg."

"Not one decent knife or fork," said Odetta, banging pots from their hooks. "You don't eat here?"

"No, I eat—" she stopped. Why *hadn't* she eaten in here?

"Where do you eat?" Odetta asked, still distracted by the neglect of the kitchen.

"I could get something from Genadie's cottage," Amalina volunteered. "Some more grain for the mash."

"Mash! Did you hear that Kralov? Worse than I thought. Didn't I tell you, Kralov? Didn't I?"

Kralov nodded and flipped a hand over his head, as if to say 'So who cares?' His eyes were growing larger, and filling with concern the longer his search continued. He was opening any door and drawer he could, moving in a slow, methodical fashion. Perhaps he was doing his own inventory. Or was he looking for something specific?

"At least the fire is going," Kralov growled.

"You didn't say where you eat, Mouse," said Odetta. It was as if her nerves wouldn't let her stop talking. "Mouse, Mouse. What kind of name is that? That's not a proper name. Your name really isn't Mouse, is it? Of course it isn't. What is your name?"

"It's Mouse," said Amalina. "Whatever the Count says."

"That's the way it is, is it? Well, you don't look like one. You're a pretty one. He only has eyes for gold, I suppose. And where do you eat, you said?"

"I didn't say."

"Well, say it. Where do you eat? Is it some secret, then?"

"I …" Amalina wasn't sure how she should answer. Her head pounded louder with each bang of a pot and slam of a drawer. Odetta's incessant talking wasn't helping either. "I have a separate place, outside the castle."

"Oh," Odetta exclaimed with relief. "Good for you, little mouse! If only I didn't have to see after Ms. Katrina, I wouldn't stay one hour within these walls. Maybe you can take Kralov with you, so he doesn't have to remain inside more than he has to. Will you take Kralov with you, then, little mouse?"

Now it was Amalina's turn to shrug.

"Let me go look for more provisions. There *is* some good cheese in that door there, if you want to have a look."

• • •

Amalina left Odetta and Kralov in the kitchens. The bustle the woman created, which would have been appreciated so long ago, was such an unwanted disturbance now; now that Amalina had grown used to the natural quiet of the castle. The babbling and clattering would take some getting used to. She wondered how long they would be staying. She also wondered how much they knew of the Count.

She also wondered who Odetta and Kralov's employers were. The two 'most talented people alive' were young and very attractive, almost unnaturally so. How did they know the Count? How were they not afraid of him?

"Genadie," she said, after locating him in his closet. He was lying on the bed with an arm over his eyes, one leg hanging over the side and touching the floor, as if he'd fallen clumsily onto it in a faint. He smelled heavily of sweat, cut with the crisp scent of snow. "Who are they?"

"Ugh," said Genadie.

"Poor Genadie, you look exhausted."

"Ugh," he said, weaker now.

"How far did you plow?"

"Ugh. Ugh."

"All right, I'll leave you alone. Get some rest. Their servants are in the kitchen."

It sounded as if he swore. His free arm smacked the bed and it creaked lightly at the childlike blow.

"Are you all right?"

The arm motioned for her to leave.

"You can't tell me who they are?"

His lips turned downwards. He didn't answer.

Amalina's head throbbed horribly. She thought to return to her room. To throw herself across her bed like Genadie. She wished she could take her head right off and bury it in the snow to cool. As she walked through the castle with a two pronged candlestick, the flames became four as her vision doubled and she felt nauseous.

She needed to get away. To rest. But also, she needed to think. What would happen now that the visitors were here? Did this mean her time at the castle was coming to a close? Could she leave with them? Could she enlist them? Could they be trusted?

She headed up the stairs to her bedroom.

A bright light coming round a turn in the stairs startled her. She thought of fire in an upper room, maybe her own. But then Erik rounded the corner holding a torch. He looked surprised to see her and grabbed his chest.

"My!" Erik laughed, recovering himself. "He was right, I wasn't expecting to see you here. Mouse, eh? You *do* get around. Were you coming to see me again?"

She didn't know if she should reveal where her bedroom was, up the same flight of stairs and still several stories higher. Of course, he was coming down from his own room, dressed in fancier clothes than what he was wearing when he'd first arrived, ones suited for the evening. He was making himself at home.

"Uh, no," said Amalina.

"Are you feeling well?"

Amalina nodded, even though she still felt as if she might cough her morning's meal onto his nice shoes.

"Are you sure?" His ice-blue eyes looked vivid and kindly in the torchlight. "That *was* you I saw earlier, wasn't it?"

Amalina looked around, and then nodded. He noticed her caution and lowered his voice.

"Gave me quite a surprise," he said. "Then you gave yourself an even bigger one, eh? Unless you are immortal, you have a snow drift to thank for your life."

"Thank you," Amalina whispered even lower than he, "for not mentioning it in front of everyone."

Erik smiled wryly and put a finger to his lips like he was shushing her. "Think nothing of it, Mouse. We know how to keep secrets. We are creatures of the utmost discretion. I wouldn't have even brought it up to you now if you didn't look a bit tired. Do you understand what I mean by 'discretion'?"

Amalina nodded.

"Sorry I wasn't quick enough to catch you when you—" his pretty blue eyes mimicked the surprise, then horror, of watching her fall. "I suppose I was wondering if you were some thief, or spy, or assassin. Never know what you'll find when you're in a castle. Or maybe I've heard too many stories. But now I'm to understand that you are just a curious little mouse."

Amalina bit her lip. Her nausea seemed to be lessening under his attractive gaze.

"Who are you really?" he asked casually.

There was the sound of movement on the stairs. It was a loud clomping of leather boots on stone. Then the Count rounded the corner and entered the light. On seeing Erik, the Count bowed.

"Mouse, I hope you are not bothering my guests," he said.

"Not at all," smiled Erik. He straightened up so that he was as tall as the Count, as if to compare their sizes. "Just on my way down, as she was on her way up."

"On your way down?"

"To see if Odetta has managed a meal yet. Kralov can be slow to see to me, especially in the winter. He says it's his bones, but really he cherishes all the holidays, and will use any excuse to avoid me."

"Yesss," the Count said absently, elongating the word, his tone and expression displaying his brutal indifference of Erik. The Count turned to Amalina. "Genadie is useless. I'll need you to bring Katrina to my private salon." He eyed Erik. He took Amalina by the elbow and guided her up the stairs. "This route will be faster. Good evening, Erik. Katrina will speak to you tomorrow morning. Have a pleasant dinner."

They walked up the stairs and could hear Erik moving in the opposite direction. Even with her aching head, Amalina noticed that the Count had arrived on foot—despite his ability to materialize wherever he chose—keeping up the pretense of needing to walk. That meant that he was preserving as a secret from these visitors at least a part of his power.

Then she realized in horror they were heading toward her room. Where the rope, which she'd hastily bundled underneath her bedcovers after she'd returned to the room (after her fall into the courtyard—and when her head was still swirling from the impact), would be so obvious.

"My private study is readied," said the Count in his mindless way, as if reminding himself instead of talking to her. "Katrina is in the uppermost suite of the opposing spire. You know where it is, as you've been there before. I believe it was your first room here. Yes. Well. Bring her to me."

"Yes, sir."

"You didn't reveal your real name to our guests," the Count more told than asked her.

"No, sir."

"They shall know you only as 'Mouse'. Do you understand?"

She was afraid to nod for fear of vomiting. "Yes, sir."

He placed a key in her hand. He gave her instructions on where to find the private study and what doors the key would open. The way he described it, it was as confusing as listening to the solution to a labyrinth. Though, in reality it was simple enough.

Then they were at Amalina's door. If he opened the door, he would see the rope. Even now, he might feel the cold breeze from under the door, as she hadn't yet gotten the window closed, and he might grow curious enough to enter.

Her head pulsed. She teetered on her feet.

The Count didn't notice. He was already gone.

21

Allies

Katrina didn't say a word to Amalina when she led the thin, beautiful, oddly commanding woman through the castle, the woman preferring to communicate by nods and smirks and flashing her eyes. She held her head back at all times, as if her spine was bent like a back-turned crescent, and though her narrow limbs were as languid as tendrils of grass in a vacillating river current, her body was as rigid as a scimitar. As she proceeded from her suite to the Count's private study, her large, hooded eyes roamed freely, grasping at all the details and character the castle provided. She gulped a couple times, shallowly, as if she were inwardly preparing herself.

Only when she arrived in the Count's study, which was modest in size compared to the reception halls but decorated lavishly in purple and red velvets, did she speak, not even waiting for Amalina to excuse herself. It was as if she wanted an audience.

"My Odetta is right," Katrina told the Count, who was lying across a divan in the style of a maharaja. "This is a miserable castle."

"Given time and money ... " he said, off hand and unconcerned.

"No." Katrina began to shake. "I thought this would be a proper castle. That there'd be interesting people here to talk to. Parties with music and dancing and great food and delicious wine, and the atmosphere to perform."

"I never promised you such things."

"Listen to me," she said, either ready to scream in anger, or to bawl, the small nostrils on her upturned nose flaring. "Right now, I could be in any city, in any palace I wanted. But you convinced me to come here, deep into the mountains. To think that I, Katrina Flauna, was lured to a freezing, rundown hunk of worthless stone on the promise of—"

"You weren't promised anything but one thing," said the Count with a look of amusement, his hand stroking his mustache like it was a pet cat. "There weren't to be parties, or galas, or soirees. Save your sensual appetites for later. You can always have that, dear Katrina. You are here today to enact an agreement, and prepare for perhaps your greatest role."

"You're right," Katrina nodded with a full-lipped pout, but sounding immediately convinced. She sauntered to the opposite side of the room, appraising the ancient paintings, and the solid gold candlestands there, caressing them lightly with the tip of her finger. "It was money that brought me. Now that I think of it. But I regret the error."

"Sir," said Amalina, backing up toward the door, feeling it rude to stay, "Should I leave?"

"Stay, Mouse," said the Count.

"I don't need rodents here," said Katrina, flicking her hand to dismiss her.

"As Katrina Flauna wishes," he said. "Mouse, run along to your hole."

Amalina bowed—as she felt she ought to—as if she was living a fairytale, and she was a servant. And then, awkwardly—as she'd never seen a servant in real life perform these actions, unless one counted Genadie—she exited the room. The keyhole, in the anteroom outside the study, was as good a place to listen, she thought.

She first brought her eye to the iron-plated keyhole, the size of a quail egg, and, seeing nothing but furniture, then turned her head to better hear the continuing conversation.

"My dearest Katrina—"

"Huh!"

"Was that really necessary?"

"I don't like mice and rats."

"I don't mean sending her away, I mean making such a fuss in front of her. I only call her Mouse. She is an excellent girl. And I don't want her led to a bad attitude by example. One willful woman is enough, and that's all I will stand for."

Katrina laughed.

Erik's handsome face appeared in front of Amalina. She almost fell into the door, but his hand steadied her. After putting a finger to his lips, he nodded and winked, and pointed with his head to the keyhole. Amalina nodded in return. He put his ear to the hole.

"You will pay me what you promised?" Katrina was asking the Count.

"Do you doubt me?"

"I trust no one. But more so someone who chooses to live in a place like this. Even my servants are offended."

The Count laughed. "I have financed you for a long time, no? All the while living here and there. This is only one of my properties. Though it's one I am very fond of. Please don't insult the high castle."

Erik took his perfectly sculpted ear away from the hole. He motioned for her to take the position. He put his hand on the latch and quietly, with expert precision, opened the door. Amalina could not believe what she was seeing. Her heart hammered. She thought they would be caught instantly. He cracked it enough to see into the room. Erik grinned at what he saw inside, fearless of consequences.

"I will declare this dump 'Count Tepsji's grand palace of pleasure'" Katrina was saying, "if what you promised to pay is true."

"You will be paid every last ounce."

"*We* will be paid," Katrina corrected him.

"Erik won't be doing a tenth of the work, I don't know why you even bothered to bring him along."

"We're a team. You know that."

"Suit yourself. You both will receive full payment on completion of the … what shall we call it? Is it a 'performance', yes? Or is it a mission?"

"Everything in life is a performance," she said. "So yes, you can call it that."

"And *you* can call my lovely little home 'the grand palace of pleasure'. I like the sound of it. Whisper it with your sweet voice into all the right ears."

"As long as I don't have to live here," she laughed her sarcastic laugh.

"So then it's settled," the Count sounded satisfied. "The preparation will not be long. We can go over it now, and be ready to begin in the morning."

"Whatever you want. The quicker the better."

"Oh, don't be like that," the Count hummed. "As cold as winter. You know you are my favorite above all else. I am so glad to see you. So glad you are here."

"Me too, my darling patron," she said warmly.

They spoke for a quarter hour longer. Amalina didn't understand most of what they were saying as they were so far away from the door, and not being contentious, their voices dropped to a more comfortable level. And what she did hear didn't make much sense to her. From the look on Erik's face, he knew what they were talking about.

Just before they said their goodbyes for the night, Erik closed the door noiselessly and waved his hand that Amalina should follow him. They quit the room and went through the halls that took them back to the great entrance. Here the air was much colder, the fire in the fireplace was burnt to nothing. Erik patted her on the shoulder as if to say 'goodbye and good night'. Then he left her in the direction of the tower where his room was. He did not look back.

Amalina waited dutifully in the entrance hall, building a new fire there until Katrina was shown into it.

"Good, you didn't wander too far," said the Count. "Take Lady Flauna to bed so she can have a good night's rest."

Again, Katrina did not say a word along the return trip. Except "Leave" when they reached her suite. Where Erik was waiting for her.

"I sent Odetta away," Erik explained to Katrina, shooting a guilty grin at Amalina.

"Leave," Katrina repeated to Amalina coldly, saying the same with her eyes.

Amalina nodded. As she turned in the hall, she heard Erik behind her: "Come. Let's talk."

. . .

Amalina was more than haggard, she felt as if she could collapse. The thought of walking to her own corner of the castle and the endless climb to her bed seemed impossible. She felt she would rather snuff out her candle and just go to sleep in the hallway until Genadie came for her. Just as it happened that night when the Count had blown out her candle, leaving her lost and directionless in the dark.

How many hours had she been awake now? Up since early morning, to ready the first meal. Then came her taxing descent outside the tower, which ended in a steep drop into a shallow snow drift (which only lightly cushioned her landing). And then, head throbbing, vision swirling, was the rushed, attempted cover up of her rope climb and its consequent fall: sprinting through the castle and up the stairs, and hauling back into the room the rope, which felt like it weighed ten times more than it ever had. Then forever sweeping the narrow courtyard of the drift and her prints in it. Then preparing the next meal. Then the official admission into the main room of the surprise visitors. Then the running around and escorting everyone, and everything else which followed. It felt like she'd crossed and recrossed the castle seven times, and gone up and down it seven times more, not counting the fall from the tower.

But still, something stirred in her. There was something she needed to do.

She thought of Erik, with his broad shoulders, and his unnaturally handsome face with those keen blue eyes, and his luxurious mane of blond hair, and how he'd shown her his allegiance by keeping her secret from the Count. This was someone she could count on. But he was behaving so cavalierly, sneaking about like a thief within the Count's home, he didn't know into what danger he was putting himself.

He did not understand that this castle was no ordinary castle, and Katrina's patron was no ordinary man. If he continued to sneak he would be caught. Not knowing what the consequences could be, she feared for his life.

Amalina decided she should warn her new ally of what he was up against. Tell him the whole truth, so that he couldn't dismiss her warnings so lightly. She wanted him (and his lady friend, despite her snootiness; and wanted even their charming attendants Odetta and Kralov) to get out of this alive, whatever they and the Count were up to.

She turned around and headed back up the hall. Better to catch him sneaking out of Katrina's room. If the Count appeared suddenly, and without warning—and he really *could!*—she could say she'd brought Erik to her as a courtesy, and kept watch over them both.

That's a good excuse, she congratulated herself, as her head and vision swam in the darkness.

When she reached the door, she could not help but put her ear to it, to listen if Erik was still inside.

She could not have expected what she heard next. So surprising was it, she put her *eye* to the keyhole, just to make sure it was true, before she felt the impulse to knock on the door and force her way in.

• • •

"I don't like it," said Katrina with her customary pout.

"Neither do I. And to place my room so far away from you ... On the other side of the castle."

"You think he did it on purpose?"

"Certainly. He doesn't like me. He wants to keep us well apart. If he could, he would separate us permanently."

Katrina let out a growling, sarcastic laugh. He joined her with a short, light laugh of his own.

"If only the prune knew," said Erik.

"But better he didn't," she warned. "How does it look, do you think?"

"All according to plan ... " he hummed confidently.

"But do you ... uh ... um ..."

"Do I what, Katrina?"

"Do you have any idea how to kill him?"

"He's old, isn't he?" Erik sneered, sounding surprised she'd asked such a thing.

"Not that old." Katrina said lazily, but with a hint of worry that he was being careless.

"It'll be easy enough," he reassured. "He is rich, he is royalty, and he is old, which means he is soft, he is stupid, and he is weak. Everything I am not."

"Weak? Haven't you looked into his eyes, Erik? There's a goodly power inside him."

"I think you've been looking too much into those eyes," said Erik, testily. "You think he's stronger than me?"

"You must take care, my love. All I'm saying is he may have strengths we don't know."

"No matter what hidden strengths he may hold against us, he has one fatal flaw of which *he* is completely unaware."

"What flaw is that?"

"He's in love with *you*. Have you seen the way he regards you? Crossed halfway across winter just to invite you here and embroil us in his plans, when he could have hired any woman at a quarter the price and with even less the frustration. Anyway, all this and more means one thing: he's in love with you." Erik held up a long knife. "That means he will present his back to me at some point."

"Our patron will die," Katrina's eyes glimmered greedily. "And we will have his money. All of it."

"His castle," he added.

"His lands," she concluded.

"Let's make this quick."

The two lovers kissed.

22

The Strigoi

There was a knock at the door. Erik and Katrina froze in their embrace. They looked in horror as the door opened.

"The Mouse?" Erik laughed in relief, as Amalina entered with large, rounded, fearful eyes.

Katrina flew from Erik's side, with Erik's knife in her hand. She shoved the door closed and had Amalina in her grasp before either of the others could react. Amalina gasped in surprise, then stared at the knife point just above her chest.

"What's the matter with you?" Katrina hissed at Erik. "She's his little spy!"

"No," said Erik, directing his bright blue eyes to Amalina's. "She's just a curious little mouse. Isn't she?"

"She heard us. She heard everything."

A flash of concern crossed Erik's face. His mouth became a small comma. "Were you listening at the door, little mouse? If you were ... I suppose I should have known better."

"What should we do?" asked Katrina, her voice husky in fear, driven further into madness by Erik's concern, which verified her own concern that Amalina just might have heard. She pressed the knife to Amalina's chest. It didn't hurt and she saw that the woman wasn't ready to kill her. But Amalina stared as the sharp metal point disappeared into the first layer of cloth.

"Easy, Katrina. You're scaring her."

"Erik!" she snapped.

Erik crossed the room. Getting down on one knee, putting him below Amalina so that he looked up at her, he asked: "Why did you come to Lady Katrina Flauna's room, Mouse?"

"To ..." Amalina had been sure what she wanted to say when she'd knocked, and then when she had dared to enter without permission. But now, with her blood pumping, the feel of something sharp against her rib, and the pulse of pain in her head, she was confused. She couldn't remember what it was. "I ..."

"What did you hear?" Katrina asked into her ear, the hot breath tickling her neck. Some of Amalina's hair had come out from under her cap, and got into Katrina's mouth. The woman spit the lock out irritably. She felt the

                    C.L. Holmes

woman's chest press against her back with every heavy breath. Her thin, bony arm was painful across Amalina's neck.

"What did you hear?" Erik prompted in a softer voice, and with a warm, hopeful smile that was entirely false.

"You said you were … Were going to murder … to kill … him," said Amalina, still trying to recover her thoughts.

Katrina squealed nervously, and her breaths quickened at Amalina's back. She twisted her arms tighter, as if she thought the girl would buck her and attempt an escape.

"Erik!" Katrina hissed again.

"What? Do you want me to stab her for you?" Erik laughed, though his pretty, dread-filled eyes were pinning Amalina in place. "You thought you heard us say such a thing, little mouse? That we were going to kill the old Count? Did you, little mouse?"

Amalina nodded.

"You made a mistake," said Erik, as if trying to beguile her with his words and charming stare. "You thought you heard us say so, but it isn't true. Not at all."

"No," said Amalina. "I did … You did … You said it …"

"Erik!" groaned Katrina.

"But you didn't scurry back to him, to warn him," said Erik softly, his voice still kind. The light rimming his hair made his true-gold mane brighter than his face, which was mostly in shadow. So she could see a golden outline, and his great sparkling eyes, which made her feel like she was facing a lion. A gentle lion, from his gentle tone. "Why didn't you go warn him?"

"I … I wanted to warn *you*."

Katrina's nervous grip tightened even more. Her body shifted to turn away from the doorway.

"Warn us what?" asked Katrina, again blowing a lock of Amalina's hair out of her mouth.

"You have to be careful," she whispered. "He … He can hear anything. He can be anywhere in an instant."

Katrina's tight, painful hold slackened. She brought her head forward to put her ear closer to Amalina's mouth.

"He may look old to you, but he is very … very, very powerful. I have seen him kill people. A man. He is very quick."

"That geezer?" scoffed Erik.

"It's an act," she told him. "If you've never seen him do it. I'm telling you, you have to be careful."

"Why are you telling us this?" Katrina asked, her voice a whisper to match Amalina's. "You *want* us to kill him?"

Amalina nodded.

"Why?" asked Erik.

He's a monster, she thought.

"He must be stopped. I feared I'd have to do it alone. But I didn't think I could …"

Katrina released her hold on Amalina, but left a hand tentatively on her shoulder. Her hand massaged the shoulder, prompting Amalina to continue.

"*You* do it?" asked Erik.

"He's killed people I know. A dear friend." Amalina could never understand why she kept insisting that Lucinda Skeldar was her close friend when she spoke of her. They must have seen the strange tick in Amalina's expression when this irk troubled her, because the two exchanged looks. "Her name was Lucinda. She was just a girl just like me, and innocent as a lamb. He didn't have to—"

"You saw him kill a man, you said."

Amalina nodded. "Yes. He's killed lots of people."

Erik blew out a breath. "I never would have guessed. I thought he was just a regular."

She didn't know what he meant by 'a regular' but she quickly shot in: "No, he's a monster. A real monster. You mustn't take him lightly or he could kill you, too. The man I saw him murder was armed with pistols."

"Pistols!" Erik whistled.

"Keep your voice down!" Katrina growled at him. "I told you there was something strange about him."

"Did this man shoot our Count?"

"No, he didn't have time. He couldn't move fast enough. The count tore him to pieces."

Erik smiled a crooked smile. "You aren't telling us this in order to put a scare into us, are you, little mouse? You didn't come as a saboteur, to save your benefactor?"

Amalina shook her head, vigorously.

"I just want to help you. That's all. If you succeed, you will have saved hundreds of lives and avenged thousands more. You will be a hero."

Erik looked unsure of all this information. Especially the last bit.

"I'll be satisfied with his money. He has money here?"

Amalina shrugged. He'd paid for the equipment and the food, and the constant rotation of livestock in his stable, he must have money.

"Never mind that," said Katrina. "It's fine she's on our side, then. We've got an ally in his little mouse. But what does she want out of it? Eh?"

Katrina shot a look of suspicion at Amalina.

"I just want to go home," said Amalina, feeling a tear welling up. Feeling the warm hope that what she said could actually happen. "I don't want to be here anymore. I am *not* his little mouse."

"What of Genadie? Can we trust him?"

"No."

"Then what else do you have that can help us?"

"I know how he can be killed."

• • •

Early the next morning Amalina escorted Erik from his room to Genadie's hovel. After she made sure that Genadie was not inside—he hadn't been back since nestling himself in the castle closet, no matter that he was now mostly recovered—she ushered the handsome talent in and had him sit at the grey table, while she busied herself with preparing the morning mamaliga.

Erik surveyed the room and shook his head. "I didn't think it could get worse."

He took out a silk kerchief and held it in front of his nose, though trying not to be obvious about it.

"Does it smell in here?"

"I'm sensitive. Especially to smoke."

Amalina nodded at the lie, and shrugged it off. She swung the pot over the fire and began to stir the contents.

"I'm sure Odetta can do better than that," said Erik, looking at the mash dubiously. "Why don't you just let that go and show me what I need?"

"I have to make everything appear normal," said Amalina, stirring the grain in the black pot. "Or he might get suspicious—erm, Genadie or the Count might get suspicious."

With a last look into the pot, satisfied it would hold without her stirring for a while, Amalina nodded and went to the far end of the room. From underneath the collapsing grey bedframe, Amalina pulled out a long length of iron, the tip of which had been flattened into something that looked roughly like a fish head.

"What is this?" asked Erik with pursed lips.

"A spear," said Amalina, looking embarrassed. "It's a spear."

"I need a spear?"

Amalina nodded and leaned it up against the table beside him. He gripped it at the middle to test its weight.

"You said he's so fast that a man with pistols had no time to kill him. A spear will do the trick?"

Amalina pulled from her dress the small book she had hidden there. She set it on the table, feeling her heart beating fast, wanting him to see it and believe.

"I've read through this whole thing," said Amalina, pressing her index finger on it, pointing out the title. 'Demonologae: Monsters In Our Lands And How To Destroy Them.' "I have systematically determined—"

"Systematically?" said Erik with amused condescension, eyeing her from behind the kerchief like she really was just the little child he considered her to be, and she trying to speak above her age.

"I have determined which ones he is not. So now I know which one he is. He is a Strigoi. Do you know what that is?"

"Of course. How would I not?" The fact that she'd challenged him, as if he wouldn't know such a simple thing, only made his condescension grow worse. Of course she was a young, foolish child, he thought, who took every discovery in the world as if she were the first to learn it. By his sorry smirk, Amalina saw this thought inside him, and thought in return that, in the light of day, he looked more vulnerable than beautiful. "Doesn't everyone know about the Strigoi? Where are you from that you'd need to learn it from a book?"

"I heard the word mentioned now and then," she said defensively. "I guess they were protecting a stupid little girl from nightmares. But, anyway, it doesn't matter if I knew what it was or not. Now I know all about *all* the monsters in our lands, and I know which one he is. And he is Strigoi."

"How do you arrive at that?" he asked.

She opened the book and went through the catalog of evidence against the Count. She realized, while reading through the list, that she'd come to her conclusion that the Count was a Strigoi more because the Count definitely did not fit within the strict definitions of the other monsters contained within the book, rather than meeting absolutely and concretely all the attributes of a Strigoi. This sudden realization did not convince Amalina that she was wrong, since she knew she was right, and she must be right: the Count was a Strigoi. But she recognized that arguing to Erik—who preferred to remain coolly skeptical to all reasoning—convincing him the man inhabiting this castle was such a fantastic spirit-creature, was going to fall flat, even when she added some of her own accounts of his super-humanity—which she knew, even as she said it, sounded like the imaginings of a child.

"It says the Strigoi plague their own families," Erik pointed out helpfully. "But you said he's killed many different people."

"Strigoi start with their families," she countered. "Those people are long gone. He is over a—well, I know for a fact that he is very, very old. His family must be dead. So he has moved on to plague the rest of the living. It then says in the book it's been heard they prey on infants, too, and not just their own family's babies, you see ..."

"You're actually saying our man here is dead?"

"A creature of death."

"How long have you known him?"

"Since the Spring."

"I've known him for years," Erik said as if playing a trump card. "You say he can appear at will anywhere. Well, why not here now?" He said loudly to the walls: "We are plotting against you—!"

"Please don't!" Amalina whispered quickly.

"All I know of him: he is a connoisseur of the arts and a filthy rich one at that. I've seen many men such as him and they are all eccentric—do you know what that word 'eccentric' means? And I know at least two of them who can pull that same trick, appearing here and there as they please—but it's always in their own homes. They are benefactors to magicians, who teach them to install false walls and hidden corridors, so they can startle their gullible guests when they like. But now, how about this, Mouse: I know our man here is filthy rich. How does he make his money if he's so busy killing people? And how does he remain above the law?"

"First, he's a count, and he doesn't spend on anything he doesn't have to. You can see that from the state of this castle, can't you? But, I mean, he owns a castle!"

Erik made a face.

"There are plenty of destitute royals," he began with a sigh, "always flouting their titles without the wherewithal to purchase so much as a cup of tea. Gripping their last holdings: some square bit of useless land or a decrepit castle, usually. But this man has never mentioned he was a count, or any other bit of royal blood, even though it would have furthered his cause. Not mentioned it once did he, as it happens, until he met with us last spring. And, for the years I've known him, he has the tastes, desires and free-spending habits of one of the most sodden merchants I've ever met. Which means he's making money somewhere. So I'd more believe that he's an export magnate who's bought himself a castle and a title off of one of those deadbeat aristocrats, and has hurried us out here to impress Lady Katrina Flauna over it, than he was a mystical 'creature of death'."

"I don't know how he has appeared to you, or even why," Amalina countered, feeling hotter out of frustration than if standing over an oven. She moved to the pot to stir the mash (and blow off steam). "I don't even know why you are arguing with me. I'm telling you—I am warning you— he is an inhuman creature who thrives on the blood of the living. I have seen it."

"And I have never seen one hint of such a thing, and it runs contrary to the reason Katrina and I are here. In fact, he could have killed us many a night if he'd chosen to, but he did not. Why go through this charade, build up such a wild plot for us, if he could make off with our lives instantly?"

"He has a purpose for you," Amalina concluded with a smirk. "Just like he has for me. And whatever it is, you can go along with it, and maybe end up stuck here as long as I've been, or Genadie, or even longer. But since I know you had some plan to try to do away with him, I thought you'd better have the weapon to do it and not get yourself killed."

Erik took this in with a sudden serious look.

"Still, though … this spear?" He looked at it like it was as potent as a lengthy sardine. He patted the knife in his belt. "I know how to use this one."

"And you'll get to use it. But assuming we can't find where he rests, though—and I'm sure we can't because I've been searching for it for almost half a year—you'll have to catch him by surprise when he's awake. If you can take him by surprise you'll need to run him through with this," she touched the spear, it felt as if a tingling current was charged through it, "best from behind, through the skull, or otherwise through the chest. And you pin him to a wall, or a table. You make sure that he can't move. Then you cut off his head."

Erik stared at her for a quiet moment, with his beautiful blue eyes.

"You were planning to do that?" he asked.

Amalina stared into the bubbling pot. She shrugged once.

"If I could ever find where he rests, that would have been easier. I could've killed him in his coffin without a fight. But if I couldn't find it … I had a plan—you don't have to look at me like that. I *did* have a plan. You know that massive chandelier in the great hall? You know how it has a chain to it, to raise and lower it? Well, I would fix this spear up there with it, and have a second chain attached to the spear which is then attached to a release. Then I would ask for his help to bring the chandelier down so I can clean it and put in some candles. When he stands in the right spot, I drop the spear through him." Amalina mimicked the spear shooting down from the high chandelier and through the Count's body. She'd felt very proud of her plan, but with his continued look of astonishment she felt it was weaker than she thought. That it was shot full of holes. "I'd have to test it out, of course. To make sure it would hit him just right … if I got him standing in the right spot."

"But how would you get the spear up there in the first place?"

"I'd have to sneak it up there myself, probably when I knew he was away from the castle and Genadie wasn't around."

"And create a release mechanism? And what if you fell and hurt yourself?"

"I've fallen from higher places," she said, ironically.

"And what would you tell the old geezer if you missed him?"

"What do you want?" she shrugged again, feeling defensive. "This way is ... Well, it looked like this plan was really going to be my only way to do it. I'd have to give it a try, wouldn't I? Whatever the danger or the cost."

"You are a very brave girl," said Erik with a big, admiring smile.

Amalina blushed. Even she didn't know if she would have ever really gone through with such a convoluted plan. Doing so would risk dying, and never seeing her father again. She saw herself spending years hammering out and perfecting the tip of the spear, never being satisfied with the catch release, balking at climbing up to the top of the chandelier to set the trap, always finding excuses in order to avoid actually making the attempt. Instead biding the time for her release from the castle.

That's why Erik and Katrina were sent here, maybe.

To help her accomplish her goal, she hoped.

"I'll need to speak with Katrina, of course," said Erik.

A Plan in Motion

"What's the matter with Genadie?" the Count asked Amalina, looking irritable so early in the morning.

"I don't know," she said. "All he does is lay there in bed moaning. He looks in pain. He probably shouldn't have driven the plow all the way—"

"Does he eat?"

"I can't say. He wouldn't let me feed him. I left the bowl yesterday, and when I came back this morning it was empty. I gave him another bowl. Doesn't look like he's touched the water."

"Haven't time for this," the Count muttered to himself. "You'll bring Lady Flauna to my private study. I'll be waiting. No matter what she says to me or you, you will stay in the room."

"Yes, sir."

The Count had lost more of his color. He'd obviously tried to cover as best he could by using a tinted face powder. His hair was slicked back. His large eyes, as always, rested both on and through her.

"Do you know who she is?" asked the Count.

"Who?"

"Lady Katrina Flauna, of course. Have you ever heard of her?"

"No."

He smiled and slitted his eyes cleverly.

"She is one of the most talented actresses in the country," he bragged. "She and her male friend are performers. They recite poetry, sing operas, reenact classic and modern plays. They are both beautiful and geniuses at their craft.

"So it is surprising," he continued in a different tone, and as if he were talking to himself instead of Amalina, "and entertaining from a different aspect, the way she fashions herself as something like an empress. These entertainers have no wealth or power. The little money they make only keeps for a day or so, and it is the leash that leads them about from city to city, dragging them into the company of whoever can afford them—and wishes to afford them—no matter how disagreeable the personality. She is a prostitute of the mind and social grace. And she thinks to humble me, to humiliate me, by insulting my high castle. While I offer her—I offer them both—the opportunity of their lifetimes."

His smile shifted, then closed.

"No matter what she says, you will stay in the room."

"Yes, sir."

"You will observe her. Watch closely and study the way she moves, the way she carries herself. This is important."

"Yes, sir."

"Get her."

"Yes, sir."

Amalina brought Katrina to the private study. As it was the night before, the beautiful woman said nothing to Amalina—beyond a cold reception of "Oh. The Mouse. You understand that whatever you've said to *him*—(meaning Erik)—nothing has changed."

But along the route, her beautiful eyes, which roamed and appraised every piece of furniture and decoration, landed on Amalina several times and seemed to want to cut into her.

The Count lifted effortlessly off the couch, and after embracing Lady Katrina Flauna, and dabbing kisses on her hands (which were the home to four enormously jeweled rings), circled her like a tiger sizing a kill.

"Dazzling," he said. "And I see you've worn my gifts to you, how thoughtful. Do you always wear them?"

"Yes," she said trying to be charming, though rather impatiently so. "But may I say—?"

"But I think," the Count interrupted, "while magnificent on those delicate fingers, they might be a little too much for our assignment. Be assured, they are befitting a woman of your standing within the community, and in the arts, or I would never have insisted on them. But in the circles you will be traveling they may be considered vulgar expressions. You will remove them of course."

"And what? Wear silver?" she asked cuttingly. "Now, I need to say—"

"No, no, no, Katrina. Never for you. Silver is so far below you, and does not compliment your natural color. It will always be gold for you, my precious one. Fine gold. White gold if it needs a different hue, but nothing less than gold. As I have always insisted for my finest maiden. But the stones on these rings are too large, and they would only invite derision and contempt flowing from pure jealousy. And we can't risk the slightest misstep."

"Shall I remove them now?"

"No, no, no, Katrina. Always wear them in my presence." He circled her and kissed her hands again, his nose rubbing on the rubies, emeralds and diamonds there. "Now! Let's get down to—"

"But before all that," she interrupted hotly. "I have to tell you something—"

"You've something to say?"

"Yes, I've been trying to tell you," she muttered in high irritation, regarding him like she might an inn keeper of the lowest order who'd been snubbing her. "My servant Odetta came to my room last night in quite a state of panic. She said she heard screams."

"But … she's in one of your suite's servant's rooms, isn't she?"

"Not anymore. She insisted on sleeping with me in my bed!"

"Your suite is on the far side of the castle, she shouldn't've heard anything," he said in his absent, inwardly conversational way, as if nobody else was in the room.

"What does that mean?" asked Katrina, for the first time looking less than confident in her complete command of the room. "Was she right?"

"Many people complain of the wind through the mountains. It's the wind. But I placed you in the tower least likely to be bothered by it. But it is the wind. So, let's never mind that and get down to—"

"I heard it too," she cut him off again, her head thrown imperiously back. "She made me open my window and I heard it, too."

"As I said," he looking unconcerned, "it's the wind. There's nothing to be done about it but shut your window again. Fortunately it only comes at night. Just go to sleep and it won't bother you."

"Better to be done here as soon as possible so I don't have hear it again. Let's get down to business."

"Mouse," the Count called to Amalina, "We will need your assistance."

"Yes, sir?" said Amalina, creeping in from the corner. It felt strange to enter into their circle, for their eyes, both hot and calculating, to be focused on her.

"Lady Katrina Flauna is a woman of remarkable intelligence. She can speak more than ten languages."

One brow arched over her arrogant eye, and her lips turned downward to form a haughty pout, to confirm her superiority over Amalina—and any other mere mortal. Her concern about the midnight wail had been instantly dispelled by the compliment.

"Let us begin," said the Count.

"With her?" asked Katrina, pointing to Amalina in surprise.

"She will be …" he mulled something over. "She will be a princess of the Franks, perhaps even related to Charles, who you've encountered at a wedding reception."

"Hello, Princess," Katrina snapped at Amalina in High Deutsch, as if to whip and punish her with the words—she obviously not believing that Amalina could understand, nor could adequately simulate being a princess.

"No, no, no, that won't do," groused the Count. "'Hello, Princess'? What are you doing, passing by on the way to market? Who would ever say such a common thing to a woman of rank and not expect execution by morning? Since you want to live to see the next day, my dear Lady Flauna, let's develop some sensibility. Oh, you know better."

"Apologies, beloved patron," Katrina curtsied, abashed by her impertinence. Her natural stiffness withdrew from her body and she became a supple vine of roses, her face as delicate and inviting as its glorious flower. She directed herself at Amalina, "My grace, such an honor it is to make your acquaintance this evening. May I say, you are even more beautiful than you've been described. Your eyes, your delicate chin, your hair. And the fairest of skin. Oh, and that dress, such an eye for—"

"I don't know if you're mocking my little mouse," the Count cut in. "But let's get serious. It was such a nice start you had there, but the princess does not need a laundry list of her favors."

"How many princesses have you met?" Katrina challenged.

"Enough," he answered, confidently.

"Not recently," she shot back. "How old are you? Times have changed since your day."

"I imagine so," he said, a sad frown setting in.

"And it's not the same with a man, anyway. Not to give away secrets of the toilet, dear patron, but one must set the princess on the highest pedestal, and before she can act embarrassed by your compliments you immediately set to placing your own self on a lower pedestal: 'If only I could get my hair to behave in this weather. Why can't my seamstress understand the new style? My hips won't allow anything that fetchingly small.' And then, if one is quick enough, on the next volley you find some target of derision, a common enemy for you both to pick over."

She had the Count's full attention. He was no longer the preoccupied, self-involved boor. He studied her every word, drinking them in with his eyes and ears greedily, as if hoping not to lose a single revelation. But her lesson was already done.

She turned to Amalina, and said in a neutral voice, "Now, do you understand what I said?"

"Yes, Lady Flauna. All of it, I think," Amalina answered in High Deutsch. "Your pronunciation is very good. It's impeccable. I still have a lot to learn, but I hope to speak as well as you one day."

Katrina's eyes widened. She stared in shock.

"Yes, the Mouse is not *untalented*," the Count said. "She knows the language very well, too. But let's move on. If at all possible, you will have been properly introduced to your peers beforehand, but let's hear you identify yourself. That is most important, of course."

"My name is Katarina Tepsji," she said, nodding. "The princess of Netz. We're cousins through 'so-and-so'—"

"Frankish," the Count reminded her helpfully. Katrina's shocked eyes still hadn't fallen away from Amalina, but they were hardening.

"—we're cousins through uncle Freidrich whose daughter married prince Baruk—"

"—My uncle—" the Count prompted her.

"—My uncle, who is Count Tepsji of Netz, has sent me here because he thought it would be good to meet our distant relatives, receive instruction in modern ways, and maybe make a name for myself." Katrina's eyes flashed evilly at Amalina. "Now, who exactly, may I ask, are you?"

"Katrina!" reprimanded the count.

Refocused, the rehearsal continued for hours. It was an endless repetition of introductions, recitals of family lineage (her 'own' family and those of the people she might encounter), the singing of traditional Ardeelian folk songs, etiquette, and dancing. All done in the languages Amalina knew, and the ones she had been studying, with Katrina growing ever more annoyed at Amalina's level of fluency and ability to keep up. Amalina surprised herself at the amount of language she had learned and retained in such a short amount of time, feeling that it was Katrina's inexplicable enmity that turned it into a competition, and the drive to prove herself was feeding her successes in this match. Katrina may be young, Amalina considered heatedly, but was old compared to Amalina, and she could out-do and out-dance this utterly practiced and graceful snob-squash if pushed. *Who does she think she is? With that little snout and stick legs, she's lucky to be considered so beautiful.*

At the end, when it was early afternoon, all were exhausted but the Count, who, though looking paler than ever, and his skin shriveled, had simply withdrawn his energies into himself. His eyes looking unattended, his expression one of supreme contentment.

"Satisfied?" asked Katrina, obviously resisting the urge to pant, or throw herself helplessly over the nearby divan.

The Count nodded blankly.

"You said I'd be introduced," she said in a challenging tone. "Who will introduce me?"

"Your partner, of course."

"Erik is up to the task, but he won't be convincing at all unless he is given the proper credentials. And he must have a letter for my introduction, by your own hand, and authenticated with your seal. I can wear whatever antiquated clothes you want to dowse me with, stuff me inside any rotten old carriage, nobody will open their door to me without a letter of call."

Amalina was impressed. Just as she was wanting to lie down to rest her aching feet, Lady Katrina Flauna—suffering the same pains as Amalina—

pulled herself up with invisible strings and stood imperiously over the Count. The Count glanced at her.

"Hm? What?"

"The letter of calling. To properly introduce me. To establish me as your true relation. You have drawn it up, haven't you?"

"Of course, it will be done."

"You haven't already?"

The Count's eyes reignited. He looked at her curiously. "You aren't leaving right *now*."

"But I need to see it. I need to know that you've done it to perfection. I've seen them by the hundreds, patron. And I've seen charlatans attempt to pass a counterfeit and be undone. I have my good name to protect, and so I will not continue in your employment unless I know you can deliver on your end … not just the money, but the most crucial of documents and verifications. I must see it."

The Count nodded. "The Lady Flauna is right. I have overlooked an important piece of our work. Forgive me, Lady. But, of course, that is why I had you come here to prepare instead of sending you off on your mission right away. So that we might equally test ourselves and discover any faults. This mission must be a success."

"This *performance*," she corrected. "Admirable foresight. Only you forgot the most important piece."

"But is it really needed?" he asked.

"Is my 'mission' then to be revealed as a hoax, and for my name to be disgraced? The only hope for my success is to carry the letter, written in your own hand, and sealed with your seal. That's the way it is done. That is the *only* way it is done."

"I suppose you're right," he smiled. He pulled the end of his mustache in thought.

"Write it up now, so I may correct any mistakes."

He glanced at her, but then stared at the wall for a minute.

"Patron," she prompted him.

"You may go," he told her.

"But the letter. Please write it."

"I will."

"Now."

"Now?"

"Yes, now," she said. "Why put it off. I must see with my own eyes that it'll pass muster, or we can call things off right now."

"But there's no reason. There are days before us."

"I have rehearsed, and rehearsed again, for hours on end. Pushing myself to the fullest, without eating, without drinking, without excusing myself over the slightest pains. Even without having seen the first coin of payment for my services. And now you would tell me, Lady Flauna, that you're too tired to write the most important item to the success of our mission?"

"I said nothing of being tired," laughed the Count. "I questioned the need for it now. You are tired, as you said. You are hungry and thirsty, no doubt. Your servants are waiting to receive you, and tend to you, and so why not take advantage of this time to rest? I was only thinking of you, my sweet Lady. This letter can be written any time."

"I say the time is now, Count Tepsji. Write it this moment. Prove to *me* you are a proper count, and the owner of this castle."

The Count smiled, nodded, then, pulling on the end of his mustache, went to a large mahogany desk with many drawers. He took a piece of old parchment from a drawer, and wrote on it using a pen with an extraordinarily long feather. The feather swished this way and that as he spelled carefully the letters. Katrina watched over his shoulder like a ravenous vulture. Amalina stifled a yawn as the process continued on for nearly half an hour.

When he was done, the Count blotted and salted the document, turned in his chair, and slid the paper with his fingertips across the desk, to where Katrina could best look it over. She nodded.

"I will take it with me to study it further. I'll have Erik look at it, too. He's seen them and may better be able to spot a mistake. But … the seal."

The Count picked up a stone cylinder off the desk and presented its chiseled end to her. She regarded the design of the seal, and looking satisfied, nodded.

"There is nothing to question about it," said the Count, still looking amused at Katrina. "It is as authentic as the sky and the earth."

"But," she said with thinning lips, eyes aflame with greed, "You have to put the seal on the letter and the envelope."

"It will be done," he said, "When I am satisfied all is perfect—"

"—But—"

"—and you are ready to begin your mission. Hopefully sooner than later."

"Amen to sooner," said Katrina, petulantly. "But why not place the seal now?"

"Because there is no reason in the world why it should be done this very instant," he said, tossing the seal into his jacket pocket, "the looking for the wax, and preparing it, while keeping you from the necessities of life. It's time for my afternoon rest. Mouse, show our Lady out."

24

Pocketbook and Pedigree

"It wasn't the wind," snarled Odetta. "It was a scream. You heard it, Lady 'Launa."

"Nonsense," Erik patted the air in reassurance with his perfectly built hand. "I heard it. It's louder in my room, actually. And it is, plain and simple, the wind. Let's not get your Lady worked up over nothing."

"It isn't *nothing*," hissed Katrina.

He sneered. "You're listening to Odetta now?"

"Oh! I knew I should never have come here!" Katrina continued. "Why must I be so greedy? Of course it was too good to be true. What an awful place. Screams in the night! What more?! We have to leave before the next storm, or we might be stranded here for a week. Oooh, such an idiot. I could have been in Istanbul!"

"Did you get the letter?" he asked calmly, as if to restore order.

"Yes!" Katrina threw it at him. He juggled it before catching it completely.

"Katrina!" he protested.

Then he opened it up and studied it.

"It's done," he said, with his eyes becoming sharp as he reread the letter of introduction. "We have it."

"The seal," Katrina pointed. "Without a seal it means nothing."

"Odetta," he said in a sweet voice, "Why don't you get us some wine to celebrate. Kralov told me he found bottles in the cellar."

"I don't want to leave the Lady," Odetta quivered. "Have the mouse do it. It's her place."

Amalina, who'd been observing the scene with interest—if nothing else because she was still unaccustomed to visitors, and found it entertaining to have the drama that had been playing out inside herself for months being voiced aloud by others—popped off the chair she was sitting. "Some of the wine is very nice," she said. "I can—"

"No," Erik frowned. "Odetta is Lady Flauna's maid. Odetta, you will please go get some wine so your Lady might enjoy her evening."

"I don't know where it is—eh, where they are, my lord."

"Kralov will show you." Erik motioned violently with his arm to Kralov, and the old man stood from the stool he was sitting on, bowed his head, and offered his arm to Odetta, who was trembling.

"Nothing to worry about," Kralov assured her with a warm wink. He pushed back his fur hat and led her to the door.

"Why does Mouse get to stay behind?"

"Lord and Lady have their reasons, Odi," he said as they left.

"Easy enough," whispered Erik as soon as the door was closed. "Doesn't matter if the seal is on the letter or not, we have the paper. The legal writ!"

"It doesn't count without a seal," said Katrina.

"Do you know where the stamp is?" Erik asked Amalina.

"Yes."

"We both do," said Katrina. "He put it in his pocket."

"Doesn't matter where it is, as long as we're sure it's in this castle. To hell with him. Once our patron is dead, we can stamp it ourselves with the seal."

Katrina's expression said 'why didn't I think of that?'

"But how'll it be done?" she asked, her voice returning to its calculating calm. "What if what the mouse said about him—Mischa being some king of monsters—is right?"

Amalina looked to Erik. He shrugged at her.

"I told her everything you told me," he explained to Amalina. "You knew I would, didn't you?"

"Well," said Amalina, "it's true. He is a Strigoi. And a powerful one."

"And we know how to kill him," said Erik. "It is just a matter of doing so."

"You will have done a great good," said Amalina.

"And we will have done *ourselves* a great good. We will have inherited a fortune," Erik sang, grabbing Katrina by the waist and dancing her in a circle. He smiled brightly, trying to get a favorable reaction. "You see, little mouse, this parchment is a legal declaration that our Lady here is Count Tepsji's niece. This Count has no surviving family members. And so, when he dies, and we present this writ as proof of relations, and there could be no other claimants... Lady Flauna will become Countess Tepsji. The fool. The stupid, old fool."

Erik continued to swing Katrina round.

Amalina felt sick to her stomach as she watched the handsome Erik grin wildly, knowing that a plot so conceived was a murder. Something evil. These two were coldblooded murderers. They were monsters, just as the Count was. She felt surrounded and crushed-in by malevolent forces. And only being drawn further into their world of casual, permissive violence. This was not her, she thought. *I only want to stop him. I only want to go home.*

She began to hate the sight of these beautiful people.

"Have you done this before?" asked Amalina.

"Of course," chuckled Erik sarcastically. "Happens every day that a rich, obscure, titled patron-of-the-arts, with no living heirs, hires you to do some dirty work, and writes up for you a perfect proof-of-relations! Why, that is why I am a Prince so-and-so here, and a Baron there, and a King way over there. And our Lady is a countess so-and-so here, a princess-of-the-blood there, a queen over there, and, didn't you know, an actual empress in China!"

"Yes," Katrina sneered down at Amalina. "We are already rich beyond measure. We just do this for the fun of it."

"I meant, have you killed someone?" she asked defensively.

The dance came to a stop. Erik, with his handsome face, looked guilty and embarrassed. His face flushed.

"He's tried," said Katrina.

"I've done it. But I don't like to talk about it."

"He is a man of many confident words. But there's been little evidence."

"Watch me now," he said with a dark grin. "We've never had a chance like this before. Every reason not to act cruelly has been removed—he is not even a man at all, but a cursed spirit, demanding the sword of justice. With the convenient advantage of possessing the pocketbook and pedigree of a high nobleman."

Odetta and Kralov returned with the wine, five cups, and bread with a chunk of cheese. Katrina and Erik put on a show of celebration for their servants. But Amalina saw fear and hesitation in their eyes.

• • •

Wracked with doubt and confusion, and tipsy from the wine, Amalina found herself wandering into Genadie's closet. He was still on his bed, but now had worked himself into a ball, looking like a rolled up worm.

"Genadie," she said, touching him, fearing he might not move and was dead.

"Are you all right?" asked Genadie with a soft scraping voice.

"Yes, of course. Are you okay? Why don't you get up?"

"No need," he moaned. "No need. All is taken care of. Master does not need me."

"I need you," she said. "I'm doing everything now."

"Let *them* do it," he moaned.

"I can handle it," she said and patted him again. "Take your time and rest until you're better. You don't like them?"

"*They* aren't needed here. I don't understand why Master does the things he does sometimes."

"Do you ever think what your Master does is wrong? That it's evil?"

"Whatever Master does ... is what is right!" he croaked quickly. "He decides what is evil. He names it."

"*I* think what he does is evil," said Amalina.

"Never!" he hiccupped.

"Maybe he's an evil person, or maybe he isn't—"

"—person, huh!—"

"—But what he does—sometimes—is wrong and bad."

"Only natural for you to think that. Master says you are one of the innocent. And too good for your own cause."

"But now I am wondering about that," she said, idly smelling her hand to see if his musty scent had transferred to it. "What if you encountered something positively evil, and you wish to stop it, but the only way to do so is by using the services of another evil?"

Genadie's head shot up. He turned his body excitedly, like a flopping worm now, to face Amalina. His eyes were as bright as ever under long strands of greasy hair.

"You don't like them," he said with a smile. "Do you?"

"Them? Well, no."

"You think they're bad people."

"I think they're bad and wicked. And—"

"And you want Master to kill them—to destroy them!" he gasped.

"Well ..."

"No, it's all right, Ms. Dalca. So do I!" He was positively gleeful, his crooked fingers were tapping together (or missing each other by their mismatched crookedness) at the top of his cupped hands. "They are false people, aren't they? They are pretenders. It's all right to admit your hate for their kind, girl, because that is what they are. And such useless scum need destroying. Yes, I know you are too innocent, and too good for your own cause. Master has said so, hasn't he? But now you mustn't despair over such thoughts that naturally come in life. You've identified something as evil— those silken make-up artists—and you've perceived rightly a thing which should not be! You also see a way to remove their offensive presence from Olymp—uh, from the castle Send the world. But only by asking the assistance of someone you also consider—rightly or wrongly—'evil'. By this I mean our Master. Is it not wrong, you ask yourself, Ms. Dalca, to use one evil to remove another evil? Does this not also make *me* evil? But consider this, my star pupil: Are you not committing a greater good by doing this thing? They are both evil. Okay, we will grant you that it is so. But when a larger fish swallows a smaller fish, are you not left with one less fish? So then, won't you be left with one less evil?"

Amalina laughed.

"What?"

"You make things seem so simple."

"They are," he said. But then he flopped back down onto the bed with a groan of dismay. "And also, they are not, Ms. Dalca. I'd have you ask Master to cast them out, to kill them, to remove them from this plane of existence. But he will do only what is right. Which means, he'll do whatever he wants. And rarely what we ask of him."

"Oh."

"I'm glad you hate them, too," he said.

• • •

Erik studied the spear's fish head, then he set it back down across the stone anvil and sharpened its edge with the side of an andiron. Sweat beaded on his lovely forehead and soaked his linen shirt so that it clung to his well-formed shoulders and back. With his looks, he'd fit the description of any hero in a fairytale.

"You don't look like an actor," said Amalina, admiring his form from the small grey bench next to the fire. The effects of the wine had waned, but the morning's workout and the warmth of the lingering fire—or was it her lingering head injury?—made her feel drowsy. Watching him stirred something inside her and kept her awake with pleasant thoughts.

"I'm one of the most accomplished actors in the land," he said matter-of-factly, his mouth a straight line from his continuing work on the spear.

"The ones I've seen all look starved and ratty."

"Those fellows are the least accomplished ones."

"And they mostly look and act like women."

"I suppose the only ones you've seen are the ones who visited your village, the kind that roam the countryside in their colorful wagons like gypsies. Performing for coins for a few nights, stealing what they can get their hands on in the town before they move out."

"I don't know about stealing, but they do get our loaves from charity. They look so sick sometimes. As if they haven't had a meal in a week. How could you deny them?"

"Hm, loaves, yes," said Erik with a quick nod, his eyes still fixed on the spear's blade's edge. "Well, I'm not one of those kind. I never travel far from the cities, like Tsobl or Pest. I've played for Governors and Kings."

"You've seen the King?"

"Yes. But I've seen better and stranger things than him. Your King's just a regular soft-headed aristocrat wrapped in dreams of exploding cannons and legal paperwork."

"What's more interesting than a King?" asked Amalina.

Erik turned around, holding the spearhead up, and at an angle to the light, so he could see the edge better. His damp shirt stuck against his body, and she saw through its fabric the rounded details of his chest, and a line of darker hair that ran down his stomach. He pursed his lips and squinted his eyes while appraising the spear's sharpness. He shook his head. Then he looked at her.

"So ... you're from a bakery," he said. "In a small village. Is it near here?"

Amalina covered her mouth.

"Come now, Mouse, look at those muscles on you. You're no fairy princess. Look at those old provincial rags you wear today. And how about this bread you just made? It's as good as I can get in the capitol. Has the same knots and folds as what sits on the Governor's table. You know what you're doing, you little baker. The Count here hired you out from a shop, eh?"

"Uh," Amalina hesitated.

"Or he took you." Erik squinted at her. "He took you away, did he?"

She kept her hands to her mouth, but looked away to the loaf of bread he'd already eaten half of, then quickly—out of guilt, or shame—to the pot.

"Hmm, whatever for?" he murmured. He set the spear on the stone. "You know too much, I guess. Or something ... Hmm. He likes you. I can see by the way he looks at you. But he doesn't *love* you. So it isn't romance. No, it couldn't be that. Because if it was, he wouldn't have you stuck in here, serving meals. No ... "

He continued to stare at her. She felt uncomfortable being the subject of his appraising blue eyes.

"I couldn't say," she said, feeling forced to say something. "I'm not a servant, really, only helping out because Genadie's ill."

"Well, I've guessed the better part of your mystery, haven't I?" he pointed to his eyes, which seemed to glow in the light of the fire. "I'm an actor. We study people very well, and can size them up pretty quickly whether they they like it or not. Did I get you?"

Amalina nodded.

"What's your name?"

"I'm not supposed to say."

"So you'll help me do this," he said, putting his hand on the (theoretically) deadly spear, "but you won't tell me your name because *he* won't like it?"

"I, uh ... "

"That's all right. I get it. He told you not to tell us your name—for some reason. And so you obey, because you are a good girl." Erik grinned, and pulled his damp shirt from his skin. With a wink he said, "But he never told you not to kill him. That's an order you don't have to worry about disobeying."

Again, Amalina's stomach turned at the thought of it. To kill. To Murder. To assassinate. Even if it was the Count, the Monster who deserved the ultimate death, she felt to her core that it wasn't in her to do. That it was wrong.

"What's the matter?" asked Erik, putting on his jacket.

"Am I a coward …? I just don't want to … "

"You're a good girl," he said. "These aren't the things that good young women do. Men fight. Men kill."

Erik shivered. There was the look of fear, of apprehension, of doubt in his face.

No matter how bold, or cold-blooded, or cavalierly he spoke about killing, Katrina had already said that Erik hadnever done something like this before. That he was as innocent as Amalina when it came to murder.

"You said he must be pinned," said Erik.

"The book said you have to remove a Strigoi's head from his body," whispered Amalina. "But they aren't going to stand still for something like that. They are only helplessin their coffin, when they are at rest. Outside his resting place, he must be held down to the ground, or floor. I couldn't see any other way to hold him. The book … it describes a burgher finding a lance through a beheaded Strigoi, which had stuck the Strigoi's body to a tree."

"We really don't know where our employer's coffinis?" asked Erik, his eyebrow raised hopefully. "In the Castle, no doubt? There's no nearby mausoleum. Here now, we're assuming he sleeps in one. Have you seen where he sleeps?"

She shook her head.

"I've looked everywhere. Here …"

Amalina got off the bench. Her limbs felt sluggish. The air outside the range of the fire was very cold.

She led Erik back into the castle and up to her room. She pulled from underneath her bed—which was also stocked with the long, hand-knotted rope—her dress with the map on it. She pointed out the rooms she knew, what they were, and the parts of the building she was still unaware.

"Oh, I forgot to add this," said Amalina.

She took the piece of chalk rolled into the dress's hem, and added several new rooms in a central rear location that had been blank before. She was careful not to make the rooms too big, as she didn't know how they fit in, or noticed if there were extra doors leading off of them.

"This is his private study," she said. "Which I now have the key to. And its anteroom before it."

Erik's eyes jumped all over the map quickly. "This is the ground floor? Then these are the upper floors? This is your room? This looks like Katrina's room. Yes? Yes?"

"I also forgot to add in your rooms, on this level of the tower," she said, quickly correcting the omission.

He pointed to a small, childlike human figure in the ground floor area, which was fitted inside a box. "Here, what's this? This looks like a man in a coffin. That isn't him?"

Amalina laughed. "That's Genadie. He's sleeping in his little bed."

Erik frowned. "Oh, right. Forgot about that one. Could he be trouble for us?"

"He's still sleeping," she said to reassure him. "The Count hurt him terribly. I thought he'd die."

"He cleared the pass just the other day. He mustn't be too hurt."

"I don't think he'll be doing that again any time soon."

"So he's nothing to worry about," murmured Erik. "Assuming your Monster doesn't know what we're up to, and he isn't listening right now ..." he paused and looked around, allowing the Count an opportunity to appear in the room to contradict him "... maybe we can find him where he's sleeping. Right now."

Amalina's heart pounded against her chest. Suddenly her lethargy cleared, and she felt more aware and quick-witted than she ever had.

"Now?"

"You said he's resting. Why not look for him?"

"In his coffin."

"Right."

"So you believe me, then?"

Erik shook his head slowly. "It's hard to believe. But either way, there needs to be a plan, and for that, I need to know the true layout of this place, which means our searching this castle. If we happen to run across him during our search, and he's at peace in a coffin, it would be a good indication you are right. And we'll take advantage of the moment."

Erik arranged the knife at his side.

"What do we do if he is awake and he finds us out?" she asked.

"We tell him the truth: That his mouse is giving 'the Illustrious Erik Kosche' what even great crowned kings have given the illustrious Erik Kosche, and given to him gladly: a tour of the castle."

25

The Illustrious Erik

They stood in the hallway just outside Amalina's bedroom. Erik's jacket was pulled back over one hip, and there his hand twitched nervously on the hilt of his long knife. Illustrious Erik's features were somehow sharpened, his disarming smile and observant eyes thinner, more angular.

"And where did you say he went?" he asked her, pointing to where she'd told him the Count had been standing.

"I don't know where he went," she whispered, reminding him to keep quiet. "I didn't see him go anywhere. I just went back and took the other way that leads down the other hall. And he was there. Then, when I came back this way, he was here again."

"Show me."

Amalina led him to the opposite passage, and showed him where the Count had blocked her way. Here a glassed window let in the afternoon light, which was still bright because the sun hadn't fallen behind the mountain yet. It was warmer in this passage, but they could still see their breaths.

"Where?"

She stood in the spot and held up her arms to show him 'this is it.'

He went to her. Then he circled around her. Looking here, looking there.

He continued down the hall

"Where are you going?" she asked.

"This doesn't connect to the other hall?"

"Not at all," she said, following after him. "You'd have to go halfway down the tower before you can come back up on the other side, coming the other way."

Erik peered down the flight of stairs they came to. He stared at the wall. He shook his head, but with a look of cunning.

He went back to where she'd stood with her arms in the air. He circled again, observing the walls, the floors and the ceiling.

Breathlessly, he brought Amalina back to the first hallway and directed her to stand exactly where the Count had been. She did, this time pulling herself up as tall as she could and mimicking the Count's glare.

Again Erik circled Amalina, his gaze shooting across her body, over her shoulders, past her head, to pick out the walls, the ceiling and the floor. She could feel the imaginary beams of his sweet blue eyes as they warmly passed over her skin. Even deep in concentration they looked innocent and clear of subtlety. Like a faithful dog but with the weight and power of a young man.

Erik went to the wall. He spread out his hands and placed them on the stones. Then he pressed here and there, moving from one stone to the next. Then he rapped his knuckles on them. Then, with his fingertips, he tickled the spaces between the stones.

"Hidden corridor, I've seen it before," he was saying.

"He was here," Amalina told him, "but then, when I went past him to take the stairs, he was at the bottom of the stairs."

"Yes, a corridor," he said, still working the stone's joints, gritting his teeth at the effort.

He blew out a breath, and pushed away from the wall. He kicked the floor. Then he shook his head.

"Did he whistle or make any sounds?" Erik whistled softly, and snapped his fingers, looking round to see what effect they produced.

"No, he didn't," she was saying as he did so. "Not at first. But then he just talked to me."

"Did he repeat any words?"

"I don't remember. Maybe 'Ms. Dalca.' He's always saying that. Very annoying."

"Ms. Dalca. Ms. Dalca. Ms. Dalca," he said to the walls. He lowered his voice to imitate the Count's deep, growling basso. "Ms. Dalca."

"Just like that, yes." she said. "What are you doing?"

"He does something to activate the door."

"But what if there is no door?" she said. "I'm telling you, even if there was, he couldn't jump through it faster than a blink."

"Are you faster than a blink?" he whispered with a smile.

"No."

"Well, you see, he doesn't have to move as fast as a blink, he only has to be faster than you."

As much as he'd won the argument with her, Erik's expression wore the dismay of someone who hadn't won the silent argument. He hadn't actually *disproven* her.

"Mirrors, maybe? But there aren't ... I don't know. Let's move on," he suggested.

Amalina gave him a quick tour of the castle. At each turn they paused slightly to listen to the room or passage ahead. It reminded Amalina of the way Genadie would tentatively move through the place, shy of meeting with the Count. This similarity irritated Amalina. But caution was necessary now, she reminded herself. Erik hesitating made it all the worse, though. It made him look weak somehow.

What should he do? Parade through the place, belting out songs at the top of his lungs?

She nodded with a thought, and said as they approached the inner areas of the castle, "And here, Mr. Kosche, is a hall to the kitchens. Let's see if anyone is there."

Erik was surprised by her sudden voice, but then he winked at her with a smile.

"Thank you, yes," he said loudly, but not over-the-top. It was a cheerful, slightly bored tone. "Let's see if old Odetta might be stirring up something for the Lady in there. Maybe we can have a taste. I don't smell anything."

The kitchen was empty. Erik smirked and shook his head.

"Damned Odetta," he whispered. "She's probably still hiding under the Lady's covers. Makes matters all the worse, infecting dear Katrina with her superstitious nonsense." Speaking louder, he said: "Odetta! Odetta! Get to work you rascal!"

"Be careful," Amalina hushed him, "you might wake him if you're too loud."

"How much time do we have left before he's gotten all of his rest? He's either up by now, or if he isn't, he's such a tired old sack he'll be out until dinnertime.

"Meanwhile," he said loudly again. "Let's see if we can't scare up something real tasty!"

Erik tried all the drawers and cupboards and side tables and closets, testing all the walls and stones and any surface he could fondle. He even took a scoop shaped andiron, and through the fire poked at the hearth's rear wall.

"Cellar?"

"There's the cellar. Then there are the lower chambers. Probably that's what they used as dungeons."

"We can get there?"

"Yes. Just bring that torch."

He did. Down the stone stairs was the cellar, with some extra storage space for empty boxes and bags. Racks of wine, mostly empty, lined a side room. Then, along a lonely stone corridor, came a series of rooms that were empty except for thick mounds of dust gathered in the corners.

"I swept it all out. But that was months ago," Amalina told him. "I'm not scared, but I don't really like it down here anyway. And there's no real reason to keep it clean. But I like to keep things clean."

Still holding the andiron, Erick knocked it along the walls. Almost carelessly so. Instead of acting as if they were closing in on their foe, he had the air of someone who'd lost patience with the hunt and knew they weren't even close. His tappings didn't reveal any hidden corridors.

"You said the family hasn't a mausoleum?" he said loudly, for the Count's benefit. "No crypts for their cherished ancestors?"

"Not that I've ever seen."

"Strange, for a family of such renown. But I've seen stranger things. Maybe in another of their properties, perhaps."

He smacked the wall one last time, with a frustrated stroke.

"All right, let's go back up."

Amalina took him to the last place on the tour, the set of rooms where, she considered now, the tour should have begun. It was the area leading to the Count's private study. Now there was little time. They'd spent so much of the day, it was only logical the Count had had his rest and would be out of his coffin, and reenergized for any kind of conflict.

She put her finger to her lips to keep Erik quiet, but, thinking better of it, said loudly to him: "I'm not sure if he's in, but it really is a nice little chamber, and I don't think he'd mind you having a peek, as Lady Flauna has already been inside."

The study door was locked.

Amalina felt her blood surge. She hadn't locked it when she left. The Count had another key. Had he locked it from inside? Or was he already up and about?

She took out her key and used it.

The study was extremely dark and cold. The fire that had once blazed in the small fireplace had long burnt out. She took the torch from Erik and poked it inside the room. It reminded Amalina of the street lamps on the night Lucinda died, the way the torchlight seemed to fail in the overwhelming darkness, barely bringing the bookshelves and cabinet and divan to light. The cabinet and desk and back wall were out of sight. It was creepier here than in the dusty 'dungeon'.

Amalina pulled out of the room and locked it.

"I think he's still napping," she told Erik in a low voice, though she didn't know why she felt that was so. "Let's go."

"Bring me back to the library," he said.

• • •

The light outside the glass windows was darkening. Evening would arrive soon.

The room that was to be the Great Library was still relatively untroubled by books. There were several large stacks on the floor, but the shelves were empty. It seemed a very lonely place, but one that could come alive in the right circumstances. If the fireplace were lit. If the large chairs were occupied. If the giant wood shelves were fully stocked. At this point it was a vast gutted husk. Or, with a positive frame of mind, more like a pleasing, large shell awaiting occupation.

Erik nodded with a grim look.

"Here," he said in a low voice. He bent his finger at her. She came close to him.

"This is the place."

She thought he was about to tap and scrape at the walls again, the way he was looking around. But then he lowered himself as he had once before, this time getting down onto one knee. He looked up into her face.

"Easy enough," he said darkly. "And it's the only place for it. You see it, don't you?"

Amalina looked around, not sure what she should be seeing.

"All the other rooms, their walls are solid stone. This is the only room where the walls are completely wood. Every angle. You see?" He pointed this way and that. "If I'm looking to peg the poor bastard someplace, here I can't miss."

"Oh, yes," she said. "I hadn't considered that."

"Yes, your plan was more dangerous than realistic. I'm glad you didn't get a chance to try it. Better to leave the killing business to me."

He ran his hand over his forehead, wiping sweat away from a brow that should have been dry in such a cold room. His fingers were trembling. But he noticed this and steadied them.

"So what is going to happen is, tomorrow, when you and Katrina are rehearsing in the study with our good man, the Count," his voice hit sarcastically hard on '*our good man*', "I will bring the spear here to the library. I will get behind the tapestry there, and maybe bring one of those stacks closer to hide my feet."

Amalina watched as his eyes traced the action in the room, envisioning it in reality.

"When your rehearsal is over, and he is hopefully more tired than we'd usually find him, I'll have Odetta announce that I want to speak with him. About something important which jeopardizes my participation in the coming mission and that I must speak to him immediately and alone. I will have Kralov dress up in my housecoat, the one the dear patron has seen me wearing, and prop him up in front of the window there at the far end of the room. The light will make his figure indistinct to anyone just entering from the hall. And the distance will require someone to enter the room fully to get a better look.

"Whether the Count enters the library through the door," Erik continued with a quick flick of his tongue on his lips, "or from a secret side passage, or he materializes from the air like a Strigoi, he will be facing Kralov's back, thinking he is me, and I will strike from behind, and drive the spear into the wall as hard as I can.

"The rest is butcher's work," concluded Erik with a brave smile that shook terribly.

"The Count doesn't like bright light," said Amalina. "He might come into the room if the window is open, or he might not."

Erik considered this for a moment.

"All the same … No, even better," he said. "You'll accompany our good man to the library. You make sure to seal the shutters and drapes over the windows, like a good little mouse. Tell him it's all safe and sound. I'll have Kralov make up a nice roaring fire in the fireplace, to stand in front of. When he comes in, he'll either be looking to make sure the windows are closed, or he'll be concentrating on the Illustrious Erik Kosche's well-upholstered backside at the fireplace. Either way: distracted.

"And so on …" he finished with a sad sigh.

He looked at Amalina, to see if she understood, or approved, or had something else to say that would foul his plans.

Not knowing what else to do, she nodded.

He wiped his forehead again, and then stood up with a bolt of resolve that didn't appear to last very long.

Before they quit the room, he gave it one last look. "Just make sure to get out of the way as quickly as you can. Find Katrina, and take her to her room. Don't move until I've come for you."

As romantic and chivalrous as it was meant to sound, his voice sounded lost and pathetic. Amalina didn't know how to tell him that she'd already seen a much worse crime, perpetrated on an innocent, than what he proposed. And more than that, that the walls in this room—in the whole castle—had been the stage for much, much, much worse.

• • •

Erik's steps were slow. Labored. He didn't say where they were going, but Amalina followed beside him and saw that they were returning to his room. It was like his whole body was a burden and his breaths were getting heavier and heavier.

As the reality of what he was about to do sank in, he was like a man walking to the gallows.

She'd seen this walk before. Years ago, a traitor to the crown had been caught outside her village and dragged to the sheriff's jail. When Tsobl's traveling court pronounced his sentence of execution, the gallows pole was set up, and the village—every man, woman, and child—was assembled by the soldiers to witness what becomes of a traitor to the government.

And Amalina had seen the wretch, a tousle-haired, bruised, bloodied man with eyes goggling vacantly with helpless terror, his lips quivering like ecstatic worms, walk the walk of the doomed. Each step toward the pole in the center square, it seemed a new hundred-weight was added to him, until he sank to the ground. He would have had to crawl to his final reward if the jeering soldiers hadn't been there to poke him with swords, to keep his spirits up and his body off the ground.

Erik's march to his room reminded her of this man.

She looked at him, at his face, trying to understand what he was thinking … The innocence Katrina had accused him of earlier must have been truer than Amalina suspected.

They stopped outside his door.

"I have killed," said Erik, almost under his breath.

Amalina froze. She didn't know what to say. Erik, with his handsome face lowered, and his soft blue eyes now looking levelly at her, was the picture of remorse, and oh so pitiable.

"You can never tell Katrina this," he continued, seeing something in Amalina's expression that told him he'd have to confess everything. "Nobody knows. But … you see … there was a man … no, I will tell you the truth: her brother. He blamed me for her becoming a player-of-the-stage. He said she had had a respectable future and that I had ruined her. But it wasn't true. It was my friend, Aldo, she'd fallen in love with. He drew her to our company. And the first time she performed before an audience, she learned how much she loved the power to move people's souls, and to feel the warmth of their adulation. Money meant nothing to her. The only thing she wanted from that very first moment was to capture and own every man and woman's heart.

"Ernst, her brother, for some reason fixed his wrath on me—and not Aldo. Maybe because we were once friends. But he soon saw that, whatever he might do to me to provoke her, she was never going to return to her family. Even threatening Aldo wouldn't turn her head, she was so far gone. So, seeing Katrina as forever lost to them, a bitter betrayal he could not stomach or die, he decided to stab her in the heart. He told me he'd do it, he warned me he'd do it … and I caught him, after he'd already killed Aldo … with the bloody dagger in hand … on his way to her tent."

Erik smiled grimly.

"It was easy to convince her that Ernst had killed her lover and run away, never to be seen again," he said. "But you see, little mouse, I can do what needs to be done. When I have to."

His awful, tortured smile spoke of an innocence torn up unfairly by the roots.

His inner pain made Amalina want to break down and cry, sensing he was, perhaps, a like-minded, soft spirit, one who had simply lived longer than she had and had been forced to act, where she was only now reaching the moment of her own trial and crisis.

"I keep wondering if there's another way," Amalina confided in a whisper. "Maybe it doesn't have to be this way."

"It's a perfect plan," said Erik. "Katrina will always be an angel to me, but she will not be beautiful forever. And then what will become of her? This is an opportunity we can't let slip."

"If you think so," said Amalina. She wished she could tell him to stop before it was too late. But the anxiety of being so close to the Monster's just end made her feel that, if she were to actually convince him not to do it—that if she were to see the Count in the months to follow still alive, strutting around with his complacent bloody grin—it would shatter her.

Erik saw her apprehension.

"Katrina may have put me through much more than you think is right, but I am always hers for the asking. She's found a way to elevate herself in the world—and by association me. I will now gladly help her reach the first golden step of her ascendance."

"You're not doing this just to make an actress a countess," Amalina reminded him—reminded them both. *This is something that needs to be done.*

"Tomorrow, it happens," he said before closing his door.

Back in her bedroom, and though it was still early in the evening, Amalina lay her weary head on her pillow, and waited to see if exhaustion would draw her into sleep quickly, or if the accumulating frets and fears of the next day would render impossible any rest.

She wasn't aware when she entered absolute unconsciousness.

26

Midnight Cries

Somewhere in the middle of the night the shrieks began. Amalina threw aside her covers, and sat at the edge of the bed, listening.

It was intermittent, much higher pitched than the wail, seemed like two voices at times, and came from beyond her doorway.

By the time Amalina lit a candle and was down the stairs, the shrieks had diminished to loud sobs and moans. And it seemed to emanate, as she now saw, from inside Erik's bedroom.

His door was open. Inside, Erik was holding Katrina, who was in a dramatic swoon, while Kralov, still in his fur cap and winter coats, patted Odetta's hand as she lay sprawled but flailing on the bed. Both women were crying and choking with some outrageous fear, their eyes either closed or, in turns, gaping at the window. The two were lacing their cries, each one driving the other louder, shriller, more intense, or levelling the other off. Their panic coming like waves.

"Please, Katrina," Erik was saying. "This isn't like you."

"What's the matter with you?" she shouted into the air. "How can you not hear it?"

"It's the wind, it's just the stupid wind!"

"It isn't the wind, you—" here she swore at length. "Listen to it! Oh! This castle is haunted! Haunted!"

"If I don't leave," groaned Odetta, "I will die."

"We must leave now," shouted Katrina. "Do you hear me, Erik? We won't survive the night with this horrible noise."

"What's come over you?" Erik pleaded.

"We have to leave! We must leave now!"

"What's going on?" Amalina asked. It was obvious what was happening, Amalina just hoped her voice might calm things.

Erik's handsome face had the hint of dark circles under his eyes. His blue eyes, looking intense, turned to Amalina, implored her to help, as if he were wrestling an impossible wild animal.

"They were frightened by the sound of the wind," Erik growled angrily. "They came to me to protect them—"

"It's even worse here!" Katrina snapped at Amalina, as if it was her fault. "What is the matter with you? Can't you hear it?"

"Will you tell her it's the wind, Mouse?"

Amalina hesitated, but Katrina didn't notice, anyway. She and her servant sobbed loudly in unison.

"The mouse can—" Katrina swore some more, and creatively. "That is some tormented soul crying out! Crying for our help from beyond the grave. But we can do nothing! Nothing!"

"She will blame us," Odetta groaned from the bed. "She will haunt us. She will curse us! Ow-wooooo!"

Odetta's cry matched sympathetically with the wail.

"Quiet with this foolishness!" Kralov shouted above them, though he continued to pat Odetta's hand tenderly.

"Let's leave!" Katrina begged, her eyes flowing with tears. "Please, let's leave. Leave!"

"Certainly," said Erik with a calming coo. "Yes, we will. Never mind the Count and all that business, we will leave straight away. Let's just calm down and get some rest and in the morning—"

"We leave now!"

"It's the middle of the night."

"We must leave this castle this instant!"

"Impossible. We have to pack—"

"We'll send for our belongings later," Katrina implored him. "But please ..."

"And where will we go?"

"Anywhere! Anywhere but here! I can't take that hideous cry another minute. I swear I shall kill myself."

"It *might* be just the wind," Amalina ventured lamely.

Katrina swore at the top of her lungs and launched from Erik's embrace. She was still in her house dress from that morning, and almost tripped over it as she threw out her arms to rake her fingernails at Amalina's face. Amalina fell back in surprise, and Erik and Kralov, who came off the bed in a bound, caught the most unladylike Lady Flauna. She dropped to the floor like a dead fish as soon as she was netted, and sent up a soul-shivering moan.

"All right," said Erik. "I'll get the horses and the carriage ready."

"Don't leave us alone!" said Katrina, grabbing hold of his arm with two hands. "We go now! Together! All of us!"

"Can you walk?" asked Erik.

Katrina, using Erik's body as leverage, got to her feet. Her mouth was a gritted, toothy frown, her nostrils curled, her eyes were wide but sunken into black puffy sockets. She moved like a machine for the door, whether Amalina was in her way or not.

"Come! Off the bed, you!" Kralov barked at Odetta. He held her around the waist and swept her large old body along the floor.

Amalina leapt ahead of them all, holding the candle high in the air and guiding them.

"It's freezing outside," said Erik.

"There are blankets in the carriage," Kralov said helpfully.

"Our coats!"

Erik swung his jacket off and, with a short shiver, wrapped Katrina. Kralov did the same for Odetta.

They moved as a tight package to the castle's great doors, all the while the castle's wail—or the thought of it—surrounded them. Katrina and Odetta had gone silent. All that could be heard besides the wail was everyone's nervous breathing.

"They won't open," muttered Erik, as he tried again and again to pull or press the front doors. "Is it locked?"

"Maybe the snow," Kralov suggested, adding his weight and muscle against it. He mentioned, lower with concern, "Or barred."

Odetta moaned, then Katrina joined her. They clutched each other and sank to their knees, their eyes focused on the great doors that wouldn't open.

"The window won't open," said Kralov, trying there. "I think the snow—"

"Mouse, where else?" asked Erik.

There were several doors and a handful of large windows which she knew accessed the other courtyards. She led the procession to them, one by one. Each one was closed as firmly as the last. And each failure to exit the castle increased the torment of Katrina and Odetta.

The final door would be the small one in the rear, just off the kitchens, that led to Genadie's hovel. She, like Genadie, rarely used it, preferring to use the front doors and circle around the courtyard, giving her more snatches of quiet time to herself—that is, until the winter months arrived. She hadn't even shown it to Erik on the tour, having decided that the less of the castle's secrets she divulged to the visitors, the more the Count would be satisfied.

Now was a good time to show them.

Amalina led them through the kitchens and into the cramped corridor that led to the exit. Running into a stone wall, she excused herself for being muddleheaded this late at night and turned them around. But then, once heading in the other direction, she realized she had been right in the first place. She went back and confirmed, with a sick feeling, that the door was not there. The door was gone.

She put her hand on the cold stone wall, and finding it to be real, she felt for a joint or a hinge of some kind between the stones. What had happened to the door? How did this wall get here?

She got the sudden feeling they had been sealed into the castle.

"What's the matter?" asked Erik.

"I seem to have forgotten the way," she said, avoiding all their eyes. "There's another. Let's go this way."

She didn't know where she would take them, she hurried ahead hoping to buy time to think.

Amalina heard the bell. The one that Genadie used to summon the Count. It wasn't loud, so it must have been coming from a room some distance from them.

The sick feeling grew.

She led them on.

"What's that sound?" asked Erik.

"Sounds like a bell," said Kralov.

"Mouse?" Erik asked Amalina.

"It's a bell."

"Why is the bell ringing, you worthless piece of—?" Katrina demanded, colorfully.

"Do you know what the bell means, little mouse?" Erik rephrased for her. "What's it for?"

"I'm not sure," she said, not wanting to panic them. "It could mean anything."

"Genadie?" Erik guessed.

"It would have to be him."

They moved down the hall.

The bell was still ringing.

Erik sniffed the air.

"This isn't an alarm of some kind? I don't smell a fire."

"Maybe he's in trouble," said Amalina. "And he's calling for help."

"Help from you, or Count Tepsji?" asked Erik.

"Never mind all that," said Katrina. "Get us out of here!"

Katrina broke away from old Odetta with a toss of her hands, she yanked the candle from Amalina and charged back toward the front doors.

"Wait," Erik called after her. "The doors won't open."

"If you can't open them, I will! I'll chop it down if I have to! I will burn it down if I have to."

The package shuffled in her wake.

When they entered *l'entrée grande*, Genadie pointed at them from the doors which were now open.

"There they are, Master!" he shouted gleefully. "Right there!"

The Count entered through the doors and shut them. He wore his thick cloak with the hood pulled back. He wiped a stain of blood on his lips, but only managed to smear the stain onto his cheek and chin.

"Dear Lady Flauna," he said with a polite grin, but with the rumbling tone of someone at the end of his patience. "My guests ... Are we having a celebration?"

"A celebration?" Katrina shouted, shaking her fist at him. "We are leaving!"

The Count stood very still in front of the doors.

"Our rehearsals are not yet complete."

"To hell with them. Find someone else. Maybe Umma Linz would find this horrorshow to her taste. But we are leaving this castle, right now."

"It's the middle of the night."

"That isn't your concern."

"Calm yourself, my lovely. There's no need to be this way. Tell me, what has upset you so? Has Mouse offended you?"

"This castle is haunted! Can't you hear the scream? That awful, awful scream! I can't stand it anymore! If I don't leave, I will die."

She took a few steps toward him. At first willful, but then each step after that was more difficult. As if he were a strong wind pushing back on her. Her steps faltered. He did not move, and when she stopped short of him—never mind the door—he stroked his mustache once.

"It is only the wind," he said.

She screamed at the top of her lungs.

"Who are you?" she cried, circling round in her spot. "What do you want? Leave us in peace!"

"It is the wind," he said again.

Erik came to her and put his arms around her shoulders.

"The Lady wishes to leave," Erik told the Count.

"There is no reason to do so. Let us not be childish. Morning will come and everyone will feel better with some rest."

Katrina closed her eyes and moaned.

"No," said Erik, "The Lady wishes to leave now. Tonight."

"Where will you go? There is a snow storm coming that will close the pass, if it hasn't already."

Katrina shrieked again. It made Amalina's head pound.

"Our carriage has sleigh rails, we will manage. Kralov is an expert at these things."

"I can get us through," Kralov affirmed. "The women are frightened."

"Not Lady Katrina Flauna," said the Count, irritable, sarcastic. "Not her."

"Please, Mischa ... Count," Erik said firmly. "We don't want to make a scene of it."

"Hasn't that already happened? But, no, you are right, let's not make anything of it. Let us all be reasonable. It will work out richly for everyone."

"Stand aside," said Erik. "We need to see to the horses and the sleigh."

"The door is frozen shut."

"We just saw it opened."

"No, it is late. It is dark. You are tired. You don't know what you saw. Even I could not open it if I wanted."

"We can cut it down if need be," Erik said hotly. "Kralov."

Kralov, old as he was, made an impressive figure when he stood straight up. He summoned a great power from somewhere inside and he looked as much of a match to the Count as Amalina could imagine. As Kralov moved for the door, the Count shifted his position to block him.

But Kralov continued forward, only now he pulled his sleeve back, readying his great arm to pulverize the man standing in his way.

Candle and torchlight lit the large room, leaving most of it in blackness, so nobody could swear to what they saw. There was a sudden blur, and the flames on the candle and torches fluttered. Then Kralov was hitting one of the remaining crates in back of the room with a groan.

"Kralov!" Erik shouted as he ran to him. Kralov held his capped head and shook it.

"Sorry," he said to Erik.

The Count stood where he always had, as if big old Kralov had been picked up by a hurricane and thrown across the room, but had left the master of the house standing.

"What I'm saying is, let's just give it another day," said the Count, calmly, his large eyes focused on Katrina, the gaze slightly weary but unblinking. "I can see only a few more days left of rehearsals."

Katrina moaned, but softer now.

"Or two, maybe, and I will be satisfied," the Count smiled gently. "Then you can leave, and never come again if that is your wish. But by honoring our plan, you will be so much better off. Is that not so, Lady Flauna—Lady Tepsji?"

He stroked the mustache with confidence now.

"But the screams," she said quietly, her voice hoarse.

"You will get used to it," he said. "Everyone does."

Kralov stood up, staring at the Count with open fear. Erik patted the dust off him.

"It's late," said Erik. "We should get some sleep. It was a long day, and our minds are not the best suited for travel. You can speak about it again with our kind patron in the morning, Katrina, dear."

"Take me to my room," she said. Her body slumped in defeat, she turned to the door that would lead her to her suite.

The Count added nothing. He stood there keeping them under his watch, stroking the mustache. Genadie was off to the side and looking disappointed that there weren't dead bodies to dispose of.

"You will not object," Erik told him, "Kralov and I will accompany Lady Flauna, and her maid, to her chamber. And we'll stay with them so long as their nerves are still touched."

"Mouse will see that you are all made comfortable," he smirked. He turned: "Mouse?"

Amalina went to the Count as Erik and Kralov quietly ushered the two women away.

"What happened, Ms. Dalca?" the Count hissed angrily into her ear.

"I don't know everything," Amalina said defensively. "I was asleep. But see, it's that terrible scream that did it."

"Didn't even have time to feed," he was saying to himself. "Not even a good drop. But it got all over me when that damned Genadie started ringing."

"What's that, Master?" Genadie leapt close at the mention of his name.

The Count warded him off with a wave.

"Bring two bottles of wine to Lady Flauna's room," he told Amalina. "Make sure they are comfortable, and make sure they get to sleep."

"Yes, sir."

"And see if you can't convince them the sound they hear is just the wind."

You're an idiot, she thought testily.

27

The Soft Opening

"**D**id you see the blood?" Katrina cried into Erik's shoulder. "It was all over his face like a mask. He didn't even notice. His shriveled little servant said nothing. Mouse said nothing! As if it wasn't even there! And did you see what he did to Kralov?"

Erik nodded. He looked at Kralov, who was sitting stiffly on a chair and staring without expression at the wall.

"Did you see, Erik?" she pleaded, grabbing a handful of his shirt.

"Of course I saw it," muttered Erik. "Everyone did."

Amalina kept quiet, and stayed in the corner of the room, stooped and exhausted, feeling annoyed at having become like a shadow of Genadie.

"It's true. Everything she said is true." Katrina looked at Amalina with fear in her eyes. "Our patron is nothing but a bloody fiend. A Strigoi. He'll kill us all."

"Unless we do as he wants …" Erik trailed off.

"Who knows what he's planned for us. Listen to that sound. Listen to that wailing! This castle is a prison. It'll be us next." She pushed her head against his chest. "No, Erik, I can't stay. I won't stay. Not another day. Not another hour. I'll leave, even if that means throwing myself off this tower to do it."

"Okay, okay," he soothed.

"I mean it," she said, shoving away from him. "Now. We leave now."

"No," he told her, holding her shoulders tightly with his large strong hands. "If we hope to live, we need a plan."

"A plan for what? You can't possibly kill him. Look at Kralov."

Kralov glanced at them guiltily and then back at the wall.

"No, my precious, the plan can still work," he said, with a cheerful note.

"I'm not staying here," she said.

"No, you aren't. You'll leave as soon as you can. But I can still make this work for us. I swear. It's just, now that I know what we're dealing with, I have to make some adjustments. That's all."

Katrina stared into his eyes.

"What are you talking about?"

"I swear it'll work. And we'll all get out of here. Just give me a couple hours, and it will work."

. . .

Erik sat for some time, with his hand over his face, thinking. Odetta sang folk songs at Katrina's request, to cover the faint but constant wail outside the window. Katrina fell to sleep first. Then, with Kralov picking up singing duty, Odetta slept by Katrina's side.

"Bring me that ridiculous rope of yours," Erik said to Amalina. "And your dress with the map. And better bring your heavy coat, too. The one you wear outside."

Amalina did so, fearing Genadie, or the Count, would be around every corner to catch her. When she returned, everyone was asleep except Erik. Kralov was laid out on the floor, his snoring completely blocking out the ghostly wail.

Erik shoved the rope and coat under the bed, then he studied the map printed on the dress, with his lips pursed. His features were shrewd and pointy once more, despite the darkening circles under his eyes.

"It's almost morning," he said. "You'll take Kralov down and prepare the morning meal. While you are doing that, I'll go to the library—or try to get down to the library, anyway. Watch out for me. Signal with a shout or something if you see 'our man'. We'll make this quick. Can't have the ladies waking up and going out of their minds. Then we'll meet up here again."

"Should I get the spear?" asked Amalina.

"Can you?" he asked. "It'll make things much easier."

She thought so.

"How about a bell? Like the one Genadie used."

"I have one."

"Even better. Make sure not to let it ring when you're carrying it, you understand, or they'll have you, the bell and the weapon. And, anyway, don't let anyone—well, don't let Genadie—catch you on the way back."

That was something she'd already begun to worry about, but his saying so amplified her nerves.

They woke Kralov. The only items Erik added to the instructions he'd given Amalina was that Kralov was to be as loud as he could be in the kitchen, and make the breakfast smelly.

"Burn something good," he told Kralov. "Have Amalina get you what you need, give you some of her dough to singe. Sing as loud and merry as you like. If and when Genadie comes, you make sure to keep him busy with distractions. Make him think you might accidentally set fire to the place. Then get him to help you check our horses and the carriage. Tell him we plan to leave here in a day or two, no matter the weather."

"What if *our patron* comes?" said Kralov, his eyes not betraying the fear carried in his words.

"Well, ask him if he wants to share a bowl of your famous 'Comfort Soup'." Erik winked.

"That man," Kralov said in a hushed voice. "That … *thing* … Erik. It's stronger than—"

He patted Kralov on the back. "I know, I know. Let's not think about that now."

"Not human." Kralov whispered even lower. "I know him … I saw him before … a long time ago …"

There was nothing else to say.

Amalina and Kralov descended to the kitchens. He set up the fire and banged around looking for ingredients. He started up the song he was singing the night before, but this time he made it booming and boisterous, as if for a wedding dance. Just as Erik had winked at Kralov to comfort him, Kralov did the same for Amalina.

"Do you want fresh goat's milk?" she asked him, after getting all the other ingredients he asked. "I can get some for you."

He shook his head. "I've all I need."

Amalina went to the small corridor, whose end had been sealed with stones just hours before. In the wall was the tiny wood door with metal fastenings. The wood was blackened, with hints of green mold on it. She touched the door to make sure it was really there.

The courtyard was cold, the sky was grey, and she didn't need a candle to get to the hovel. After making sure Genadie wasn't inside, she took the spear and her bell (stuffed with a blackened cloth to deaden the clapper), and with heart pounding, snuck her way back to Katrina's room.

Everyone was awake now. Katrina and Odetta sat next to each other on the bed, holding hands. Katrina looked nothing like the steely conqueror from just a couple days ago. From the way her body was so collapsed into the old woman, she had become, so it looked, a small, frightened child. But her eyes were large, rounded and haunted. They were focused on a spot of air just beyond the tip of her small, upturned nose. Her eyebrows and lips worked to form an expression of resolve, troubled though it was. Her head turned only slightly when Amalina entered. She said nothing, of course.

"Great," said Erik, taking the crude spear from Amalina. He slid that, too, under the bed with a light clank.

"Did you get to the library?"

"Didn't take long at all," he said with a proud, though off-kilter smile. "All done."

Katrina opened the window. The cold air swept in so that Odetta shivered and pulled the blankets around her. Katrina stuck her head out of it.

"What are you doing?" asked Erik.

"I can't hear it anymore," she answered, and closed the window.

She moved slowly, as if she were floating, looking like an apparition. She began to pace the room this ghostly way, filling the room with ominous tension.

"Now here," said Erik, taking Amalina aside. "When Kralov returns, it begins. You will go downstairs and wait at the private study for our man to wake. When he tells you to bring Lady Flauna for the rehearsal, you tell him 'right away'. Then you come back up here as fast as you can."

"And then what?" asked Amalina.

"We play it from there."

"What about the library?"

"What about it?" he asked.

"That was the plan," she reminded him.

"Not anymore."

"You went down there. What did you do?"

"Got things … ready," he said with a clever grin. "But with luck, you and I won't see it ever again."

Kralov entered soon after with a board of cups, bowls, wine, a smoking, blackened loaf of bread, and a large pot stinking of rotten cabbage and onions. Katrina made a face at the smell and Odetta crossed herself.

"Woof!" Erik smiled. "That should do the trick."

"Comfort stew," Kralov said without humor, removing the iron lid to let the odors fly.

"Go down and make some more." Then he asked: "Did Genadie show?"

"The imp is taken care of."

* * *

Amalina could only wonder what Kralov meant by 'the imp is taken care of', as she waited for the Count to appear. She hadn't much time to search the castle for Genadie—which she did, fearing Kralov had done some great harm to the worm. Not finding him right away, she'd been forced to return to the script and go to the private study, full of nervous energy and worry. The smell that now permeated the castle's lower floors—Kralov's 'Comfort Stew'—made it all the more difficult to remain in one place.

I'll wait for 'Master' inside the study, she thought before too long, unable to contain her restlessness and thinking she might escape the stench.

She took the key from her pocket and opened the door.

"What are you doing here, Mouse?"

The count was turned from his desk. He was partially bloated with blood, and wore that bland look of satiation he got after a successful hunt. A clothespin pinched his nostrils closed.

"What do you want?" he asked, nasally.

"I was checking to see if you wanted us for rehearsal."

"It's a little early," he said with a light belch. "I thought after last night Lady Flauna would sleep in. A mercy I was more than willing to extend to her."

"That's very kind of you, sir, but—"

The Count cocked his head to the side as if listening to something above his head.

"But, yes … I believe they're all awake. Or the rats have found something to play with. Difficult to tell with that racket from Kralov. At it again, is he? I believe he's ruining the peace of my household with his wretched voice and merciless peasant cooking on purpose. I'd wager Erik put him up to it, in payment for last night's scare from the 'wind'."

"I can tell him to sing a little quieter," Amalina offered.

"Genadie should've done that by now. It appears you'd only be encouraging that backwoods ruffian to sing louder still. It's the Muscovite in him." He delivered this last line with a look that Amalina would describe as tribal pride. Apparently the Count was enjoying the morning's unpleasantries, like they were moves in a game among friends. If nobody else in the castle had had a good night, the Count had, and he was preparing for a good day. "Ah, he's settled down now. If my Katrina is up to the task, by all means show her down. Maybe see that she's had something to eat first. We'll try to get this over as soon as we can."

"Yes, sir."

"Oh," he said when she'd reached the door. "I should ask: How is Katrina? Did she get some sleep? Has she calmed down?"

"She did sleep. Can't really say much more than that. I'll go get her now."

. . .

Erik was waiting outside Katrina's suite. He rushed to Amalina when she reached the top of the stairs.

"He sent you for our Lady?" asked Erik, his blue eyes eagerly scanning for the answer on her face.

"Yes."

"He's waiting down in his study?"

"Yes."

"He didn't act suspicious? Um … odd or anything?"

"No. Why?"

"Good," Erik sighed. He took Amalina by the arm and led her to the door, which was closed. Standing outside the door was a small table and two chairs, with some parchment, quill and ink, and a wine bottle and cup set on the table. "It's unfolding, and the old fool's playing his part brilliantly."

The look on his face was growing darker, even as his smile widened, the cheer in his smile was beginning to curdle. He stopped at the table.

"What's this?" asked Amalina.

"A distraction. All part of the plan." Erik picked up the cup and gulped from it. "Ah! Not everything here is awful. His taste, as usual, is exquisite. Here," he offered Amalina the cup, "before we begin, some 'Courage from the Gods'."

The way he looked so pathetic, with a dribble of wine on his lip and chin, his eyes ringed black with worry, she obliged him a sip. There wasn't much left.

"Finish it," he told her. "I'll pour another."

Amalina drank the remaining bit, and handing the cup back, she wiped her mouth. He poured another cup.

"Do we really have time for this?"

"Mouse," he said with an expression that seemed entirely lost. "I just want a little more time. To enjoy myself."

Erik came closer, whispering: "Katrina may have loved Aldo more than me. I'll never know. But he never loved her like I did. I've committed many crimes for her. I've killed for her. I'm willing to do anything for her."

Amalina nodded. She turned her head to check if the Count was there.

"I could have saved myself from this fate," he whispered on. "So many times I could have left her and enjoyed a simple and happy life. But I didn't. I couldn't. I knew she was my only light in the world, even if everyone else saw her as something to be used, or regarded her as trash."

"You loved her," said Amalina.

"You have someone that you love more than anything else in the world, don't you?" he asked, lowering his eyes to hers. "Your parents?"

"Yes."

"Your mother. Of course, your mother."

"She's dead," said Amalina. "Long ago."

"Your father?"

Amalina nodded, feeling a large throb of her heart when she thought of him—and how dangerous the hour was growing. Though if all went well with the plan, she might see him sooner than not.

"He is someone you would do anything for. Someone you would do anything to save, right? Even at your own peril."

"Of course," she said. "I know what you're say—"

"Yes, yes, of course." Though his eyes still glimmered blue in the torchlight, his expression couldn't be any grimmer. "Then you will understand why I'm doing this."

He set the refilled cup on the small table and took Amalina into the room.

28

The Four Friends

The entire bedroom had been altered. The beds, and tables, and chairs, and benches, all the furniture, had been crammed close on either side of the doorway. Strewn across the center of the open floor were metal plates and wood stands. On the plates, and stuck into the stands, were torches of all sizes; all burning brightly and spilling like a chaotic trail from the now blazing fire inside the fireplace. A cool draft swirled in from the open window.

Neither Katrina, nor Odetta, nor Kralov were there.

Erik shut the door to the hall and moved into the room with purpose.

"Here," he shoved a heavy dress into Amalina's hands. "Get this on quickly."

"What?" It was one of Katrina's dresses. It had bright flowers and birds and patterns all over the fabric.

"Don't be bashful now," he said as he busied collecting items from a pile in the far corner. "We haven't the time. Get it on. Quickly."

"But what's this for?" she asked, as she removed her shoes and loosened the waist of her own dress.

"Kralov would never fit into it. And even if Odetta could, she doesn't have the courage to do what needs to be done."

"Where is everyone?"

"Out of the way." He was lighting more torches. Sweat beaded on his forehead and soaked his shirt. His blond hair looked dark and greasy and disheveled. "The plan is just about the same as I told you. Different room, of course. And it will be down to us."

He began unwinding Amalina's makeshift rope, taking care not to let it touch any of the scattered flames. She looked at the open window, and something dreadful occurred to her.

"We aren't climbing out there, are we?" she asked worriedly.

"Wouldn't think of it," he said, now blank-eyed, distracted by his labor and private thoughts.

Amalina already had her housedress off and was slipping her legs into the beautiful dress. At another time, this might have been a great pleasure: donning the elegant and fashionable clothes of a notable woman. Now, her legs felt weird as they entered something so foreign. It felt so odd to her, it was as if this fancy dress that Lady Katrina Flauna would hang off her slight, slim figure was made of lead. How could Katrina even carry it? she wondered.

"All part of the plan," he was saying.

She began to feel sweaty despite the cold. The dress had a silk over-layer, with thick woven cotton underneath. She shook the dress up and over her shoulders, shoving her arms through the holes. She shook her arms. Her legs had been tingling against the fabric, and now her arms felt the same sensation. Sweat covered her thickly, even when the cold grew more intense.

"Now this," he said, helping her into the large fur coat Katrina had worn when she came to the castle. It now smelled mightily of some clove perfume.

"We aren't going out the window?" she asked again.

"Cold in here, isn't it?"

The fur felt like it added another fifty weight. Her body shook. The costume was so heavy, and getting heavier. She felt like she needed to catch her breath.

She saw a chair and started for it. Her legs shook and they seemed to lose coordination.

"Ah," Erik said, catching her in his strong arms. "Here, you look a bit shaky. Let's get you into the chair. Yes, that's a good girl."

Amalina didn't sit as much as melted over the chair and its arms. Her head drooped. Her bottom, which now also felt the same tingling sensation of her limbs, and assisted by the smoothness of the fur, slid forward awkwardly on the seat. Erik pushed her back onto it before she fell off.

"Ah, yes, ah, yes," he said, low and somber now. "A bit quicker than I thought, but all for the better."

"What …?" Amalina said. Her head hummed. Her sight seemed to retreat half a foot behind her eyes, so that there was a fuzzy black rim around the edge of her vision. Her tongue felt thick in her mouth. "What …?"

She couldn't move her body. It was embarrassing the way her neck drooped, dropping her head onto her chest. The long, course hairs of the coat cushioned her cheek, but also invaded her lips and nose uncomfortably.

Erik began tying her wrists to the arms of the chair with black silk scarves. He looked into her eyes from below, reading them for consciousness, looking ashamed.

"I'm sorry I had to do this, little mouse. As I explained to you, she is someone I would do anything for. And this is all part of the plan.

"After last night," he said, lashing her ankles roughly to the legs of the chair, "I was convinced you're right. Our ancient benefactor, he's Strigoi. Too bad we couldn't catch him in his coffin, then. Because, you see, after what he did to Kralov … his incredible strength and speed … I knew my plan to murder him wasn't going to work. He's just too … too fast …

"Here we are," said Erik, pulling open a small box of theatrical make up—almost exactly the same as the one the Count had shown her so long ago in the carriage, on the way to Neku's graveyard. He pulled out a scarf, and after freeing Amalina's head from the fur's hair, tucked it all around it, protecting the coat's hood from whatever he was about to do to her face. He rubbed his fingers in a dark, ochre looking cream, and then, after dabbing it here and there on Amalina's cheek, chin, forehead, neck, and hands, began spreading it across her skin. "Very good.

"So, little mouse," he continued in a hushed voice, "I knew that if I tried to kill him but failed—which is now almost certain—he would punish us all severely. But most importantly, he'd punish Katrina. I couldn't risk that. I could never allow even a chance that she'd die. Not before me. I couldn't continue living if she were no longer in this world. If only we hadn't begun on this stupid plot. It was her idea, but we all went along with it.

"You understand, little mouse, we four are a team. Kralov and Odetta were once a celebrated pair of players—the handsome strong man and talented beauty, both extraordinary tumblers—who aged out … as we all do. But they both were clever, and they taught us how to work the patrons and relieve them of their money. And though 'our good man' here approached Katrina directly with his generous offer, for the most elaborate play in history, and Katrina was the one of us who cleverly devised a more cunning counterplan, to establish herself as his lone legal heir, and then see him off the stage, we all went into it. And so when this creature revealed itself for what it was, we knew we'd made a terrible blunder, and we were in the most dangerous peril we've ever faced. We understood one of us would have to be the sacrifice, to allow the others to escape. We drew for it. When my beloved plucked the fatal card, I wouldn't stand for it. I took it for my own

"I know you think Katrina doesn't deserve such devotion," he said, now applying a darker makeup with a stick to Amalina's eyebrows. Each brush stroke set off a weird tingle. "But nobody deserves it. We're all the worst creatures in the light of truth. We only elevate ourselves by selfless actions.

"To preserve Katrina's safety—as well as the others in our team—in the face of this creature," he applied a red-purple cream to her numb lips, "I volunteered to sacrifice myself. I must assume I will die, and my only saving hope is to delay and distract that being for as long as I can before he does me in, so that my beloved can get safely away unnoticed. In this, you must be my assistant."

He pulled necklaces out of the box. He compared them to the dress, and chose two thin ones with paste jewels to put around her neck.

"From my years associating with him, I was aware of his disdain for—and peculiar sensitivity to—sunlight. And his aversion even to fire. I had forgotten about any of it, until you reminded me when you corrected my plans for the library. That is why we have torches here. And sunlight from the window. That should piss him off, especially if he does imagine he'll just pop in here through a wall without looking first."

Now it was time for one of Katrina's wigs. It looked like he pulled her entire scalp from a drawer in the box. He used a brush to quickly smooth it and sculpt it. He put it on Amalina's head and repeated the action, though she couldn't see what he was doing and only felt her head being pulled in different directions, her face crinkling the protective scarf.

"I knew he was observant, but you, if you remember, told me about how acute all his senses are. His hearing, his smell. For any hope to trick him, during all our activity to prepare for the moment and then to allow their escape, we had to make sure he could not track us. Better to keep him from getting even the least bit curious, or to decide to check on us in person. And so Kralov's performance this morning, with his off-key arias and heavy-scented breakfast. He covered our subtler movements, while hopefully also keeping 'our man' brushed back and at bay in some inner chamber of the castle.

"And all was readied for this."

Erik removed the protective scarf and stepped back to admire his work.

"As good as it'll get," he muttered ruefully. "Ah!"

He took from a napkin from his pocket all the glittering rings that used to be on Katrina's fingers: gold, and white-gold bands that gripped flashing jewels.

"Presents from our patron," he explained as he worked them onto her limp fingers, "which he insisted we never sell. Something he wouldn't miss. Ah, those nails!"

He flung open a drawer on the box, and gawped helplessly at a set of clear-glass vials filled with so many colors.

"Endless!" he grumbled, then slammed the drawer closed. "No time for this. Women are so much more complicated! Well, this will have to do."

He curled Amalina's fingers into her palms, which accentuated the rings and hid her plain, rough, chipped nails.

"Now," he said more loudly, "That's that."

He blew out a loud sigh and then took in a breath as if to prepare himself for a new phase.

From behind he dragged Amalina in the chair to the window. He ran across the room, and after a nervous pause opened the door to the hallway. Very quickly he upended the bedframe (now free of its goose-down mattress), the desk, the room's table and chairs, to create a deep, interlocking, but very porous barrier to block the doorway. "Yes," he laughed when it was done, "That should hold him."

He set the iron spear in front of Amalina. He took the makeshift rope, and after feeding out some length from a great coil, fastened it around the back of the chair and Amalina's midsection. He cinched this very tight, so that it forced her to blow out a breath—she didn't feel it as her whole body was numb, but only experienced a small pressure and heard the sound—and she worried she might get sick.

Erik looked into her eyes again. The pupils of his beautiful blue eyes were like pin pricks, and there was something flat to them, as if they only perceived to the end of his nose, though he looked right at her.

"Still with us?" he asked. "Good. Good. I hope you aren't cold. Do forgive me. But it really doesn't matter if you do or you don't approve, this is really the only way."

He rolled more torches in front of him, and checked the stock of wood near the fire. Then he took out his large dagger and set it onto the floor next to the iron spear.

After looking at Amalina again, in one last sweep of appraisal, he took more large black scarves from a case.

"Nothing that can be done about the eyes is there?" he said as he stuffed one scarf in her mouth, then cinched a gag around Amalina's head, pulling the scarf so tight it pushed between her lips, and shoved the scrunched scarf inside her mouth further back. She thought she would choke the way it tickled the back of her throat. She tried to breathe hard through her nose, but she had no control of her body. She felt faint. He was saying: "But this will help."

He folded up the last scarf loosely and bound that around her eyes. The fabric was so sheer that she could see through it; if only just a little where it wasn't tripled up.

"I'm warning you now, little mouse, do not, under any circumstances, make any noise or move, even if this drug should wear off, no matter how scared you might feel or uncomfortable you are. With all this light and fire in the room, it should make it difficult for him to see you well, but if he sees your hands or your face—the shape of it—or your eyes clearly, or so much as hears a groan, which could never match the sound of Katrina's melodious voice, the game is up. Don't even think of betraying us, little mouse. If you even hope to survive, you must not let him think you are anyone but Katrina.

"If this should come off properly," he said, "If by some miracle all goes as planned, he will come to rescue you. He may move as fast as lightning, but this obstruction should give me enough warning, and when he goes for you, to save you, his beloved Katrina, and he gives me his back, I will strike him."

Erik lifted the spear and banged its blunt end on the stone floor.

Even with the drug coursing at strength through Amalina's system, with her body completely separated from her control, and so that she had to fight to remain conscious, she thought in alarm: *He won't come for me! He'll come straight for you!*

But she could say nothing. Though she tried, she could not move her lips, or force a breath into her throat. She could not warn him of the flaw in his plan. Oh, this love-struck boy was going to die, all right. And right in front of her. And even though the blindfold reduced the light in the room, he was still a visible grey shape, and she could not close her eyes or turn them away. She would witness everything.

It looked like he pulled out another bit of the rope, and looped it in a weird way around the spear. Tucking the rest of it underneath his arm, he turned to Amalina in the chair.

"Now, for this last part."

He groaned as he seized either side of the chair she was sitting on and lifted the whole package high off the floor. He didn't have far to walk. Reaching the rear set of legs over and past the sill, he set the bottom of the seat down onto the sill itself. Amalina felt a vague sensation of coldness on her back. Erik reached up and pulled the fur's hood down.

She watched as Erik's feet, well below the margin of blackness created by the hood and blindfold, moved back and forth, the length of rope from her midsection following him. It was as if he were testing his range and freedom of movement. His arm dipped into view as he rearranged the torches.

Still she tried to find her voice to warn him. Whatever he had planned, it seemed it was going to go very, very wrong. The fact she was sitting on a very narrow perch, and with a sheer drop to doom at her back, did not frighten her as much as it normally would. Perhaps numb complacence was one of the effects of the drug.

Holding the spear in one hand, he nonchalantly set his large dagger on Amalina's furry lap. After a pause, and a quick grunt of reconsideration, he took the dagger back and put it through his belt. He tested the speed of drawing it out. He wasn't very fast. The dagger went back to the belt.

The cord swung far to the left, as he walked out of her sight. Then he came back. In his hand was Amalina's bell.

He rang it, and he rang it hard.

"Come Mischa! Come Mischa!" Erik shouted, his voice cracking as he strained it to the highest volume, even louder than the clang of the bell.

"Come Count Tepsji, or whatever you want to call yourself! Come here! Come here! Come here!"

She watched as he spun himself around, wrapping some of the rope's slack around his waist. Then he came to the window and shoved hard into Amalina's chest, pushing her and the chair up, then right out the window.

29

The Escape

The chair teetered outside the window. Amalina's body rested on its angled back, the chair clinging to the sill by the very tip of its front feet, and was kept safely in place by the grace of the taught makeshift rope which Erik held between his arm, and which was also caught in a twirl around the spear.

Because of her shifted, slanted view, she could now see most of the room, as well as the tower's old stone walls on either side. Though the rope vibrated with tension, it didn't appear to take much effort for Erik to keep her from falling out the window and plummeting to the stone courtyard. So this was his plan? To keep her suspended awkwardly by a rope, between security and death, while he played with the Count? To what end?

He rang the bell again and again, tirelessly.

"Come here! Here in the tower! Come Count! Come Count! Come Count!"

He threw the bell hard to the side. Suddenly the rope was over his shoulder and his dagger was in his hand, while the bell still banged off the wall and skittered noisily on the floor.

At the same time, the Count's head appeared in the doorway, peering through the spaces between the interlocked slats of furniture. He shouted in surprise and fell back.

"Too bright for you?" taunted Erik.

The Count came back to the opening, but with a black hood over his face.

"What's going on here?" croaked the Count in annoyance.

"What does it look like?" Erik said slowly, with a grinning, sadistic relish.

"Katrina!" the Count called to Amalina, mistaking her for the actress. As was Illustrious Erik's plan. "Katrina!"

"She … can't … hear … youuu," said Erik, very slowly now, drawing out the words in a weird way. Who knows how the Count interpreted the stretched out vowels and long spaces between the words. But it fitted nicely into Erik's scheme, making sure he had the Count's full attention for as long as he could. "She's fast asleep, and doesn't know that she is on the very brink of death, should you make the wrong move."

"Asleep?" said the Count, his voice dripping with doubt. "Katrina! Katrina, listen to me!"

"I drugged her, Mischa ... I'm sorry, *Count Tepsji*. However you like. I put it in the wine. And I had her drink it. If you doubt me, you can see for yourself. The bottle's there beside the doorway. There is a full cup, too, if you're daring enough to sample it."

The count brought the cup to the opening of the hood, then he set it back. "Satisfied?"

"Why have you done this, Erik?"

"To have my way."

"Not likely," scoffed the Count from the shadows of the hood. The hood turned and called down the hall: "Mouse! Mouse!"

"No," said Erik, prolonging a hideous giggle. "She drank it, too."

"Genadie!"

"Count Tepsji—Mischa, you don't really think I am as dumb as all that. Your little rat of a manservant was the first we sacked. Then little mouse. Then, when I knew it was safe to enact my plan, Katrina and Odetta together. It was only Kralov and I, you see. So now, here I am with our beloved Lady Katrina Flauna hanging by a thread out the window, while Kralov makes away with Odetta, your mouse and your Genadie."

The black cloak shuddered.

"I know you don't like the sunlight, so you probably won't try to rescue them first. But they are probably too far away at this point to catch them. If you're fast enough, you might still be able to see them from the battlements, making their way down the mountain. But probably not—"

The cloak was suddenly gone, with the sound of a loud flap, before Erik finished the sentence.

"—what with the sunlight and all," he concluded. He stared at the empty hallway. "Count Tepsji?"

After a pause, Erik swore and jumped as fast as he could to the fireplace, reeling out the rope as he did. The chair bobbed dangerously, more so when he came leaping back, trying to wind the slack in the rope as fast as he could to prevent the chair from falling out the window entirely.

He'd hooked a thin metal pot, what looked like two deep plates pressed together, and, pulling Amalina in, inserted it into the fur. Warmth blossomed dully at her midsection.

"Oh, my, I completely forgot," he said apologetically. "You're going to definitely need that. I can't have you freezing to death."

Am I freezing to death? she asked herself. She tried to feel toward her extremities. There was only the vaguest sensations of temperature beyond the encapsulating numbness. The warmth spreading presently, feeling like a light linen sheet being drawn across her body, was from a bed warmer straight out of the fire. She realized with a fright that her legs and stomach might be blistering and she wouldn't know it.

Erik pushed her out the window again, and took up position.

The timing was perfect, because the black hood appeared. The Count's mouth and chin were visible. He had a very wide, toothy smile. One born of tremendous, though tremendously sour, appreciation. The Count said nothing, but stood mute, apparently staring—as much as he could, considering the open window—at Erik, his newfound foe.

"Well?" said Erik, his nerves overriding his need to prolong (as much as possible) the inevitable events of this moment. "Are you satisfied, Count Tepsji? Kralov has on that sleigh Mouse, Genadie and Odetta, all succumbed to my poison, fast en route to Netz, where they will serve as hostages until I am safely out of your reach; which you can do nothing about. And here, where the outcome of events you *do* have the power to influence, is Katrina ... on the edge of death."

"Erik Kosche," said the Count, equally slowly, but with almost a giggle of amusement. A sleeve came up to adjust the hood, making sure to cover his mouth and chin, shading it from the light. "What is it you want from me?"

"First, that's the last time you'll move," Erik warned him in the most serious of tones. "Until these negotiations are done—or unless I allow otherwise—you will keep yourself in my view. If you should leave, if even for an instant, I will drop Lady Flauna."

Erik demonstrated how true his threat was by letting out the rope so the chair tipped dangerously backward. Then he tugged it back. For Amalina, the feeling of dipping backward lagged shortly after seeing it happen. But she understood the danger and would have cried out if she'd had the ability.

The Count did not react.

"Do you understand?"

"I understood the situation already. It's simple enough. Now I repeat: What is it you want that that you could not ask from me politely?"

"Katrina is mine," he answered with hot-blooded passion.

"Of course she is," the Count's laugh rumbled.

"You love her! I know you do. If you didn't love her you would leave this very second and let her die."

"*What do you want from me?*" he repeated. "The stakes have already been placed."

"Katrina!" Erik blurted in exasperation. "I'm saying that I will have Katrina, and you will not."

"And I already granted this, you may have her, you will have her, and that you have her now. So why have you done this?"

"How can I have her, if *you* do? I'm not willing to share her love."

"So take her for yourself. I have no earthly love for my darling Katrina. And if I had, I know I wouldn't ever hang her out a tower window."

This statement gave them both pause.

"Now, is that really her?" the Count wondered absently. "If you care for her so much, why would you do such a thing? Now I wonder. I wonder. Who is that, there in the fur, really?"

Erik, keeping his eye on the black hood, reeled Amalina in a little. Enough so he could use the tip of his spear to push back the hood from Amalina's face—though not too much—and while doing so, clever as it was, "accidentally" pointed to the rings on her hand. The Count's black hood pushed forward, arm lifted defensively against the light. His chin could be seen.

"Don't move, Katrina," Erik whispered warningly to Amalina. She could not, though she was trying. The heat of the warming pan was increasing. She wanted to be able to buck it off of her if it became too much.

The hood retreated from the opening, but still kept in view in the hallway.

"Satisfied?" said Erik.

"I'll rip your tongue from your head, my friend, if you ask me that again," he said, almost jovially, still not understanding that Erik would be repeating himself a thousand times more if it could buy the real Katrina another mile toward freedom. "Now tell me, Erik Kosche, how you will be satisfied this morning, so that we can return to our business."

"You will pay me."

"Do you mean more than I already intend to?"

"You will pay me for *her*. For Lady Flauna's hand."

"I don't want her *hand*, or her heart. I just want her—and, until now, *your*—services. Am I not making myself clear?"

"So you were just *using* her, then?" he sounded like a miserable wreck, bellowing accusation.

"What do you mean?"

"Leading her on. You understand, she thought you loved her. And that you intended to marry her."

"What?!"

"It's a good thing she can't hear you right now, or she would be devastated. You stole her love from me, and here you cared nothing for her? Her heart will be broken."

"What is this?" the Count was caught between amusement and confounded irritation. "You're talking nonsense. Have you gone out of your mind?"

"With jealousy!" Erik crowed, stage melodrama shaking his words. "I cannot live without her. And now that I know she has had her head turned, and by none other than an old, heartless rake, I can never look at her in the same way. Even if she were to love me again, I could never bear to return to a love that has been shattered and ruined."

"You're mad. Here, bring her back in and we'll warm her up. And then we can have a sensible conversation, and see if all cannot be set to right."

"L-listen to you," he stammered. "So coldhearted. Unable to recognize the crime he's committed by seducing the most beautiful, the most sought after actress in ten kingdoms …"

Here Erik took off on a wild tangent, recounting the names of all the kings and dignitaries, all the notable clerics and the bishops and the cardinals, and the highest of the merchant classes who had offered proposals of marriage, or massive bribes to take her as a mistress or concubine. It lasted for nearly two rambling hours, so that Amalina thought she might have fallen in and out of consciousness while he carried on.

All the while the black hood remained where it was, unmoving.

"All right, come on," said the Count, when Erik seemed to finally come to the pointless end of it. "You said there's a price. What did you mean?"

"If I'm going to give up what is mine," he said, "then you will have to pay me for it. And you will pay dearly, after the value that I've just shown her to be. Her real value. Or must I run through it again?"

"So all you are asking is that I pay you off, and you won't have to accompany Lady Flauna on the mission?"

"In so many words."

"'*In so many words*'!" brayed the Count. "You've just wasted an encyclopedia of words to get to this fine point. What is your game? Have out with it. How much are you asking? It couldn't really be more than I was going to pay you for the mission, could it?"

Erik explained the mission was to be for a brief period. The Count had robbed him of a lifetime of fulfilled companionship. For the criminal, the price must be substantial.

"Come to it, how much?"

"You will give me half of your lands, this castle, 800 bushels wheat and 80 gold a year."

The black hood shook even more than it had when it discovered this scene.

"I robbed you of nothing!" the Count protested, with real indignation. "And I supported your entire company these many years, you ingrate."

"You robbed me of all that matters: Lady Katrina."

"And I said you can have her!"

"But I can't have what you've stolen. You can't return someone's love like an ill purchased gift."

"Look here, I never loved her, I never seduced her, and I never lead her on in any way!"

Erik took this opportunity to conduct the Count in another great circle of argument. This time he invoked the many times they had met with him in this nearby town, or that one, and recalled in vivid detail something the Count had said to Katrina which could have double meanings, or be construed as amorous attention. Erik performed beautifully as the tormented cuckold, who watched helplessly on the sidelines as his woman was lured away by sweet words and promises of riches. This felt to Amalina as if it took another several hours of back-and-forth, with Erik charging, and the Count refuting it all coldly.

Erik was tireless, but his energy flagged from time to time. He obviously had to work at it. The Count, however, was like a machine of argument, willing to engage, and without let up.

"Isn't she cold?" asked the Count after a while.

"Don't move," said Erik.

Erik threw more logs into the fire. He relit some torches. Then he brought out another bed warmer, and after tipping Amalina up, replaced the old one. Now Amalina felt the heat like she hadn't before. She actually felt a pinch and ripple in her stomach. Her body jerked, ever so slightly. She concentrated on that, trying to get her stomach muscles to move again. To move her bottom. But along with the heat, the cold worsened. She saw her hand, even with the ochre stain, had gone white.

"You cherish her so much you couldn't put a cover over her?" observed the Count, dryly.

Erik almost turned, then double-checked to see if he was in earnest.

"I'll allow it," the Count assured, with a strange, amused look.

Erik, with a discreet grin of his own, happily prolonged the moment: he crossed slowly and warily to the left, then came back with a blanket, threw it on top of Amalina and petted it down. When Erik tipped her back in place, the blanket tented on top of the rope, letting the whirling breeze outside the tower blow in underneath it. They didn't notice.

"Whatever you think I've taken from you," the Count said in the end. "I'm not paying your price. It's ridiculous."

"Of course you will, or you'd have let me drop her by now."

"You seem to think I value her for a reason which I do not. And you've miscalculated the value I do consider her to have. She means invested time and effort to me, nothing more. And I'd still hope to see her safely into this tower to continue our work. But if that's going to happen, you will have to bring the price down."

Here they haggled for an hour. With the Count always howling, "Be reasonable, be reasonable."

And Amalina became ever hotter … and colder. Her lap felt like it was singed and scalded, while the numbness of her face and limbs was replaced by the sharp, stinging pain of ice on flesh. She believed she'd gotten her wrist to move. Yes! It moved, she thought. And she tried again. Not even considering the significance of doing so while hanging over a mighty drop to the paving stones.

Eventually they settled on a price. The Count would write a letter bestowing a hereditary title to him, looping him into the estate; 80 gold per year, firm; and one castle or home of Erik's choosing. Erik insisted the Count write out the deal, and read it out, before he'd consider bringing Amalina in.

Amalina thought she'd be well dead of cold or baking by the time it was all through. If only she could keep her hand moving. Her fingers, numb as they were from the cold, had begun to respond to commands. They uncurled ever so slightly.

Erik noticed. He looked tired—amazing how he had held her weight all this time—and as if he didn't much care she was regaining movement.

Erik directed the Count to the parchment and writing instruments that were sitting on the hallway table along with the poisoned wine bottle. The Count began to write out the purchase under Erik's unhurried dictation.

"You do understand," said the Count while writing, "That I've entertained this conversation for so long because I had no other choice."

"Yes."

"I don't mean because you're hanging poor Flauna out the window."

"No," Erik agreed. "You could do nothing about it because of the fire and the daylight."

"But the days are very short this time of year," the Count said with a rising amusement. "And though you set up this ransom perfectly, evening is coming."

"Yes, I know."

"You haven't much longer."

"You are a monster," Erik told him defiantly. "And your days are at an end."

"To the contrary. Any minute now, your day is."

"Your *time* is at an end," Erik corrected himself, patiently. "Your unnatural *life* will be snuffed out."

"Too many people have said that to me."

"But they didn't know how to kill you."

There was a silence between them. Amalina felt the urgency to free herself. The moment was coming to a head, and she might suddenly find herself falling if she didn't get out of the chair. She began to wriggle. The hot pan shifted and fell to her side, burning her outer right thigh. She worried the pan might have come open, spilling the contents into the fur. Her fingers could move, but not enough. To get out of the restraints on her wrist, she began tugging with her whole arm, hoping to pull through the holes the frozen balls of dough that were her hands. But the rings snagged on the scarf.

Erik took a second to glance at the sky. It was still bright enough, apparently, to ward off the Count. But the light was visibly dimming.

"Now, now, dear Katrina," whispered Erik. "Take it easy. There's still a little more time. You don't want to hurt yourself."

"I had been hoping for a dark, dense cloud," said the Count. "That would have been enough for me. But I don't always get what I want. Sometimes I have to wait. But I'm very patient. I have all the time in the world."

"I was hoping you'd need to rest," Erik admitted, admiringly. "If for just a little, to give my arms a break."

"No, only *you* need rest. And sleep. So … I have all night to wait you out."

"Not so," said Erik with some dramatic finality, "It'll happen when I say it does."

No! Amalina thought.

She wanted to say something, though she didn't know what. "Stop" would probably have been it, but she couldn't get her mouth to work. And even if she could, there was the gag that would have stopped her. But she wanted to do or say something that would prevent what was about to happen from happening, because she saw only her own mortality in it. How dare they coldly barter for her life? As if she were an utterly meaningless trinket! A pawn on a chess board! In a rage, and with a ripping sound as a ring tore through the silk, she got one hand free, and she bucked and heaved to get the next one out. Then she thought better and shoved the blindfold off her eyes.

"Katrina," the Count called to her. "Don't be scared. I won't punish you."

The look on Erik's handsome face was one of absolute delight. One of utter victory. The Count still thought Amalina was Katrina. Even now!

Though the lower edge of the blindfold still covered her upper lashes, she now saw the black hood clearly in the firelight. She saw the hood rise. And when she saw fully the Count's giant, dark eyes within, she knew what was going to happen.

The Illustrious Erik Kosche let go the rope.

The black shape burst through the furniture barrier and torch stands, sending shards and fragments off like missiles.

Amalina and the chair fell out the window. And as she fell she saw, in the dark blue-purple, crystal-clear winter sky, the sun set behind the mountain ridge.

30

The Wolf

For the second time in a week, Amalina felt her head throbbing as if it would burst. For the second time in a week, she opened her eyes knowing the last thing she'd seen was the sky as she fell from a castle tower, her makeshift rope rattling on the shrinking hole of a window. This second time it had been from a greater height.

Instead of waking in a pack of snow in the courtyard, as she had done after the first fall, she opened her eyes to a fire. It was burning in a large fireplace. She felt its warmth and was glad for that.

She was in *l'entrée grande*, lying on the large table usually reserved for scientific apparatus. It was now pushed as close to the great fireplace without the chance of it catching fire. She sat up. Her head swam. An all too familiar feeling. She leaned over the side and vomited.

She was still wrapped in Katrina's fur. Over that was a blanket. The blindfold and gag had been removed. She still wore the gaudy rings.

The room was dark but for the roaring blaze. All the doors were closed.

"Genadie?" she asked the air. Her head hummed at the sound, but then she tried a shout: "Genadie!"

Her voice reverberated around the stone walls.

"Sir?! Count Tepsji?!" Should she try the next option? "Erik?!"

She found a torch and lit it in the fire. It took several minutes to decide where to look first. All she really wanted to do was to go up to her room and lie in her bed. But there wouldn't be a fire there. So lying back down on the table, rolling up in the blanket and falling back to sleep was more tempting.

She felt a drop on the back of her hand. At first she thought it was a spark from the torch, but looking down, she saw it was a red splash. Blood. Touching her crusted hair, she found fresh blood.

"Genadie?!" But he was gone, wasn't he? Off to Netz with Kralov. If what Erik had claimed to the Count was true.

"Count Tepsji!" She called his name as she wandered.

Out the front doors, the courtyard was in complete darkness. It was nighttime now. The wail wandered in faintly and she closed the door on it.

Nobody was in the great hall, or the private study, or the kitchens. The door leading out to Genadie's hovel was still there, not replaced by stone like it had been the night before. She could see from the doorway that the hovel was dark and silent—well, silent but for the scream, which was a little louder on this side.

Nobody was home. But someone had taken her inside the castle and placed her on the table. The odds were it was the Count who'd done it. Unless Erik's plan had worked. When the Count had burst through the barrier he might have bypassed Erik to rescue what he thought was Katrina—either by grabbing the rope or maybe plunging out the window—and, presenting his back to Erik, had the spear plunged right through it.

"Erik?" she called.

On the way up the stairs to Katrina's room, she thought of the wine she'd drank, laced with a powerful tranquillizer. But she'd only had a little, while Erik had gulped down more than half the cup. How had he not been paralyzed, or worse? Had he taken some antidote beforehand? Or did he have some immunity to it? Or was it just that he was an actor, and he'd pretended it was a full cup, and mimed great swallows, making sure to leave some convincing drops on his lips and chin?

The wine bottle and cup were still on the table.

The bottle of ink was broken on the floor, a large dried black puddle extending out from it. Stuck in it was the quill feather and pieces of blank parchment.

Right outside the door was the parchment the Count had been writing on. The purchase agreement Erik had been dictating to him. Curious, Amalina kneeled to see what had been written. In the Count's peculiar spidery and cramped lettering it read: *Lady Katrina Flauna lives. Erik Kosche does not.* This repeats continuously down the page until it stops at some random tapping and scratches and blots.

The fire was down to red embers and small flames. A good number of torches were still flickering in the draft coming from the window. Judging by all this, it had been at least an hour since she'd dropped out the window, but not more than two.

With all the broken wood and debris, and the scattered sheets, blankets, pillows, clothes and Amalina's rope, it was surprising any of the fires hadn't caught and turned the room into a charred hole. To avoid doing this herself, Amalina stepped carefully and tried not to move anything, while she checked through the various piles to make sure nobody was in them. The rope still hung out the window, its coil had been tied to Katrina's massive (and obviously heavy) trunk.

The rope reached all the way to the courtyard below, where pieces of the shattered chair mixed with its unraveled end. She could see it very clearly against the white background. She also saw Katrina's wig and the spear lying at an angle next to it.

No Erik. No Count.

She came away from the window.

She thought of returning to her bedroom, or the entrance hall with the big warm fire.

But something told her this was not what she should do, despite her lightly aching head and familiar swirling vision when she moved. So what was bothering her that she couldn't just go to sleep?

Did she need to know who had won the fight?

She crossed the castle and went to Erik's room. He wasn't there.

The whole castle was dark, with no lights but for the few lit fireplaces and torches, and no sounds but what was usually there.

"Count Tepsji! Count!" She yelled over and over again. "Anybody?!"

Erik must have died.

Or been caught?

Amalina made her way to the cells below the kitchen. They were empty.

As far as she could tell she was all alone in the castle. Abandoned there.

But alone.

Free to do what she wanted.

Like escape.

. . .

Amalina didn't bother to add on any more clothes. The hood would be enough against the cold. She threw off the bulky rings when she tried to work the door leading out to Genadie's hovel—for a second time—and the bulky stones got in the way. They clattered to the paving stones as she headed to the small barn just beyond the hovel.

There was one horse. A whinnying, impatient courser. It was very large and all white and had a bit and reins fastening it to a post outside a stall. Kralov had probably not had time to hook it up to the sleigh and so left it there. It did not like the torch, so Amalina set the torch in a stand and stood with arms on hips trying to decide how to get on.

Amalina had never ridden a horse in her life. She'd seen it done. She'd watch her father and others hook up horses to carts, or throw saddles on them. But she'd never done anything like it herself. But the only way she was going to make a proper escape from this castle was on one. By foot, she would be dead by exposure if not eaten by a pack of wolves—or something else she wasn't considering. No, it was winter, and she'd need a strong horse for transportation.

It should be easy enough to ride, even without a saddle, she thought. *It's just a matter of getting up there and throwing your legs over the sides.*

She tried to steady the horse but it wouldn't stand still. When it saw her reaching her leg up, it shifted, or when she finally was so frustrated she jumped at it, it bucked. She tried pushing the courser alongside the stall, but recognizing that's what she wanted, it sidestepped, sounding a smug nicker.

"Come now," she said gently, patting its side. "Let's be friendly and let me up."

She climbed to the top of the stall and stretched her leg out to climb onto its back. The closer her boot got out and over, the more the horse shuffled around, pulling hard on the lead connecting it to the pole.

She jumped for it, bounced off its side and landed on the straw.

Amalina cursed.

She pushed the horse's side. And though it shot out a hoof to warn her not to try it again, the courser brought itself in line with the wall. Amalina ran around, climbed up the slatted wall and slid herself awkwardly onto the horse's back. Then she suddenly found herself falling right off its slick round sides and back into the straw.

The jolt made her head spin and she heaved emptily a few times.

Gasping for breath in the straw, she looked angrily up at the courser. All she needed was to get on its back and she'd be free.

She took the reins from the post, and with torch in hand led the handsome white horse out of the barn.

Coming around the castle on the other side, she went to the tower with the smashed chair and the rope below it. Lowering the torch close to the ground, she saw there were large, coin-sized drops of blood around the fallen spear. The blood could have been hers. Could have been anyone's.

She continued on, looking for a more convenient spot to try to board the horse, which was bobbing its head antsily behind her. For the first time since she'd come awake, she became very aware of the castle's wail. It was very loud here. Which was strange, because it should have been louder on the other side. Then, as she moved further along, it seemed to die down.

She stopped.

Backing up, the wail grew louder, and seemed to have an echo to it that she hadn't noticed before.

She tried this again, moving forward, then back, the horse looking confused and annoyed but not appearing affected by the wail itself. The sound grew quieter and louder as she did so. She looked around and saw the well. Approaching it, the wail grew louder still.

"Hello?" she called into the well's mouth. "Hello, can you hear me?"

As always, the inexhaustible cry—which sounded so agonizingly human—carried on without letup, without acknowledging it was being spoken to.

"Hello?"

She turned away and headed for the castle wall's main entrance.

But the trick of the wail happened again. Growing louder, then quieter.

This time Amalina determined it was coming from a drain along the inner wall.

"Hello!" She yelled. "Hello! Talk to me or I am leaving!"

She didn't stay long, but marched steadfastly in the direction that would take her out of the castle.

With each drain the sound rose and fell.

She came to the last drain before the turn toward the main entrance. The grate was large. The hole it covered large enough for a man in full armor to fall into if the grate weren't there.

Amalina squatted and listened. The wail was much louder still. Its source, it would seem, was down underneath the castle. She rubbed a finger on her chin.

If there was a person down there making that noise … It would be inhuman to leave the poor suffering soul behind, she thought.

Thinking of the handsome Erik, and his willingness to kick her right over the window ledge, rankled her pride enough that she thought, in the moment, that she should match—and outdo—his treachery with kindness and goodness. If she were going to escape, she would not have the blood of another on her memory, she thought loftily. *I am good, and I will do good!*

She grasped the bars of the grate and then pulled on them with all her might. The metal did not budge. She tried several more times.

She almost laughed when she thought of it: Amalina looped the reins around one of the bars and knotted it, then she encouraged the horse to move. Any direction should do. The courser tested the weight of the grate with its head. Then, unhappy with the resistance on its lead, it bowed its head and began licking at the bars contentedly.

"Yahhh!" Amalina charged at the side of its head, its eyes.

The horse bucked and leapt to the side taking the grate with it, the metal clanging and grinding. And then, after a startling snap of leather, the grate came crashing back down. The grate had come off and away from the hole only a little. But that was as far as it was going to using the horse. The reins were broken.

"Hello?"

She tried sitting at the edge of the hole and pushing the grate with her legs. It didn't move. She put her feet in, dangling them down into the darkness. *Am I really going down there? Where am I going?*

But she had to try.

With the tight squeeze rucking up the fur around her waist, she managed to slither down in up to her thighs, and there she wedged. Her legs kicked helplessly at the air. Where the metal pinched at her thighs, just below her butt, it felt like the grate was trying to eat her.

Panic set in.

She dropped the torch and used her arms to shove back out of the hole. Before the torch could be fully dowsed by the snow, she had it in her hand again and brought it round.

She could see a grimy bottom below, but it was deeper than her height. There was a rung of metal along one side of its wall. She could climb down, but only if she could squeeze through.

"Hello? Are you down there? Can you hear me?"

The wail continued as always, without break.

Looking at the sky, she saw she had hours until morning … but did she even have that long before the Count returned? She didn't know if he wasn't actually still inside, having never left. If she wasted her time trying to figure out how to save a creature that didn't even have the sense to answer her, they could both be lost!

"Forget it," she muttered stonily, taking her feet out of the hole. "I'm leaving. Your door is open if you like."

Trudging through the main entrance of the courtyard, hand pulling the now very shy horse by its shortened rein, she saw the doors to the outer castle walls were open. Kralov had opened them to get the sleigh out and hadn't bothered to close them. The Count, perhaps in pursuit hours later, hadn't taken the time to close them either. All the better for Amalina.

As she emerged from the castle walls, still troubled at leaving the mysterious wailer behind, and still wondering how and when she'd find a good spot to get onto the horse's back, she saw the body.

It was lying a short distance beyond the gates.

Amalina pushed her torch forward to cast the light as far as she could, to see past the boots and identify who this was. At almost the same time, when she saw clearly that it was Erik's body, and that he was missing his head, ten shining eyes and five sets of fangs came up into view.

Wolves. She'd interrupted their supper. Of Erik. They stared at her with their common vicious looks. A menacing growl rose from the pack.

The horse bucked against her, and with a twist of its head yanked the reins from her hands. It bolted back through the doors.

The largest wolf, with a nasty stare and black cowl of a mane, stepped forward confidently.

Amalina backed up. She waved the torch in front of her, warning it off. But it kept coming. His fellow pack followed eagerly behind him.

She picked up her pace. So did the wolf.

Moaning, risking glances behind her to see where the entrance was, wondering *how far did I go?* Amalina began a backwards trot. This encouraged the wolf. It growled hungrily.

"Sh! Sh! Go on! Get out of here! Leave me alone!" She remembered all those times the wolves had attacked her and Dragomir on the way to the mill, and knew that this was one of her greater fears realized. She'd had nightmares as a child, and even now, of wolves tearing her apart. And here, just behind the lead wolf, was Erik's gory example of what they intended to do.

Blood dripping off muzzles, shreds of flesh and sinew hanging from snarling fangs, the pack moved forward as one.

She was inside the castle, but she didn't know if there was enough time to close it off. She calmly walked to one side, praying quietly that they wouldn't get the notion to charge in through the entrance. They were still being cautious and had paused when she'd ducked out of sight. Now she swung one of the great doors shut. When it did shut, the sound was a loud blast of wood on stone, which echoed through the courtyard and back at the wolves. All but their leader leapt back.

The leader lifted its head, showing its fangs, growling in a way that said: "You are only making this worse for yourself."

Amalina moved slowly, still waving the torch, and got hold of the other door. Bringing it around, and with the outside ramp coming back into view, she saw the lead wolf charging at her. Amalina screamed.

She threw the torch at the great black wolf. It dodged the blow, but by doing so dodged to the wrong side. This allowed her enough time to build the door's momentum, so that it was going to slam shut before the wolf could adjust its trajectory and get in.

Or get *all* the way in.

It threw its shoulder against the door, and slowing the door, shoved its mouth into the opening. White and blood-red fangs tore at the edge of the door in a rabid fury at being denied its prey. One angry eye glowered hatred at Amalina's screaming face. Then the terrible mouth fell away as the door banged closed.

Amalina dropped against the door, bracing it shut. She could hear and feel the wolf ramming itself against the opposite side of the door. She did the same on her side, barking back at it.

There was silence (except the wailing).

Her head hurt. She wanted to throw up but gulped down the bile from her already purged stomach.

She saw the large slide-bolt that would seal the gate. Rising slowly, she kept her back to the door. As long as the wolf only went for this door she would be fine.

She reached the bolt and locked the door.

. . .

"So I'm not going to escape," Amalina swore angrily. "That wasn't meant to be. What am I supposed to do, then?"

She knew.

The moonlight in the clear night sky was bright enough to see by once her eyes had fully adjusted. But to get around, she'd need a torch. She went back inside and got another one, with the horse prancing and dancing at a safe distance from her and as if it were keeping an eye on her.

Amalina looked at the partially opened grate. Unless she took the fur off, there was no way she was going to get into that sewer duct. But even if she did take it off, there was no guaranteeing she would make the squeeze. She needed to open it just a little more.

The horse backed off at her approach. Its reins wouldn't really reach to the grate and allow her to knot it there anyway.

She took off around the bend, then returned with the iron spear. She found some leverage against the grate and threw her entire weight on the iron. The grate moved about half a foot. More than enough.

"Hello?"

She wondered once more if it wasn't just a strange sound of wind through the passage. That thought only lasted a second, though. The voice was gut wrenchingly human.

With a sigh she climbed down the rungs using one hand. She swung the torch around and found the direction she thought the wailing came from.

If it wasn't for the black, oozy grime on the floor, which also rose in places along the wall, it might have been any other hallway in the castle (though one with a very low ceiling). This made moving further in less scary than it might have been. She only had to watch her step so that she did not fall. Her foot slid on a couple slick steps and she almost pitched over.

At a junction, she wasn't completely sure where the sound was the strongest, so she made a guess and turned to the right. The duct angled downward at a shallow slope, and considering how far she had walked, she decided she must be under the castle, if not underneath one of the outer walls.

Echoing around her in the duct, the wail was definitely getting louder. Amalina wanted to plug her ears against it.

She came to a dead end. While the wall in front of her was solid, by using Erik's method of feeling up the wall, probing the spaces between the stones with her fingers, she found several wide slits between the stones. The seams were so wide that they seemed, despite their roughness, to be intentional. Or could it have been the work of rats?

Putting her ear to the holes, she heard the piercing cry of the wail, and barely below that a strange wooden grating noise. She felt a warm breeze coming through the holes. Whoever it was, they were behind this wall. Or at least in a room not too far beyond it.

"Hello? Hello? Can you hear me? Stop screaming and answer me!"

Once again, Amalina searched the walls the way she'd seen Erik do it, hoping to find some mechanism that would open a hidden door. When it didn't reveal itself, she stood, hand on hip, torch roaming over the surface.

She cursed briefly.

Why didn't I bring it with me?

Back up the passage, her feet skiffling much more as she fought against the gravity of the slimy slope, and then, coming out of the hole and finding what she needed, it was right back down again. She wanted to run, but she had to keep her pace even or she'd be sliding headfirst to who-knows-where in who-knows-what.

Back at the wall with the holes, and seeing there was enough room to come at them at an angle, Amalina rammed the spearhead into the mortar between the stones. Holding the torch in one hand and the spear tucked under her furry armpit, her gripping hand guiding the spear's tip, she looked like a bizarre jousting bear. Bang, bang, bang! She rammed at the sides of the holes, trying to widen them. Whack, whack, whack! The white sandy mortar chipped away easily.

She elongated the holes, and aimed at other crevices which needed digging out. But she saw it was going to be a long time to get the mortar completely stripped away. Amalina was tiring fast, and after so many shots to the wall, she ran her shoulder into stones here and there to see if any would move. None did. She'd need some kind of leverage against them, when the time came. When the holes were big enough. But how much time did she really have?

All that work, and the wail didn't so much as drop in intensity to thank her.

Back to it.

Crang!

Amalina froze.

Why?

It's not that the tip of the spear had pierced through the wall. No. Yet she felt it was important to stop. Sensed there was a good reason.

What was it?

The point was buried to only a finger tip's depth into one of the seams.

Was there something to it?

What about what she was looking at was so important?

The spear tip nipped shallowly between the stones.

She felt alarm rising inside her, but couldn't understand its meaning.

She looked to the tip again.

What was it? ... A spear tip.

On a spear.

The spear.

The Count.

The Count would be returning.

On his return he would have plenty of time to assess what had happened yesterday.

Whether Katrina or Odetta or Kralov—when the Count eventually caught them—accused Amalina of being in a plot against him, there was a body of evidence for him to piece together her guilt. Her complicity. The first and foremost clue—the critical, condemning clue—would be the spear. And what would be his sentence against her for her treason?

She saw Erik Kosche's torn body in the hungry, snarling mouths of the wolves. *That* would be *her* next.

The spear, he would say to her. Where had Erik gotten the spear?

Amalina tore back up the passage, nearly landing face first as she slipped in the grime.

When she got out, she used the spear shaft to work the grate back over the hole. It took five tries before the grate clanged solidly in. Then Amalina ran to the hovel. She had to hide the evidence. She wrestled the anvil stone out and back to its original position. She took the wood hammer and set it in the abandoned wood shop where she'd found it.

Who knows where Erik'd gotten that spear? Amalina hadn't made it for him, that's for sure! Maybe they'd brought it with them.

Returning to where she'd found the spear in the snow, Amalina placed it approximately where it had been. The snow in the courtyard wouldn't be too much of a problem because the horse was running around, making tracks everywhere. No need to look suspiciously at the horse's presence, roaming out of its sty. It had obviously broken free from its post in the barn. And snowflakes were beginning to trickle down from the sky. Maybe there would be a storm and her more human tracks would get covered.

Panting, she looked at the rope running all the way back up to the window. With a tug of dread, she remembered that it wasn't just old lengths of bedding and tapestry she had used to create the rope, but there were pieces of the castle's leftover dresses that Genadie had given her. If the Count saw that, he would suspect her part in its creation.

Amalina ran back upstairs to Katrina's room. She found the end of the rope, and with a note of panic, reeled its length in as far as she needed until she ran out of the clothes that would damn her. She used Erik's dagger to pry at the solid knots. She looked out the window. How many hours had it been already? This was going to take forever!

But she continued on, even when she recognized the howl of the wolves in the mountains. It was just like those other times in the past months, the howling that heralded the Count's return. When it started there was maybe an hour to go before he arrived—at most. But when had it begun? How long had they already been howling?

The muscles in her arms were burning. She felt like her hands were pieces of hard clay that would not respond to her demands.

When she got all of the dresses out, she quickly refashioned the rope by tying sheets and tapestries from the room, pulling them free of the broken bits of wood when she had to. While doing this she discovered her skirt with the map of the castle. She distractedly threw that on top of the pile of unknotted dresses—she hadn't decided what to do with them yet—then turned back to the real work.

Eventually the rope reached the ground again.

Amalina dropped the knife and ran down the stairs, across the castle and up the stairs to her room, dresses and skirt slung over one arm. Her lungs burned, her legs felt like jelly. She was thankful she didn't need her hands anymore. Using the strength of her body, she tossed the dresses under the bed.

What now?

That damned book! If he searched her room, he would find it and he would know that she'd been learning who he was, and the ways to kill him. Maybe she was the one who had given Erik ideas.

But when she looked for the book in her drawer, it wasn't there.

Where was it?

She'd shown it to Erik in the hovel.

She ran downstairs. Out she flew and into the hovel. But the book wasn't there, either.

Her mind screamed.

What happened to it?

Maybe it doesn't matter, she thought as she calmed herself, listening to the steady howls of the wolves mixing with the wail like a haunting chorus. What would it really mean if he found it anyway? *You could always tell him the truth: That you found it while cataloguing books. He must know he had it, and that you'd see it. So what's the offense? And you can always put it on Erik that he took it from the stacks and tried to use it against him.*

So what else? Amalina wondered with a pang of fear. What might he find that would implicate her in the plot? As long as there was nothing out of the norm, she'd look innocent. A victim of Erik's—just like him. As long as he found nothing suspicious.

All he must know is that he left me on the table in the entrance hall, so he must find me there, completely unmoved and unchanged from when he first found me. She ran down to the table and hopped onto it. She threw the torch into the fire, which was still burning.

The torch!

Amalina had thrown a torch at the wolf, thrown it outside the castle at him ... when she closed the doors. Her torch was outside! And the outer doors had been standing open! Now they were bolted closed!

She leapt off the table, lit a new torch and ran to the outer doors. She put her ear to it.

All she could hear was the far off howling, and the wail behind her. The wolves didn't sound anywhere near the entrance.

She threw the lock.

Pulling the door open, she peered out.

The fangs of the wolf missed her nose by half an inch. She screamed and fell back from the door.

The big black wolf smashed its shoulders at the door and muscled in. The next blast of its legs sent it straight at Amalina.

It struck her solidly in the chest. She fell backwards, feeling the teeth biting through the fur and scraping at the inner layer of clothes. Amalina slammed her elbow against its head and it slid off of her, trying to dig its claws in to stay on top. The deep, thick fur wouldn't allow the claws traction.

She only had time to sit up when it leapt at her again, jumping half the height of a man to come straight down upon her and her throat.

As she brought her arm across to protect her head, she didn't notice she was still holding onto the torch. The wolf's mouth fell straight onto the shaft of wood. She brought her other hand up to keep the torch's fiery end from falling onto her shoulder and igniting her fur coat.

The wolf growled ravenously, twisting back and forth, trying to score her with his claws if he couldn't with his bloody fangs, the light of the torch adding a hellish glow to its eyes. She rolled as it rolled, keeping the baton of the torch firmly lodged in its mouth.

It tried to pull back and lunge again, and seeing this, she went with the movement, hoping to throw the wolf on its back. It was too strong and it pounded her back into the ground.

But as she landed, she smacked the wood with her right hand, and with a snap-pop the torch sent sparks flying.

One spark went right into the wolf's eye.

The beast howled and flew off her, as if the horse had kicked it in the jaw.

Amalina leapt to her feet. There was no time to check if any of the sparks had set her coat on fire, the wolf had a second vicious thought and boomeranged back at her; its left eye closed shut, its mouth still wide open and full of menacing teeth. But the side of its face with the wounded eye contracted in pain to give it the look of a crooked grin.

She slipped the burning torch right into its greedy maw.

Now it blasted a high-pitched squeal. The wolf fell backward, rolling awkwardly, looking confused, its mouth opening and shutting, its chest heaving and coughing.

Amalina brought the torch down on its head.

The wolf's paws skittered on the icy stones, trying to launch back out the door.

Whap! The wolf's head was smashed to the ground. Whap! It fell to the side. Whap! The snout was driven against the stone again.

Sparks were flying off the torch. Flames seemed to reach out and into the wolf's fur.

It finally righted itself and ran out the door. Amalina followed it, screaming at the top of her lungs, and swinging at it again, and again, striking with brutal success.

The big black wolf bounded off faster than she could pursue it. Its four companions just some yards distant watched it dash for the tree line of the forest, sparks still flying off of its head. They turned to her, their mouths caught open, staring querulously at the strange fur beast holding the fire stick.

She didn't give them too much time to think. The howling in the mountains had stopped, which meant the Count would be there any minute, if he wasn't there already. She backed up, waving the torch at them.

She collected what she'd come for, the torch she'd thrown at the wolf earlier. With that in hand, she opened both great doors wide, causing the pack to take a step forward, even more curious now. One offered a short protesting bark. She sprinted without looking back. Her lungs felt like they were on fire. Her heart was hammering. Every part of her body ached. She flung herself inside.

Tossing both torches into the fire and kicking the logs to mix them in, Amalina then collapsed onto the table, not one ounce of energy left. As she stared into the fire she saw her hands.

The rings!

Amalina wailed.

Where had they gone? What had she done with them?

She fell off the table and ran as fast as she could to the rear door of the kitchen. She must have looked like a drunken llama running through the halls the way she flopped her legs and arms, willing herself forward, always nearly dropping, finally, to the ground. She grabbed at the rings, both inside and outside the door. The ruby one, the emerald one … the diamond one so difficult to see in the dark, hidden in the snow. How could she have been so rash, just to toss them away? What had she been thinking? She found them and raced again, not believing the Count hadn't yet stopped her. Hadn't caught her. That she hadn't already keeled over like a spasming fur fish, gasping for air, unable to locomote on land anymore.

But she made it to the table again, shoving the rings onto her fingers so hard they scraped her knuckles, surely drawing blood. She'd forgotten one! She'd forgotten one of the rings!

No! She'd shoved two onto one finger. Who cares?

On the table, in the waning firelight, she began to cry, having endured the greatest physical and emotional stress she'd ever suffered.

"Ms. Dalca?" came the deep basso voice from behind her.

"Ms. Dalca?" came the high, scraping echo of Genadie.

She rolled, letting her head flop to the side. She was sobbing. She could barely see them standing there, just inside the entrance. Snowflakes, coming heavier now, blew in around them.

"Is Ms. Dalca all right?" asked the Count, watching her body shake uncontrollably on the table, tears gushing off her face, soaking into the fur and the wood, her cries eclipsing the wail that was fading off as the dawn came.

The Count glanced down at the shredded fur cap in his hands—Kralov's fur cap—and like a bashful school boy he hid it behind his back, and looked to see if that might have been what had caused Amalina's meltdown.

The way she was carrying on, she felt stupid, and she began to laugh madly. And she didn't stop laughing, even when she saw her obvious grimy boot prints on the floor, wandering here and there, back and forth, in and out of the front door—exposing all her night's activities.

31

The Lesson

"**M**s. Dalca," said the deep voice, just as it had last night. Or this morning. Or was it yesterday?

"Ms. Dalca," Genadie echoed, just as before.

"Amalina, are you feeling better?" asked the Count.

Amalina rose from her pillows. Then she brought her knees up to her chest and hugged them. She looked at the two men staring back at her. Her joints ached. Her throat felt raw. She touched her hair and it was still matted with blood. But she nodded gently.

"You look it," said the Count agreeably.

"What happened?" she asked in a soft voice, almost incuriously, as if nothing mattered. Seeing the windows shut off by wood boards, she didn't know what time it was. In the fireplace was a large, healthy fire.

"I must apologize for what happened here," the Count said in his inward way. "I should have foreseen the possibility and dealt with it before it even began. I should have employed Katrina alone."

"Here are her rings," said Amalina, removing them uncomfortably from her swollen, raw-knuckled fingers. "She can have them back."

The two stared at her silently.

"Is she dead?" she asked.

"The wolves attacked when they left the sleigh and tried to hide in the woods," he answered matter-of-factly.

"All of them?"

"Nobody was spared in the attack."

"I see that Genadie made it out just fine," Amalina said without sarcasm.

"Yes, Ms. Dalca!" Genadie chirped positively, appearing pleased that she'd recognized him.

"Genadie did not leave the sleigh," said the Count. "He wasn't one of their double-dealing kind. I don't know how much you cared for them, but they were not here long enough, I should think, for you to establish intimate attachments with … *any* of that lot …"

Was he intimating something dark about her and Erik? she wondered.

"I liked their servants, Odetta and Kralov," she said. "They were nice, innocent people."

The Count's mouth fell into a lopsided grimace and he shared a look with Genadie.

An odd silence, one with the ratcheting tension of a building storm, fell on the room.

"You are Strigoi," Amalina stated as evenly as she could.

The Count's eyes widened.

Genadie choked.

"*Strigoi?*" the Count stared at her, his lip curled now in light bemusement.

Genadie's face, usually so grey, like a boiled potato, was worked into a red fury. His teeth gritted. "Strigoi? Strigoi?! You dare say that to Master, after all he's done for you, Ms. Dalca? After all he's *shown* you?"

"I'd thought you too innocent to have known a word like that," the Count murmured.

"I might have been innocent when you brought me here, sir. But I've learned," she said.

The Count produced the slim book from inside his black cloak. Amalina recognized it instantly and felt a wringing knot of guilt in her stomach. But it was a faraway sensation below the aches and pains of the rest of her body. She stared at the book without expression.

"From this?" he asked, pointing to it.

"Yes, of course," she admitted, jutting out her chin, to boldly show defiance even now.

"That look," he chided. "But this is trash. Worthless. Entirely false."

"It tells the truth. It explains who you are."

"I found this on Erik's body. Did he show it to you? Or did you show it to him?"

"He showed it to me."

"And yet it comes from my own collection, Ms. Dalca," he said. "You already logged it."

"I entered it in, but I didn't read it. You know how fast I'm working." She thought quickly and added, "Erik found it when he was wandering around during our lessons. He said he thought it would help him with a play he was writing. But then he saw similarities shared between you and one of its monsters, from the years he's known you. And when he decided he knew exactly what you were, he came to me. He accused you of being a creature of death, and accused me of working darkness on your behalf. I denied him as best I could."

"But you believed him. What he showed you in the book."

"You are Strigoi."

Genadie let out a plaintive cry.

"Shut up, Genadie," said the Count.

"Yes, Master."

"*Strigoi*," the Count declared the word dramatically, as he flipped open the pages of the book. He ran his fingers through it until he found what he was looking for. "Strigoi. It says here they are men and women who have died and come back to prey on the living. But I have never died, Amalina."

"You kill people at night and feast on their blood to live. I've seen it with my own eyes! Lucinda Skeldar—"

"I've already told you not to raise that subject—"

"Master is innocent," Genadie groused, waving a finger at her. "Her death was not his fault."

Where he might have shoved Genadie into a wall, the Count, demonstrating restraint for Amalina, put a finger to his lips. Genadie fell to the ground like a whipped dog anyway.

"You kill people at night and feast on their blood—their vital essence— to live," she repeated. "I know it's true. You can't lie."

"Yes," said the Count, pointing into the book. "I see that as a possible attribute here. Under the first, primary part about having died. Which, as I told you, I haven't. I never once died … And it also comes under the part about leaving their grave to do so. I do not live in a grave, Amalina, I live in an ordinary room inside an ordinary castle, as I have done for centuries. I would never rest inside a coffin, or a crypt, or a mausoleum. As I am not dead. I am powerfully alive!"

"Not if your head is removed," said Amalina. "Or a piece of wood or metal is driven through your heart."

Genadie gasped.

The Count smiled.

"Try it on yourself," he said, his eyebrows lowering into a mean 'V' above his eyes. "Try it, and see how long you live. Anyone would perish with their heart run through, or their head removed. But it would be impossible to do to me—to even attempt to do to me—because I am too powerful."

Genadie clapped and cheered.

"Quiet Genadie," Amalina shouted at him.

The Count looked amused that she'd become so enlivened now. He tossed the book to her. His throw was incredibly accurate. It landed flat beside her.

"It's worthless," he said. "What else does it say about me? About *Strigoi*? Read it. Tell me who I am."

"They prey on their relatives. Killing them one by one," Amalina looked up defensively. "But you've been here for hundreds of years. Your family is already dead, so how could I prove you did such a thing?"

"My family is still alive," he countered. "My family line is one of the greatest families of this country. I am estranged from them, and I've changed my name to protect them, but I have never killed one, nor would I ever. Go on!"

"If not their family, then … to survive they take the lives of infants."

"Never. Again, never. I loathe small children and would never touch one for my purposes. The thought is preposterous and disgusting. But you know the particular choice of my victims, Ms. Dalca. You know on whom I feed. So, go on!"

"They can be recognized, after feeding, by looking pink or red, and bloated."

"As does anyone who has finished eating. Some more than others. I show it."

"But it is human blood!"

"Not my relatives', though, and never small children," he said with a snide look. "And why not blood? Am I a cannibal? Blood is fortifying, with the maximum energy I require, without resorting to the meat. Which would be monstrous. And on that point, Ms. Dalca: it says Strigoi live by syphoning their victims' 'vital essence' or 'soul'. But, see there, in that informative book, nowhere does it say, specifically, that they drink blood. Where does it say that a 'vital essence' and 'soul' *means* blood?"

"What else would a vital essence be?"

"What else?" he asked in return, sarcastic grin firmly set. "I can't imagine. But the author could easily have written blood, but he did not. And so the essence being drawn would more likely be something else besides blood, and then I am not what you think I am." He folded his arms. "Go ahead. More. Tell me what else, Amalina, and I will refute it."

Amalina scanned the page, barely being able to recognize the words by how enervated she was. Here he was, this monster, and he was quibbling with her on the finer points?

"What else, Ms. Dalca?" sounding haughty now. "How else can you verify that I am Strigoi? Read it out so that Genadie can learn my true identity."

"Oh, no Master," he burbled unhappily on the ground, his eyes regarding his master with those of a worried pet.

"You hunt at night."

"I should hunt in the daylight? Come, Ms. Dalca, you are repeating yourself now. Anything else? Is there anything else that that book can shed light on me as this Strigoi?"

She turned a page and was surprised. Her face flushed. How had she not seen this passage before?

"It says," she began tentatively, feeling an irresistible surge of electric excitement building, "that if a bag of grain, or rice, is spilled before this being, a Strigoi, it will be forced to stop and count them all before it can move again."

"Genadie, bring a sack of grain," the Count ordered, his eyes closed imperiously, his lips tightening into a small downward curve. "At once."

"Yes, Master," Genadie pulled a small bag from off his belt. "Will raw millet do?"

"You carry millet on you, Genadie?" he asked in amazed bemusement.

"Just in case I am hungry, Master."

The Count held up his finger to indicate Genadie should wait.

"Why didn't Erik Kosche do this simple thing—pouring out a bag of grains before me—instead of engaging me in his overblown farce with you?" he asked Amalina. "I'd still be counting at this moment if he had, no?"

"I don't know. Maybe he didn't read that far," she said, cursing herself for not having turned over the page to read into the more far flung anecdotes. It seemed a giant oversight on her part now. Or maybe the pages had stuck together? That must be it! In any case, it was something she should have known and attempted. She flushed again, this time with embarrassment. "I didn't notice it, anyway."

"Is there anything else you see there in the book that will define me as Strigoi?"

Amalina looked blindly at the page.

"No."

"Then before we proceed to this final test, I will inform you now: Strigoi is a word invented long after *I* came to this earth," the Count murmured his derision. "They created that word out of fear, to try to *explain* me, to *understand* me. And over the centuries they've embellished the word, embroidered its superstitions with fetishistic heart piercings and under-the-ground-resting, and created a whole mythology, with a race of such creatures—*Strigoi*—it seems for which to indulge their fears and to entertain their idle thoughts. And to fashion a weapon against their own mortal foes. A terrifying name to malign and destroy their enemies' legacies through gossip and lies once they are in their graves and can't deny the accusation. There is no such thing as a Strigoi, Ms. Dalca."

The Count pointed at the ground in front of him. "Genadie, pour the grain."

Genadie looked sheepish, and fumbled with the bag, and then hesitated before pouring it, glancing again at his Master for permission.

"Get on with it!"

Genadie opened the mouth of the small bag, and in front of his Master's feet splashed hundreds of bits of grain onto the floor. Genadie shook it all out, creating an uneven island of millet. His eyes twitched rapidly, his crooked forefinger started to bounce nervously, and his lips moved silently, as if he himself—in desperation—were immediately setting to add up the grains for his Master.

The Count smashed his foot down onto the pile with a satisfying crunch, and then he walked stiffly over it and to the door, ignoring it entirely.

"Now clean the mess up, Ms. Dalca," he said as he left.

• • •

"*Strigoi!*" Genadie was still apoplectic, his Master's calm defense not rising far enough to satisfy his absolute outrage. He'd gotten Amalina a small pan and broom to clean the floor. "Can you still not see what is so obvious, girl? Master is the Father God, Zeus! He is Zeus, come down from the heavens to enjoy our world."

"Zeus?" Amalina was still confounded.

"There is no man on this earth so powerful." Genadie waved his finger, apparently beginning an enumeration of his master's atmospheric qualities. "There is no man so eternal. There is no man so invulnerable. There is no man so wise. There is no man so swift. There is no man so capable of flight. There is no man so capable of transformation and transmutation. He is God. And he has condescended, as he so wishes, to live with us on Earth. Has made this castle his Olympus."

"Then why does he behave like a Strigoi?"

"Ha, ha!" Genadie barked with his delighted, scraping voice. "He's disproven that! He's shown you clearly you are wrong, wrong, wrong!"

"But why does he behave like a cruel, rotten, inhuman monster, anyway?"

Genadie looked wounded. He slunk out of the room, throwing a sad look back at her.

32

The Secret of the Wail

"**I** can't allow insubordination. But to remove a meaningless distraction and return everyone to their duties … is simple enough." The Count's face was as stony as his tone, which told her that this was going to be a favor given grudgingly.

It was morning, and Genadie had brought her down from her room and into the cellars, where they took a turn into a passage that she'd never seen in her previous ventures below the castle. She was positive that the entry Genadie led her through hadn't been there before. There was no possible way she could have overlooked it. But there it was now, and she'd been led, twisting and turning, and down its steps, so that she couldn't imagine where she was in relation to the rest of the building.

Then he'd delivered Amalina to a door, with the Count standing stone-faced before it and who, after a stern clearing of his throat, delivered his cold admonition. So now Amalina, the Count, and Genadie (who held a candle), stood before a single locked door at the end of a long, lonely corridor.

What was behind the door, though … she knew with rising anticipation what would be there waiting for them. It was the answer to her question: *Who screamed at night?* The door only had to be unlocked and opened and she would see. The Count held a key in his hand, but he didn't look in any hurry to use it. His eyes, as ever, held her in place as they looked at her and somehow through her.

"Thank you, sir," she said, shy and uncertain.

"You must understand, Ms. Dalca, I could, at my own choosing, destroy you utterly. It is at my mercy that you continue to live."

Amalina felt the impulse to contradict him, to challenge him. But she knew if she spoke now she would not see—finally—who was on the other side of that door. Perhaps not ever.

But in a flash she understood just who it was. Who it must be.

Of course!

Why hadn't she thought of it before now? All these months, and it never occurred to her. Who else could it be, but the Count's wife? The one he'd rescued from that graveyard. The body had been a lifeless hunk of bone and dried flesh back in the graveyard of Neku Jonker. But in some fantastical fashion he had given her new life, so that he could be with her again. Only

... had something gone wrong? She screamed so terribly. So constantly. Every night. These were not the cries of a happy wife.

Even now, the cries were not fully abated. Maybe they never stopped. But with the sun up the wail had died down to a low blubbering, which could be heard just outside the door. Amalina could picture the figure inside the room, still dressed in the velvet dress she'd seen dragging through the grass behind Neku, now sitting on a small, padded bench, her upper half sprawled across an opulent dressing table, her skeletal head buried in her arms. Weeping.

This circumstance was a tragedy for the Count. An embarrassment. And Amalina had selfishly forced her way into a scene where she did not rightly belong. Her cheeks flushed.

"Does this child listen to me? Or does the curiosity of womankind dissolve all decency of social discourse?"

"I don't know, Master," answered Genadie in a careful whisper from behind his hand.

"Yes, I understand," she said.

"It is out of respect and pity for your father and your family line that I did not kill you that night when you leaned out your window, which would have meant nothing to me if I had. Nor when you fouled me with accusations of cheap murder. But try my patience further, and you will find that patience in short supply, and the consequences for you everlasting."

"Yes."

How could she have forgotten the lesson he'd taught her so recently? It was almost as if he didn't realize he had pushed her to the brink of death already. She and Genadie exchanged glances.

"And it is not just for your idle interest I am doing this ... to placate the selfish whims of a child. Genadie has rightly reminded me that this sound, as loud as it is, could stand to ruin everything I am working towards."

"Oh."

"So if I am to open this door," said the Count, looking more sober now, "and reveal to you this castle's secrets, you will do something inside of it."

"Huh?"

• • •

Up.
Down.
   Up.
   Down.
The movement so relentless, so monotonous.
   Up, then down.

Up, then down.

Or was it: Down, then up? Down, then up?

A motion seemingly designed to rob all energy and thought. Which it had. So that there was not much memory to hold onto, it all slipping away to the extremes of the up-down-up-down motion. Even the curiosity once felt over why a turn to one side or the other—left or right, east or west—why one side or another did not leave any impact on the senses when reached, rather than when it struck all the way up or all the way down, that curiosity was a weak remembrance of a long ago marvel. All that mattered was North and South, Up and Down.

And, of course, the agony. A thorn scraping out the insides. An anguish consuming the whole body. The pain abated regularly like the throb of a slow pulse, only to return. Never once stopping. And without the power to move a limb, to lift one's body, under the crushing weight of a thousand feet of earth—or so it felt—all that was left was to cry out against this constant torment. Cry and cry. The cry's fueling breath never-ending, eternal, as if a constant wind was blowing through the body. Never requiring rest or needing to stop. Just like the 'Up, then down. Up, then down'.

Voices.

That was something new.

Not far away.

But not very strong. Hidden.

Hard to tell which direction, with the constant movement.

What were the voices saying?

Listen.

"… will throw the lever. Then you act. There will be little time."

"Why can't you do it? You are stronger than me."

"You must prove yourself."

"That isn't a very good reason. If you need it done, and fast, there would be less risk if *you* do it."

"I will not enter that room."

"Why not?"

"You don't need to know."

"And why not Genadie?"

"He pulls the lever."

"I can pull the lever for him."

"You don't know where it is, and you aren't strong enough to do it, even if I allowed you to try. And Genadie has already proven himself. He entered that room once. Now it is your turn, Amalina. If you want to know what's there inside. If you want to prove yourself to me, Amalina Dalca …"

The name, the voices, they mean nothing.

Shut them out. Just wait.

Someone is coming.

Make yourself presentable.

Yes, that was important once, wasn't it? You must look good. But how can I, without a mirror? Without light? Well, somehow. Your moment of opportunity is coming.

. . .

The door opened.

Two eyes peered in through the narrow parting. One below, one above.

The door opened wider.

Light shot into the room.

Two silhouetted bodies in the hallway. One large, one small.

The small one stepped forward.

Stepped once toward the wheel in the center of the room.

In the small one's hand was a chunky block hammer.

The other hand was clutching something. Something …

The room vibrated with the scraping movements of the turning wheel. The wheel stood vertically. It was a smaller version of the water wheel found at a mill house. Its wood was old but sturdy. You could tell just how sturdy it was by the deepness of the sound it made, its resonating voice as it spun.

The small one moved cautiously, studying the wheel and what was lashed to it.

It must have been difficult, in the minimal light, and with the unceasing turning of the wheel, to make out the exact details and proportions of the spinning body upon it. It was slender, and pale. It wore a light gown and had long blond hair. Its skin was withered on top of thick veins and the protruding, but closed, orbs of eyes. It was a woman. Hard to tell the age. She was thrown out across the wheel, spread eagle. And she was bound to the wheel at the waist, the wrists, and the ankles, by what looked to be hundreds of strands of chain. More chain than would seem reasonable to secure such a weak figure.

The small one's head began to lift up and down, to circle to follow the rotation of the woman's head as it made its circular journey from ceiling to floor. She stopped within half a foot of the wheel. She appeared mesmerized.

The larger shadow, in the hall, seemed to disappear then reappear within the space of a second.

Somewhere a lever was thrown, and a loud protest of wood and metal followed. The walls groaned.

And the wheel stopped.

. . .

The head of the body lolled drunkenly, eyes still closed. But there was an extra movement to the head not to be attributed to the stopping of the wheel. The body was alive. Unconscious, but stirring.

Stirring.

The Count was right. There wouldn't be much time.

Amalina studied the woman's face. This wasn't the woman from the graveyard after all. Someone very different. She must have been pretty once upon a time. Though wrinkled and drained, the skin still seemed *fresh*. And it wasn't hard to imagine that with the sags and crevices plumped out, she might even be stunning. But now she was sickly. And dangerous, if the Count was to be believed.

The head shivered.

Amalina placed several long bits of metal—carpenter's nails—into her mouth and clamped them hard between her teeth. The metal had warmed in her sweating palm, but the nails still felt cool next to her tongue. She tasted the sharp bite of iron.

With her left hand, she brought a single nail up to the wheel, near the lolling head, and pounded it once, twice, thrice, very quickly. The nail was sharp and went into the wood fast, solid and deep. The eyes on the head shivered.

"No," said the Count. "Closer. It will need to be closer, Amalina!"

Amalina took another nail from between her teeth, positioned it a hand's width from the body's mouth—its teeth—and drove in the nail with the same three determined blows. She nearly smacked the body's cheek on the final strike.

The eyes on the head fluttered like the wings of a panicked butterfly. A moan sounded.

"Amalina!"

Amalina went to place a new nail on the other side of the head. The body's mouth, with withdrawing lips, followed her hand. She gasped but carried on as the moan grew and the eyelids opened just a little more … a little more.

Wham, wham, wham.

"Wh … Wh …"

Its voice was so dry and hoarse. Sounded like the scraping of two planks.

"Quickly!"

Amalina found the loosest length of chain, which was threaded across the torso, and pulled it free. These chains were as cold as river water. Her fingers stung faintly at the touch. They were shinier than any iron chain she'd ever seen.

She hooked one side of the chain around the closest nail.

"The mouth!"

Quickly, and with a shocking tremor of sadistic glee, Amalina pulled the chain taught across the woman's mouth, the growing moan driving her movements, in the hopes of stopping the sound before it rose into a scream. Into that awful wail. She wiggled the chain, separating the lips, forcing the teeth apart. Like setting a bit in a horse's mouth, she thought.

As the chain leapt past the teeth and wedged deep into the corners of the mouth, the woman's eyes shot wide open. Eyes dry and wrinkled and dull, but full of fury. Amalina wrapped the chain's far end around the nail on the other side of the head. The woman gasped but the sound was just a low inward hiss, her head held fast against the wheel, her mouth gagged. All efforts of her neck and throat discouraged; blocked by some power in this chain. Amalina brought down the hammer to bend (and lock) the second nail through the eye of a shiny link, and it secured the chain tight.

This chain was so oddly bright. Amalina stared at it. It wasn't made of iron. Not any iron she'd ever known, at least. It outshone the luster of fine steel.

Somewhere Genadie threw the lever and the wheel lurched with a burst of stored energy, and the wood and metal cried out. So did the body. But she could not cry out as before. So weak and muffled now. The shimmering chain paralyzing her head, her tongue, and smothering the sound.

• • •

"That chain is the only thing that seems to work on her," the Count explained.

"Why?" asked Amalina.

"I don't know."

"What kind of metal is it?"

He didn't answer, his blithe expression fixed into place like a hardening plaster, and his eyes rooted themselves somewhere beyond the walls in front of them. This reaction was as good as just another 'I don't know.'

"Who is she?"

"I don't know that either." he said patiently, if a little dull and distantly.

"Then why did you do this to her? You *did* put her on that wheel, didn't you?"

"I did," Genadie leapt to his master's defense.

"He told you to do it then," said Amalina.

"He needn't tell me to. I knew what needed to be done and I did it."

"You knew that poor woman needed to be thrown on a mill wheel and hitched there with that chain, did you?"

"I knew she needed to be stopped," retorted Genadie, indignantly. "She dared to invade Olympus—"

Genadie stopped short of his full comment, looking very shy.

"Where did you say?" she needled him.

"Where do you think you are, girl?" he growled defiantly. "This is our Master's home."

"And why did you call it 'Olympus'?"

Amalina looked to the Count for his reaction. The Count was staring at his servant as if he was interested to know himself.

"Stupid girl," he dismissed her quickly. "Master knows all about it. And no one, no mortal—no simple mortal—may enter the mountaintop without our master's permission. Much less defile it with her curses and her violent, destructive behavior. She had to be stopped and she rightly was. *By me.*"

The Count's eyes gained that glimmer of amusement again as he observed his quaking servant carrying on. It was telling enough, his lively but somehow detached, condescending look.

"I don't believe it happened quite that way," said Amalina. "She's not a 'simple mortal'."

"She is."

"That woman on that wheel is not any normal human being."

"She was. Once upon a time."

"But she wasn't when she was put to the wheel, because something like that, a torture on a spinning wheel, it would kill someone. And you bound her there with a chain of strange metal, like your master said, because it was all that would hold her, when any old iron chain would do the trick for a regular body. So: not a human, after all, Genadie."

"Well, I … Well, I … She *was* normal, if you listened to me. *Once upon a time.*"

Amalina saw the count's eyes twinkling merrily at the exchange between his servants, he safely out of it.

"What happened to her? Why did she invade the castle? She was mad at you, sir?"

"She was as confused as I was," he said after a hesitation, surprised he'd been targeted in the questioning. "A girl who should have died. Fallen to me …"

"One of your victims."

"Prey," he said in a withdrawing tone. He did not care for the attention being focused on himself one bit. It seemed to bore him. "If what she claims is true. I don't remember everyone, of course. Only, this one—if it's true— she did not die, as all the others have died. They've all died for as far back as my memory goes. But she lived on this way, instead of dying. And I could do nothing to change that fact."

"And she wanted to kill Master," Genadie jumped in. "That meant a lot of trouble. We had no choice."

"You couldn't kill her at all?"

"She is almost like our Master. Only the composition of that bind chain—"

"We tried many different solutions," the Count cut in, trying to put an end to the conversation. "This was the most effective."

"You didn't try to pierce her heart?" asked Amalina.

The Count's eyes widened.

"You said that she's like you," explained Amalina. "And whether or not you are *strigoi*, you admitted that doing such a thing would hurt you. And still, you haven't pierced her heart. Why not? Or cut off her head?"

"I do not wish to kill her."

"It would stop her from crying out. She wouldn't trouble you anymore."

"She won't trouble us any longer as it is, with her head immobilized. You want me to kill her, Ms. Dalca?"

"I just think she's suffering needlessly. Cruelly. On that horrible rotating rack all this time? And how long *has* she been—?"

"She will live until I deem it otherwise. It isn't very long in the scheme of things, even if I were to allow her to live for another fifty years."

"Yes, sir."

"But I need her to live, until I can understand how she became this way."

"Why do you care?"

"Because if I knew how it happened … "

But then Amalina was already feeling a rise of shame for having helped him, whatever his purpose. She really didn't care to know what it was all about. She'd silenced the wail. Yes, in the moment the woman had been frightening, but that was no excuse. And now, as she suffered the plunging realization that she might have just made a mistake and regret fully set in, Amalina's shame grew teeth; the pang of having done wrong, having commited to something so irresponsible it was punishable, attacked her more savagely than any wolfhound. It tore at her insides. What she'd done to that poor woman on the wheel, binding her there, was a criminal act that she would never—could never, and should never—forget. But she knew it was also one she'd best to keep well to herself. Like a secret.

She had just added to this castle's secrets!

Secret #1. A being of immense, incalculable power—perhaps even a god—lived in this castle.

Secret #2. The being had long ago imprisoned a creature like himself—but a woman—in the cellars; locked her to a wheel, where her only relief was to cry out her torment through the night, eternally.

And, Secret #3. Amalina, with her own hands—and now to her utter disgrace and embarrassment—had silenced this pathetic woman forever. A selfish act whose consequence was: she herself became a part of the castle's history, linked her to it as with an invisible iron chain; also forever.

33

The Count's Confession

That evening Amalina was summoned to the Count's private study. He was sitting on the divan in the same oriental manner he'd received Katrina. Only looking a little stiffer in his posture. Genadie was sent away.

Amalina was relieved to find the Count so relaxed considering all that had happened. And relieved, too, he'd given up any suspicions against her—especially now she'd proved her loyalty by helping to restrain the weird woman on the wheel. Amalina's grimy, incriminating footprints, wandering all over the castle, created the previous night while attempting to erase her guilt, had been dismissed outright as mad wanderings after the day's extraordinarily stressful events, then having received a concussion, and then finding herself all alone in the castle, at night. Her prints outside the castle walls and specific movements in the courtyard had been conveniently covered or obscured by the frolicking horse and the storm that coated everything with a foot of dense white snow.

So now here she was, delivered to the Count, who was spread out regally, if looking a little forlorn. She noticed something else ... something else different about his face that she couldn't rightly identify. In a vague way his face looked thinner and weaker.

"I have lived for a very long time," the Count told her in his deep, rich voice, and regarding her with something more than was usually there in his large, dark eyes. "And, as I told you earlier: I never died. I was born as anyone else is born. I remember the sights and experiences of when I was a child, fragments that get clearer and more precise as it carries forward from there.

"I was very powerful, at first, when I was young. But only in the most common way of being powerful, Ms. Dalca: I was lord over these lands. All these lands. I was the owner and the protector of my people. But I was a weak man then. And for so long. My thirst and hunger was for more and more territory, more and more castles, more and more authority and adulation by the faceless horde of commoners. I did not understand *real* power until much later. After I'd acquired everything a mad tyrant could want—the titles, the respect, the fear—it was only then that I became aware of the growing gift inside of me. The internal power that would set me above all other men of this world.

"This greater power of mine came gradually. At some point I realized what was happening, and realized, too, I had to withdraw myself from the public circles of ordinary life, before the people grew aware of my unusual and increasing strength. In fear, they might conceive I was a sorcerer of some kind. In numbers, they could turn on me. At least in the beginning."

The Count rubbed his chin and grinned snidely at the thought. She realized now what was different about his face. His mustache was gone.

"I nurtured and grew my abilities, and sought to bring them to bear on all my worldly opponents. While my body was surpassing the limits of nature, my mind was still bound within the thoughts of a low being. I still craved my conquests. I still reviled my enemies, and my family's enemies, and cherished the idea of protecting this land against its invaders.

"I still do ... But, maybe not so much as before. You see, Ms. Dalca, I have lived for a very long time. And early on I was able to lure my old enemies close enough, to bring them into my lands. And then I killed them. Every one of them. I slaughtered their armies. I destroyed their families to a full end, so that no remnants were left even on their maternal sides. Everything that defined me—those enemies which I fought against—I eliminated. Entirely.

"And so, with the world cleared of opposition, I was without direction. I had nothing to live for, and yet, as it turned out, I am as eternal as any demigod. Let Genadie have his amazing delusions about me, they are as good as any. I am a being who can't be vanquished, I can tear down kings and armies, and raze whole cities.

"Have you heard of the cities of Olex and Vijku?" he asked, sending an amused, querying look at her.

Amalina thought about it, rummaging through her memory.

"No," she said.

"That's because I put them into the ground. And I removed every trace of them. From maps and histories."

Amalina looked skeptical.

"You read your sheriff's secret history of your city. Didn't you see the holes burned into the pages alongside the names of the cities of Netz and Tsobl and the rest? Didn't you notice the holes burned into the recording of the names? Those holes eliminate the cities of Olex and Vijku, and all the men from there. Olex and Vijku were renegers to the agreements laid out in the contract which the bishops of Tsobl and Netz and others forged with me—*had* forged with me. And so I took them down, to the last soul. Because that is within my power."

It seemed impossible to Amalina. To remove whole cities from history?

"Amalina, I've been on this planet for hundreds of years. How long have you been here? You know only what you've been told, and even that much extends back ... how far? How old is the oldest person you know, and how far back does *their* memory go? In time, everything can be erased, even cities and their populations. Entirely forgotten by history and mankind. Lost forever, Amalina. Never to have existed. All it takes is time. And all I have above everyone else in this world is time."

· · ·

"I was a fool." the Count continued. "When I was still an ordinary man, I never indulged in recreation, I despised leisure. I was nurtured and educated in the dogmas of a fanatical religion, and so I deemed anything carnal as sinful, to be derided or destroyed. Food mattered not. Women were commodities to provide heirs and cement alliances. Flowers obstructed my path. Blood was only important when it was being spilled to instill fear, or gain bits of ground. What mattered most was gold and land and vengeance against those who opposed me. It was all I could ever think about, even—as I've revealed to you—after I came to the fullness of my powers. I relentlessly pursued what I had always considered 'important', and only with great reluctance sought those resources which slaked my body's requirements (those of sustenance and siring, which I considered 'regrettable' at the time). I disdained the expansion of intellect beyond its 'proper' bounds. I neglected the body. I cared nothing for society.

"I was no man," he nodded with a grin and a wink toward Amalina, "I was *inhuman.*

"But I've changed, and become reflective. Over the centuries, I've grown ever weaker against the light of the sun, so that I cannot abide it. My sensitivity and vulnerability to various sensations and certain materials has increased to the point of suffering in their presence, as like a severe allergy. And my thoughts are flattening, dulling. Becoming less precise as they once were. And recently I have come to fear, to truly fear, that I will reach a point of ultimate exhaustion.

"In that realization—and through that prism—I looked around me. And I realized what I have missed. All this time devoted to the conquest of others, I did not appreciate those aspects of life which are the most interesting. In the passing of time, a measure I can appreciate from my own unique vantage point, all that stands out are the brushing of one interesting person against another, the accomplishments of the mind, and the thrill of sensations. As a creature of cold calculation I'd never recognized the primacy of *living*. How mistaken I was that I did not celebrate the magnificence of sensuality.

"But I've awoke to this reality. And now that I'm trapped here, within this thriving, exciting world, never to leave it, my power like a cage preventing my release into the eternal. I must make these prison bars silk, and every palette a pillow, and finally enjoy what was meant to be enjoyed while I have the time. Before I become as bland as a statue. Maybe this is my punishment. But I will take it."

He paused with a wry smile.

"When I rescued my beloved wife—her body, anyway—from that criminal, Neku Jonker, I ended the last concern I ever had for that old life. The final vestiges of a squalid, wasted humanity, one drearily devoted to power and the control of others, was finally put to rest. And it was time to turn my eyes forward."

The count pulled to his lap a book whose covers contained many loose sheets of paper. His eyes roved lovingly at the pages he turned, regarding them like valuable gems.

"The printing press. I am now able to peer directly across the world, as if with a telescope. To places beyond my physical reach. I've witnessed their progress in science and the arts. I've watched as their cultures have blossomed. Their clothing styles evolved. Their manners matured and honed to the best of all things."

The Count pointed to a long piece of newspaper.

"Look at this, Amalina. Galas and balls. Symphonies and recitals. The world thrives beyond these mountains, and I am missing it. I am missing all of it!"

She could not tell if it was rapture or horror in his eyes as he stared into the pages, as if he were about to plunge bodily into them.

• • •

"Katrina, that most talented woman, was to be my envoy," the Count continued on, now more hollowed in tone, passing out of his reverie. "She, the greatest actress I have ever seen, with the proper look and the correct training, posing as my counterfeit niece, would be introduced into the greater society of Europe. During the spring and early summer she would meet with all the best families, and speak well of me, and seek out all the finest available daughters that might be interested—might be convinced— to travel eastward. To enjoy the splendor of the old provinces and the company of a storied prince—um, er, count of the region.

"I put so much thought and cunning into my planning. You and Genadie would polish this castle into its former elegance, while Katrina discovered and primed the treasures of the west, to bring them here to me."

"But now she is ... gone," said Amalina, with a shudder of horror, and feeling sad at the loss of even the cold and arrogant—the criminal—Katrina.

"Her shortsighted greed robbed her of her life. And ruined so much of my careful effort, yes."

Amalina straightened with a warm bolt of realization. If Katrina was dead, that put an end to the Count's entire scheme. So that meant she was no longer necessary here in the castle, as the work would now be pointless.

"Does that mean," she dared to ask in a rising eager voice, speaking even before her mind could catch her, "that I can go home?"

The Count regarded her silently.

"I mean," she said shyly now, "since I'm no longer needed."

"Did I tell you that you are no longer needed?" The Count asked her. "Don't worry, Ms. Dalca. You will return to your village soon enough. But this castle still needs to be prepared."

"But without Katrina …?"

"You know I am very thorough in thought and planning," he said. "Katrina was to be the star of the show that is true. And I will regret her absence. But I prepared for every contingency, and as in any great performance, there is the one who is called 'the understudy'."

Amalina had never heard the term before, but she immediately understood the meaning by the way he was looking at her. Her mind went haywire. Her face flushed, her body began to shiver and shake. But she stood there in her spot, staring in disbelief at the Count.

"I've begun to suspect," he said with a satisfied smile, "that it was fortune showing me a kindness when I found you in the window that night."

He rang the bell and Genadie charged in to help him off the divan.

The Count winced as he got to his feet, muttering hotly, "That Kralov."

Then he walked with a slight limp out of the room. He was limping? She hadn't noticed it before. Had Kralov wounded the Count?

This revelation didn't excite her too much. Once he was out of the room she ran upstairs to cry.

• • •

"Ms. Dalca," said Genadie in his soft scratchy voice. "I know you're upset, but really you shouldn't be."

"Leave me alone!" screamed Amalina.

"If you will just listen," he whispered. "Please. You needn't be like this."

"And why not? He said I'd be going home soon, and now he plans to send me off as 'the understudy', his replacement 'niece', to who knows where? Never! I won't. I'll throw myself out the window!"

"You'll be back home," Genadie whispered soothingly. "Sooner than you think."

"Oh, shut up!"

"No, my pupil!" Genadie said crossly now. "You listen to me. I know what you've been through. I know what you think of our Master—"

"*Your* master! To me he's nothing more than a living monster!"

"He is Zeus!"

"Shut up!"

Amalina threw a pillow over her head.

"I was thinking about what you asked me, Ms. Dalca," Genadie whispered again, in the opening under the pillow, his breath smelling like foul herbs. "About why our Master behaves like 'nothing more than a rotten Strigoi', was it? Well, you see … this is my answer, Ms. Dalca: How our Master amuses himself is our Master's will, and above question. Why does he read a book? Why does he indulge in crude sciences? Why does he choose to allow certain materials to be materials he cannot abide? Why does he allow that horrible woman-thing to continue to live underneath the castle? … And so he behaves like a Strigoi? How can you dare question the life of a god? You should be on your knees before him, girl. Kiss your knees. Pray for his forgiveness.

"But, listen," he whispered, oh so softly now, so that she could almost not hear the words. "He may be Zeus, but we are all men of free will. The legends of the pantheon abound with willful heroes disobeying their direct commands, when they thought it just to do so."

Amalina turned her head under the pillow. She saw Genadie's eye blinking at her.

"Listen, Ms. Dalca … I know what you've suffered here. And I remember the kindnesses you've done for me, and how you've looked after me, and how you tended to me and would not see me suffer one lump. Better than any mother I could've hoped for. You're a very good person, Ms. Dalca. The nicest, kindest girl I've ever met. And I don't abide children.

"In payment for your kindness," he continued, "I am willing to do what is right and just. I see how upset you are. I know Master wants you to go far away to help him on a quest. And that I'm to take you there. And that it is important for his will to be carried out. 'Straightaway to Antwerp', he said."

Genadie stuck up one of his crooked fingers under the pillow, wagging it. "But I'm a good person, just like you. I remember what you want, I know what your kind heart longs for, and I am willing to do it. When we leave this castle, it will be at daybreak. The Master can't follow us. He won't know where we are going. He thinks we will be going straightaway to Antwerp, because his servant Genadie is faithful and will do his bidding. But as payment for your kindness and goodness, Ms. Dalca, we will not be taking the road to Antwerp. We will be taking the road to Korr, your village … and your father!"

"Oh, Genadie!" Amalina could have kissed him if he didn't look and smell so unclean.

34

Dragomir Rejoices

"How's your daughter, Dragomir?" asked the deputy sheriff. Dragomir looked at him with dark-pitted eyes and shrugged his large shoulders slowly.

"She's fine. But doesn't write as often as she should." A morose laugh rose from him like a soft belch. He was hunched over. His chin nearly resting on his chest.

"Where did you say she went? Berg ... ?"

"To visit my aunt, in Breck. Which is in Germania."

"All the way there?" the deputy sheriff gawped, just the way he'd reacted first time he'd heard it. "Germania? For such a young girl!"

"I thought it might help her in her education. Besides, my aunt doesn't have a daughter and she is old and needs help."

"Amalina being away doesn't help *you* very much." The deputy sheriff took one of the loaves of bread and knocked it on the counter. It sounded like a rock. "Not as bad as your comrade's logs on the other side of town. But hasn't really been the same since she left."

"No, it hasn't." Dragomir thought he should apologize for the bread. People had been complaining for months how burnt, or undercooked, or tough, or flaky his bread was now that Amalina had gone away. Some had even left off as customers. Were they traveling across town to buy Argus' crummy stock? Unbearable a thought. Dragomir had been an excellent baker long before his daughter was born. The only accounting for why he was no good now, now that she wasn't around, was that his heart was heavy. Even after so long a time.

If only he could see her, or hear from her, he thought. To know she was well and in good care. If he had some reassurance to buoy his spirits he could attend to his craft with proper diligence, instead of finding places in the store to hide his tears. Or consuming his time with fears of what might be happening to his daughter, far away in that creature's castle.

How hard it is, he thought, to keep this secret. To maintain the lie to all his friends and patrons that his daughter had gone to visit some fictitious relative in a city whose name he'd only ever seen on a map. He was sure a dark train of gossip was circulating about what might have happened for a father to send a daughter away. A fight? A broken romance between Amalina and an unsuitable boy? Had she run away from home? Had she been plucked from the forest by the wolves (or the Monster)?

The men who comprised the village's enlightened inner circle knew this for a fact: Dragomir had packed his daughter away to a foreign relative—*"all the way to, Breck! … in Germania!" they would say*—in order to keep her out of the Count's hands—*"even if the poor man's unwilling to admit it!"*. And who was Dragomir to disabuse them of their smug, cynical certainty? Let them have it. It kept them quiet not wanting to shame their friend. And quiet was good. It meant they asked fewer questions, and that he and his business still had some degree of standing in the village, no matter how diminished.

Dragomir figured Sadra had already spread this "secret truth behind Amalina's absence" to certain women. To those who weren't aware of his daughter's encounter with the Count. Bless her.

"Yes, I'll have to get a better flour," Dragomir said abashedly. "It doesn't hold its body, then it burns. I'll make sure it's right tomorrow."

"Good. Wouldn't want to have you lose customers to that man across town. Oh, and while she's gone," the deputy sheriff grinned, "you might take your mind off her absence by visiting Widow Lidsz."

Dragomir smiled politely. The deputy sheriff knocked the bread on the counter as a way of saying 'you know what I mean' and then left.

Dragomir's shoulders slumped.

Why did the deputy sheriff have to mention Amalina? He hadn't thought of her since the morning, and now he would be in a bad mood for the rest of the day. Maybe the next.

When he turned he saw the strange man with the long greasy hair and the dirty suit bowing to him.

"You!" Dragomir bellowed. His rage boiled and he stood to his full height. But then he had a second thought. "Why are you here? Is it Amalina?"

"Please," said the strange man, holding up a crooked finger. "I can say nothing to you. I've said nothing to you. I was never even here."

Then he presented Dragomir with a large, leather bound book.

"I've broken none of *His* laws," said the strange man, bowing and retreating out of the store.

Dragomir followed, but stopped in the doorway, watching the Count's toady scurry along the snow-clogged streets like a nimble rat, not looking in any direction and keeping his head down and covered with his hat.

Dragomir's heart was pounding with excitement andhe resented it. Why should he get excited at the sight of his enemy? Just because he was lightly attached to Amalina?

It made his blood boil.

Well, what's the book about?

He opened the book and was immediately mesmerized. By the crisply delineated pieces of machinery which his eyes tickled over, he could tell this book was a guide to engineering. He couldn't grasp the exact purpose of the first illustration's detailed mechanism, but he always enjoyed well-crafted diagrams, whether he understood them or not. *And look how clear and neat the edges are*, he thought, admiring how fine the printwork was. *What craftsmanship!*

But what was the purpose of giving him this book? Why had that rat delivered it? Was it some present from the castle? From Amalina? Or did the Count have a reason for it?

He searched the book for an envelope or a note.

His eye was caught by a tiny childlike drawing of a flower below the first paragraph.

It looked like the kind of flower a child draws.

It looked like the kind of flower *Amalina* drew.

But what was it doing there on the page?

He flipped to another page and spotted another flower.

This continued on until he spotted a flower in one of the diagrams. There was a small letter "h" next to it. It was in Amalina's handwriting. His heart began to thud hard again.

Searching the book, he found more and more of the letters, some at the top of the page, some in the middle, and some at the bottom. There were more to be found in the diagrams, sprinkled here and there.

Dragomir tore off a sheet of parchment and took a pencil. He then began writing the letters down as he found them.

> "hi papa i am well i hope you are well too i miss you here is a book you will like write back to me in the book they won't notice they are stupid love AMA"

Dragomir wanted to shout to the heavens. He laughed and his tears flowed. And the next day the bread was going to be the best he'd baked in nearly a year

• • •

The carriage shook. Genadie had climbed back onto it.

"Dragomir was very happy," Genadie shouted down to Amalina "He gives you his love!"

Genadie made a tch-tch sound and the carriage jolted. The horses began to pull at a fast pace.

Amalina, inside the carriage compartment, screamed: "Genadie! This isn't fair! This isn't what I wanted! I want to go back home!"

"And you will," he called cheerily. "Very soon! We just have a mission before us, commanded by no less than our beloved Zeus!"

She cursed him.

"If you keep that up I'll put on the gag," he warned.

She looked at the shackles on her wrists, and the chain runnning through the bolt on the floor. She used her legs to try to break the bolt free. If she got it loose, when they reached the next city she could leap through the heavy blankets that covered the windows.

Thinking again, she kicked at the blankets. She knocked one aside and then brought her head to the window. She hoped to see Gulgas, or Jenz Timer, or anyone else from the village. Someone who would see her and recognize her and rescue her.

Of all people, she saw the minister and his wife, Sadra, all bundled up and walking alongside the road, they having moved aside for the raging carriage, staring up at it with looks of surprise.

Amalina gasped and fell back to the floor. It was a reflex that had done it. All the children, whether they were up to something naughty or not, had the habit of running and hiding when the minister—well, when Sadra— appeared suddenly. They would hide and laugh to themselves. Laugh for whatever reason, as if they'd gotten away with murder. Only now Amalina cursed herself. She saw in her mind the minister's lips purse, his expression changing from one of surprise to one of confusion—unsure of what he'd seen. But Sadra's face hardened. She was no longer surprised, but confident of what she'd seen. And what they'd seen was very curious, wasn't it?

If only I'd stayed at the window and shouted at them, Amalina thought.

When Amalina realized her mistake and put her head back to the window, they were already out of sight. She didn't bother to yell. She felt her defeat.

It's all been mistakes for me, hasn't it? she lamented as, in her despair, it all became clear to her. Every time she'd helped the Count—in the graveyard against Neku, laboring with Genadie in the castle, silencing the wailing woman—they'd been tests. And while she'd passed them by surviving, she hadn't been smart enough to see they'd really been tests of loyalty, she proving her ability to serve him. She hadn't been clever enough, instead, to escape.

She looked at the bolt securing her to the floor and went at it again with her legs. There was always the next city to get free. Any place would be good enough to turn around, before they got too far.

As they traveled through the mud and snow and the deeply rutted roads on their way out of the mountains, destined for the never-before-seen western kingdoms, Genadie was singing: "You'll be back before you know it! You'll be back before you know it! You'll be back before you know it!"

Only the Beginning, pt. 2

"The darkness which hid itself away, which lay dormant for so long, has now chosen to emerge; and to expand its foul breath into our living space," Attila the low constable announced with a dramatic flip of his wrist. His eyes remained half-shut and were the study of boredom.

The old, fat high constable rapped the table irritably to get the attention of the other men in the room. But he addressed Attila directly: "Your words mean nothing in defense of the charges against you."

Attila was about to die, and he knew it.

With his impeccable perception, unparalleled deductive reasoning, and that touch of Ardeelian mountain intuition, the low constable could almost read his death sentence as if it were written in fire across the eyes of these ambitious old men staring at him now—even the odd one out, the one in the back of the room, who had no reason to be there. That this was Attila's day of execution was so without question, he could already feel the rope around his neck, the blade skewering him and opening guts to the air, the horses plucking his limbs in all directions, the flames licking up his skin and choking him—whatever was to be his end. Still, he did not honor these men with anything close to a look of fear, but leveled at them the stoniest of expressions, which could only be read as confidence or contempt. Even to that one in the back, looking somewhat bemused by it all.

Attila Bronk wasn't wrong: death *was* approaching. At the very moment Amalina Dalca was being flown away to parts of the world yet unseen to her, ruing her naivete and her decisions that led to her being chained inside that carriage, and cursing the fool-hardy, impetuous curiosity that had so upended her world, the low constable was about to suffer a death no less reproving of his own faults—his own peculiar naivete and his arrogance.

Good enough to sense the arrival of an end, but not fully understanding it yet, he pushed on—pushed against the stupidity of these old men, so that, even if they were to be rid of him this day, they would be forced to accept the truth; even to the man in the back!

. . .

"I couldn't care less about meaningless charges," murmured Attila.

"You consider these charges meaningless, do you?" asked the mayor, his voice as irritable as the high constable's rapping on the table. "If nothing else, they will certainly discharge you from your post, constable."

"Or banish you from our territory. But you could also hang," added the prosecutor. "Or burn."

Attila's eyes betrayed no emotion. At length he nodded his head in acknowledgement of their points.

"Attila," began the mayor, "I'm trying to honor your family name by viewing your crime in the most charitable of lights. But you must help us all—us *all*—by cooperating in the effort."

"There are families with as good a name as your own, and far better," said the judge hostilely, "who'd be content to have a malcontent such as yourself, one who promises nothing more than a reign of petty tyranny by abusing his post and power, to enjoy a swift end."

Without moving his head, Attila turned his eyes to the judge. He stared at the man for a long time.

"Attila," said the fat high constable, trying to attract his attention, "you seem to view the position you are in—in this court—as some sort of stage to spout your fantasies. Nothing that happens here in this room will be known by anyone, other than those *in* this room. The wild and dramatic content of your imagination will be contained herein, and wastes our day. Respond as a man of the law, and in a relevant way to the charges before you."

"You are charged, Attila Bronk," the judge shot in impatiently, preparing to sum once more the low constable's offences, his large nose shaking back and forth with the vehemence of his words, "with having disturbed the peace of Tsobl on the day of ..."

Attila stifled a yawn. He cleaned his right ear with a handkerchief.

"... You were observed in a state of drunkenness. You sounded the bells of our central church in the manner of alerting invasion. You caused the disquiet of two of our most beloved citizens, who either collapsed in fear of impending death, or were injured in the panic which followed, in the form of broken limb (the right and left legs). You did this, and stand guilty before our eyes. Now, what say you to the charges, Low Constable Attila Bronk?"

"I was drunk," said Attila. "Inebriation is not an enumerated crime in Tsobl's law, no matter we jail those who are intoxicated. Lest you mistake the reason we do so: we jail the drunks to preserve order, and to prevent them from hurting themselves or others. But it isn't punishable by any statute. And jailing me as a precaution is just what the high constable did. While I cannot forgive the abusive length of my incarceration—*months*, sirs—meant for my own benefit, but would suggest vindictive punishment against me by the honorable high constable—I will set that matter aside for the greater good; as I would ask that you men here in this room, the very elite of law and order in this land, would follow my lead. My request for leniency extends also to the governor, who has shown his interest in this matter by attending this morning's proceedings."

The governor, the man in the back, a man with a pink-red face the complexion of a roasted ham, wearing a vested suit made by the most fashionable tailor of Tsobl, pursed his lips and steepled his fingers. Out of boredom or to acknowledge Attila's statement, couldn't be positively decided.

The roasted ham waited for Attila to continue without further movement.

"But ringing those bells," said Attila, "that was not a malicious prank, or an abuse of my powers. It was the warnings of a true, loyal citizen of this city and country, to a menace known all too well—or at least should be known, and *recognized*—by the men sitting in my judgment here today. It was a warning of a rising danger. One as serious as any invasion by pirates or the Ottomans, as this danger has the power to wreak unfathomable carnage upon us all if it were to exercise its full strength. I simply gave warning. Gave warning."

"Do you feel there is a conspiracy against you, low constable?" the prosecutor scoffed.

The judge just admitted as much, Attila thought. He stared dully.

"Do you feel there is a conspiracy against you, low constable?" the prosecutor repeated, more seriously this time, but with incredulity at how ridiculous such a conspiracy would be.

But if a conspiracy were so ludicrous, why then was this trial, delayed for so very long, being attended by the highest ranking leaders of Tsobl? and conducted inside private chambers? with no secretary to record the event or their words?

He had hoped the trial would be public. That there would have been someone to transcribe faithfully his speech, so that his important words might be broadcast louder than any bell—*to alert the farthest reaches of Ardeel!*

Instead he was enclosed here with the browbeating elites, the purpose for these jealous men to crush him or to kill him; willing to kill him; waiting to; possessing the power to do so. It was enough to make Attila give up.

Attila shrugged at his own hopeless thoughts.

Several of the men in the room chortled at the unconscious gesture, taking it as a sad confession of his impotence against them.

Though his dull eyes never flickered, he allowed himself a soft sigh at the recognition that he would indeed be executed this day and never see the full fruition of his work.

But, again, he had to try. To continue to sound the alarm. To strive as hard as he could, despite his despair.

The whole world depends on it.

• • •

"My superiors," Attila began warmly, cordially, his final attempt. "How could there be a conspiracy against me? Conspiracies are enacted only in the face of an overwhelming threat to those conspirators' power. That would mean you'd have to perceive me as some kind of threat; that I had some force that could destabilize your stations. No, there's no conspiracy against me. There is, however, a conspiracy against *the people themselves*." At this Attila lifted a small book from a pocket of his jacket. "Written in black and white. A compact between those that claim to serve the people," he pointed the book in a jabbing way at each member of the court, "and a force almost equal to the Almighty's reckoning, but was forged in the furnaces of hell."

The faces gaped at the book in wonder. The high constable wrapped his thick lower lip with his pudgy fingers. The roasted ham simmered silently.

"No, I am not here to judge you," the low constable told them, though his tone was basted with ridicule. "I am here to draw your attention. I am here to remind you. There is a threat to us all, and could destroy our way of life here if we do nothing, if we waste our time prosecuting blameless members of the community; if we *let* it *do so*.

"I have been to the St. Grigori church," he told them. "I have seen the activity of this monster that was once constrained by heaven's power, no longer bounded by it. It has either increased in might to match our heavenly Lord, or it has shrugged off its superstitions and torn its unholy agreement in the bargain. To reiterate: *It* has violated sanctified—that is, *protected*—ground. It has touched blood that is inviolable. It is breaking the bonds that the Ardeelians, in their moment of weakness, fashioned for it. While it chose to humor their—and now our—hopes for the longest time (in its own private, centuries-long game that eternals can afford to play; to entertain its own strange, inconceivable mind), it has at this time, by its actions, announced its intentions, clearly, to break the bonds. And we are *all* at risk. Every man, every woman, and every child. Every home, every town, and every city. Whether one is native or new arrived here. Anything standing in the way of his infernal ambitions … will be destroyed. Can you not see that?"

"You will return that book to where it belongs," the high constable said from behind his pudgy fingers.

"I already have," replied Attila. "Come closer. You don't see that this book is much smaller than the book you hide in your safe? This is a *copy*. While I waited for this day of trial to come—and long was I waiting—I had the History of the Tsobl Constabulary printed. So that I might have my own copy. And the printer might have a copy. And every church might have a copy. And any good man of this country, native or newly arrived, can have a copy if he so wishes; and read of its true history; and understand the scourge that has plagued these our lands for generations; and recognize the betrayal of its governing citizens, both before our arrival and after our taking control. And so they might fear for their future as they realize the disadvantageous position into which they've been put: how a power of utter evil has been allowed to fester (and now grow) in the bosom of these our mountains, so that it might take one terrible bite, and at once have us all. And so—whatever you think you might do to me today, this bound-up and printed truth is out, and it is in their hands—the people will see how they have been misled for so long, and they might then prepare themselves to march and root this evil out, and destroy the menace once and for all."

The book was wrenched from Attila's proclaiming hand.

. . .

The small court was cleared. Attila found himself in a small private library. He faced the roasted ham, dull eye to glistening eye.

"That was a close one, wasn't it?" asked the Governor, the pink-purple of his hammy complexion pulsing lightly. "Not sure how Arvik"—the printer—"managed to slip you a copy of the History of the Tsobl Constabulary before he was executed. You *do* know he was executed?"

Attila's heavy-lidded eyes became only more bored than they already were. "When?"

"After smuggling that copy of the book to you, obviously. I'd thought we'd recovered them all. Too bad."

"Why was this done, executing an innocent—?"

"For printing obscene and heretical works. A common hazard for men in his trade. These printers always want something new and exciting to sell. Then they succumb to their basest instincts and the filthy tastes of their clientele. Trust me, nobody wants to know what he was printing. The people were relieved to see the pages burned along with his press. Nobody knows the true reason."

"And why am I still alive?"

"Well, what do you have to do with Arvik and his depraved activities? Completely unrelated."

"I mean to say: There is a reason you did not have me killed. A reason you created my sham trial. A reason that I, the low constable of Tsobl, am now speaking privately with the governor of Ardeel."

"You are no longer the low constable of Tsobl," the governor informed him. "There was some hope we could get you to see the light. You are not a stupid man. But you *are* a bit thick in the head on some matters. Unsuitable for the position, I'm afraid."

"But you know relieving me of my rank won't silence me."

"Thick head, big mouth. Luckily you are unpopular, and by your own device now considered a drunkard and a lunatic; your little ploy with the bells saw to that well enough. You may have some excitable and superstitious partisans in the city, but they've all been scared away by Arvik's example. They aren't as thick as you. Anyway, to further answer the mystery, you are not one of *them*, but one of *us*, a King's man, and by your family's petitions to my office—and their generosity spread all around—they might have just convinced us to spare your life today. We'll see how long that lasts."

"I know I should be flattered that your highness, the governor, is condescending to tell me all this. But still, there are plenty of others who could. So why you?"

"I just wanted to let you in on a secret," smiled the roasted ham, his toothy smile breaking the duel of inexpression.

Attila stared as he waited for the secret.

"Very well," the roasted ham carried on. "So you understand: that book you sought to publish is a living covenant. Every man who signed into it, ancestors and descendants, may have come to a terrible bargain with the Count of Ardeel, but it is a serious pact. One that, despite its disuse and forgotten words in this modern age, is still in full effect, let me assure you of this. As long as we—the territory's newest arrivals and its authority—do nothing to violate our end of this old agreement, fashioned by those we now rule, we are perfectly safe from harm. Should we stir up the population with forgotten bloodshed, should we seek to reengage with this count on his own terms, the disaster you are predicting *will* be realized."

Dryly, Attila murmured that if they did nothing at all it'd still be realized.

"You did, in fact, read the book, didn't you?" croaked the ham. "Nothing could kill him. He was invincible and close to omnipotent."

"Centuries ago," Attila said with a yawn. "We are now more numerous and more powerful than clattering knights and bowmen. We can erase the stain of blood these forefathers smeared across this country's history."

"There's no righting that shame," said the ham, looking dismayed. "No righting their dereliction at all. No matter if we should ever remove that monster from this earth, *their* embarrassing history will exist forever."

"It's *our* history now. Especially if we choose to continue it."

"That embarrassing history will exist forever, especially if we begin assembling armies, announcing to the rest of the civilized world what is happening here—and therefore broadcast to every corner of the world what once ago happened in these mountains. And bring to light that abominable agreement. Let it rest, and the world will never know."

"We can't do *nothing* when the creature is building its strength against us."

"I don't believe it is."

"It's already reclaimed its wife from consecrated ground."

"And still it's done nothing against us."

"How many victims has it claimed this year?"

"Well," said the roasted ham. "As per the agreement. Nothing excessive."

"Look at the book."

"Which book?"

"You know which—"

The governor took out the book that used to be held in the high constable's safe. The original, which Attila had taken and studied. The one he had copied by hand (and then sent along his perfect copy to Arvik the printer for mass publication). The one that had gotten Arvik killed.

"You mean this one?" the governor said with a ruddy smile, the hamminess at a glow. "What about it? Tell me about it, child. Do."

Bored expression set in place, Attila snatched the book and ripped through the pages.

"There! There!" Attila pointed at a name. "Look. He killed Neku Jonker, the grave tender. Neku's bloodline began this agreement. You see the signature there. His family has stuck to it, down the many ages and throughout. He is untouchable. And yet, the monster killed him just to get what he wanted: his bride-queen. The paper means nothing anymore. The signatures mean nothing. He is striking out at will now. We must strike him in return, before it's too late!"

The governor shook his head.

"You need to steady yourself," the roasted ham grinned slyly. "This thing, this monster, this Count of Ardeel, cannot be killed."

"He can be," Attila countered. "I'm sure he can be."

"Oh, I'm sure he *can* be. At some point. If we should ever figure out just how to do it. But for now—and I will presently explain to you just what I mean, and I am confident you will come to see it my way—while he is alive, he is quite useful." The roasted ham now had Attila's undivided attention. "The Count must live, you see; because for all of us—including you, Attila Bronk—he is, in a word, indispensable."

With these words, and a small shudder from his body, the world Low Constable Attila Bronk had known and believed in from infancy—one of piety, and justice, and moral righteousness—died.

This was the death Attila had sensed coming. And now it had happened.

And this death, this change in reality, unforeseen and quite shocking, presented him—this once loyal footsoldier of the King's Law—a rebirth; an entirely new path to walk. With his keen mind he knew at once the greatness of the challenge should he take it, but also the nobility and surpassing richness of its reward. And so he thought, even as the ham explained on in lazy confidence:

Now I must act. Now I will act!

AMALINA'S DARK ADVENTURE

THROUGH IMPOSSIBLE CHALLENGES ...

... AND EVER GREATER DANGERS ...

FOLLOW AMALINA DALCA ... AS SHE BATTLES HER WAY OUT!

www.badhoundpress.com